MANDY

I0639695

Hamid Yusof

First published in 2017 by

Becomeshakespeare.com
Wordit Content Design & Editing Services Pvt Ltd
Unit - 26, Building A-1, Nr Wadala RTO, Wadala (East),
Mumbai 400037, India
T:+91 8080226699

This book has been funded by WORDIT ART FUND
WORDIT ART FUND helps deserving
Authors publish their work
To apply for funding, please visit us at
becomeshakespeare.com

©
ISBN: 978-93-86487-91-9

Disclaimer
This is a work of fiction. Names, characters, business,
place, event and incidents are either the product of the
author's imagination or used in a fictitious manner. Any
resemblance to actual person, living or dead or actual
event is purely coincidental.

DEDICATION

I would like to dedicate this book to my son: Rudy, daughter: Katrina, and wife: Roha.

ACKNOWLEDGEMENT

I would like to thank everyone at Team BecomeShakespeare.com for all the great work they have done with this book.

CHAPTER ONE

It certainly wasn't a conscious decision on my part to come to live in Penang after my wife and I had decided to go on our separate ways after twenty-two years of marriage. I guess the feeling of rejection was too much for me to bear - I had to get away from her - anywhere will do I had thought.

About three months ago I had left my in-laws' house and had move to an apartment. Now three months later, on an overcast afternoon, I had boarded a taxi to take me to the airport. All my worldly goods were in a suitcase and a hold-all. I had left everything else behind including all my precious hand tools at my mother-in-law's house. The house was a landed one as opposed to an apartment where most Singaporeans tend to live in. Twenty-five minutes later, in a taxi on route to Changi Airport, I decided to change my plan and told the taxi driver to take me to the railway station instead. He tilted his head up to look at me in his rear view mirror, after a short pause, he asked, "The railway station?" I said, "Yes". He stopped at the next traffic lights and made a U-turn when the lights had turned green. Half an hour later we arrived at the Tanjong Pagar railway station.

The building was in a richly ornamented Art Deco style. On its exterior were four reliefs of white marble, allegories of Agriculture, Industry, Commerce and Transport. They were works by Rudolfo Nolli.

The hall had a barrel vault roof. Inside the main public hall, the walls bear panels with scenes depicting economic activities that were historically significant in Malaya then: rice planting, rubber tapping, shipping activities, bullock cart transport, copra growing and tin mining.

These panels and the original floor slabs were manufactured locally, using rubber to deaden noise.

The two long platforms were capable of accommodating the longest mail trains, covered by umbrella reinforced concrete roofs.

Half an hour later I was sipping the putrid-tasting coffee I had bought from the station's café. The nasi lemak that I had bought with it was rather tasty and so I went back to the counter and bought another packet.

I had several hours to kill before the train to Butterworth was due to arrive. I unzipped my hold-all to get a book to read and moved to a sofa in a quiet corner of the not-so-crowded café. Only two tables were occupied. The one facing the door had a local gentleman, in a Hawaiian shirt, reading a newspaper. A Caucasian young couple were standing near the table I had just vacated, the man waited for the waiter to clear the remnants of my nasi lemak and my empty coffee cup and saucer, while the young woman was looking at the menu above the counter. Both of them sat down at the table and began discussing what to order was my guess.

After nearly a quarter-of-a century together, all of a sudden my wife thought it might be best that we should do all the things we used to do together only this time we'd do them separately. A novel idea I thought and so I agreed, albeit reluctantly, after a lot of persuasions with her over several days in which I had failed miserably to counter her suggestion.

In the end I could see that she had already made up her mind and nothing I could say would change that. Besides, our two kids were no longer kids and so there was nothing left to bind us together, not even money - especially money - since I had lost everything during the last recession. For a couple of years after we had sold our house and had moved into my mother-in-law's house, we had delved into our savings and we could see that it was depleting fast. My wife's decisions, of course, was a practical one – get out now before everything was gone, which presumably, made this earth-shattering decision somewhat easier for her to make. Talking about timing - was it perfect for her? I guess so. As for me it was lousy, but I had no choice.

I seem to recall once at a party, although it may have been said in jest, I overheard my wife saying to a group of her friends that her motto was *"No Money No Talk"*. Well, in that case, my wife was true to form then!

So here I am in Penang – alone - and I haven't a clue what I am going to do here. Sure, I have been here many times before, during happy times, with my wife and our two boys. I had always loved Penang – loved its people, and its food, but most important of all I love the way most of the people here seemed to mind their business and not anyone else's. As a family then, we had enjoyed our stay at the *Rasa Sayang Beach Hotel* most of all because of its close proximity to the beach.

Tourists from the four corners of the world seem to know Penang better than they know Kuala Lumpur, the capital of Malaysia. They had come in droves to Penang for the sun, the sea, and the sand. Batu Ferringhi, their favourite destination, has got some of the best beaches south of Phuket. Besides, in Penang you don't need any translator either; even the rickshaw peddlers speak reasonably good English.

Not too long ago I remember people living in other parts of Asia like those in Indonesia, from Thailand, and even from its closest neighbour, south of the border, Singapore, sent their children to some of the elite schools in Penang because of their high standard of education all conducted in

English. Today we're even behind India in our proficiency in English.

What I like most about Penang is its lack of the hustle and the bustle that pervaded most cities like Singapore, Kuala Lumpur or Bangkok, where life gets stressful most of the time. However, the very laid-back attitude displayed by the people here can be frustrating sometimes, especially when you want things done fast. But as I got to know a few of the locals better, I too became afflicted with the same infection, but guess what? I found myself loving it. *Hello care-freeness; goodbye stress!* Now, that's a slogan for Penang to adopt.

Life before Penang was one big rush for me, rarely would I find moments of solitude, whereas in Penang I came across it every day. The place is like a balm to me: it soothed away all my pain. Life in a big city like Singapore where I came from is like a non-stop roller-coaster ride with its occasional spikes that could almost touch the sky – too exhilarating to describe, but for the most part, it's downhill, with the gut-wrenching feeling like one gets when the car you're in got slightly airborne. For instance, before coming down a hill suddenly. In Penang I don't necessarily get myself all wound up if things don't go according to plan. Committing *hara-kiri* when things go wrong is definitely a rarity here; sure people do jump off the Penang Bridge now and then when the going got tough, but only a few would do that.

After nearly a week of trying to persuade my wife to give our marriage another chance, but to no avail, I got on the train for Penang with just a suitcase and a holdall - there wasn't even a job waiting for me in Penang. I had no idea what I wanted to do in order to put bread on the table or a roof over my head, so why did I come here in the first place? I guess part of the reason was to be as far away from my wife as possible and still be within a flying distance to Singapore in case she changed her mind. The other reason I chose Penang was because it has an environment not too far removed from my previous place of abode.

As a creature of comfort, after checking out places like Kangar and Alor Setar in the north, Kuala Terengganu and Kota Bahru on the East Coast, I decided that Penang was the next best thing to Singapore to come and live. You must have noticed that I didn't say ex-wife - that was because we weren't divorced yet, although I guess, it is as good as done from the attitude she was giving me. During the week prior to my jumping on the train for Penang, any attempts at reconciliation on my part would send her running in the opposite direction – it became too humiliating for me.

Coming back to Penang, I had always thought that with a bit of copying on what Lee Kuan Yew, the Prime Minister of Singapore, had done for Singapore, I should imagine the sitting Chief Minister, Koh Tsu Koon, could turn Penang into a

Singapore Mark 11 easily enough. In time, who knows it too could overtake Singapore and become a model even Singapore could emulate – a rather tall order to all, but the blind. It could be done if it wanted to though, Penang, after all, is bigger than Singapore, and unlike Singapore's Lee Kuan Yew, Koh Tsu Koon needn't have to carry the burden of the defence budget and all the other trappings that are needed in running an independent country like Singapore. In Penang's case, the Federal Government would be taking care of all that high expense budgets. All KTK needed do was to focus on attracting investors, foreign and local, and run Penang like a CEO would with a corporation; exactly like what Mr. Lee Kuan Yew had done with Singapore. If Singapore can do it why can't Penang? Lim Chong Yew, KTK's predecessor, had turned a sleepy hollow, which was Penang, into a vibrant state attracting investors from all over the world especially in the electronics sector. Chong Yew had set up Free Trade Zones close to the airport – a smart thing to do since electronic factories shipped all their finished products by air. As a matter of fact Chong Yew had left Tsu Koon with a number of completed projects including the dated 66-storey KOMTAR, an administrative centre of the state government, and the 13.5 km Penang Bridge that bridge the island with Peninsular Malaysia.

When it was completed, KOMTAR was for some time the tallest building in Asia, and the

Penang Bridge one of the longest in the world. Somehow during the ensuing years Penang had run out of steam. That is always the problem when planners overstayed – they run out of ideas and prefer to seek the comfort zones of their offices thus the reason why spring cleaning are always done in all progressive countries of the world. Keeping over-staying leaders are definitely not de-rigueur nowadays.

If one wanted to compare apple with apple, Koh Tsu Koon, after all was a smart person, if not smarter than LKY academically? Wasn't he a university professor before he became a politician? While LKY was just a lawyer and a trade unionist who had nowhere to go but up when Singapore got booted out of Malaysia in August 1965.

Since I had decided to come and live in Penang I can only hope and pray that improvements will come eventually, especially towards cleaning up the place. With rubbish clogging its rivers and drains, Penang looked a bit jaded and Third World. I'm not here to criticise, but to find out if this place is suitable for me to continue with the next phase of my life.

I had taken a night mail train from Tanjong Pagar in Singapore and had arrived in Butterworth early the next morning. The crossing by ferry to Penang island was pleasantly refreshing after being cooped up in the train all night. I had checked into one of the hotels on Penang Road - Penang's main thoroughfare - and that evening I had decided to walk the short distance from my hotel to KOMTAR – the sixty-six storey edifice with its shopping complex on the first three floors that surrounded it. It was already time for dinner and I had wanted to see if I could find some place to eat there. Along the way I must have walked past dozens of places where I could have stopped for dinner, but since I had wanted to check out KOMTAR first, I proceeded as planned.

Penang was famous for its food and one well-known eatery is a the *Hameediyah Nasi Kandar* restaurant where they served their fantastic *Nasi Biryani*. It is just off Penang Road midway from my hotel and KOMTAR. From where I was standing on Penang Road, a few minutes from my hotel, I could just make out the sign board turning into it. I made a mental note to have lunch there the following day. After the twenty minutes brisk walk it was refreshing to step into the air-conditioned comfort of the shopping complex beginning from the ground floor KOMTAR. The 66-storey tower can be seen from as far away as the mainland itself.

A quick glance at the directory on the ground floor informed me that there was a food court on the third floor. As it was already way past my dinner time, and lunch seemed a long time ago as far as my stomach was concerned, I decided to take the lift instead of hoofing it up the escalator.

The sound of people eating and the smell of food greeted me as soon as the lift door opened was enough to put me in the right mood for dinner. The food court was still full of people despite the lateness judging from the queues forming in front of the various stalls. Business all around me seemed brisk. In Asia anytime is a good time to eat.

After dinner of chicken rice and a bowl of ABC – a concoction of shaved ice, red beans, cendol, fruit salad and gula Melaka, I took a leisurely stroll through the concourse on the third floor where it was teeming with people - always a good indicator that such an attraction should be checked out. I noticed that the majority of the people there were window shoppers, but a trinket shop on my left and a McDonald outlet up ahead seem to be doing brisk business. The trinket shop was packed with young ladies looking for costume jewellery, headbands, colourful plastic bracelets and so on. The McDonald had a good mix of tourists and locals and the queues were long at the counters. I like their *Big Macs* and their *Double Cheese Burgers*, so it was good to know where to come next whenever I was in town.

After reaching the end where a departmental store was located, I retraced my steps and stopped at a *Kopitiam* next to the trinket shop I had walked past earlier. I took a table on the front row facing the concourse area and did what everyone else there seemed to be doing - watching the throng of people going by. The sharp proprietor, a thin middle-age man of average height, wearing a Hawaiian shirt, seeing that I was a new face, came over and introduced himself.

"Hi! I'm Eddy," he said, extending a hand which I shook.

"James," I murmured, slightly startled at the unexpected show of friendliness which I thought was quite alien in Malaysia. I quickly recovered and gave Eddy's hand a couple more shakes as an afterthought. He smiled broadly showing his cigarette-stained teeth.

A *kopitiam* is actually is a just a coffee shop like any other, however at Eddy's it also served his famous home-made ice creams. He was quick to inform me that his ice cream machines came from Italy. Pride was written all over his face when he said it. Fortunately I remembered that Italy was famous for its gelatos. Didn't they discover how to turn snow and shaved ice into syrup-laden slush like they have in Hawaii? It was a precursor to the ice creams as we know it today.

"Really?" I said. He looked pleased when I said that.

"Are you here on holiday?" He asked, cigarette dangling from his mouth.

"No, I'm here to stay if I can find a decent flat which shouldn't cost me an arm and a leg".

The next day I began my hunt for a flat. After checking out the two units that an estate agent had brought me to, both of which were in George Town itself, I was so repelled by the shocking state they were in, I told the agent that I don't want to stay in town. I asked him to find me a flat somewhere in the suburbs but not too far away from town. What I didn't know was that since most flats were located in a rent-controlled areas in George Town, it was left to the tenants to spruce it up at their own expense, the rent however was cheap.

I continued with my search the next day and the next, but it wasn't until the fifth day when an agent named Tony brought me to a fifth-floor flat among five blocks of flats in a place called Sungai Nibong, a suburb of Penang some thirteen kilometres away from KOMTAR. The first thing I did was to check it out if they had another lift to the flat. It may be an ideal way to do some exercise but I certainly had no desire to walk down and up again five flights of stairs whenever I want to go out and to come home to if the one lift were to malfunction. Since I liked its location and the view from the top was magnificent, I was thrilled to find another lift on the opposite side of the U-shape building. What struck me as unusual was the fact that the inside both lifts were relatively free of graffiti and the floors of both lifts were clean. After a half-hour inspection of the flat, and since I felt comfortable with it the minute I had walked in, I agreed to sign up on a two-year lease with an option for another two years.

The flat had a large master bedroom and two small single ones, one of which I had decided to turn into a study-cum-guest room. The smallest room which was close to the kitchen I turned it into a dining room. Most tenants would put a dining table in the living room for their meals and afterwards for their children to use to do their homework. Without the dining table in the living room I had ample space to put a couple of bookshelves and park my music system there when eventually I had them. The place wasn't totally in the woods for it was only about thirteen kilometres from George Town or about thirty minutes' drive away according to Tony. At that time I didn't have a car and the buses took a bit longer, but since I had no job to go to the extra few minutes didn't matter at all to me.

I was again at Eddy's two days after I had moved into the empty flat. I didn't want to stay in the hotel longer than necessary and so to the departmental store I had gone to and bought myself a couple of pillows, a light blanket, and a roll-up straw mat. It was rather primitive, but it'll have to do until I get some proper furniture.

Eddy saw me as soon as I entered his shop and asked if he may join me at my table, I welcomed the company.

"Have you managed to get your flat yet?" he asked, his cigarette dangling between his lips.

"Yes. I found a flat in Sungai Nibong. It's on the top floor of a five-story flat. I think there are five blocks of flats there".

"That's good", he said as he removed his cigarette and flicked the ash onto the floor despite an ash tray being on the table in front of us. I looked down at the ash on the floor thinking what a filthy habit this guy had got until I saw at that moment one of his staff was sweeping the floor just behind us. Eddy did that just to make sure his staff wasn't sleeping on the job. The young man neatly scooped up the ash with his broom into the long-handled scoop he was holding in his left hand.

Since I hadn't had breakfast that morning I ordered eggs over-easy, toasts and a mug of cappuccino. I was about to open my newspaper when I noticed a startling good-looking young woman chatting with a Caucasian man two tables away from where Eddy and I were sitting. According to Eddy the man came from Bosnia and the girl was local. He could be thirty-something but I can't be sure how old the girl was – about twenty-something I reckoned. The waiter brought my breakfast, and since I was hungrier than I thought, I ignored the couple and dived into my breakfast with gusto.

I spent the next few days doing up my flat, and since it was only about eight hundred square feet in size, it only took me a day and a half to slap on two coats of paint of slightly cheerful colour over the colour pencil scrolling and other miscellaneous dirt that were all over the walls. For good measure I had the terrazzo floor resurfaced and polished which set me back two hundred Ringgit. I figured it was worth it for after the final polishing was done I could see my reflection clearly on floor and mopping it would be a breeze, I thought.

Penang had got some good antique shops whose prices on the items I had liked I couldn't afford, however I managed to buy a round rosewood dining table with six chairs for eleven hundred Ringgit at a second-hand furniture shop. For the living room, I bought a three plus two-seater sofa set for seven hundred Ringgit and for my bedroom I chose a Queen-size bed and two bedside tables to go with it and these set me back another nine hundred Ringgit. After checking my bank balance I thought I'd better stop at that; besides there wasn't any more room left in the flat for anything else except for some prints to put on the walls and two book shelves. Other objets-d'art will have to wait until I start to earn some money.

As it turned out during the following visit to Eddy's, the good-looking young woman, who was the centre of everyone's attention during my last visit there too was there with her Bosnian boy-friend.

Eddy saw me and grabbed my elbow and practically dragged me towards the couple to introduce me to them.

"I'd like you to meet two friends of mine", he said to me.

The man got up from his seat and extended his hand to me. "Hi, I'm Chris. How do you do?

"James". I shook his hand. "I'm well, thank you".

"Hi, I'm Mandy", the young lady said, extending her hand out to me.

"Hi Mandy". Her grip was firm that belied her small frame.

Chris, it seemed, was a refugee from Bosnia and had been living in Malaysia for almost a year. I recalled reading an article not too long ago about the Prime Minister Mahathir Bin Mohamad who had been one of the strongest supporters of the Bosnian cause during the war, was the only Asian country that had accepted Bosnian refugees.

At their invitation, I pulled up a chair and joined them. I casually mentioned to Chris, from little I knew, that I thought Yugoslavia was better off under Tito. Surprisingly he agreed with me. I remember an old adage that talking politic leads to nowhere except trouble and so I quickly changed the subject.

"Have you visited many parts of Malaysia, Chris?" I asked. He mentioned he had and so I listened for a while to his tale of his Malaysian Odyssey before I excused myself citing having some shopping to do.

Ever since I arrived in Penang Eddy's Kopitiam was my favourite haunt and before long Eddy and I had become friends. It was a good place to be for people watching. Since it was located facing the concourse area, there were shops selling anything from shoes to fashion wear on both sides, it became a popular spot for the locals and for the tourists alike. Unlike most thoroughfare I know, this one was located on the third floor of a shopping arcade.

Eddy's Kopitiam was where I had spent many pleasant hours pretending that I was really at a Paris side-walk café doing what comes naturally over there too - people watching. In my mind's eye I had renamed Eddy's Kopitiam *Chez Eddy*. One day, several days later, Eddy caught me looking at some chic-looking ladies coming out of the food court.

"James, stop those lustful thoughts of yours", he intoned as he approached me, his cigarette dangling from his mouth.

"What do expect from a man at my age", I replied, trying to sound as casual as I could. "Look but don't touch, that's my motto, besides, I'm a bachelor, remember?"

"Yeah! Yeah! Undressing ladies with your eyes should be made a crime, don't you agree?" he shot back at me revealing his blackened teeth.

Eddy did not notice at that time but Mandy had just walked past his shop and it was her I was looking at. She wasn't with Chris but with a young woman about her age, and both were in their school uniforms. I wasn't gawking as Eddy had put it crudely, although my stares may have been longer than what may be considered cursory. By this time I had considered Eddy as a friend and so I didn't mind his ribbings at all.

In her school uniform, Mandy looked no more than eighteen years old, or perhaps even younger, I thought. I suddenly felt ashamed of myself. Here I was almost reaching the half-a-century mark and was I having unclean thoughts about an eighteen-year old girl? Eddy was right; I should be hauled up for questioning. Then I realized I was unattached, I felt exonerated.

Here I was in a country which had an officially-sanctioned snoop police force to catch couples caught in close proximity situations. Believe it or not, these officials who were authorised by the religious departments even pay people who had tipped them off on such activities by couples wherever they may be. Imagine that, they pay *Peeping Toms* in this country!

Some of these stool-pigeons were workers in hotels who wanted to make a few extra bucks. Some were security guards working in car parks, and of course there were those who had grudges against the intending targets. If found guilty, the people who had committed *Khalwat* could face a maximum penalty of two years' imprisonment. In some cases when these couples were caught red-handed they had often ended up marrying each other hoping to get their sentences reduced when they got to court. They would cite love as their excuse for their behaviour. In the end most of these shot-gun marriages ended up in divorces not too long afterwards. Contrary to the intended purpose by these holier-than-thou employees of the state, their very actions in turn created more problems than they had cured. Have they ever wondered why there are so many single mothers around?

The constitution of Malaysia provides a unique dual justice system - the secular laws (Criminal and Civil) and Sharia laws for the Muslims. The Islamic courts which applies the Sharia laws can try Muslims who dominated the multi-cultural population in the country for religious and moral offences. Non-Muslims however are not at risk for they have their own criminal and civil courts.

After having lived in the west and then in Singapore for many years, I find the idea of people snooping on each other revolting. These ill-thought out schemes like all ill-thought out schemes everywhere always have a tendency to fall apart. These despicable religious bigots don't realize that they were creating more problems than they were solving. Nevertheless, like it or not, with those thoughts in mind, I intend to watch my steps very carefully.

The next day while sitting at my usual front table at Eddy's, I almost choked on my toast when I saw a picture of Chris with a hand shielding his face and Mandy in dark glasses behind him. The caption said in bold letters **"Couple Caught In Close Proximity In A Car At Ferringhi Beach"**.

A week later at Eddy's I met Mandy again. This time she was sitting alone at the table where I would usually sit whenever I came to Eddy's. I looked among the crowd to see if her boyfriend Chris was around, he wasn't. Mandy looked up as I approached her table. I waved my hand and said hello. She was startled at first, but slowly to my relief recognition finally appeared on her face. The couple sitting next to her table were looking at her, apparently recognizing her from the photograph in the papers. They were giving her dirty looks and were whispering to each other.

I asked Mandy if she would mind if I joined her. She gave me a smile and waved her hand to a vacant chair next to her. Since I had no desire to remind her of her skirmish she had with the law, I got her talking about Penang as it was going to be my home for God knows how long.

For such a young person, she appeared to know her Penang quite well. After nearly an hour, just as I thought we were beginning to get along fine, Mandy, all of a sudden became very touchy when she thought I was prying when I asked her something about herself. Startled at her reaction

I tried to apologize, but she stood up and gave me a look that said it all – nice to meet you, but good bye!

She mouthed the words, "Mind your f. . .g business!" before showing me her back and strutted away. She must have thought that I was prying into her life when I asked all the usual question people of my age tends to ask of school children – why aren't you in school, especially on a Tuesday morning? I didn't know that she was in the afternoon session. She could have told me that fact, right?

Mandy, who was about to sit for her SPM examinations, felt irritated with me, I guess, when I tried to enumerate to her all the merits of having a good education. It was something she had heard often enough from her form teacher, the same things I had often told my own children when they were Mandy's age. Like Mandy, my children too had had the same reaction.

As a father with two grown boys, I had no inkling whatsoever that unlike most kids her age, mine included, Mandy had always aimed to have a good education. I had found out that piece of information from Eddy. Despite his nonchalant façade, he had dug out this bit of information for me, why? I had no idea, but it did however make me think of Mandy in a different light.

According to Eddy, Mandy had once told him that she aimed to have a good education because it was not only the key to her future, but to her freedom as well. She had looked forward to sit for her High School final examinations like a child had looked forward towards Christmas.

"What do you mean her freedom?" I asked, giving him an incredulous look.

"Her mother may be grooming her so that she could live off her income someday".

"What the hell are you talking about, Eddy?" My raised voice made a few heads near our table turned in our direction. Eddy looked at me but didn't give me an answer.

"You mean as a call girl?" I probed; more heads turned towards our table. Eddy, by this time looked embarrassed and uncomfortable, decided to change the subject.

CHAPTER TWO

I had not laid eyes on Mandy ever since she had walked away in a huff about a week earlier. To be honest I hadn't expected ever to see her again after our last encounter – I remembered she had more or less told me to fuck off. This time, however, it was she who had tapped me on the shoulder, when I had my head between the pages of a newspaper. Startled, I looked up and saw her looking at me shyly. She looked stunning and friendlier too if her smile was anything to go by. Born in Singapore, but had grown up mostly in Australia, I instinctively I stood up, said hello, and asked her if she would care to join me.

She readily accepted my invitation and sat down. I signalled for a waiter. She ordered a banana split. Fearing another scene, I consciously avoided asking her anything that was remotely personal in her life. To my surprise it was she who began telling me all the things she had avoided telling me the last time we had that disastrous conversation. For some reason she seemed eager to tell me her life story. Perhaps she had decided to accept me as someone who was quite harmless - a father figure even.

Right through her banana split, comprising of two bananas, three scoops of ice creams of three different flavours and a multitude of sauces told me her life story - even about her dreams – her daydreams - her wish list really.

I remembered how she had flared at me before and so I switched tact and decided to become more of a listener than a talker. This worked very well because I could see the animation in her voice and the twinkle in her eyes, I could see that she had eager to talk. What she was telling me was incredible and I was getting to know her life's history - at least the part she could remember - from the time she grew up in the village not far from Batu Ferringhi. She began by telling me about the time when all of them were still living with her maternal grandparents to the time when she was raped by her uncle at the age of fourteen. More of this tragic episode later. She mentioned the rape incident without rancour, to shock me perhaps, and I was truly shocked. As I looked at the pretty young girl in front of me, I can't really imagine how hard her life must have been if what she was telling me was the truth. Young children tend to make up stories and exaggerated their stories, sometimes, in order to shock.

At the end of her tale I could see that Mandy was certainly desperate to get away from this island – most tourists thought it a paradise, that much I can tell. She would repeat the same things to me on the three different occasions in the days and weeks to come. We had been seen together so often people were beginning to suspect that I was her new boyfriend. I was tempted to ask her what happened to Chris, but then again, why do I care about Chris when she was right here with me.

Mandy kept repeating to me what she would do once she'd received her SPM certificate; with her savings she'd buy herself a bus ticket and board a bus at KOMTAR's basement bus terminal.

"Where will you go?" I asked her.

"To Kuala Lumpur to get a job", she replied. I asked her why the rush to leave Penang?

"I can't tolerate living with my mother anymore", she replied.

I looked at her and said nothing; this much I knew from Eddy. According to her, once she reached Kuala Lumpur she'd be going to a couple of interviews and then she would land herself a job. How naïve she was I thought – two interviews and she had expected to get a job straightaway. The fact that she had nowhere to stay there and didn't know anyone at all over there didn't seem to bother her. All she could picture was the job she would land a few days after a few interviews. To live a life of freedom from her abusive mother seemed paramount to her.

As I listened to Mandy relating her story my own thoughts began to stray to my two boys who were with their mother in Singapore; I have often wondered what their hopes and aspirations were? My children as I recalled never took anything seriously; Mandy on the other hand was so intense.

I know I had given my two boys all the opportunities to better themselves academically, but like most kids who had never experienced hardship, they chose the easy path by dropping out of college when the going got tough. They even have the gall to lecture me that having a college education wasn't everything. They cited Bill Gates as one of the few well-known names that had done very well for themselves despite having dropped out of college.

Unfortunately, true to what I had predicted for them, they ended up hopping from one menial job to another. They claimed they were happy in what they were doing, but I knew as well as they did that things weren't as what they had claimed them to be.

Mandy, on the other hand had had a rough life and therefore she was looking forward to her forth-coming SPM examinations as a ticket out of repressiveness she was in. A good result was important to her and that was her incentive to study hard. Her mid-term tests according to her had shown that she was sufficiently prepared with all the subjects she was going to sit for with the exception of mathematics and biology. She told me that she knew she had to put in a lot more efforts on the two subjects in order to obtain at least a "B".

Eddy came to my table as soon as Mandy had left and took the seat Mandy had vacated. I could see that he was curious about why Mandy and I were talking to each other again. He wasn't the only one; I too was curious as to the reason why Mandy had decided to make me a father confessor.

About two months before her SPM examinations Mandy met me again at Eddy's, and with tears in her eyes she recounted what her mother had said to her when she had come home from an all-night out. Her mother had told Mandy she needn't have to study too hard because she may not be in school much longer! When Mandy asked her what she had meant by that, her mother told her that it was time for her to go out and start earning a living, not only for herself, but to support the whole family, herself included. She told Mandy that it was time that she took her long-deserved rest by quitting her job at the restaurant where she worked as a waitress - once Mandy had got her job.

It seems that her mother had dropped the bombshell when she had come home inebriated and had brought a man home with her. Her mother had often brought men home according to Mandy. This time he was someone Mandy had never laid eyes on before. He was a much younger man than all her mother's previous boyfriends. According to Mandy he had smiled at her as he helped steady her mother with his arms on her shoulder as they walked towards her mother's bedroom.

At that time Mandy had been studying at the dining table in their living room and hadn't realized the time when she suddenly heard the front door key being turned. Frantically she tried to clear the table, but froze on the spot when she saw her mother's head emerged through the door. She had no time to pick up all her books from the dining table. She had been doing her homework ever since she came home from school that afternoon. The table was in a mess with her empty bowl in which she had her instant noodle still on the table. Normally she would do all her work and studying in her own room, but when she saw that her mother had already gone out, she decided to use the slightly bigger dining table instead.

Mandy had often mentioned to me that her mother, a night bird, would go out practically every night after work and would only come home late, or rather early the next morning. On most occasions, a man would accompany her home, and more often than not, the man would end up staying the night. Mandy had often heard whisperings from the neighbours that her mother was a prostitute. At first she didn't believe them or rather she didn't want to believe them, but after she had lost count as to the number of men her mother had brought home, she became resigned to the fact that the neighbours might be right after all. She once tried to tell her mother not to bring men home anymore, her mother got so angry she gave Mandy a slap so hard Mandy could have sworn that the ringing in her ears didn't stop for at least a week after that. From that day onwards, Mandy had kept to her room as soon as she had done all her chores.

That morning her mother found Mandy in their living room where Mandy had decided to do her studying instead of her tiny bedroom. She had needed more space and had decided to use the dining table. The solitary 25-watt fluorescent light in her bedroom being so dim she could hardly see the words in her books. The light in the living room was a 40 watt one and was brighter.

Her mother who had walked in become livid with anger when she saw Mandy in their living room. She accused Mandy of spying on her. Mandy, startled by her mother's sudden entrance, tipped her chair backward with a loud bang, and almost fell flat on her back in the process. Only her swift reflex action saved her from losing her balance altogether. She hadn't realised the time when her mother and her beau for the night had walked in.

Her mother took a few unsteady steps towards Mandy and when she saw her pile of books on the coffee table, she went berserk. She strutted across the room like a woman possessed, pushed Mandy's books, pen, and pencils – everything off the table. At that time of the morning, the sound of all the falling objects became exaggeratedly loud.

"I thought I told you to forget about school and to start looking for a job?" she screamed. She bent down unsteadily and pointed to some ancient scratches on the table and cried, "Look at all the scratches and look at all these lights," waving her hand at the solitary fluorescent light high on the ceiling. "Why are you wasting all my money on all these electricity, huh? You should have been in bed hours ago".

To save money all the lights in their small three-bedroom house were fitted with fluorescent tubes; the brightest, a 40-watt tube, was fitted in the living room above the sitting area.

Her mother, oblivious to the fact that her date was beside her, went into her usual tirade of how she had to struggle to look after her and two brothers when their father had abandoned them. Since Mandy had heard all this before, her mind went into an automatic suspended animation mode, where all sounds coming from her mother was completely blocked out.

For the umpteenth time, her mother was telling Mandy how sick and tired she was looking after them all and that it was time that Mandy started working so that she could take her well-deserved rest.

As always, she used the opportunity to condemn her father for all the ills that had befallen her. For years Mandy had hated her father for what he supposedly had done to her mother, but lately she seemed to be siding him more often than not perhaps just to spite her mother.

After seeing, how irrational her mother had often behaved, especially how easily and how often her mother would condemn other people for the wrongs she had perceived they had done to her, she concluded that her father must have been so fed up and had walked out on them. Often all her mother's accusations were without any foundation or justifications. Mandy had hated her father for not taking her with him and lately, no matter what her mother had said about him, she was convinced that it *was* her mother who had driven her father away in the first place.

Despite her drunkenness, and like most Oriental mothers who do not tolerate any show of disobedience from their children, her mother gave Mandy a searching look for any tell-tale sign of defiance. When none was visible, she screamed. "Remember what I said. Tomorrow, I want you to tell your teacher that you're quitting school, do you hear me?"

Mandy stood motionless as she tried to concentrate on a spot on the floor. With her inner switch turned off, she waited patiently for her mother's ranting to end. The unexpected stinging slap on her left ear deafened her momentarily and brought involuntary tears to her eyes. It was a sign of weakness, she knew, but the flow of tears was something she had no control over. She had learnt long ago that tears had no purpose in her life except to give satisfaction to her cruel mother.

Each time she cried she hated herself for it and after each slapping she'd promise herself she would never cry again. But each time she got hurt, whether physically or mentally, she'd end up blubbering like an idiot. The cuff on her ear was painful, but what was most painful was her mother's demand that she leave school. Not now, not when it was so close to her final examinations, she thought.

Mandy remained silent as she waited for her mother to stop her ranting, which could happen suddenly, or it could go on for another half-an-hour or so. She only hope that this threat, like the ones she had heard before, was nothing more than just that – a threat. With her ear still painfully humming steadily, Mandy slowly bent down and began to pick up her books, her pen and pencils. When she noticed some were lying near her mother's boy-friend's feet, she walked over towards him to pick them up.

As she was about to bend down to pick them up, he suddenly stooped down and picked up the pen she had treasured most and handed it to her. Unexpectedly she felt his hand brushed lightly on her right breast. Before she could react, he quickly turned his back on her and began walking towards her mother. Mandy saw him put his hand on her mother's hip and steered her in the direction of her mother's bedroom. It looked as if he had been in their house before, otherwise how would he know in which direction was her mother's bedroom? She hadn't seen him in the house before so he must have visited her mother when she was in school.

Not wanting another scolding from her mother, Mandy quickly tidied up the living room and disappeared into her bedroom. Once in her room, Mandy could hear their lovemaking through their paper-thin walls as if she were in the same room with them.

Disgusted, she wanted to leave her room and go back to the living room, but was afraid that her mother might hear her. Resigned to the fact that she had very little choice but to endure the noise their lovemaking was making, Mandy shut her eyes and tried to sleep, but sleep would not come. As she laid there listening to the noise her mother and her lover was making, she was surprised to find her hand between her legs and she was playing with herself.

Mandy noticed for the first time how nice it felt when she began to rub her clitoris and dipping her finger in her sex. She reached her climax just as her mother gave out a low moan followed by a louder one coming from the man. The last thing Mandy remembered before she fell asleep was her mother asking her lover for a cigarette.

The next morning Mandy left for school without having any breakfast fearing that her mother, or worse, her mother's lover, might walk in on her. On the school bus Mandy reflected on what was happening to her last night in her own bedroom – she felt a little apprehensive and somewhat guilty – thinking that whatever that made her feel good must be bad for her.

ℵℤℵℤℵℤ

CHAPTER THREE

Mandy's face turned red whenever she recalled the first time she had her menstruation. She remembered how frightened she was, had cried when she saw blood had stained her underwear which had seeped through her school uniform. Her friends had laughed at her when they saw how panicky Mandy had become. They suspected that Mandy must have been having her period for the first time. They themselves remembered how it was when they too were having their period for the first time and they stopped laughing suddenly.

Having had no one to tell Mandy about the birds and the bees, she went into a fit of terror and began crying. Her best friend, Carol, who heard her crying, took Mandy to see the principal where, for the first time, the fifty-something-year old spinster told Mandy about the reproductive system.

After that incident, the Principal, realizing how ignorant some of her students were, decided to include sex education in the curriculum of her school. She found out that, like Mandy, there were many young girls in her school who had no idea that it was normal for them to bleed once a month. She blamed the parents mainly for not taking the trouble to explain to their daughters about sex and the reproductive system. In her opinion, it was the main reason why many young girls got pregnant in the first place.

Mandy knew that the sensation she had felt last night was unlike the period she normally had. And unlike her period, it wasn't painful, but nice. But before she became a laughing stock again, she thought it best to go to the library to check it out. Unfortunately for her that day was filled with all kinds of activities and her trip to the library was postponed. Besides, her mother's threat about her leaving school was crowding out most of her other thoughts.

Full of apprehension Mandy had come home to a surprise she hadn't expected - to find her mother in the kitchen preparing dinner. She quickly assumed that new man in her mother's life was coming to dinner that night; it was a rare sight to see her mother cook dinner for her and her brothers. Dinner to Mandy and her two brothers were something that came out of a packet, poured into a bowl with some hot water added to it. They call it instant noodle and practically the entire nation thrived on it and made the manufacturers rich.

To Mandy, her mother was someone to fear and to loathe and not someone to look up to. She had never known her mother to dote on her or on her two brothers. Seeing her cooking dinner for them was something none of them could recall.

Her grandparents, who lived not too far from them, would occasionally sneaked in some home-cooked food for Mandy to share with her brothers. And each time Mandy would end with the bones or the crumbs her brothers didn't want to eat or couldn't eat. Not once would they think of sharing their food with her. If they like something, even if it was on her plate, they wouldn't have any qualms about taking it from her. Caring and sharing with each other weren't the norm in the Lee's household.

Under these circumstances perhaps Mandy had become more matured than her two siblings. Another reason may be why she found her school more appealing than most kids her age did was because to her it was a sanctuary where the environment felt safe, with less unpredictability, unlike her home. According to Mandy her mother had never cared if she went to school or not. Her concern was only for her two younger brothers!

I find this odd, it could be because her mother would perceive a more educated Mandy would be more of a threat to her authority than her two brothers would. It is a well-known fact with some Chinese families that sons were preferable to daughters.

The simplistic logic was that sons will one day be able to care for them in their old age, whereas daughters will be under the control of their husbands, who in turn will be looking after their own parents. To make things worse for herself,

Mandy had made it amply clear to her mother that she had always preferred school to home.

"You know, I can't remember an occasion when my mother had asked me anything about my school or even about myself. There had never been any communication between us, only her demands," she said. "If I had been ill, I'll try to cure myself because no one else would".

"How?" I asked.

"I always keep some Panadols with me", she said. "I would take one or two tablets with a glass of water and would lie on my bed for a while. Not when my mother was around, of course. I would get a belting if she found me in bed during the day", she said with a straight face.

It seemed to me that every utterance coming from her mother had invariably come out as a reprimand or in forms that resembled it - or demands – mainly demands it seemed.

When thoughts of her mother came to her mind, Mandy found it hard-pressed to find anything good about her.

When I asked her to tell me about her mother, surprisingly she had insinuated that she had looked a bit like her when her mother was younger. Despite her age Mandy still thought her mother as a good-looking woman, with a body no bigger than hers, she had added.

"A lot of people thought that my mother and I looked alike".

"She must be pretty, then!" I asked.

"Well, some boys in my school have described me as being pretty, so my mother must be pretty", giving me a cheeky look.

If what Mandy had told me was true, then to the string of men who had bedded her mother, far too many for her to remember, Shirley Lee must be one voluptuous, sexy woman.

I ordered her an iced lemon tea, something she immediately liked. After she had taken a few more sips, I urged her to continue her story.

"I like it," she said referring to the ice lemon tea. From that day onwards, she'd order it whenever she was with me.

On the way home from school that afternoon, Mandy, in her mind's eye, saw visions of her mother confronting her whether or not she had told her teacher about her leaving school. On arrival home she was surprised to see her mother wearing an apron over her house dress, cooking dinner. She looked up when Mandy entered the kitchen to go to her room. Mandy could feel her heart beating furiously when she sensed her mother looking at her.

"I'm sorry, Ma, for being late".

"That's all right," replied her mother in a tone that sounded almost friendly. "I'm making chicken rice; we'll eat as soon as your brothers are home".

Mandy stopped in her tracks and looked at her mother. She wasn't sure if she had heard her right. Didn't her mother say that they'll eat when her two brothers reached home? Even her tone sounded positively friendly; this can't be, she thought. Her mother has never been this friendly to her, ever! Something must be wrong, Mandy thought. She was going to ask me to leave school.

Mandy scrutinised her mother's almost flawless face for any tell-tale signs behind her actions. Her mother certainly looked different; her hair was done in a bun and she wore a dress underneath her apron that looked as if it has been ironed and not her usual crumpled house dress she'd normally wear at home. Mandy rubbed her eyes before continuing to stare at her mother in disbelief. Her mother was actually standing in front of her worktable with a cleaver in one hand and the other holding what looked like a well-done chicken on a chopping block. With even strokes, she saw her mother sliced the chicken. Even though she was seeing it, Mandy couldn't believe what she was seeing. Mandy continued to watch in awe as her mother chopped and sliced the brown crinkled chicken into bite-size pieces and arranged them onto a big plate with slices of cucumbers neatly arranged around its rim.

Their dining table looked as if they were expecting some important people for dinner. The aroma in the house was positively appetising. Mandy was struggling to restrain herself from picking a piece of the chicken and putting it in her mouth. The thought that had kept coming back to her mind was that her mother's new lover was coming to dinner, otherwise why should she go to all this trouble of cooking? Not for us, surely!

All of a sudden Mandy had lost her appetite. Dejected she was about to walk to her room when her two brothers walked in through the front door. They ignored her as they were about to walk past her, holding their shoes in their hand, and their school bags slung across their shoulders.

But as soon as they saw their mother busily pouring the clear chicken soup in little soup bowls while the dining table looked as if a banquet was being prepared for some special guests, they stopped in their tracks and gaped in disbelief. They looked questioningly at Mandy, but before Mandy could respond with the sign language they always use among themselves, her mother turned towards them and said, "Go and wash your hands and then come quickly for dinner, otherwise everything will get cold".

Without speaking, they quickly disappeared into their room which the two of them shared while Mandy went to hers. To see their mother cooking dinner was certainly a strange sight for all of them. None of them could remember when they had seen her do that – cooking real dinner!

If ever their mother were to cook anything, all they can remember her do was to cook a dish that could sometime last three to four days. She always did this in order to save time. Very often, a few days later, they'd find the dish had turned rancid, but bereft of anything else to eat, and to avoid being scolded by their mother, they'd force every morsel down their throats.

More often than not, Mandy and her two brothers would eat noodles or takeaways from the nearby stalls before coming home from school. If they ran out of money, which was often, they would eat instant noodle at home. Their mother had made sure instant noodles were always available at home. She'd buy a carton at a time.

If they had come home and found their mother in the living room watching her favourite soap operas, they would wait until she had either gone out or had gone to bed before they came out to make their *Maggi noodles*. Any noise from the kitchen would result in a roar from the living room berating them that they have no consideration for her well-being. She would berate them by telling them that she had been on her feet all day long and now even at home she had no peace and quiet. Sometimes if she or her brothers didn't feel up to having another bowl of noodle, they would settle for a cup of *Milo* with a slice of bread.

Although most kids their age were allowed to watch occasional television, Shirley Lee had imposed a strict rule that they were not to watch any TV without her permission and very rarely she would give her permission. Besides, with all their schoolwork to do, they hardly had time to watch TV. Occasionally, if they want to watch, they could only do so when their mother had gone out. And if they were hungry, they would not come out until the coast was clear and not before, no matter how hungry they were.

If Mandy were around she'd sometime cook for all of them. Constantly fearful that they may break something, or they would mess up the kitchen, they'd sit quietly at the kitchen table and wait patiently for Mandy to serve them. Once they had broken a bowl while trying to make an instant noodle, their mother came out of her bedroom and gave her two brothers a trashing using the handle of a broom. To most Asians it was considered bad luck to hit someone with a broom. Their mother, however, had never any qualms about using a broom to hit them with.

Despite Mandy's devotion to her two brothers, they had never once shown their appreciation to her. All they seemed to do was to take advantage of her. Without a doubt, they seem to prefer her cooking of the *Maggi noodles* to their own, but to show their gratefulness? Never! They knew that their sister would to try to make it interesting and tastier for them by putting in some vegetables and some dried mushrooms. Sometimes, if eggs were available, she'd add them in to make them even tastier. On their own, they would just add hot water to it and would then have their noodles *au naturel.*

That night, fearing that something ominous was about to happen, Mandy quickly went to her room as soon as dinner was over and she had washed all the dishes and put them away. The chicken rice, she had to admit, was one of the best she had eaten in a long time. She was convinced that her mother could certainly cook if she really wanted to.

As she stood in her bras and underwear in front of the mirror, Mandy realised, not for the first time, that her breasts were getting to be as big as her mothers'. She remembered not too long ago when, in one of her mother's rare good mood, they had bathed together and her mother had asked her to lather her body with soap. She remembered too that besides the mole under her mother's left breast, she saw how bushy and shiny her mother's pubic hair was just as hers were about to evolve.

A fearful thought came into Mandy's mind when she realised that physically she was becoming to be an exact replica of her mother. She placed her hand on her stomach and rubbed it with a circular motion and was thankful that it was still flat whereas her mother's now looked as if she was permanently pregnant.

If she was her mother's daughter, would she then one day become as mean and as cold as her mother had become? She shuddered at the thought as she unconsciously stroked her pubic hair. Before long, like the night before, she was slowly swept into a blissful tempest. Just like the night before, her strokes became more urgent and before long an ecstasy came along. Just like the one she felt the night before, her climax overcame her. And just like the night before, she dug her finger into her sex and felt its silky wetness and the accompanying niceness that resulted when she began to stroke her vagina.

Mandy, who had been lying on the bathroom floor, turned and laid flat on her stomach, her hand under her. She continued rubbing in a circular motion and before long she climaxed once more.

The next morning Mandy woke up early and had quickly showered and was about to put on her school uniform when she realized that it was Saturday and there was no school. She quickly changed into a pair of shorts and a tee-shirt. In the kitchen she boiled a kettle of water and prepared to make a cup of instant cup of coffee. Thinking about last night made her wonder what was her mother up to. The loud whistle from the kettle jolted her off her chair and she ran towards the kettle to turn it off. She was afraid her mother might wake up and things will be back to normal. She wanted to savour the peace and quiet a while longer.

As it turned out, her mother hadn't come home last night. She had left as soon as dinner was over. That night, dinner was another unusual affair; her mother actually ate with them and even attempted to make small talk with them.

Mandy made herself a slice of bread with *kaya jam* on the top. The smell of coffee brought her two brothers into the kitchen. They poked their heads around the corner to see if their mother was around. When they saw that Mandy was alone, they quickly asked her if their mother had woken. When Mandy told them that she hadn't come home, they gave a loud whoop. But as far as Mandy was concerned, the mystery deepened.

ƔƔƔƔƔƔ

CHAPTER FOUR

Penang Island is a small place and KOMTAR seems to be the focal point where people made a point of going to at least once a week. KOMTAR was like a city within a city where you could get all your necessities in one place. On the same floor where Eddy's café was there was a food court run by *Yaohan*, above it was the *Yaohan Departmental Store*. Not long after I had arrived in Penang, a stall had become vacant and for wanting of something to do I asked *Yaohan's* management if I could rent it from them. *Mr. Hito*, a no nonsense manager, asked me what did I want to sell there. I told him that I had wanted to sell *Nasi Padang* since restaurants selling *Nasi Padang* in Singapore, where I had come from, was very popular there. I had thought that since Penang's racial composition resembled that of Singapore, it should be popular here too. Fortunately for me my assumption turned out to be correct, even though it took me more than three months of sweating it out with hardly enough income to pay my staff, before I finally broke even. About three months after that it became quite profitable.

Mandy would come to my *Nasi Padang Stall* late in the afternoon almost every Friday after school. She told me she had to save for a week just to have a meal of fried chicken or fried fish and vegetable with her rice at my place. I guess my staffs tend to be economically correct whenever I was around. Mandy, however, would top her rice with a lot of gravy. Some times when she had less money than usual, I'd ask my staff to throw in a small piece of chicken or a fried fish on her plate of rice. I would sit there with her while she had her meal. If she had her friends with her I would leave them alone.

Whenever we were alone she would tell me things that had been bothering her, or about something that she had found exciting, at other times she would just concentrate on eating her food would leave as soon as she has finished.

During her next visit to my stall she seemed very upset. I asked her what the matter was and tried to calm her down by ordering a glass of ice-cold herbal tea she had always loved. When she finally had calmed down she told me that her mother had wanted her to leave school and to find a job.

I told her she must have made a mistake because as far as I know no mother would want her children to miss out on school. Mandy wasn't convinced because for the first time since she had begun to patronize my place, I have never seen her lose her appetite. On that Friday evening she had left her fried chicken practically untouched. Normally I would see her pick the bones clean. She only drank half a glass of her herbal tea before rushing off. As soon as she had left the *herbal tea* and the *Prawn Mee* sellers came over and sat with me. Judging by the looks on their faces, they thought that I was one lucky guy having a young girl like Mandy as a girl friend!

* * *

The whistling of the kettle jolted her back to the present. The moment she turned the stove off she heard her mother calling for her to come to the living room. Fearing the worst, Mandy shuffled towards their living room where she found her mother standing looking out of the window.

Earlier that morning, as she was putting on her dress, Mandy thought about her mother's unusual behaviour during dinner last night. She had practically dotted on them like she had never done before. Even her two younger brothers were bewildered with their mother's sudden change of behaviour. As dinner progressed, her two brothers kept looking in her direction with questioning looks on their faces. Not wanting her mother's mood to change, Mandy signalled to them to behave themselves. Having been subjected to their mother's constant berating for any slight slip-up during most of their young lives, they were happy to comply. Mandy too felt happy that evening, perhaps because she saw her mother happy for the first time. All three of them ate in silence.

The subject of her wanting Mandy to leave school was never brought up that night. After she and her two brothers had cleared the table and had washed up all the dishes and put them in the wooden cupboard, Mandy walked to the living room where her mother was sitting watching the television. She could feel her heart starting to pound, she was sure her mother could hear it. She forced herself to stand in front of her and bowed slightly while her brothers stood stiffly behind her.

"Ma, thank you very much for cooking such a lovely dinner," Mandy offered.

"Oh, did you enjoy it?"

"Yes, very much Ma."

"Sit down," her mother said, still in the same friendly tone. Her two brothers seeing that they were not being asked to stay, said their thanks and quickly fled to their room.

"I know I've asked you to leave school before, but now I want you to forget about what I've said. I want you to study as hard as you can so that you can obtain the best result in your SPM."

Mandy couldn't believe what she was hearing. "Do you mean it, Ma?"

"Yes, I do. Now go on and do your homework", her mother replied.

* * *

Peter was the name of Mandy's mother's new male companion. That weekend he had come for her mother, and while waiting for her mother to emerge from her bedroom, he had introduced himself to Mandy and had offered his hand. Mandy took it and shook it a few times as Chinese were inclined to do, but when she wanted to pull back her hand, he held on to it for several moments, rubbing the back of her hand with his other hand. Mandy felt uncomfortable but before she could react, she heard her mother's bedroom door opened and shut. Peter quickly dropped her hand and pretended to look for some imaginary thing by tapping his shirt and trousers pockets a few times. Mandy took a fast exit through the side door that led to her grandparents' house a few doors away.

Shirley Lee saw them as soon she opened her bedroom door and was immediately consumed with anger. She was tempted to storm into the room and pull Mandy away from Peter, but somehow had managed to contain her anger. She shut the door loud enough to stop Peter from going any further with Mandy. She forced a smile when both of them looked at her. She saw the way her Peter had looked at Mandy and knew that if she didn't nip it in the bud this amorous feeling he was having for Mandy, it'll be just a matter of time before he'd walk out on her, and she wouldn't have that.

She decided to change her strategy by encouraging Mandy to do well in school. She had always known that Mandy would leave home once she had a good grade in her final examinations. It was for that reason she had wanted Mandy to quit school so that she'd be able to contribute to their support. But now, with Peter in her life, she wanted to make sure that Mandy got out of Penang as quickly as possible. She planned on doing anything to help Mandy do well in her forth-coming examinations.

Once Mandy was out of the way, she'd have Peter all to herself. Her two boys wouldn't be a problem; she could always rely on her parents to look after them. She'd give them money of course. Peter, as a senior government servant, who earned a good salary, is her best catch thus far. She could afford to be generous. What if Peter wanted a family, would I still be able to have children? She quickly dismissed that thought from her mind; she'd cross that bridge when the time came, she thought.

Shirley realised that at her age, Peter may be her only chance to have someone to look after her in her old age. Even her body, once the envy of every women she knew, was beginning to show signs that things were not the way they used to be. Her breasts reminded her of the papayas in the backyard of her parent's house – gravity at work! Lately she noticed that despite the gallons of lotion she had put on her skin, it still felt like it was slowly turning into leather. Even sex was no more fun for her. Each encounter with Peter was like a big show that had to go on.

With Mandy's examinations just a few weeks away, she could afford to be extra nice to her. She'd do everything in her power to encourage her to study. She had always known that Mandy would leave her once she had her results. That thought had previously irked her, but now it became very appealing to her. With Mandy gone she'd make sure that Peter would have his show anytime he wanted.

Shirley had often heard stories from her friends that some Malay women take some herbal concoction called *Jamu* to tighten their vaginas, especially after giving birth. She made a mental note to get some for herself. As for her sagging breasts, she decided to put more efforts into her exercises and also by massaging them into shape.

The prospect of living the rest of her life without a man seemed daunting to her and she was determined that under no circumstances will that become a reality. How would she live unless Peter married her? Peter, the government servant, was a catch she'd never thought she'd land! Didn't they say that being a government servant was like having an iron rice bowl?

* * *

Mandy welcomed her mother's change of attitude towards her although it was puzzling to her, but she had no time to dwell on it. She had quickly dismissed it as a result of some sort of hormonal changes in her mother. She heard stories that women of her mother's age get what they call menopause. And one of the things they say happened when they had this thing was that they'd go through a personality change. How long will this change last, Mandy wondered?

If it was menopause, then it was the best thing that had ever happened to her mother, Mandy thought. The alternative would have been unthinkable! Imagine leaving school just weeks before her final examinations? She knew that if her mother had forced her to quit school, she would have left home. Where she would go, she had no idea, but she was sure that was what she'd do.

The last time her mother had threatened to pull her out of school, Mandy had concocted up a story for her by telling her that the school principal had wanted to see her personally. Mandy had rightly guessed that the thought of seeing the principal in person would put her mother in a state of panic. Mandy had even hinted that it was something to do with the law that children must go to school otherwise their parents will be in trouble. Mandy had vaguely heard something to this effect, but the details had eluded her.

Shirley's fear of the law stemmed from a brush she had had with the law not too long ago, and she had never forgotten it. Her short spell in a police lockup for being caught in a police raid together with a number of illegal aliens working as Guests Relation Officers or GROs was something that was etched permanently in her brain. It was a traumatic experience for her. She'd tremble whenever she saw a policeman. She had never recovered fully from it although she had never told anyone what actually had happened to her in lockup. Mandy knew about the incident from a friend whose uncle was a policeman. She never felt so embarrassed in her life, but fortunately her friend hadn't mentioned that incident again.

She remembered the first time her mother had asked her to leave school, her mother in a frightened voice, told Mandy to tell her school principal that it was all a misunderstanding - she had no wish for Mandy to leave school. Mandy told her that perhaps it would be better if she gave her teacher a letter. Her mother agreed and asked Mandy to prepare the letter for her. Mandy went to her room and took out the letter from her desk drawer, the one she had already prepared and brought it to her bed to read it once more. She had spent a good part of an hour to write the letter. For effect she subjected her mother to a fearful anticipation by allowing several more minutes to pass before she came out of her room with the letter for her mother to sign. Her mother had quickly signed it without reading. Mandy smiled when she remembered how her mother had paled when she lied about the school principal wanting to see her. It certainly felt good when she didn't have to cower to her mother, even though it was only for a few moments.

Unfortunately for Mandy, her mother did not take long to discover from friends who played

Mahjong with her that a child needn't have to attend school if her parents didn't want him or her to do so. That same evening, Shirley Lee, her face twisted in anger, waited for Mandy to come home from school. She held in her hand a piece of twig she had cut from a nearby tree and had made a few practice strokes on its trunk to see how it felt in her hand. As soon as Mandy walked into the door she started beating Mandy with it until Mandy's back and legs were bloodied and the twig split into two.

Mandy was only saved from further beatings when her grandfather, who had walked past their house, heard her screams. He rushed in the house and grabbed whatever left of the twig from his daughter's hand and immediately stopped her from inflicting more pain on his granddaughter. From that day onwards, her mother had always used the threat to pull her out of school whenever she felt like it, knowing very well that there was no power on earth that could prevent her from actually doing it.

* * *

With one worry out of the way, Mandy's other worry was her forth-coming examinations. So far she felt comfortable enough with most of her subjects except for two subjects with which she was having a hard time trying to get to grips with.

Mandy wanted her SPM certificate so badly she could almost taste it. Although she has studied very hard in school, she wasn't all that confident that she could obtain the grades she was aiming for due to the two weak subjects. Even her own class teacher thought that she was only good enough for grade three unless she had extra tuitions. A grade three would only qualify her for a factory job, a far cry from what she had always pictured herself to be doing after she had left school!

She knew that she had to have tuitions for her two weak subjects, but where in the world would she get the money to pay a tuition teacher? She kept asking herself that over and over again. A good SPM result was something Mandy had wanted more than anything else in the world. It was her ticket to freedom! With it she could leave home and never look back. Home, as far as she was concerned, was her hell on earth. Home was worse than being in a prison because home was where Mama was.

After each thrashing from her mother she would hate her mother more. Mandy would picture her mother as someone who had become so fat and flabby she had pictured some faceless fishermen had harpooned her mother while she was swimming in the sea near their house when they thought that she was a whale. That would never happen, of course, because Shirley Lee was terrified of setting foot in the sea again, where once she was almost drowned.

Once, while she was swimming at the nearby sea with a friend, an undercurrent swept her out to the sea. It was dusk when the incident happened and the beach was already deserted, her friend, who wasn't a good swimmer had tried to save Shirley but was swept away by the strong current and had drowned. Fortunately for Shirley, a returning Malay fisherman in his small boat who was on his way back to his kampong saw Shirley in trouble. He immediately dove in and quickly managed to pull her out of the water.

Although only six years old and had just come home from school when that incident happened, Mandy, already an abused child, felt nothing when told that her mother had nearly drowned but was saved by a fisherman and now resting and well.

Very often during the ensuing years Mandy had often wished her mother had died then, because Mama, despite having cheated death once, was never a sweet or a caring person. All she can think of her mother was that she would hit her for any slightest mistake and that usually followed by a barrage of words so foul, it would put any sailor to shame.

Mandy will always think of her mother as a vulgar person, unfit to live in a refined society like Malaysia, where its people were usually polite and considerate with each other. To Mandy her mother had always been mean, cruel, vicious, fierce, brutal and abusive. Sometimes in her black mood, her mother would develop into a person with a combination of all these "attributes" and used it effectively on Mandy. Sometimes after a severe beating from her mother, Mandy would convince herself that her mother was really the devil in disguise.

> *If you strike a child, take care that you strike it in anger, even at the risk of maiming it for life. A blow in cold blood neither can nor should be forgiven.*
>
> George Bernard Shaw (1856–1950),

* * *

Mandy would daydream often, always with the same objective, which was to get as far away from her mother as she possibly could. Often she would count the money she had saved from doing odd jobs over the years. She'd work some more after her exams were over, while waiting for her results. With the money she'd buy her one-way bus ticket to Kuala Lumpur where jobs were plentiful according her friends, most of whom she knew would end up in KL. After working for a few months, she'd imagine herself moving into a nice flat, then another six months down the road; she'd get herself a car.

Despite lapsing into these occasional daydreams, Mandy would work very had in school, never missing a day no matter how bad the weather may get sometimes. Each day she would psyche herself with a thought that if she'd work harder, with luck she might get a good grade; although she knew luck has nothing to do with it.

"I wish I have some spare cash for tuitions," she lamented to Carol, her friend since grade one. "I'm weak in at least two compulsory subjects. I don't know what I'm going to do. What I have saved so far wouldn't be enough to pay a tuition teacher for long."

"You could try teaming up with some of the bright students and study after school with them," Carol suggested.

"I can't even do that! My mother insisted that I come straight home after school," Mandy replied dejectedly.

"What is wrong with your mother? Doesn't she want you to do better than she did?"

"I guess not. All she wanted to do is to play Mahjong all day with the neighbours and at night, to make love with that new boyfriend of hers," replied Mandy.

"Really?" Carol asked, curious all of a sudden. "Can I ask you something? Have you ever peeked in their bedroom to see how they were doing it?"

"Of course not!" Mandy replied angrily. "How dare you think such a thing?"

"I'm sorry," said Carol. "I was just curious, that's all!"

"Well, if you must know, I haven't peeked, OK! But I can hear them do it," said Mandy, no longer angry with her friend.

"Really? Come on, tell me about their lovemaking…"

Carol, who had just begun working, was one year Mandy's senior, and had been her close friend for several years. After having witnessed on several occasions from the bruises on Mandy's body how cruel Mandy's mother could be, Carol had encouraged her friend to study hard so that she could get a good job. She herself was happy to have landed a good job in one of the factories in the Industrial Zone, and she according to her mother, was poised for a promotion soon.

Unlike Mandy, Carol, despite having lost her father at about the same time as Mandy did, had had a happy childhood. Her mother had seen to it that despite her husband's untimely death, she was determined to see her Carol had a good education and a happy home.

Mandy took her friend's advice by sounding out some of her classmates to see if she could study with them. To her surprise, many were willing to let her study with them. That evening she told her mother that until her examinations were over she'd be home late so that she could do her studies with some friends. Her mother asked her who her friends were, after Mandy mentioned who they were her mother seemed satisfied and gave Mandy her permission.

Mandy's progress was slow at first but improved considerably as her friends took the trouble to take her through the difficult passages in literature and to try to make her understand the true meaning behind the words or phrases. Other students helped with her biology and mathematics, her two weakest subjects.

With less than two weeks before the examinations, Mandy was still not confident enough that she had come to grips with biology and mathematics. One day after school she had gone to the library with some of her friends and studied until 9.30 PM and while she was waiting for her bus, a car stopped right in front of her and to her surprise she saw Peter waving at her from behind the steering wheel of the car. Thinking that her mother might be with him, she approached the car, but when she saw that he was alone, Mandy backed away from him and went back to the bus stop. Peter got out of the car and called out to her. "Let me give you a lift home," he said.

"No, thank you, I can take the bus," replied Mandy curtly.

"If you are afraid that your mother might see us, I'll drop you off some distance from your house, OK?" Peter came close to Mandy and grabbed her hand and pulled her towards his car.

Mandy tried to push him away from her but his grip was strong. She struggled to get away from him but he wouldn't let go of her. As they were struggling the bus arrived with a loud hiss from its hydraulics as the door opened to let some passengers out. Peter immediately released his grip and Mandy ran quickly towards the bus and got on without looking back. As the bus pulled away from the bus stop, Mandy saw Peter got back into his car and had followed the bus. All of a sudden the relief she had felt dissipated as fast as it came.

The moment she got off the bus, she looked towards the rear of the bus to see if Peter's car was anywhere near. Satisfied that he wasn't following the bus, she ran as fast as she could in the direction of her house.

Home didn't look so welcoming to Mandy that night because all the lights were either turned off or they had a black-out. When she saw lights in the neighbours' house, she had assumed that her mother hadn't come home yet. That night she knew that her two brothers will be at her grandparent's. She thought it strange that her mother wouldn't leave a single light on as she normally would before going out.

With trembling hands Mandy opened the front door and almost died of fright when she saw a dark figure looming in front of her the moment she walked in. She fumbled for the light switch and turned it on. Her mother, still in her evening clothes, was lying on the sofa with the back of her left hand covering her eyes.

Mandy approached her and stood close to her not sure what else to do. After several minutes her mother pulled away the hand that was covering her eyes and began to sit up on the sofa. Mandy was taken aback when she saw her mother's hideous face streaked with her mascara. Her mother had been crying, she knew that much, but why? Her eyes were all puffed up and apart from her mascara that had streaked down her face; there was a slight bruise on her upper left cheek.

Judging from the dress she was wearing, Mandy guessed that her mother had been out and was home rather early judging from her mother's usual habit - the wall clock indicated 10.05 PM - far too early for her to be home. Normally she wouldn't be back until two in the morning.

"Ma, are you all right?" Mandy asked as she stood gingerly in front of her mother.

"No, I'm not all right. The son of a bitch had just dumped me," she scowled.

"You mean, Peter?"

"Yes, Peter. Who else?" She gave out a sniff before wiping her nose with the back of her hand in the same manner she herself had often done as a kid and her mother used to reprimand her for it.

Mandy had wanted to say something, but had changed her mind. Any utterances from her might upset her mother more and she didn't want that.

"I should have guessed it when I found the packet of condoms in the glove compartment of his car recently. We never use condoms…" She stopped when she realised she was talking to her own daughter.

Mandy took the seat opposite and looked at the pitiful figure of her mother. She thought of telling her mother about how Peter tried to force her to get in his car a while ago but decided that it might just inflame her mother further. It was obvious to Mandy that Peter dumped her mother for her. She wasn't sure whether she should be angry or flattered but a glance at the clock on the wall told her that she should be in bed soon.

"I'm sorry about Peter, Ma," said Mandy. "I think it's for the best." Regretting it immediately.

"Best for whom? For you?" Her mother snapped. "I saw the way he fondled you. Keep away from him, do you hear?"

Disgusted, Mandy stormed to her room without a single word and slammed the door behind her.

That night she had a dream whereby she saw a couple fornicating and as if by some inner force she found herself drawn closer and closer to the two wriggling couple. She immediately saw Peter as the man on the top of the woman. Instead of running away from them, Mandy stood rigid with excitement as she watched Peter ramming his member in his partner-in-sex. His motion was rhythmic at first but as he began to accelerate his strokes, his partner switched from being passive to active and began to meet his thrust with an equal counter-thrust of her own with equal intensity. Moments later Mandy watched them reached their climax that brought a loud groan from Peter and a gasping sound coming from the woman underneath him. She saw the woman opened her mouth, and with her eyes closed and soon after she let out a loud moan. He lit the cigarette and offered it to his companion. The woman got to a sitting position and took the cigarette from Peter's outstretched hand. As she put it to her mouth to take a puff from it, Mandy looked in dismay when she saw that the woman was herself.

Mandy woke up in a sweat and out of breath. She realised that she must have masturbated for her finger was in her vagina and it was wet with her juice.

CHAPTER FIVE

Mary could read and write, but just barely, and she never held a job in her life. While her husband was alive, they lived a fairly comfortable life with a small house of their own not far from the Penang Hill. As a matter of fact Mary and Joseph's two bed-room wooden house was at the foot of the famed hill now known as *Bukit Bendera*.

To make things simple, the British Colonials called the tallest hill on the island, Penang Hill. Her postman husband was killed when some drunk driver knocked into his motor cycle while he was making his rounds.

Mary could have continued living comfortably with her husband's gratuity and other payments the government had given her if she hadn't been swindled out of her money by one of her late husband's old friends.

For several months after her husband's death this so-call friend was Mary and Carol's regular visitor at their house. The man, a widower, was nothing but a con artist – an impostor. His modus operandi was simple; he would befriend people who were about to retire. His main target would be government servants, whose particulars he would easily get from friends who were still working with the government. Once he got their names he would then check them out to see if they were people he could easily make friends with.

In Mary's husband's case, it was simple for Thien to befriend the easy-going and trusting Joseph. Since Joseph and Mary were church-going people and even though Thien was a Buddhist, he nevertheless forced himself to attend the same church that Joseph and Mary went to. Almost immediately they struck up a friendship and not long after he had their trust.

Neither Mary nor Joseph, of course, had any inkling that this trusted soul was nothing but a person waiting for the opportunity to con Joseph out of his money once he had retired. From the information he got, he knew that Joseph would be retiring soon.

Thien couldn't believe his luck when Joseph suddenly died less than five months before his retirement was due. With the exception of their priest, Joseph and Mary had no other close friends. Some weeks after Joseph's funeral, Mary who had received some papers the government, had gone to seek help from her priest. Unfortunately he was on a sabbatical leave and a new priest was in his place instead, someone Mary did know that well. Instead of going to him to seek help she turned to Thien to help her with some documents pertaining to some payments she was about to receive from the government.

Once again Thien couldn't believe his luck and saw this as his golden opportunity. As he helped her get her money, he began to formulate a plan to part her from her money.

During the next month or so, he talked constantly about a business venture he was about to embark into that was going to make him a very rich man. He never actually approach Mary and ask her to put money in the business but each time he came to visit he lamented on how difficult it was nowadays for him to find somebody he could really trust to look after his small office while he was out to put in place his business plan for the company. As it were, he had already several out of state visits planned but had to be postponed because there was no one he could trust to look after his office while he was away.

After a couple of weeks of moaning about the same thing, he came out and ask Mary if she would consider working for him and look after the office for him. He offered her a pay that was more than double than what she was getting from a fix deposit at the bank.

"Me?" Mary retorted. "What do I know about running an office?"

"There's nothing to it. All you need do is to answer the phones and to type a few letters".

"I don't know. Perhaps I could give it a try since there is very little for me to do at home now".

"Of course, it would be nice if you were a partner in the firm too," he said. Realizing that he may be pushing things a bit too fast, he quickly added. "But that's something we can talk about later".

Carol tried to make some sense as to what her mother was telling her that evening after school. She also had no idea as to why anybody would be excited about going to work every morning when she didn't have to. Although she hadn't told anyone, Carol didn't really like Thien. She found him obnoxious, especially after he had tried to kiss her on the cheek one day. Carol had regretted for not telling her mother about that incident.

Mary found the work was simple enough, all she had to do was type simple letters which Thien had prepared in long hand for her and to answer the telephone. The most interesting thing about her job was answering the telephone. She seemed to be talking to some very important people by the sound of their names, some of whom had high sounding titles, all were keen to speak to her boss. What Mary didn't know was that the important people who had been calling were friends of Thien. For a cup of coffee or a few dollars from Thien, they were more than happy to make these calls.

By the time Mary receive her first pay check, she was convinced that the company she was working for had a good future and her boss was certainly a man with important connections. The next day, without telling Carol, she withdrew all her money from the bank and bought a bank draft made out to the company.

Once again the man Mary worked for couldn't believe his good fortune. He disappeared as soon as he transferred the money into his account in another state, and was never seen again.

The next day Mary found herself locked out of the office. On checking with the agent, she found out that it was only rented out on a month-to-month basis and it was in the name of her own church with the Pastor's name as a reference. The Pastor told her that neither he nor his church had anything to do with the renting of the office. It soon dawned on Mary that she had been swindled and she was penniless.

With all her savings gone, Mary had no choice but to find ways and means to survive for herself and for her daughter. It was doubly hard when she wasn't trained for anything, apart from the short stint at the conman's office, except to keep house and to look after her family. She took in washings and did some sewing, something she had liked to do as a hobby. It was difficult and it didn't take her long to realise that the hand-to-mouth existence wasn't what she wanted either for herself nor for her daughter. She told herself she was going to make some changes with their lives and not just leave everything to fate.

The first thing Mary did was to stop feeling sorry for herself, and the second was to stop thinking about the money she had lost. "It's gone," she told herself, "there's no point crying over it". It was easily said than done, but she managed somehow. The next thing she did was to work doubly hard so that she could save some money.

To achieve that end she took in more washings and hired herself a part-time worker to cope with the extra workload. After she had saved some money, she began making and selling cakes and *nasi lemak*, a type of Malay rice which people normally eat for breakfast, which she sold at her make-shift roadside stall from seven in the morning. All the preparation had to be done the night before and she would arrive at her stall around six-thirty.

While she was busy at her stall until about three in the afternoon, she kept her laundry business going by hiring another worker. She gave up her sewing job because that needed her full attention.

Mary soon found out that her food business gave her a better return, not only on her investment, but her time as well. Not wanting to disappoint her customers who were mainly single office workers living in rented rooms, she left the entire laundry business to her two workers and concentrated on her food business. By this time she offered to do ironing as well.

Mary soon found out that many people who worked in the city hardly ever come home for lunch. She decided to expand her menu by including plain rice and numerous other dishes and delicacies for her customers to take to their office for their lunch. She was told that many offices nowadays have microwave ovens for their staff to use to heat up their food. To make it easy for her customers to heat up their food, Mary had them packed in polystyrene boxes so that heating them up in a microwave oven would be a snap, even if they had kept their lunch boxes in refrigerators all morning. It had cost Mary an extra ten cents for the polystyrene box, but it was money well spent.

Her customers had shown their appreciation by their return visits. In the beginning Mary had only a pushcart in which to carry her things, and each morning around five o'clock, she would load it up and pushed it for nearly a mile to a spot close to a road junction where she set up her stall. It comprised of a folding table, which she found the hardest to cart around in a pushcart, a small stool on which to sit on while waiting for her customers and a large umbrella to shade her from the harsh Malaysian sun and from the occasional rain.

With her table under the brightly-coloured umbrella, she arranged the food, which she had packed in clear plastic containers, in neat rows on it. On a good day, people would start coming in as early as six-thirty and she would continue serving them until about half-past two in the afternoon.

One of Mary's enduring habits is that she was a neat person. Each day around two-thirty, before she left for home, she'd sweep up all the debris her customers had left behind and put them in a plastic bag to be disposed of in a proper manner on her way home.

Going home with everything sold gave Mary a nice feeling, not only because she had money in her purse, but also the wheelbarrow felt much lighter for her to push. However when it rained and the business was slow, she'd end up with plenty of food to take home with her. She would struggle with the wheelbarrow, for it would feel heavy in her hands, especially when she had to push it through some muddy stretches along the way. Occasionally the wheel would get stuck in the mud.

Although it was about a mile from her home, Mary had chosen that particular spot to do business because it was close to a busy road that led to the city. There was an open field where her customers could park their cars without hindering the traffic flow. In the beginning she only made a little money from the sale of her breakfast fares, but it began to pick up after she included her lunch fares.

Before long her business began to increase and kept on increasing when the news about her food began to spread, the wheelbarrow she'd used to cart her food became no longer adequate to carry all the food she had to sell. Mary's business principle was simple, she'd only sell the food she herself would eat and would only use fresh ingredients.

Mary sold whatever jewellery she owned and bought herself a three-wheeled cart, which she could push to and from her *Air Itam* house. She also bought some folding stools and tables for her "eat-in" customers to have their meals in comfort. She also added some cold and hot drinks to sell. As Mary's business became increasingly brisk, she asked Carol to come straight from school to assist her. Mary had made a policy of providing good nourishing food at her stall, and despite the fluctuating prices of foodstuffs, she'd always try to maintain her selling prices whenever she could, increasing them when it was absolutely necessary. In no time mother and daughter became as well known as the food they were selling.

Two years earlier, when Carol was in the midst of preparing for her SPM examinations, she asked her mother whether she should leave school and help her full time at the stall.

"How can you even think such a thing?" Mary replied angrily. "The only reason I've worked so hard all this time was to see to it that you have a good education".

"How can you say that, mother, I've worked just as hard too! When I'm not in school I have to be, not only here to help you sell, but at home too to help with your cooking? Each day I have barely the time to do my homework and to study. This year is my SPM year, I don't even have time even to go to the library, how can I make it, mother?"

Mary looked at her daughter and cried. "Oh, Carol, I'm so sorry. I guess I got so carried away with our business I have forgotten the reason why we've worked so hard for".

That night Mary took out her *BSN Savings Account Book* and looked at her balance. She was mildly surprised when she saw that she had more than three thousand ringgit in her credit balance. It was more than enough to engage at least two workers, she thought. She picked up the telephone, which she had installed two years ago in order to help her with her purchases and other related business use, and made a few phone calls. As soon as she hung up, she went to Carol's room and knocked softly on the door. She waited until she heard Carol invited her in. On entering the room she was as usual glad to see her daughter busy with her studies. The thick books on Carol's desk looked impressive to her. And in front of her was an open exercise book on which she could see Carol's neat hand writing. She had often wished she could be a better reader, at least to be able to read what her daughter had written. Unfortunately all she was able to do was to pick up one or two words which had very little meaning to her on their own.

"Carol, from tomorrow onwards, all I want you to worry about is your school work. You needn't come to help me after school anymore. I want you to start preparing for your SPM examinations right away. Go to the library if you want to, because from tomorrow onwards your mother will become a boss lady. Come morning I will have two ladies to help me do everything from cooking to serving the customers. We'll do some of the cooking at the site so that we won't mess up our kitchen like we used to do. And during lunch they'll be helping me to serve the customers, and at the end of the

day they'll help me clean up. How do you like that?"

"Oh, mother! Are you sure you can afford to hire anybody? And did you say two ladies? Who?"

Carol gave her mother a suspicious look. It occurred to her that her mother might be trying to do everything all by herself just to deter her from disrupting her studies. Even though her mother was a strong woman with not an ounce of fat on her body, Carol doubted that she could handle everything all by herself. Besides, due to an increase in business recently, she and her mother had to get up earlier than usual to prepare for the extra food. And at night Carol had noticed that her mother would doze off right in the middle of her favourite

Cantonese show on TV. She was afraid that the strain might be too much for her. Her mother was all she had got; she didn't want anything to happen to her.

"Ma, are you sure you've got people to help you with the cooking and to serve? Please don't lie to me, okay?"

"I'm not lying to you. I have got two women who'll join me first thing in the morning. Please don't worry."

Mary planted a kiss on her daughter's cheek before leaving her to her books. The next day on the way to school, Carol, despite her mother's instruction not to come, decided to drop in on her mother. On arrival she saw only one person helping her mother with the cooking. She recognised Ah Chai, one of their relatives who were recently widowed. Carol tried to see where the other person could be, didn't her mother say that she was employing two ladies, but where is the other one?

"Ma, where is the other person who is supposed to work for you? I only see Auntie Chai helping you."

"She'll be coming in the afternoon just before lunch. I'm only paying her part-time," replied Mary.

Carol could see that her mother seemed to have everything under control, most of the food seemed to have been cooked with only a few more dishes to be done and it was almost seven-twenty.

Satisfied that her mother wasn't lying to her about getting some help, Carol bid her mother and her Auntie Chai goodbye and peddled her bicycle as fast as she could to school. She didn't realise that she had spent more time than she should chatting with her mother.

* * *

Several weeks later during the school holidays, on her way to the library, she decided to visit her mother at her stall. Carol had a great shock of her life when she found that her mother no longer was at her usual spot. She felt guilty for not visiting her mother at her stall for quite some time, but when she couldn't find her stall at her usual spot, she began to worry.

The entire street was empty and it even looked different; the field where her mother's customers used to park their cars were all fenced up with corrugated iron sheets. She saw a billboard indicating some sort of development being built on that site. On it were pictures of tall buildings, shop-lots and two-story terraced-houses judiciously featured with their selling prices written in bold red letters across it.

Carol knew she was in the right place when she recognised the worn-out spots where the tires of her mother's cart used to stand on. She was further convinced when she saw other little things she had recognised around her, but where was her mother?

Carol walked quickly to the end of the fence towards her right, and when she turned the corner, in the distance, she saw what looked like a large wooden shed with zinc roof, something that resembled her school canteen. And like her school canteen, there were a number of people seated in there on picnic-styled tables and bench sets instead of tables and chairs like she had in her school.

Carol noticed that most of the people there were workers in the hard hats, some of whom were eating while others seemed content reading their newspapers and smoking their cigarettes. As she walked nearer, a smile appeared on her face when she saw her mother sitting behind a counter talking to a man in front of it. It looked as if he was buying a packet of cigarettes from her mother.

Her mother selling cigarettes too? That was something new to her. Her mother never sold cigarettes before because she said she didn't want to contribute to people getting cancer. Carol had no doubt that her mother had a change of heart because there, on the counter top in front of the man, was a packet of Marlboro and her mother was giving him back some change.

Mandy was the first to see Carol and she shouted excitedly: "Auntie! Auntie! Carol is here!" Mary, whose view was blocked by her customer, poked her head out to see where Mandy was indicating. She smiled when she saw the look of surprise on her daughter's face.

"What are doing here? I thought you'd be at the library," she asked, at once anxious, thinking that her daughter might not be feeling well.

"I am on my way to the library. I thought I'd stop by and see how you were," replied Carol. "What happened to your old place? And where is your tricycle cart?"

"Well, as you can see I've moved here and it is a much better place, don't you think? As for my old rusty cart, I sold it. The workers told me that they are turning it into a mixed-development project that comprised of office blocks, shop-houses and condominiums".

"This place is certainly nice. How can you afford to build all this?" Carol gestured with a wave of her hand.

"The developer allowed me to stay on to provide food for their workers, provided my prices were reasonable, I agreed. They also built a proper eating-place for them, as you can see. And not only that, we have running water and electricity too. And do you know how many workers they have working here? Nearly two hundred. Can you imagine that? I'm feeding a lot of people for breakfast, lunch and dinner."

"I see you are also selling cigarettes too," Carol said.

"Oh, Carol, I had no choice. Some of the workers complained to their management and they came to me and insisted that I sell cigarettes too, or the deal is off."

Carol saw in her mother's eyes something she had never seen before, at least to her. She was begging for her understanding.

"Mother, I understand. You don't have to explain anything to me. I think it's wonderful that they've done all these things for you. What about business? Is it all right then?"

"Better than before. Not only I have all these workers to feed, my regular customers too are beginning to come back. I may have to find another helper to replace Mandy once the school holidays are over".

Mandy, who had been busy washing dishes, came over and gave Carol a hug. "Your mother was kind enough to give me this job, I'm so grateful to her. And I'm saving every cent I've earned from this job. When I get my SPM next year I am going to get myself a job in Kuala Lumpur."

A few days after she and Carol had that talk, Mary went to look for another relative of hers and asked her whether she'd like to work for her. Unlike Ah Chai, Ah Lian's husband was still alive, however he had recently been laid off because the Japanese factory he was working in were moving their entire operation to China. As luck would have it, he was knocked off his bike and had to have an operation. Although the company had compensated him when they ceased their operation in Penang, his medical bills had practically drained their savings. Without any hesitation Ah Lian had grabbed at Mary's offer. The next morning when Mary and her two relatives arrived for work, they found Mandy huddled up underneath some burlap bags under a table near a wall.

"Mandy! What are you doing here?" Mary asked.

"My mother beat me up and locked me out of the house last night. I came here to look for you and to ask you whether I could spend the night here. But you were not here...no one was here, so I waited. I must have fallen asleep..." When she stood up, Mary saw the bruise marks on Mandy's hands and shoulders.

"Oh! My God!" Mary cried out. "Mandy, I want you to stay here while I have a word with your mother. Don't go anywhere, do you understand. I'm going to ask your mother whether she'll let you stay with Carol and I while you work here. Would you like that?"

"Oh yes, I would! Thank you very much - do you think my mother will let me?"

"I'm sure of it," replied Mary. "Don't you worry about a thing now." Mary turned to her relative and said, "Ah Chai, please take Mandy to the room at the back and let her freshen up a bit. After that give her something to eat, and when she finished, show her what to do, all right? I'm going out but I'll be back in an hour"

"Yes, Mary," said Ah Chai. "Come along, Mandy."

"Mary, if you're going where I think you're going, bring back some of her clothes, will you?" asked Ah Chai.

Mary's meeting with Shirley Lee was short and sweet. She began by telling her that the police might want to have a talk with her regarding Mandy whom she and her workers found at her canteen this morning.

"She was covered with bruise marks and was hungry. She said you beat her up and locked her out of the house. The authorities will take a dim view with parents who abused their children".

Mary could see that her last remark caused Mandy's mother to shake like a leaf. Mary let it sink for a while before continuing.

"It is up to Mandy, of course, but just this once I may be able to talk her out of going to make a police report".

"Would you do that for me? I'd appreciate it very much. Tell her I'm sorry, I didn't mean to lock her out of the house. I thought she would go to my parents' house as she normally would. Mary could see that, like most bullies, she would cower like a scared rabbit when the tables are turned on them.

"I don't know...you've done these things to her before, haven't you?" Mary gave her a long hard look, but Shirley turned her head away and didn't reply. "I don't want to be involved in any court case, which I certainly will be if this gets to trial. So I'll tell you what. Since Mandy is having a break from school now, why don't you let her stay with Carol and me for the duration? During the day she can come and help me at my stall.

"I agree. Thank you very much. I know I can trust you to do the right thing for Mandy and me. You see I love her. I don't know why I do these things to her, but I promise you I won't do anything like this again."

"In that case, why don't you show me to her room so that I can pick up some clothes for her," said Mary.

For the rest of the school holidays Mandy stayed with her friend Carol and her mother. During the day she'd worked diligently at Mary's canteen and at night Carol was kind enough to help her with her studies. At that month's end Mandy received her two weeks' pay – the number of days she had worked – while Ah Chai received her full month's wages. Ah Lian who only worked a week got her week's pay.

"Ah Chai, please take Mandy to buy a pair of rubber shoes tomorrow afternoon", asked Mary. "She's ruining her own shoes with all that water splashing on them when she's doing the washing. Here is some money".

Mary managed to keep Shirley Lee on tenterhooks with regards to the police report. She kept the suspense going by telling her that Ah Chai had insisted that a police report should be made as a deterrent. A week later, Mary cooked up another story by telling her that the police had been round to her place and asked her a lot of questions. She wasn't lying when she said that; the police were always on the lookout at most constructions sites for foreign workers without the necessary permits.

Mary had no qualms about putting the pressure on Mandy's mother when she found out from her daughter how extensive Mandy's beatings had been. Carol told her how one day Mandy showed her the marks on her back and buttocks. According to Carol they look like tracks on railway yards except that they were welts and bruises criss-crossing each other all over her body especially her back, buttocks and thighs.

Mandy was aware that her school holiday was coming to an end and soon she had to leave for home. She was terrified at the prospect of meeting her mother again, and knowing what a vindictive person she was, Mandy was certain she would take it out of her for staying away for so long with not a visit home during all that time. She wasn't sure what Mary had been telling her during her weekly visit to her mother. Carol had told her that her mother had threatened to report Mandy's mother to the police. In fact Carol had advised Mandy to go straight to the police should her mother beat her again. Mandy was appalled at hearing what Carol had suggested, she knew she could never do that. Despite what her mother had done to her, she was still her mother, and reporting her to the police was something she could never contemplate on doing.

On the day Mandy was leaving for home she was grateful that Mary and Carol came along to give her some moral support. All morning she had been afraid, but she knew she had no other alternative but to go back home. With Mary and Carol around she was sure that her mother wouldn't dream of lashing at her either verbally or physically.

As it turned out, on that day, Mandy's mother was not only civilised but was hospitable too. She invited both mother and daughter to come in for a while so that she could thank them properly for looking after Mandy.

Mandy, who have never seen her mother entertain anybody this way before, didn't know what to make of it. Her mother actually insisted that Carol and her mother stay for tea. In a voice that was soft and close to sounding melodious, her mother asked Mandy to put the kettle on and to make some tea for their guests. She herself took out a tin of biscuits that she had in her bedroom and gave it to Mandy to bring out with the tea. While Mandy was in the kitchen, she overheard her mother saying to Mary how grateful she was for all she had done, especially for looking after Mandy.

When Mandy came into the living room carrying a tray containing the tea and biscuits, her mother actually got up and gave her a hug after she had put down the tray on the coffee table which to her surprise had a tablecloth over it. As she put her arm on Mandy's shoulder, her mother beamed at her and said, "I've missed you Mandy." Mandy was taken aback by that show of affection but tried not to show her surprised to their guests nor did she pull away as she instinctively would. She smiled lamely at her mother before disappearing into the kitchen.

The following year Carol sat for her SPM examinations, and while waiting for her results, she decided to take up a job as a trainee in a financial institution in George Town. Three months later, at about the same time she got her SPM results, they confirmed her with a slight increase in her salary. But instead of being thrilled Carol was dissatisfied not only with her pay but also with her job prospect. She told her boss that she was grateful that he had confirmed her but she was sorry she couldn't stay, and when her boss asked why, she told him. Picking the right words so as not to offend him, she told she had obtained a good grades in her SPM examinations, she wanted to do something more than what she was doing and she'd like to try elsewhere.

On hearing that, her boss offered her another, much senior post with higher pay. After briefing her on the job, Carol accepted it. She knew then it was exactly the type of work she had been looking for, besides, the pay was almost double what she earned when she first joined the firm.

Mary was pleased that her daughter had found the job she had liked and was happy for her. She too was happy because she had on the same day made a down payment to the developer for a shop lot she had been eyeing ever since they started with the project. It had an ideal location for a restaurant, she had said.

Not too long ago she wouldn't dare dream of owning her own restaurant, but as her savings began to grow, she became optimistic and began to work even harder.

When Mary returned home that night, she found Carol waiting with supper ready on the table. Over supper both mother and daughter told each other what each other had done. Mary told Carol that it'll probably be another six months before she can take possession of the premises. In the meantime, she told Carol, she had to move to another location because they have to finish the car park area where Mary's canteen was presently located.

The person she had been dealing with at the developer's office was a young executive whom she had liked, and thought him ideal as a son-in-law and not Sam with whom Carol was engaged to. If only she could arrange it so that the young man and Carol could meet, Mary was thinking. But first of all she must find out if he's married. Having her daughter married to the right man was very important to Mary, and Sam McGee, in her opinion certainly wasn't the right person for her. The next day when she saw the young man walking past her canteen, she asked him whether he'd like some *Pau* she had just made. The young man thanked her but shook his head, telling her that he had just eaten and he had a site meeting to attend to.

It took Mary several more days before she finally found out that the young man was not only single but he also lived with his mother. His father, according to her source, was a clerk-of-works for this same construction company and had died when this young man was only in his teens.

His mother who was a school teacher brought him up single-handedly like she herself did with Carol - what a coincidence, she thought, making a mental note to find out from her fortune-teller if that was good or bad.

Mary, like most Chinese of her generation and some of the younger generation too, relied a lot on fortune-tellers to guide her on a number of things. Her source told Mary that the young executive's name was Danny Cheah. She repeated the name a few times before pronouncing that she had liked it.

As the project was near its completion, Danny Cheah was seen darting about at the site, but so far he had never been in Mary's canteen for a meal or even for a drink. She wondered whether he was the snobbish type who wouldn't dream of being seen in a place like hers.

About a month before Mary was to take possession of her shop lot, she met with Danny Cheah again. This time he came in with a number of people, some of whom Mary recognised as sub-contractors who used to patronise her place. He came directly to her to inform her that with luck she might be able to take possession of her premises in about a month's time - two at the most.

Mary was thrilled at the news. She asked Danny to bring his mother over for dinner when she opens for business, adding that she'd cook them something special. Danny told her that he and his mother would be pleased to come for dinner once she'd opened for business. He waved his hand when one of his friends called out to him. So, he's not a snob after all, Mary concluded, only busy - perhaps too busy to eat.

* * *

Carol was in her office preparing to go to a meeting in the boardroom upstairs when the telephone on her desk rang. She looked at her watch and frowned when her secretary told her that it was Mandy on the line.

"I'm sorry Mandy, I don't think I can meet you today. Why don't we make it some other time, okay? I have meeting to attend to and I am already late as it is. I did warn you this morning that I might not be able to make it, didn't I?"

Mandy was disappointed that she couldn't see her friend that day, for she had wanted to seek her advice on what to do with her mother's demand that she left school immediately and to go to look for work. She didn't want to leave school before sitting for her SPM examinations but she was afraid of defying her mother. Carol and her mother had helped her once before and now she was seeking their help again.

Mandy was so deep in her thoughts she didn't realise that someone was talking to her. She looked up and when she saw that it was Sam McGee, she smiled broadly, thinking that perhaps Carol had managed to get away from her meeting after all and that she had come with Sam. Sam was Carol's boyfriend, someone Mandy thought Carol should not have anything to do with. On one occasion she saw Sam with another woman and yet she had seen him with Carol earlier that same evening.

* * *

Several months had come and gone from that day, but as far as Mandy was concerned, it seemed to have gone so excruciatingly slow. She marked each day on her calendar just like a prisoner would on the wall in his cell, except in her case there was no cell in her house and no barbed wired surrounding it, nevertheless Mandy felt more a prisoner in her own home than a prisoner would in the state penitentiary.

And if she were a betting person, she was sure that her mother would put the warden at *Pudu Jail* to shame in any competition involving cruelty inflicted by a human being on another on a sustained level without showing any remorse.

For example, if she were angry at Mandy over something trivial in the morning, she would still be angry with her by the time they got to bed that night. All day long she'd be picking on Mandy and would beat her on the slightest provocation.

Although Mandy didn't know it, prisoners were having it easy nowadays, at least in comparison to what she had gone through, and was going through as long as she lived at home.

Unlike her, prisoners don't get beatings anymore, at least not while they were carrying out their sentence. They may have got a few strokes of the *rotan* in the beginning, if they were part of the sentence, but not while they were serving their sentence. And unlike Mandy, they have their rights. For instance, if they have any grievances against the prison authorities, all they have to do is to inform their lawyers and they'd see to it that they'd get heard. They even have parole boards to hear their cases and possibly got their sentences reduced through good behaviour.

Mandy would be surprised to know that even those hardened criminals who do hard labour seldom get bothered once they were in their cells for the night. Her mother wouldn't have any qualm to pick on Mandy at any time of the day or night.

Compare to the prisoners, Mandy had no such rights and no one to go to air her grievances and no boards to hear her case. She would have to be on beck and call of her mother twenty-four hours a day, except when she was in school, which would explain why she loved going to school so much. It was her sanctuary, a place she could feel safe from her mother. School, as far as Mandy was concerned, was akin to the exercise yard whereby the prisoners, in any jail, wouldn't be hassled by their jailers except maybe by other prisoners.

Mandy's mother on the other hand, wouldn't hesitate to wake her in the middle of the night for a glass of water or if she wanted to go to their outdoor toilet. Mandy had to stand guard outside the to[let door, bitten almost to death by mosquitoes, while her mother did her business.

What she hated most was when it rained, and for some unexplained reason, nature always seemed to call to her mother during some of stormiest nights, and for some reason it always took her forever to do whatever she had to do. And when it was all over, despite using an umbrella, Mandy always got soaked to the bones.

ЖИЖИЖИ

CHAPTER SIX

When I first laid eyes on Mandy, she had no idea how old I was, except that I looked old to her. To a girl her age, anybody over thirty was considered old, so she told Eddy that I must be over thirty. I couldn't say if she was pleased to have met me or not, but I remembered her being annoyed with me when I started asking her all sorts of questions about her school and the subjects she liked or dislike. I could see that she became anxious to get away from me.

She told Eddy she had never met anyone so inquisitive like me before.

"Do you know that he had the gall to suggest to me that I should take tuitions for my weak subjects?" she exploded. "I don't need him to tell me that!"

"I told him to mind his own business. Damn him!"

Eddy told me she knew she needed tuitions, but how in the world could she afford it?

"Doesn't he know that tuition teachers don't come cheap?" She practically screamed at Eddy.

* * *

After she had left James, and had finally cooled down, Mandy began to envy and despised all the rich kids - each and every one of them could afford tuition teachers, which, she reckoned, must be the reason why rich students seldom fail to do well.

James would be pleased if he knew that Mandy had placed him in the thirty-something category. Being thirty or anything over thirty was a long time ago as far as he was concerned.

He was forty-seven, a fact he could clearly remember, because he was repeatedly reminded of it by Sophie, someone he and his ex-wife used to know when they were living in Singapore.

Sophie had insisted that James should celebrate his birthday together with her husband, Brian, who happened to be born on the same day but not in the same year, with James. Brian, an Australian, was born in *Carlton* in Melbourne, while James was born in *Rantau Panjang* in the state of Terengganu, on the east coast of Malaysia.

Sophie, it seemed, had taken it upon herself to look after James ever since she and Brian had bumped into him in KOMTAR in Penang one day. They hadn't seen each other ever since James and his wife were separated five years before. Sophie and James's ex-wife were close friends. In fact they belonged to cabal of very close friends comprising of five other women of similar background and interest whom, according to Sophie, still met from time to time for coffee mornings or buffet lunches or dinners.

* * *

That night Mandy was in her bedroom by nine-thirty, a rare occurrence, because her mother was feeling poorly and was already sound asleep. It was the flu, according to her *Akong*, who had popped in to enquire how her mother was doing.

Actually the real reason her grandfather was there was to give Mandy a small bottle of ointment to put on her hand which was hurting her when her mother had given her a beating the day before for coming home late from school. Mandy had smiled inwardly at her mother's discomfort – serve her right, she had thought.

Mandy had gone to the library to do some work instead of coming home straight from school. To make things worse, her mother was infuriated when she discovered she had run out of cooking oil halfway through her cooking, and had to run to the provision shop for it herself. And in her haste to get to the shop, she had forgotten to turn off the fire for the soup she had on the stove. When she returned she found her soup had all but dried up, and on the top of that, the family cat had eaten the fish she had prepared for frying. She was in a foul mood when Mandy walked in about ten minutes later. She vented her anger at Mandy, shouted at her for being irresponsible, and without any warning, picked up the broom and began hitting Mandy with the wooden handle.

The next morning, her grandfather, who was working in his vegetable garden, greeted Mandy as she walked past him. When he noticed the bruises on Mandy's hands and had asked her about it. After making him promise not to mention it to her mother, she told him about the beating she had got. As Mandy laid on her bed to rest for awhile with the light turned off in order to save on electricity, she began applying on her hand the ointment her Akong had given her, and while doing so and for no apparent reason, she thought of James.

She thought it strange that she should be thinking of him when she remembered clearly she didn't particularly like him when they had met. She was thinking of him now, because like her grandfather, James seemed to have the caring nature about him. Maybe when I get to that age I too may have the same feeling of concern about other people. Take yesterday, for instance, he looked concerned when she had said that she might have to leave school and get herself a job in order to support her family. He was aghast that she was even thinking of such a thing. And when he started to lecture her about the importance of having a good education, she couldn't help thinking how different he was compared to all the other men she had met. Sure, she was mad at him!

Without exception, all the other men she had known couldn't care less whether she went to school or not. All they were interested in was in her, whether or not she'd go out with them - all of them would promise expensive gifts and money in return for her favours.

Mandy remembered that she was annoyed at James's condescending behaviour. Even her own father, wherever he may be, and from what she can remember, had never been interested in what she was doing when he was around. And now that he is gone, the last thing she wanted was a substitute father. She didn't need James' advice whether she should continue with her schooling or get a job. What was it to him if she had left school six months before taking her SPM? It was really her fault for telling him and Sam, who happened to join them while she and James were at Eddy's, that her mother had asked her to leave school immediately and start looking for a job. She had no idea why she had said all those things to them except that she was probably unhappy at the thought of having to leave school without sitting for her SPM examinations.

She suddenly felt ashamed at the thought of how she was trying to gain some sympathy from James and Sam by revealing to them the sordid details of her home life. James was shocked at the very idea and had implored her not to leave school until she at least had sat for her SPM exams. James told her to aim to get as many "As" in her SPM exams as possible. These "As" would make it easier for her to get a good job, according to him. As if she didn't know that! She knew that with a bad or mediocre result, she could end up just like her mother doing menial work.

She was determined to make her mark in this world and nobody was going to stop her, not even her mother. She got up from her lying position and began to jot down all the plausible reasons to give to her mother in order to convince her to let her continue with her schooling at least until after her SPM eaminations. The next day Mandy found out the real reason why her mother had wanted her to leave school.

The next day Mandy happened to come home early from school because her teacher was on sick leave and there was no substitute teacher around to replace her for her afternoon class. The headmistress had allowed them to go home for the rest of the afternoon. On reaching home Mandy was drawn by some noise to her mother's room. She was about to knock on the door when suddenly heard her mother's laughter and then - nothing, not a sound.

Filled with curiosity, Mandy turned the doorknob slowly and peered inside. What she saw made her see red - her mother, stark naked, except the part of her covered by a man - not Peter - but someone new, equally naked, lying on the top of her.

"So! This is the reason why you have changed your mind and now you want me to leave school?" Mandy was so furious, she felt no fear from her mother. "Well, I'm not going to quit school so you can lie in bed with him", pointing to the naked man who looked younger than Peter was. "And if you force me or even touch me again, I'm going to tell everybody you're nothing but a whore!"

Her mother, her face turning red, pushed the man off her and without bothering to put her clothes on, came rushing towards Mandy and gave her a tight slap. Mandy, for the first time in her life, stood up to her mother by giving her mother a tight slap in return.

Shocked and mad with anger, her mother screamed on the top of her voice as she grabbed Mandy by the hair and began hitting her wildly.

Her grandfather, who was watering his plants at the back of his house, came running in and when he heard the commotion. When he saw what was happening, he quickly broke them apart. But Mandy's mother, seething with rage and apparently had forgotten she was naked as the day as she was born, stole a slap at Mandy, hitting her in the mouth.

Khong, noticing blood oozing from Mandy's mouth became so infuriated, he gave his daughter two tight slaps that sent her reeling to the floor landing at the feet of her lover who was as naked as she was. Her lover, in a daze, just stood there with his limp member hanging grotesquely towards the floor. And like Mandy's mother, he too seemed oblivious to the fact that he was naked as a jaybird.

Mandy's grandfather glared at him and shouted. "Who the hell are you? And what are doing in my daughter's bedroom?" Without waiting for a reply, he pointed to the door and said, "If you don't get out of here now I'm going to call the police."

The man hurriedly put on his pants, grabbed his shirt and bolted out of the room and disappeared. Khong then turned his attention on his daughter and spat at her.

"Look at you! What a slut you've turned out to be. You're not fit to be a mother. All you know is to terrorize your own children. I've kept quiet all this time because I thought as their mother you should know what you're doing and I didn't want to interfere. But from now on, if you ever lay your hand on any of them, you'll have me to answer to. Do you hear?" he shouted on the top of his voice.

Ah Khong turned to Mandy and demanded to know what was going on. Mandy she told her grandfather that her mother had asked her to quit school and to get a job. On hearing that, Khong poked his forefinger hard against his daughter's forehead and hissed out the word, "Stupid! Go get dressed, you whore, and then come back here. I want to talk to you." He then turned to Mandy and said, "Mandy, I want you to continue with your schooling and I want you to study hard, do you hear me?"

"Yes, Akong. I will try my best," Mandy replied.

"Now go get your things, tonight you'll stay with us." As soon as Mandy had left the room he turned to face his daughter who had returned and was wearing her caftan, her usual attire when at home.

"From now," he said, "I want you to make sure that you work doubly hard so that you can support your all children without burdening your mother and I as you've been doing. We will continue to look after our grandchildren while you are at work but from now on you have to make some monthly cash contribution and I don't want to see you bring any man home or to come home drunk ever again, otherwise I will personally report you to the police for abusing your children. They would come on hard on people who abuse their children nowadays, so take me seriously."

"You'd do this against your own daughter?" she asked, her composure all but returned to normal.

"Yes I would," replied Khong. "And don't you forget it. I won't give you any more warning."

She looked at him and saw, not her father whom she had often looked down to, but a father who looked determined to do what he had promised to do, and not someone she could bully any more.

The next day James was still very much in Mandy's thoughts. She can't wait to see him and to tell that she wasn't going to quit school after all.

She felt she had to do this otherwise she couldn't do anything else for the rest of the day. Besides, Mandy still felt guilty because she was rude to him. She had realised that he had meant well.

All of a sudden she found herself desperately wanting to get in touch with James and to apologize to him.

Mandy called her friend, Carol, and asked her if she would ask Sam for James's telephone number. Carol told her she'd ring back as she got the number from Sam.

A few minutes later Carol called back and told Mandy that according to Sam, James had gone abroad and won't be back for several months. Sam had lied about James being abroad. He did it deliberately because he was jealous that Mandy should be looking for James and not him. It wasn't a total lie, Sam thought to himself: James had gone to Singapore for a couple of days and since Singapore is a foreign country, James has gone abroad.

Physically and mentally abused by her mother almost from the moment she was able to walk, Mandy was starved for affection and someone to care for her. With the exception of her grandfather, all the other men she had known had only wanted to use her. Even her uncle who was like a father to her had raped her when she was only fourteen years old. What hurt her the most was the fact that her own mother had sold Mandy's virginity for five hundred ringgit to her own brother. She did this just to settle a gambling debt!

Her uncle who was obsessed with the idea of deflowering as many virgins as possible in a believe that by doing so, he could slow down the aging process in him. He had somehow managed to convince his elder sister that she was doing him a great favour by letting him take Mandy's virginity from her instead of letting her squander it on someone else.

"Wasn't it not an old custom with our ancestors for an uncle to take the virginity of their nieces?" he asked his naive sister. "So, why not let me, your own brother, take it from her." When he saw the look of uncertainty began to register on his sister's face, he quickly added,

"Besides, I'm willing to pay a great deal of money for the favour."

"How much money?" asked Mandy's mother eagerly.

"Three hundred ringgit," he replied.

Although unlettered, Mandy mother quickly detected an opportunity in the making. "Six hundred ringgit," she said.

"Come on, *Jie-Jie*, six hundred is too much, her brother replied. "Four hundred is all I can afford." After five more minutes of haggling, they came to a compromise – five hundred ringgit. While the discussion was going on, Mandy was sound asleep in her bedroom.

After giving his sister the money he had immediately gone to Mandy's room and had forced himself on her while her mother had arranged it so that they'll be alone in the house by going next door to her neighbour's house to play *Mahjong*.

Abandoned by her husband when she was carrying her third child, Mandy's mother had been tempted with rich offers by some businessmen for Mandy's hand, not in marriage but as a mistress. She had refused not on moral or any other ground, but out of fear from her own father and mother, who like her, hadn't hesitated to trash their children for any wrong-doing when she was young.

Khong had tried his best to protect Mandy from his tyrannical daughter but it wasn't easy. For one thing, in the early days, he was a lorry driver working at all hours and more often than not would be away for days on end. And Shirley would make sure that whatever punishment she thought Mandy had deserved, would be met out while her father was out of town. Invariably the welts would have disappeared or almost gone by the time he got home.

Khong had loved Mandy so, perhaps more than his two grandsons - Mandy's two younger brothers. Like the fairy tale's proverbial ugly duckling, which Mandy certainly was, until the age of twelve, he noticed that Mandy had suddenly turned into a beautiful girl.

Shirley, he noticed, became jealous of Mandy instead of being proud of her beauty like most mother would. She envied Mandy's fair skin and her fine-drawn features and especially her nose, which was straight and well-shaped whereas hers had that cruel flare of the nostril that made her look hard and unfeeling - savage even.

As she began to grow up, and despite having two dotting grandparents who treated her with special care, or perhaps because of it, she still got beatings from her mother for any misbehaviour, however slight. These beatings would be done behind her grandparents' backs and Mandy had found out the hard way that complaining to them would only resulted in more beatings, so she quickly learnt to suffer in silence.

* * *

Several months had passed since her *Akong* had forced her mother to let her continue with her studies, she found that she was making progress with all the subjects she'd be taking for her examinations. During that period of relative freedom from harassment from her mother Mandy had work very hard to prepare herself for the forthcoming SPM examinations. During that time too, her mother's boyfriend had kept away from the house for fear of running into her grandfather; Mandy was sure her grandfather would go after the young man with a meat cleaver. However, lately her grandfather was making more frequent trips to as far away as Singapore in the south and to Bangkok, Thailand in the north. And instead of staying away two to three days at a time like he used to do previously, he would be gone a week to ten days at one stretch.

Mandy's mother was quick to take the opportunity to revert to her old tricks by having her boyfriend stay with her during that period. To get even with Mandy, Shirley sometimes forced Mandy to do her shifts for her at the restaurant where she worked whenever she had her boyfriend over. This boyfriend was not the same one whom her Akong had forced out of their house, this one was new.

Unable to do much about it, Mandy tried her best to juggle her schooling, homework, revisions, and her job as a kitchen helper at the restaurant as best as she could. She was determined not to let her mother upset her from getting a proper education. Sometime when it wasn't too busy at the restaurant, she'd managed to do some studying, but more often than not she'd be so exhausted by the time she got home, and even brushing her teeth before going to bed would take an effort.

Mandy thought of telling her grandfather what her mother had done, but she realised that it would only make things difficult for herself. Her mother had done this to her not only out of revenge but most of all she wanted to break her spirit and to destroy her will to be different and to bring Mandy to her own level. Well, she's not going to succeed - Mandy promised herself.

Mandy had often wondered whether she was really her mother's daughter or was she adopted. She had often thought it incredible that the hostility, the callousness, and sometime brutal beatings her mother meted to her, came from someone who had nurtured, and cared for her in her womb for nine months. It seemed so wasteful in time and energy when all her mother did after Mandy was born was to mistreat her. If she didn't want the baby in the first place, why did she bother to have it? There were many options she could have taken to avoid having one. Or why didn't she have me adopted, she wondered. Why go through the agony of pregnancy and the pain of giving birth if all she wanted to do was to treat it like a slave afterwards, or thought of it as nothing but a nuisance to her!

Mandy had often wondered whether any stranger would do to one another what her mother had done to her? She doubted that they would, and yet, her mother wouldn't give a second thought about beating her until she bled or to hurt her with a hot object or to have her chained like a dog.

Once, while washing some dishes in the kitchen, Mandy had accidentally dropped a plate onto the floor and turned it into a million pieces. Her mother became so incensed, she took a hot ladle out of the pot of soup which had been simmering on the stove and hit Mandy on the head with it, and for good measure, she then pressed it against the bare skin on Mandy's back. A long time ago Mandy made a vow that she would never give her mother the satisfaction of seeing her cry no matter how hard a thrashing she had got, but when the hot steel ladle was pressed hard against her back and she could feel the pain searing right through to her, she forgot her vow and let out a loud scream. Moments later, she realised that she had broken her sacred vow, she became angry with herself causing the Adrenalin to course through her entire body, almost immediately the pain mercifully began to subside. She quickly wiped the involuntary tears that had flowed down her cheeks with the back of her hand and proceeded to clean the mess from the kitchen floor. Her mother, on hearing her daughter's scream became alarmed, she left the room abruptly.

The bump on Mandy's head disappeared within a few days, but the burn on her back took several months to heal mainly because her bra kept pressing against it. Each time she went back to the clinic to change her dressings, the nurse would scold her for continuing to wear her bra despite instructions to the contrary. Mandy wanted to tell her that she had well-developed breasts and to go about without wearing her bra just wouldn't do.

Of all the nasty things her mother had done to her, the one that had traumatised Mandy the most was being chained like a dog. On one occasion she remembered being chained to the grill of the living room window for failing to complete her chore of cleaning the bathroom and had instead joined her two younger brothers and played outside in the yard. She remembered another time when her mother had her chained again to the grill but this time in her own bedroom. It was punishment for going out without her mother's permission. She hadn't been out more than ten minutes to do an errand for Ah Chew, their next door neighbour.

It seemed at that time her mother wasn't on talking terms with Ah Chew, therefore for Mandy do her a favour was tantamount to aiding and abetting the enemy. When Mandy protested that she was not aware that her mother and Ah Chew were not talking terms to each other, it brought an angry response from her mother, who strode out of her room and marched towards Ah Chew's house.

Even though her room was some distance away, she could her mother's tirade directed at Ah Chew from outside her house, who, unknown to Mandy's mother, was out at that time. After nearly twenty minutes, her mother returned and promptly put Mandy in chains, which incidentally was used to chain their family dog at night, and dragged her to her bedroom and secured it with a padlock to the grille by her bed. Needless to say, that night Mandy went without dinner too.

Being hungry had its advantage, for when hunger gnaws at her vitals, Mandy became drowsy and was soon asleep. The next morning unfortunately she awoke at 5:30 because her bladder was full and her need to go to the bathroom was urgent. But at that hour her mother would be dead to the world, and at that moment Mandy wished that her mother was really dead, but not before she removed her chains first. She pictured her mother suddenly clutching at her chest, terror in her eyes as realization began to hit that the end was near, and despite her open mouth she was struggling for breath. The images in her mind's eye showed clearly her mother putting up an unsteady hand, begging Mandy to help her. The images showed her walking calmly over her mother's inert body and left the room with a smile on her face.

* * *

The watch which her Akong had given for her birthday indicated that it was 1:35 PM and there was still no sign of her friend, Carol. Mandy glanced around the room to see if Carol had walked through the restaurant's entrance without her noticing it, but when she couldn't see Carol anywhere, she became resigned to the fact that she wasn't coming after all.

Mandy had sat at the table for almost an hour and had told the waitress for the third time that she was waiting for a friend. She had ordered an Ice Lemon Tea the second time the waitress came to ask if she was ready to order. By this time the restaurant was getting crowded and people were glancing at her empty seats.

Mandy signalled a passing waitress and asked for her bill. Although she was hungry, she knew she couldn't afford to order anything from the menu. The waitress had returned and placed her bill on her table when she caught sight of Sam McGee coming towards her. She looked up anxiously thinking that if Sam was around, Carol might be around also since Sam was her fiancée.

"Sam, how are you?" Mandy shook his proffered hand. "Is Carol with you?"

"No, she's not. She's got a busy day so I've come instead," replied Sam.

Sam had overheard Carol and Mandy's conversation this morning over the extension in Carol's living room when he went to her house to fetch Carol for work. He heard Carol telling Mandy that she might not be able to make it for lunch but she would try, she had said. When he called Carol earlier and asked whether she wanted to go out for lunch, Carol told him she couldn't because she had a meeting to attend to. Sam had a broad smile on his face on hearing this and his mind began to concoct a scenario that went like this...if I were at the pizzeria and if I happened to bump into Mandy while I was there, surely Carol wouldn't object if I had lunch with her? Perhaps it'd be better if I brought a friend along...yes...it'll look much better.

"How are you Mandy. You look lovely today," Sam said holding on to her hand. "I mean...you always look lovely, but today you look exceptionally lovely."

Mandy tried to pull back her hand but Sam refused to let go, mumbling something about someone he wanted her to meet. After what seem a long time he finally released his grip on her hand. Mandy quickly pulled back her hand and was about to rub it when Sam suddenly turned round and called out to his friend who was sitting a few tables away to come on over. Mandy immediately recognised him as the man who had been staring at her for the last ten minutes or so. He also looked vaguely familiar. She felt she had seen him somewhere before. She had no desire of meeting him and was about to tell Sam a lie about a pressing appointment she had to attend to immediately. However when she saw the man was practically running towards them, she changed her mind. She smiled when she saw how excited he was by the way he kept looking at her as he approached them. She couldn't help giggling when he nearly knocked a chair over. It was right in front of him and yet it was obvious that he didn't see it as his eyes were on her and her only. Mandy had always known the effects she had on men before, but had never met anyone so eager to meet her before.

Sam tapped his friend on the shoulder and said, "James, I want you to meet Mandy. Mandy, this is my good friend, James."

"Hello, James," Mandy shook his proffered hand. She turned to Sam and said, "listen Sam, I came here to have a chat with Carrol about something but since she's not here, I'd better go." She then turn to James to shake his hand. "Good bye James, nice meeting you. Bye Sam". She quickly walked out of the restaurant leaving Sam and his friend looking rather surprised at her abrupt departure.

* * *

It was a big surprised to me when Sophie, a close friend of my wife, had suggested on giving me a birthday party at their luxurious home. Sophie who had turned up in Penang with her husband and their two sons not long after I had met with Penny, another one of my wife's friend, whom I had bumped into on Penang Road, reminded me that my forty-seventh birthday was coming soon and had suggested that I and her husband, Brian, should celebrate our birthdays together. Brian, not wanting to go against his wife's plan, quickly seconded the idea. Imagine that, two of my wife's friends suddenly turned up in Penang and both of them wanted me to organize my forth-coming birthday for me. It was too much for me to absorb.

Ever since I broke up with my wife, I tried as far as possible to keep away from people both of us had known socially. I had thought that moving to Penang was the perfect solution until one day, not only I had bumped into Penny earlier in the day, that night Sophie and her husband, Brian, happened to be at the same Nasi Kandar restaurant where Eddy and I were having dinner there. Now I'm beginning to wonder if my wife was in town too! Penny seemed to have a legitimate reason to be in Penang – she was there to enrol one of her two sons at the USM – a well-known university of science. Sophie and her family chose Penang for their holiday destination because her husband, Brian, was attending a conference in Phuket, in the neighbouring Thailand.

I bumped into Penny when I was on my way to Eddy's and she was coming out of the trinket shop next door to Eddy's kopitiam. I invited her to join me for coffee where she could wait for her husband, Jack, and her two sons. Over coffee, Penny told me that she was in Penang because her eldest son, Harry, was about to commence his first semester in Computer Science course at the *Universiti Science Malaysia*. She updated me on all that had been happening among my wife's cabal of friends. It seemed that with the exception of my wife and I, most of the old gang had kept in constant touch with each other like they had done for the past several years. And when Penny and I parted company, we parted with the usual promises people make about keeping in touch but never do, that thought crossed my mind at that time. "Give my regards to Jack and your two boys. Give Harry my phone number and ask him to get in touch with me if he needs a *Pakcik* for whatever reason."

Not long after that chance encounter with penny, James found Penang no longer the sanctuary he thought it to be, especially after his wife younger sister, Lily called and told me that she was in Penang with Derrick, her boyfriend. Since I had to be at my *Nasi Padang* stall that morning I told her to come and meet me there.

Other people too - acquaintances from James former life - began to appear at his food stall as if by accident. All seemed to be in Penang for their holidays, some of whom did come with their children and maids in tow. James couldn't but suspected that Penny may have leaked his whereabouts to their group of friends when she had returned home.

So when Sophie turned up with her husband and their two sons, James wasn't surprised. To call Sophie a busybody would be grossly unfair because she wasn't a busybody in the true sense of the word for she really never interfered in other people's affairs. But if there's a whiff of scandal among people she knew, she'd be around in no time flat to try to dig at the truth, or what she'd perceived as the truth.

Her husband Brian, a lawyer by profession, had left for Phuket that morning to attend a two-day seminar and will return to Penang to continue with their holidays.

James acted the perfect host by taking Sophie and her two boys sight-seeing around the island. The next day, after having dropped her sons at a bowling alley not far from their hotel, Sophie arrived unexpectedly at James's flat telling him that she's come to make breakfast for him.

James, who felt uneasy about having Sophie in his flat alone, nevertheless invited her in by telling her that he won't take a moment to change his clothes so that they could go out and have their breakfast at his favourite restaurant – a blatant lie – he didn't feel comfortable to be alone with Sophie.

Sophie was disappointed on hearing this but didn't show it. She had come with the sole purpose of trying to seduce James. She had mistakenly thought that James would welcome it when she thought she had seen James had looked at her with lust in his eyes during their tour around the island. She was sure she'd be more than welcome it if she came alone to his flat where they could make love to their heart's content while Brian was in Phuket. As she waited for the door to James flat to open, Sophie's thoughts raced back to last night when Brian was making love to her, she had fantasised that it was James who was in her instead of Brian. Pretending that it was James' instead of Brian's member in her had brought Sophie to her to her climax and she almost called out James name when she climaxed.

That morning however, they ended up having a nasi lemak breakfast at one of the food-stalls nearby after which James dropped her off at the bowling alley where her two sons were still bowling.

When he met them again after Brian had returned from Phuket, James in an effort to be a good host, treated Brian, Sophie and their two boys to a seafood dinner in which Penang was famous for.

Determined to get James in bed with her one way or another, Sophie, halfway through dinner, reminded James that his birthday was due soon and so was her husband since both of them were born on the same day. James told them that for several years he hadn't celebrated his birthdays because he didn't want to be reminded that he was getting older.

"If you don't mind, I'd like to keep it that way", he had said.

For a woman in her mid-forties, Sophie still had the figure and the looks that would be the envy of many women half her age. It may have true that James, like all full-blooded men, may have lusted for Sophie at one time or another but that must have been a long time ago. So when Sophie invited him to celebrate the event together with her husband at their house, although flattered, James had rejected it. He had seen the danger signs; Sophie sometimes would purposely bend her head so that James could have a full view of her breasts. He lied by telling them that he had already made other plans. Sophie, who have never taken no for an answer pleaded and cajoled him until James had to say yes. The party will not be held at their house but to be held here in Penang, albeit a week earlier.

The party was held at one of the restaurants at their five-star, beach front hotel in Batu Ferringhi, and it was a great success as far as birthday party went. Brian seemed to have drunk more Champagne than usual and was fading in and out of consciousness by the time Sophie, with James help, half-dragged him into bed.

James had waited on the sofa while Sophie was tucking her husband in bed. Her two sons had already left the party much earlier and were sleeping in the adjoining bedroom. He stood up when he heard the bedroom door opened, but when he turned, Sophie was in a transparent negligee, which left nothing to his imagination. She strode to James and held his face and kissed him with such ferocity, both fell onto the sofa. James tried to untangle himself. unfortunately Sophie's expert manipulation with her mouth and hands aroused in him what had been dormant for so long, James threw caution to the winds and gave in to both their desires.

The next day, Sophie had phoned and asked James if he would join them for B-B-Q at their hotel pool side. Not knowing what to expect, James was relieved when Sophie appeared as if nothing had happened between them. She looked well-groomed, wearing a pair of perfectly tailored pants and a matching long-sleeved blouse with a touch of jewellery here and there, Sophie was perfection itself as wife and mother to her husband and her children. Brian was apologizing to James for passing out the night before. While at the table with Sophie sitting next to him on his left and Brian was sitting opposite him, James felt a stirring in his groin when Sophie squeezed his tool under the tablecloth. He turned to look at her but her concentration seemed to be on her food as she ate with a fork held in her left hand. When she noticed that Brian's glass of juice was empty, like a good wife, Sophie got up to get him another glass. As James watched Sophie in her role as a housewife, James played back the video in his head of their wild love-making last night. The visions resulted in him having a full-fledged hard-on with nowhere to put it in. After dinner, Brian asked to be excused in order for him to finish his report, "while everything was still fresh in his mind", he had said. Sophie, still the role of the perfect wife, stroked her husband's shoulder and said, "must you, darling?" Brian leaned towards his wife and gave her a peck on her cheek. "Yes, I have to". He got up and said to James, "stay as long as you want and keep Sophie company". As soon as Brian disappeared with his two boys in tow, James suggested to Sophie that they go for a stroll on the beach. As soon as they walked past a cabana, Sophie casually took a peek at one that was set off away from the rest and was secluded. She pulled James into it and started kissing James passionately. James responded, felt his member growing, removed Sophie's panties and inserted his tool in Sophie's already wet and warm sex. After they had made love the second time, Sophie lazily whispered in James ear that it was time she picked up her role again as a loving wife and a doting mother and return to her husband. If Brian had insisted on making love to her, she would go along with it, she had said to James. James walked her to her suite door. They kissed and as they parted company, she was thinking that she had hoped that Brian would still be busy with his work for she was pooped. She would prefer to savour the wonderful glow of the after-sex feeling of the great sex she had had with James for a little while longer if she could, but if Brian had wanted to make love, she would let him. It turned out that Brian hadn't finish his work by a long shot. He turned towards Sophie as soon as he heard her walked in. "Go to bed if you want to," he said. "I'll be a while yet."

James felt that he would most probably missed Sophie now that she, Brian, and their youngest son, had gone back to Kuala Lumpur.

James occasionally would think about Sophie, especially lately, perhaps more than he had thought about any other woman he had been out with since his separation from his wife. He was thinking about Sophie when he and his friend, Sam McGee, were heading for the pizza parlour on the third level of the KOMTAR shopping complex. To his dismay, he felt a hard-on coming on without any apparent reason and there wasn't a damn thing he could do about it. He looked around to see if anybody was paying him any particular attention. He was relieved when he saw that none did.

CHAPTER SEVEN

KOMTAR, the pride of Penang, was the tallest building in the state. Its tower was circular in shape, and, at sixty-two storeys high was also one of the tallest building in Asia. It was built during the tenure of the former Chief Minister who must have felt that he deserved to leave a monument or two behind as a reminder to the people of Penang that he was responsible for turning a sleepy hollow, which was Penang at that time, into a modern city whose factories, among other things, produced the most micro-chips in the world. Others say that the tower was built as a reminder to those who had loved and lost not to despair but to love again. There were many other sayings about the tower whose phallic shape was the butt of many jokes, some of which could not be printed in this book.

Sam McGee, whose diminutive figure attracted little or no attention as they walked along the crowded street on the way to the Pizza place, was one of numerous people James had met at Eddy's. As a matter of fact, most of the people he had known in Penang he had met at Eddy's. Sam, an extrovert, who was attached with the police department's anti-narcotic division in George

Town. He had other reasons to come to this particular pizza parlour - eating pizza certainly wasn't one of them, especially not on that day.

The choice of going to Pizza Hut for lunch was his idea, not James's. James had wanted some Nasi Kandar and if Sam had told his friend the real reason they were going to Pizza Hut, James certainly wouldn't have come. James had met Sam at Eddy's and soon became friends. Being serious and cautious by nature, James had liked Sam's spontaneity, and more than once during James early stay in Penang, Sam had managed to coax him away from his self-imposed isolation by doing what came naturally to Sam, be it biking round the island or going on a drug bust with team of roughneck police officers. Despite not being that particularly keen on having pizza for lunch that day, he had gone along because Sam had asked him, and because he was returning Sam a favour.

If the truth be known, James wouldn't have minded a plate of Nasi Kandar with a piece fried chicken, some vegetables, and plenty of gravy at Kassim's corner restaurant. Kassim restaurant had become an institution in Penang and anybody who had come to Penang and had not eaten at Kassim's didn't know what they were missing. It was only a stone throw away from KOMTAR's 60-storey edifice.

"I wouldn't even mind a bowl of soup and a tuna-on-croissant sandwich at the French-style cafe nearby", James griped. "To me pizza is something you eat while watching a football game on TV, but not for lunch."

It wasn't because he didn't like pizza or anything like that, he loved it, but seldom for lunch. Besides, he had gone to the dentist earlier that morning and had mentioned it to Sam that he didn't think he should have anything solid for lunch that day for his mouth was still sore.

That morning Sam had been thinking about whom to take along with him to the pizza joint. Going there on his own would make it so obvious to his target. As a detective Sam had gone undercover so many times in the course of his job, but that morning he had found it difficult to choose among his colleagues whom he should take along for this delicate operation. He knew that if he fouled this up he'd have plenty of explanation to do. So when James called on him at his office that morning to get a parking ticket taken care of, Sam knew then he had found himself a perfect partner for the operation he had in mind.

James had tried every which way to get Sam to go somewhere else for lunch but Sam had refused to budge, pointedly telling James if he wanted the favour returned he should reciprocate by accompanying him to the pizza parlour, otherwise no deal. James repeated to Sam that he had just been to the dentist and that having a pizza might not be such a good idea.

"They have other things beside pizza on the menu," said Sam. "You don't have to order pizza. Besides, I have to meet someone there whom I'd like you to meet."

Sam felt that with James it'd be best if he told him the truth. James was by far the most intelligent human being he had ever met in his life, and in his job he had met plenty.

"Oh no! Don't tell me you're going to introduce me to another one of your ex-girlfriends," James looked at him in dismay.

"And what's wrong with any of my ex-girlfriends, may I ask?"

"Nothing. Except that all they ever talk about when we go out was about money. They'd be telling me what they'd do if only they had more money. They don't seem to have any qualms about asking me to pay for them for whenever they wanted to buy something, be it a bar of chocolate, a packet of cigarette or a bottle of perfume. And when I gave in to them, without exception they became extra nice to me. I felt that I was being used."

"What's wrong with that? You were getting what you wanted, weren't you?"

"What do you know what I wanted?" James looked suspiciously at Sam.

"Companionship and that sort of thing...right?"

"Yes... but decent women don't do what they do, do they? I've been out of circulation for over twenty years, I don't know anything anymore."

"All right, maybe some of them were a bit money crazy, and maybe some may not be so sophisticated, but this girl we're going to meet is different. For one thing, she's not one of my ex-girlfriends, so you can stop worrying," replied Sam. "I've only met her once. She's a friend of my fiancée, she's beautiful, and young. I'm not even sure if she'll turn up. She telephoned Carol because she wanted them to meet. Carol had told her she couldn't be sure if she could make because she had to be at a board meeting. This girl told Carol that she'll be at the pizza parlour around 1:00 PM and she had hoped that Carol could make it."

"Did Carol tell you all this? And did she ask you to meet this beautiful friend of hers on her behalf?" James looked at his friend dubiously.

"No, of course not! Carol wouldn't trust me with her grandmother," replied Sam. "I was listening on the extension when this girl telephoned."

"You're despicable!" James replied, looking incredulously at his friend.

"Come on. Where is your sense of adventure? Besides, aren't you curious what she looks like?"

James gave his head a couple of shakes in disgust. If the truth be known, he was curious all right. He had met some of Carol's girlfriend before and he must admit that some of them were gorgeous. Like Carol, who had changed from the school girl to a sophisticated young woman since she began working, her friends too had the classy look about them. Sam's ex-girlfriends on the other hand were some of the roughest girls James had ever met.

James was thinking that Sam, being a police detective who was attached to the narcotic division, had to deal almost on a daily basis with some of the nastiest people associated with the underworld. Understandably, the likes of those he usually came in contact with were far from the genteel kind. James had often wondered what in the world did Carol see in him. Could it be the case that the opposite attracts?

James knew he was thinking unkindly of his friend, but he was slightly piqued at Sam's underlying innuendo that he was hopeless when it came to getting dates on his own since his separation from his wife. He was nevertheless grateful to Sam for helping him pick up the pieces and to re-join the world of bachelorhood once again. Without Sam he'd probably ended up staying at home most of the time and feeling sorry for himself for the failure of his marriage.

When they'd walked into the dimly-lit, typically American pizza parlour with its usual chrome and plastic decor, James was surprised to find it fairly crowded. Although he had been there for dinner before and found it crowded, it never occurred to him that it'd be just as crowded for lunch too. So it must be the food that these people came for and not the decoration, James suppressed a smile at the thought. There was nothing to shout about the décor, it was just plain.

Despite the crowd and the establishment's dim light, James saw her, or he thought he saw her, from Sam's description of her, as soon as his eyes got adjusted to the light. But the moment he saw how young she was, he quickly turned his head away. As he and Sam continued to follow the head waitress to their table he saw her reflections on the mirrors that practically surrounded the entire room.

Mandy, who had been waiting for her friend Carol, was aware that one of the two men who had just walked in had been staring at her and it was beginning to grate on her nerves. Through the corner of her eye she watched the hostess led them to their seats. Although she couldn't see the face of the other person, she could tell that he was younger than the one who had been staring at her. For a moment she thought the man who had his back to her looked familiar and was about to see if he would turn around, but when James turned his head to look at her again, Mandy gave him a hard stare of her own. She smiled with satisfaction when she saw the embarrassed look on James face just before he turned his attention to the menu in front of him. *What a cheek! He must be older than my father, she thought.*

During the split second their eyes met, James saw the angry look she was giving him - irritation written all over her beautiful face. Embarrassed, James quickly cocked his head upwards and pretended to admire something up above her head. She wasn't convinced for she continued to give him the hard stare for several moments more before turning her head away in a show of apparent disgust.

James refrained from looking at her again for fear of getting another dose of the same treatment so he continued with his pretension of admiring the establishment's decoration.

And as his mind began to compute what his eyes were seeing, and as an architect, a scowl suddenly appeared on his face. What a gaudy decoration this place had, he thought.

He remembered thinking the same thing when he first entered one of its store many years ago during a trip to the United States, and now several years later, he still thought it gaudy. Don't they ever change the décor once in a while? he was thinking. He could only assume that the Chairman of the Board must have selected it, nobody else would have had such a bad taste or had such power in the company. James knew he was thinking unkind thoughts; perhaps all this company wanted to do was to try to make their countrymen and women feel at home when they walk in through the door or the doors of thousands of similar establishments around the world. And looking around the room, it looked to James as if no expenses had been spared to duplicate everything they had back in the USA. The company's boss may call it corporate image, James called it perpetuating dullness!

James smiled at his own mental humour. He scanned the room to see if there was any American present. He wasn't disappointed. He saw a number of them sitting at their respective tables in one corner, grouping more or less in the same area, not far from the salad bar. Like a herd of elephants in the bogs of Sudan they tend to group and nuzzle together wherever they went. However, when he saw another couple sitting quite far away from the group, he raised his eyebrows questioningly. He thought it odd for them to stray from the main group, but when he saw how young they were, he understood immediately. Despite the fact that they were far from home, the generation gap seemed evident as ever.

James's eyes reverted to the main group and noticed that a few of them had actually ordered salads. Amazing! he thought. He wouldn't have counted on them eating salads outside the USA or Europe due to their morbid fear of catching some bugs. Our standard of cleanliness must be all right then, James was thinking. Right there before his very eyes he saw them enjoying their bowl of salad just like they probably did back home. Without bothering to look at his menu, James too ordered the salad since he wasn't in the mood for a pizza.

As he waited for his friend to make his choice about what to order, James wondered whether the girl was there on her own or with a companion who had gone to take a leak or something. When he noticed that she wasn't looking his way, He took a good look at the girl again after which he began to scan the room to see if he could pick out her boyfriend – a sort of game he'd play while waiting for Sam to make his choice. He looked at practically every young man in the restaurant and after he had scrutinised almost a dozen young men there for a probable candidate, he came to a conclusion, ridiculous though it may seem, the girl was there on her own.

When James noticed that the girl hadn't look in his direction for quite some time, he began to scrutinize her again, this time with more intensity. The thing that struck him most about her was how matured she looked despite her obvious tender age. He figured that she couldn't be more than seventeen or eighteen years old.

He noticed that although she was simply dressed in a skirt and a blouse, she outshone every female from six to sixty in that place. The white short-sleeved blouse she had on had pretty little flowery embroidery on her sleeves as well as around her collar. She wore a black tight-fitting skirt that hugged her well-formed body like a glove. James couldn't believe it when told later on that the outfit she was wearing was her school uniform.

In his school days, school uniforms looked just like school uniforms - nothing more nothing less - and nobody would look twice at anyone wearing one. Sure there were exceptions, but rare; it occurred to him that maybe he was looking at one of those exceptions. James was willing to bet that even if she had a flour sack on, he reckoned that somehow she'll manage to make it into a fashion statement. Besides, no school girl he'd seen before ever looked like her, and, very few he recalled had a body like hers. It wasn't a body of a school girl he was ogling at, but one that belonged to a voluptuous young woman. At that thought he looked around the room to see if he were alone with that perception. He smiled when he saw that he wasn't; like him, it looked like any men under eighty, who were in that pizza parlour that day, found it hard put not to stare at her. They stared at her when they entered through the door, and they stared at her when they walked passed her, and finally they stared at her, discreetly if with female partners, when they had settled at their table. Like him, they'd pretend to be interested in what was in the salad bar, but in reality they'd be ogling at the girl. Well, why not, he thought. She was beautiful.

When Sam McGee finally gave the waitress his order, James nudged him in the ribs to attract his attention. Sam winced in pain and glared angrily at his friend. In his excitement James must have hit his friend rather hard. However, as soon as James had pointed the girl out to him with a comment like "Get a load of that one", or something to that effect, James was surprised to see his friend got up and strode quickly towards the girl. Apparently he knew her and judging by the smile she was giving him, she seemed to know him too. She must be the reason Sam had came here for, thought James.

James stood there looking on with envy as they went through their "Hi" and "How are you". After what seemed like an eternity, Sam finally called him over. When the girl saw that it was James Sam was beckoning to, a frown appeared on her face.

Too giddy with excitement James appeared not to notice that the young woman was far from pleased at seeing him and he almost aped Carl Lewis to be by her side. In his haste, he almost knocked over several chairs.

James realised that he must have looked clumsy and over eager to the girl, for when he looked up he saw that the frown had disappeared from her face and in its place was an amused look. His face, on the other hand, felt as if a burning sword had singed it.

For the next several minutes or so as Sam talked with her, James began to realize that not only she had a mature body but she seemed matured beyond her age. The meeting was short and sweet as far as James was concerned; or was it because of James it was short and sweet!

Several months later, the awkward encounter at the Pizza place had long been forgotten by all concern, James, Sam and Mandy were at Eddy's having coffee and the subject on ethnic-cleansing came up, James was surprised to hear Mandy's take on it: she felt disgusted when even the United Nations was unable to save the minority Muslims from being massacred. According to her in April 1992, when the government of the Yugoslav republic of Bosnia-Herzegovina declared its independence from Yugoslavia. Over the next several years, Bosnian Serb forces, with the backing of the Serb-dominated Yugoslav army, targeted both Bosniak (Bosnian Muslim) and Croatian civilians for atrocious crimes resulting in the deaths of some 100,000 people (80 percent Bosniak) by 1995. It was the worst act of genocide since theNazi regime's destruction of some 6 million European Jews during World War II, according to her. James was impressed that Mandy was very much up to date with the current affairs - local as well as foreign. James had asked her how she knew so much about such things. She told Sam and James that she liked to read about these things at her school library mostly; they don't have newspapers at home, she had said. Slowly he found himself beginning to admire her intellect more than her body. He couldn't believe that he had actually found one of those much talked about but rarely seen beauties with brains: a combination they say considered rare.

At night, according to Mandy, she would rather watch the news or the documentaries on the television, when permitted to do so by her mother, she hastily added. She had said that she rarely watched the "mind-numbing local programs or the soap-operas from Hong Kong" - her own quote, because she found them boring. James was impressed and he told her so which brought on a smile on her face.

Encouraged, he then asked her what she would like to do after she finished schooling. All of a sudden the youthful exuberant that she had been radiating vanished from her face, and in its place was one sadness.

James became alarmed and asked Mandy what was the matter. She shook her head and said nothing. It was obvious to James that although Mandy was reluctant to talk about it, it was something that she had wanted get off her chest but was afraid to do so in front of Sam. James had sensed that she wasn't too comfortable to talk about anything personal in front of Sam.

Mandy changed the subject by asking James what he did for a living. He told her that he had a small food outlet in the Yaohan food arcade on this very floor.

They talked about food for a while, and when she finally stopped talking, she looked at Sam instead of James and said in a rather nonchalant manner that she was leaving school at the end of the year and that was what she had wanted to talk to Carrol about at the Pizza place.

* * *

At that time at the Pizza Hut, as soon as Mandy had left them, James decided that since they were already he might as well go for the salad, something he had already decided on before Sam beckoned to meet with Mandy. James loved salad. Once he was at the salad bar he tried his best to make himself a small mountain of salad on the small plate they had given him.

Those who knew James well enough have always said that he can never walk away from a good challenge when confronted with one. And to him looking at the tiny paper plate in his hand, while right in front of him was a mass of salad ingredients looking invitingly at him was a challenge enough.

At that restaurant, perhaps in all their restaurant chain, they ask you help yourself at the salad bar. You take as much as the plate can hold or as little as you want. However, if you go for a second helping you'll be charged extra for it. So the idea was to pile up your plate with the salad ingredients available there at the salad bar without spilling anything, they'd consider that as one serving and will be charged accordingly.

James knew that one would think that he was being a cheapskate, but it wasn't that: to him it was the challenge, you see!. Anyway, he thought that he had succeeded quite well since he managed to pile up enough salad for two people onto the small plate for the price of one. Pretty good bargain, he thought. While James was busy at the salad bar, Sam was busy trying to make out with another pretty girl who had come alone. Mentally, James wished his friend the best of luck. As for him, he thought he was too old for any of the women in that Pizza restaurant. He smiled at that self-deprecating thought; it smacked of being such a sour grape. As a matter of fact it was sickeningly close to sound like self-pity to his ears.

As it turned out his friend couldn't even get to the first base with the pretty girl. Apparently the girl knew who Sam was: she had cut him short by asking him about his fiancée, Carrol, whom it seemed was her close friend. It seemed to James that Sam would flirt with anyone under twenty wearing a skirt!

James tried to eat his salad, which at that moment looked ridiculously huge in front of him making him look terribly greedy. All of a sudden he had lost his appetite. When a waitress came to clear Sam's plate away, she glanced at James's mountain of salad and then at James. She gave him that unmistaken look of disgust that James himself had often given others at buffets, whenever he saw them leave uneaten food on their plates. James felt so embarrassed, he wished at that moment that the floor would open up and swallowed him. Of course that didn't happen, so he did the next best thing, he tried to gobble up everything on his plate as best as he could without choking to death. But at that moment, death would probably have been more favourable compared to the humiliation he was going through.

⊠⊠⊠⊠⊠⊠

CHAPTER EIGHT

With her mother demanding that she left school Mandy felt disappointed that her friend Carol couldn't make it for their lunch date at the Pizza Hut. She had hoped that she'd be there for Carrol was her only close friend. She wanted to ask her friend's opinion about what she should do.

Her mother had wanted her to leave school and to look for a job, but Mandy would like to stay on and try to get her High School diploma at least. Mandy knew that with it she'd be able to get a decent job but if she were to leave school now, the sort of job she'd get wouldn't pay her enough to support herself, let alone her mother and her two younger brothers. She didn't know what to do. She needed someone's advice. Carol was her only close friend and now it looked like she couldn't even count on her anymore.

She was about to telephone Carol when she it suddenly occurred to her that the chance meeting with her fiancée may not be what it seemed. She had become suspicious of Sam after an incident at Carol's last birthday party when Sam tried to get fresh with her. He had earlier tricked her into accompanying him to Carol's bedroom under the pretext of helping him fetch something for Carrol.

He had grabbed her and forced her onto the bed and forcefully kissed her on the lips. Mandy managed to push him off her and threatened to scream her head off if he didn't cease and desist, and to unlock the bedroom door. Sam Had the bedroom door locked as soon as they entered and had pocketed the key. Unwilling to take a chance with so many people around, Sam had reluctantly opened the door. He then begged for Mandy's forgiveness giving his drunkenness as an excuse for his behaviour.

Mandy had, on several occasions, wanted to talk to Carol about Sam. She felt that as a close friend she was duty-bound to warn her best friend about her fiancée. She hadn't done so because she thought that it might break Carol's heart. Carol had, on a number of occasions, told Mandy that she really loved Sam and there was no one else in her life except Sam. Mandy had thought that she must be truly in love otherwise she wouldn't be this blind, besides, Mandy had reminded herself, it wasn't really any of her business.

That afternoon at the pizza parlour, Mandy felt most annoyed with Sam, first of all for coming on strong to her when he knew very well that she was Carol's best friend. And secondly when he telephoned her later at home and tried to match her with his friend to go out on a double-date with him and Carol the coming weekend, she told him she'd rather pick her own date. Sam had become angry and had threatened to get her harassed for anything he could think of, from littering the streets to jaywalking.

Mandy, far from being scared, was furious with Sam and his threats. She looked at her watch and seeing that it was only 3:30 PM she decided to call her friend Carol.

"Hello Carol...this is Mandy... "

"Mandy, I'm sorry about lunch, I was so swamped with work. Would you believe that I didn't even have time for a bite to eat until now. I'm having a bowl of wan tan noodles and then I'm off to another meeting. I'll call you in a day or two. I promise you we'll have lunch together - just you and me, and maybe with Sam too."

"Listen, Carol... about Sam... there's something I have to tell you...."

"Oh, yes. Sam told me that you and that friend of his will be joining us for Langkawi...good. Mandy, I'm sorry I can't talk now. I'll call you soon...bye." Mandy stared at the dead phone in her hand for several moments before putting it down.

That night Mandy tried to call Carol again but was told by Mary that she wasn't home and wouldn't be home till very late and suggested that Mandy called again in the morning.

The next morning Mandy decided to call Carrol. The clock on her bedside table indicated that it was ten minutes to seven. She got out of bed, stripped down to her briefs, and then put on a pair of shorts and a T-shirt she had grabbed from the back of a rickety wooden chair by the window. She went into the living room to where the telephone is. When she entered the living room a man she had never seen was sitting on one of the chairs at the dining table. He wore nothing but a sarong that hung loosely around his fat belly. Mandy was sure the sarong was one of her mothers'.

"Who are you and what are you doing in our house?" Mandy asked the stranger.

Instead of replying, the man gave Mandy a smirk before turning his back on her and walked back towards her mother's bedroom and closed the door behind him.

Mandy picked up the telephone and began to dial Carrol's number. Carrol picked up the telephone on the third ring. Without any preamble Mandy told Carol how Sam tried to date her and when she had refused, he then tried to match her with that friend of his, and when she again refused, he had threatened to harass her. Mandy was stung when Carol retorted by telling her to keep away from her boyfriend and not to make up stories.

"Sam loves me," said Carol. "You story about Sam trying to date you is nothing but a figment of your imagination. From now on I consider you no longer my friend, so don't call me again." Before Mandy could reply, the line went dead in her hand.

Mandy was about to put down the telephone when a rustling behind her made her turn around. The slap that landed on the side of her face was so hard she was thrown off the small round wooden stool she had been sitting on and landed on the linoleum-covered floor bringing the telephone crashing down with her. Through involuntary tears, Mandy saw her mother standing over her, her face black with anger.

"Ill-mannered child! Who do you think you are talking to my friend that way?" Her mother's shrieked.

"Who?.. Carol?"

Her mother gave her another tight slap. "Are you trying to be funny?" She raised her hand once more, but this time Mandy quickly backed away from her. "Oh, you mean that man in your room?"

"He is uncle Max to you. And he's come to live with us and I want you to be civil with him, do you hear?" Her shriek was even louder than before.

Mandy almost laughed out loud. Uncle Max... Give me a break! she was thinking. "Sure, mother," she replied. "Whatever you say. May I go now?"

Without waiting for a reply, Mandy bolted out of the living room and returned to her own room and prepared for school. The school bus would be arriving in half-an-hour and she had better hurry. Mandy was thinking that if uncle Max was her mother's new boyfriend, things may turn out for the better. She may not have to leave school after all!

Surely uncle Max will be giving her mother money for all of us to live on. This is my final year, I'd hate to leave school without sitting for my SPM examinations. I know if I study hard I have a good chance of getting good grades. But if I leave school now I'd be lucky to have a job as an assembler in a factory. Mandy was so deep in her thoughts, she was startled to find the driver of the school bus shouting something at her from his seat. Mandy got up from her seat when she realised that apart from the driver, whose distorted face was red with anger, she was all alone in the bus. She walked quickly towards the exit and practically ran across the lawn into the school corridor and finally into her classroom. With her face wet with perspiration and slightly out of breath, Mandy managed to reach her seat without attracting her teacher's attention. Unfortunately a snigger escaped from some of students lips causing her teacher to turn around and saw Mandy just as she was about to take her seat.

"Miss Lee, this is the third time you're late for class. I want you to report to me after class!" The teacher, a strict disciplinarian who was never known to give any student a second chance despite her fondness for Mandy. She was a forty-year-old spinster with a lesbian tendencies, had been trying to literally get her hands on Mandy ever since Mandy joined her class at the beginning of the year. Six months had passed and she still got nowhere. Mandy who had known what the teacher had in mind for her had taken advantage of the situation by getting away with a lot of things by leading her on. In fact she told herself once or twice that she wouldn't mind going to bed with her just to find what it was like. She couldn't see any harm in it because it wouldn't be the same thing as going to bed with a boy. She hadn't forgotten what her uncle had done to her when she was fourteen years old. In fact the memory of being raped was constantly on her mind and it became the principal reason why she had rarely gone out with any boys on dates. Once she had gone out to a movie with a boy from her village. After the show they went for a ride towards the beach. When the boy kissed her she returned the kiss, but when he started to put his hand in her panties, Mandy reacted so violently, the boy ended up with a bloody nose. After that incident she never went out with boys again.

When Mandy first joined her class, Miss Koh, her teacher, who first thought that Mandy must have come from a wealthy family because of her exceptional beauty and fair complexion. But after reading Mandy's particulars she had obtained from the principal's office soon revealed to her that wasn't the case. It stated that Mandy was anything but rich, and that she was looked after by her mother who worked as a kitchen helper in a restaurant in the village. As a matter of fact the village where Mandy came from was familiar to her because she herself had lived there for several years until her widowed mother remarried and moved out of there when she was about nine or ten years old. They had never returned there again until recently, when out of curiosity, she went searching for Mandy's house. When one of the villagers pointed it out to her, she waited across the street in her car to see if Mandy would come out. After waiting fruitlessly for several minutes, Miss Koh left the village and returned to her flat where she took a warm bath and thought erotically of Mandy and masturbated.

Miss Koh too had never let any man touched ever since her step-father raped when she was about Mandy's present age. To this day she had kept the ugly secret from her mother because she didn't her to be the cause of the break up their marriage. The morning after her step-father raped her she packed her bags and left the house telling her mother that she was going to be a teacher someday and that she had enrolled in a teachers training college. Before she left she confronted her step-father with a kitchen knife just as he stepped out of from his bath and poked him in the thigh. As he watched in fear at the blood oozing from his wound, she told him that if he ever touches her again, or treats her mother badly, she wouldn't hesitate to kill him. She told him that if he tried to escape, she'd hunt him down like a dog and when she'd catch up with him, she indicated with the knife what she'd do with his penis.

That afternoon after school, Miss Koh waited to make sure that everyone had left before she came over to Mandy's desk and straddled the vacant chair in front of her, exposing her white thighs as well as her knickers. She smiled when she saw Mandy looking under her skirt.

"Mandy," she said. "You have a good chance of getting good grades for your SPM this year but I can't see how you can achieve that without good tutoring. I don't know whether your family can afford to pay for your tuition but if they can't I may be able to help you."

"You can? How?" Mandy asked.

"You come to my place for your tuition, in return you have to do something for me," Miss Koh replied. "I'm thinking of redecorating my place, you could help with the painting for an example. Do you think you could do that?"

"Oh, yes, Miss Koh. I certainly could," answered Mandy.

"Thank you very much for this offer. When can we start?"

"Right away if it's okay with you. Let us both ask your mother whether it's okay with her or not." Miss Koh felt her heart almost skipped a beat when Mandy leaned forward and gave her a hug.

"Oh, Miss Koh! Thank you very much. You don't know much this meant to me. I'm sure when my mother sees how concerned you are about my passing the SPM examination, she'll be as grateful as I am." Mandy was thinking what a stroke of good fortune this day happened to bring. She was sure that her mother wouldn't dare go against her teacher, knowing what a coward her mother was when faced against authorities.

Like Mandy had predicted, her mother, when in the presence of Miss Koh, was tough as dough. In her caftan she looked like a Chinese junk that was about to sail. She was in the bedroom when Mandy arrived in Miss Koh's nippy little Honda Civic, her mother had come out with her hair in a mess wearing her multi-coloured caftan, her usual house dress. It was obvious by the expression on her face she wasn't altogether happy that Mandy had brought someone home without informing her first.

When Mandy told her who Miss Koh was, she darted about like a nervous chicken, telling Mandy to go make some refreshment while she excused herself.

By the time Mandy came back with some refreshment for Miss Koh, her mother too returned looking a slightly better than before with her hair brushed and face looking less oily. Miss Koh came straight to the point by telling Mandy's mother that with SPM examinations less than six months away Mandy should have extra tuitions, and because she considered Mandy to be a bright student, she was willing to give Mandy tuitions herself.

"Is that the only reason you're doing this thing for Mandy?" asked Mandy's mother. Mrs Lee was quick to notice that Miss Koh mannerism and make-up and the way she kept looking at her daughter was anything but normal. She wasn't sure, but Mandy's teacher reminded her of a lesbian friend she once had and the relationship they kept for over a year. During that period she made use of their relationship to get everything she wanted from the other. She was sorry that it ended when the other woman moved to another state. And now this teacher who was obviously in love with her daughter and wanted to tutor her in her home must have the same design on her as her friend did a long time ago. She remembered that she enjoyed the relationship as much as the other did and in the end there was no harm done. besides, she was sure she could persuade Mandy to cooperate to get whatever she wanted.

"What do you mean?" asked Miss Koh.

"I mean what do you get out of doing this good deed for my daughter?" Mrs Lee asked. Mandy looked at her mother in disbelief at her impertinence.

"Exactly what I said, that Mandy needed help with her school work and I'm willing to help, that's all," replied Miss Koh.

"Well in that case, you have my blessing provided you feed her first before sending her home," said Mandy's mother.

"Mother!" Mandy blurted out, looking very embarrassed.

"It's all right, Mandy. I'll be more than happy that you'd share meals with me, although I warn you that it'll be nothing much."

* * *

James Razali, a product of a civil servant father and a kampong mother, completed his tertiary education in Australia like most middle-class Malays of his time due to limited places available at the local universities and colleges. Since only the very best, or those who could pull the biggest cable, and not just strings, could get in. His father, pious, and as straight as they come, wouldn't dream of doing anything that was remotely dishonest, not even for his son, paid for James's education himself.

Needless to say, it was not without sacrifices from the rest of his family especially from his other children. He had no trouble from his daughters. At an early age he had drilled it in their heads that as females they were not required to have any academic ambition because once married they'd only end up being housewives he had said. It would be just a waste of time and money, he had reminded them time and time again. James being the eldest son was the first to be sent overseas to further his education.

As a Malay and a Muslim, it was inherent in James to be non-racial and to respect other religions and cultures. He was by nature tolerant of other people, and had always enjoyed the cross-cultural intermingling, be it at home in multi-racial, multi-cultural and multi-religious Malaysia, or when he was studying in Australia among the multi-ethnic Australians. He wasn't overtly sociable nor was he too reserved. He could make friends whenever he wanted to.

Like most Asians, James, who rarely display their prejudices in public, was shocked to see the whites in Australia blatantly flaunting their racial tendencies, especially towards the Aborigines and other Asians immigrants. What dismayed him most was how the government of Australia could endorse a policy which encourages immigration from their former wartime enemies like the Germans and Italians, rather than allow their closer and more hardworking Asian neighbours, with whom they have lived with for centuries, from entering the country.

And yet the majority of Australians whom James had come in contact with during his entire stay there were mostly nice people who seemed oblivious to their government's diabolical and abhorrent *"White Australia Policy"*. Or perhaps they were like the ostrich that'd stuck its head in the sand, or maybe like the three monkeys where one would hear nothing, another would see nothing, while the third would say nothing, pretending that everything was fine.

James found it ironic that on the one hand its government was racist to say the least, while on the other, the majority its people were easy to get along with. Not being able to tolerate the Australian government's repugnant policy, James left the country not long after he graduated with a degree in architecture. On leaving Australia, James Razali had gone straight to Singapore where he worked as an architect in a public utilities department there. As propinquity would have it, on his second year there, he met a local Chinese girl and fell in love. They eventually married. They had two sons whom he adored and dotted on. When Singapore got booted out of Malaysia, he and his family moved to Kuala Lumpur. For a while he became a lecturer in architecture at a college in Kuala Lumpur.

James, who had always regarded Malaysia as home, was in a way glad that the decision was made for him to return to Malaysia. Even if the separation between the two countries hadn't happened, he would one day want to return home to the land of his ancestors. His two sons, whom he had sent to England to study, were different from him. They were willing to trade in their Asian heritage and culture for a British one. Whenever they were home for their holidays they seemed to be more British than the British themselves which irked their former friends and classmates.

When James chided them on their mannerism and accent, they told him that he needn't be so concern about them for they planned on leaving soon. When he asked them where they were going, they told James that they were going back to England to where their friends were!

Not long after their two sons left for England, he and his wife parted ways. The breakup of his marriage was bad enough for James, and with his two sons gone and his wife no longer wanted him, it was too much for him. It saddened him greatly, but there was nothing he could do about it, both his sons were adults. He tried to reason with them but it was no use, they had made up their minds. They were determined to put their friends in England before him became too much for James and he felt terribly hurt.

James, unlike most Malays of his generation who'd rather seek the security of a job with the government, had ambitions to have a business of his own. He began saving for it as soon as he started working. After nearly a decade down the road, when the opportunity came, and the money he had saved while working as an architect, plus some borrowings had looked almost adequate, he quit his job at the architects firm and started his own business.

He soon found out that running a business was not as easy as it looks. Undercapitalized and understaffed, James plodded on, selling everything from engine oil additives to car polish, from cookware to toys, carrying the products himself in the boot of his car, sometimes working till the early hours of the morning. After a period of some years, with nothing near the success he had hoped had hoped for, he decided that perhaps he should give up the business altogether and look for a job. He gave himself three months to try to improve the business, at the same time keeping his ears and eyes opened for any suitable job. He told himself, if at the end of that period and still the business hadn't improved, he'd call it quits. But after two months with the business getting worse, he told his staff of six his intention to close down the company.

With no job and with a mountain of bills to greet him each day, James was beginning to get panicky. He knew that things will only get worse if he didn't do something about changing the situation he was in. In desperation he phoned his bank manager for an appointment, hoping that they could extend him further credit, on the basis of his longstanding relationship with them, at least until he sorted things out.

On the very day he was at the bank, he had the good fortune of bumping into an old buddy of his from Australia. It so happened that this friend was in Malaysia looking for a partner for a business venture of his and he was at the bank to see the manager for some recommendations.

James told his friend about the history of his company, the business he was in, and why he had to cease operation. His friend in turn told him about his own business and about his intention to spread out of Australia. James then asks him whether his company might be suitable. His friend said that was depending on the usual vetting by his accountants, he couldn't see any reason why they couldn't be partners in the new venture. Like a house on fire, the two lost no time in discussing the business in detail. James put a suggestion to his friend that instead of forming a new company as they had originally planned, why not use his existing company.

It took them no time at all to iron out the details such as the amount still owed by the company to the bank and other creditors, and after deducting that from its assets, they came up with a workable formula in which his friend would inject into the company funds for its equity as well as low-interest loan in order for them to begin operation straight away. The company, took advantage of Malaysia's relatively cheap labour plus the availability of the raw materials that came in from the neighbouring countries, broke even at the end of its second year in operation. From then on it became so profitable James and his partner, Steve, scoffed at rumours that was sweeping the country at the time that the recession was already hitting Europe, USA and Japan. Recession will hit Singapore and Malaysia eventually, everybody had said - it was just a matter of time.

The two friends who had made some money but not much in beginning of their business operation had made a lot of sacrifices and they were very frugal then. They had watched very closely how the money was spent, had stuck closely to their budget; they paid themselves just enough to live on.

Steve, who was bachelor, had lived in a single-bedroomed apartment but soon moved to a bigger apartment when buyers in Australia, in the USA and Europe, as well as Japan, were buying a lot of their products. The bigger apartment Steve had move to was in a more expensive part of Kuala Lumpur, James had noticed.

Within three years of their business operation, the company was generating a lot of cash and they were spending money like it was going out of style. Unfortunately for them the prediction that they had scoffed at earlier became very real, the recession had hit Singapore first and then Malaysia. Like a ton of bricks they were hit hard. Despite the two partners' bold efforts to rein in their spending, it was too little too late, they suddenly found their business wasn't there anymore. Since the products they were making were high end stuff like ready-to-wear items and accessories for men and women, mainly for the rich and famous. When the rich and famous too felt they had to tighten their belts, they had lost no time in finding out that they could do without the products that James and Steve had produced and when they stopped buying all together, Steve and James's business soon folded up.

His friend and former partner left for Australia, while James, with nowhere else to go stayed put in Malaysia. To make things worse his wife of over twenty years decided that she would like to go back to Singapore. She had advised James to stay put in Malaysia and to try to look for a job. James tried to persuade his wife to stick around with him while he look for a job. She had told him that may not be the best idea because she might be in the way since he had to go from place to place to find something to do. It sounded very logical to him and he had agreed that she moved back with her mother in Singapore.

Malaysia like the rest of the world, was in deep recession. James couldn't even get a job let alone starting a new business.

ﮞﮞﮞﮞﮞﮞ

CHAPTER NINE

James didn't see Mandy Lee again until about a year later. She appeared while he was having coffee with some friends in the Yaohan Food Arcade on the third floor of the KOMTAR shopping complex. James was sitting facing the entrance of the food arcade when he saw someone, at the telephone booth which was located near the entrance, waved at him. At that distance he couldn't see clearly who it was except that it was a young woman.

James's dismissed it thinking that perhaps it was one of his customers who had waved at him. He had been operating the food outlet in that arcade for nearly two years then, and during the course of the day he tended to meet a lot of people. Over that period of time one can imagine the number of people he did get to meet. He did what he normally would do when people wave at him, he waved back. He tried to see who it was, but the woman was already busy on the telephone with her back towards him. He returned to his companions and carried on with his conversation with them. A few minutes later James realised that it was Mandy Lee whom he hadn't seen for over a year, who had waved at him, when she, whom he did not recognize at first, approached him at their table. James felt his heart was beginning to race and his face was beginning to feel flushed. With great difficulty he managed to control his hand from shaking so much in order to shake her hand.

As he was introducing Mandy to his friends, he began to realize why he hadn't immediately recognised her. About a year ago he saw a pretty young school girl who had said some unkind things to him. But the young woman who was standing in front of him looked nothing like the young school girl that she was.

Looking very matured, elegant and beautiful, the voluptuous Mandy was a young woman who would raise any man's temperature a few degrees just by being in the same room with her, James was thinking.

This time, however, Mandy was not in her school uniform but in a light-brown skirt with a blouse that matched it perfectly. She had a hand bag slung on one shoulder, and in her right hand she held a paper bag that had *Selangor Pewter* printed on it. She had cut her hair short, but not too short to make her look like a boy. James had always fancied women with long hair, but Mandy with her short hair was an exception he'd gladly concede to. It suited her very well, he thought. If anything, it only made her look slightly mischievous.

Ever since that day at the pizzeria James had always fantasised of meeting with Mandy again. Now that he was face to face with her, he seemed to be lost for words and must have looked rather sullen as he was inclined to be when he got nervous. Why in the world would I get nervous in front of a young woman was beyond me, he thought. But it didn't matter a great deal because Mandy didn't stay very long. She left just as soon as she finished her coffee. She had said something about meeting her boyfriend downstairs and that it was time that she left. They shook hands and moments later she strode out of the Food Court and walked to the concourse area.

As soon as she disappeared from view, James had this odd feeling which he couldn't logically explain. It was a feeling of inexplicable loss, and the weirdest thing was his sudden urge to go after her and wanting to put his arms around her. It was incredible! It was as if he should run after her and try to protect her - from what he couldn't really say. This feeling came in a flash and to his dismay it stayed with him for most of the day. On a rational level it was ridiculous, but at that moment he knew that he was smitten by her and there was not a lot he could do about it.

* * *

As an architect James Rashid was quite successful in his chosen field, working practically non-stop. Malaysia was in the midst of recession at that time so getting work as an architect was out of the question. He did the next best thing: he registered with the relevant authorities as a contractor. For nearly two months nothing came out of it, then a call from one of the government department asking him if he is still working as a contractor. Without any hesitation he had said yes. After he had spoken for several minutes with the man on the line, he was asked to come to his office the next day to collect some documents. When he saw the caller at his office the next day, James was given a set of documents to fill out and signed. With that done he was given a list of work he had to do at the address given. It turned out that he was given a list of projects he had to renovate for the government. He withdrew from his savings account most of the money he had in there to buy materials for the job on hand. Looking at the drawings, he knew what things he had to get immediately and also knew he had to get a few experienced workers. Within three days he was ready to start work. It was slow beginning but with a lot of patience on his part in trying to get his workers to execute the job the way he had wanted them to do. He was thrilled a few days later to see his workers, most of whom were from Indonesia, had completed the job much to his satisfaction. He had divided the job into lots and so when he had finished a lot he immediately submitted his claim. He was fearful that he may not have the cash flow to complete all the lots. He was surprised and grateful when he received a call from the officer who had asked him to come and collect his cheque.

He had completed all the work he had been given ahead of time and on budget. A week later when he was called to come and collect his cheque, he was surprised to be given another renovating job to renovate a whole block of hostels.

James had worked very hard and in the process had earned himself a lot of money. He had always cherished the idea of one day becoming a businessman like most Chinese in the country.

Ironically, James's wife, Irene, whose mother was a Straits-born Chinese and whose father was a businessman, hated the idea of her husband becoming a businessman. She had seen in her father how uncertain life of a businessman could be, and how it affected the whole family. When things went well, it was all milk and honey at home. But during the lean times, which was more often than not, things could go so bad they didn't have enough money to buy milk powder for her baby brother and sister. She remembered the roller-coaster years with clarity and had vowed that she would never marry a businessman. It took a considerable effort on James's part in trying to persuade her to allow him to go into business.

During the time James was working as an architect in the Singapore Housing Board, Irene had enjoyed the life as an architect's wife, including all the perks that went with it like Ang Pows from contractors, sub-contractor, suppliers and so on. She also enjoyed being member of two of the country's oldest clubs, mixing with what she considered the right people, and being seen with them.

Irene greeted her husband's decision to leave the practice and start a business with a heavy heart and trepidation. It didn't help any when her husband told her that he hadn't made up his mind as to what type of business he had planned on going into when she had asked him. How naive could he be, she thought to herself, many men with more experience than her husband had failed despite the fact that they had known exactly what they had wanted to do and knew how to do it. How could her husband, who hadn't done anything else except practice architecture, succeed when others who had been in business all their life had failed?

For the next couple of years Irene watched in a rather detached manner how husband went from one business to another with regularity, all of which was doomed to failure even before they even got started. Although she was concerned, she never take any effort to try to understand whatever he was trying doing. Perhaps if she did, things may have turned differently for them. On one occasion when she asked James if he was really sure about going into business instead of practising architecture? James had replied to her that if the Chinese could do it so could he. She looked hard at him, trying to read into that statement of his, but when she saw James turned away from her gaze, she knew then for the first time in their married life a racial dig was beginning to crop up into their conversation and she was afraid. She was afraid of what it would to him and to their marriage should he fail in business. She knew that failure in business was as easy as falling off a log. She knew that it would be worse for her husband who'd be like an ant in a colony of anteaters.

Irene wasn't trying to be smug or patronising towards her husband whom she had respected but was only trying to tell him what was in store when she told him what he failed to understand was the special bond and cooperation that the Chinese business community received from one another. Once a Chinese has set himself up in business he would invariably get the support from his own community. With very few exceptions, his friends, his neighbours and all his kin would rally behind him, giving him the full support he expected from them. Will the Malays support James, Irene wondered; she doubted if they would.

Although James didn't know it or didn't want to know it, and Irene may or may not know it, the Malays, contrary to what they claim, had always had an aversion of seeing other Malays succeed. Some would even walk the extra mile just to avoid patronising a business owned by another Malay. It was the inherent jealousy in them that prevented them from helping each other.

In James's case, he had made the mistake of targeting mainly Malays for his business. Worst of all, in his last venture, he had allowed some of his customers to buy on credit. Consequently, many of them failed to settle their bills promptly resulting in tremendous hardship for James to replace his stock. He hung on for as long as he could, much longer than all his previous ventures, until he resigned himself to the inevitable and closed his shop.

Two months later Irene left for Singapore to see her mother who had suffered a mild stroke. James joined her there for a few days and had planned on bringing Irene back home with him. To James disappointment Irene had told James that she would like to stay on to look after her mother. There really wasn't anything Irene can really do for her mother, a family doctor would be on call taking care of her.

James could only assume that Irene herself wanted to be away from him. He felt saddened by the thought, but decided to give in to her wish. He said his goodbyes and left for Kuala Lumpur in his car. His mother-in-law had asked her servant to give him some mandarin oranges to take with him. *Chap Go Meh,* which signalled the end of the Chinese New Year, was still two days away.

❧❧❧❧❧❧

CHAPTER TEN

Choosing to live in Penang was something that came out of the blue, something he'd never thought of doing. Penang had many similarity with Singapore, including its people, and he had wanted to forget a lot of painful memories that had stemmed from there. He had no desire to have anything or anyone to remind him of that episode of his life so it came as a surprise even to him that he had chosen Penang, once dubbed as the "Pearl of The Orient".

When he left Singapore he thought he'd never find a place like it again, where not only its people of all races could live in harmony, but the government there wouldn't dream of butting in a person's private life - with regards to religion, for instance.

Whereas in Malaysia, some quarters with their holier than_thou attitude, wouldn't hesitate to slap a *Khalwat* charge on an unsuspecting couple, for example, who may want to find a quiet corner somewhere for having a tête-à-tête. And yet, despite all these deterrents and harassment by the authorities, the number of abandoned babies among the Malays, the main target of these policies, seemed to be in the increase. Obviously that policy and other discriminatory laws specifically targeted them hadn't worked and should be looked into, scrapped, if found to be counterproductive.

The government surely has no business in interfering in the private lives of its citizen. James had always felt that the discriminatory actions on them because of their religion, regardless of how well meaning the intention was, not only made them look like second-class citizen, but it would be a grave infringement of their civil liberty. Fortunately for the government, the Malays had, and would, never question anything if it concerned their religion, no matter how silly or ridiculous they may have looked to the general public. It seemed obvious to anybody with some common sense that education was the only way to go, and they shouldn't count too much on the parents' involvement in this.

James found Penang in many ways similar to Singapore. On the positive side, he found it less rigid, but the people with its laid-back attitude could be damn difficult to work with at times. On the negative side, he had found Penang dirtier than he had remembered it. However as he began to tally up the pluses and the minuses, he became convinced that it wasn't a bad place to settle down.

* * *

James had spent a week at Tasek Kenyir three months into his stay in Penang. There he went jogging every day before breakfast. Breakfast normally consisted of toasts and black coffee. Sometimes, if the weather was fine he'd do a bit of fishing where he would hire a boat for the duration. By about noon he'd return to his cabin with his catch which he'd sometime fry them and have for lunch. Alternately, he'd have the fish baked in foil and eat it with either baked potatoes or yams. On two occasions he had the chef at the main hotel cook the fish for him. The chef, who was from Switzerland, outdid himself with his creations; James told him that he had never tasted fish like it before. That pleased the chef very much.

The chef told James that for the moment there are no names for the two dishes he had prepared for him, not until he had them perfected. But as far as James was concerned it couldn't be more perfect, and he knew he wasn't a Philistine. The chef confessed to James that the two recipes were originally his mother's, but he had improvised on them by replacing some of the ingredients with herbs he had found not far from Tasek Kenyir.

When he came back home to his flat in Sungai Nibong he hadn't come to a decision as what he had wanted to do with his life apart from running the Nasi Padang outlet at the food court which he considered it as a hobby.

He began to formulate some plans about going into a construction and renovation business. When he telephone Irene in Singapore and told her about his plans, she told him directly that whatever plans he had in mind he should exclude her in any of them.

"I think it is good you have some things planned with your life, but please exclude me in any of them, okay?" The line went dead in his hand. He tried to call her, but was told by Ruby, her sister that Irene had gone out. James noticed the sadness in Ruby's voice.

"Ruby, please tell me what's going on over there?"

"I don't know. You have to ask Irene that yourself".

During the next several days he tried to get to talk to Irene but each time she would tell him to go ahead and do what he wanted to do. James thought that he and Irene should a talk again once he had settled down and got on with the plans he had wanted to do.

Apart from one more meeting they had had when James had driven down to Singapore to try to persuade Irene to come home with him, it was the last time he were to see Irene again.

* * *

A week later, through a real estate agent, he put up their house for sale. Since their house had had some renovations done to it, and it was well kept house, it was sold rather quickly. James gave Irene two-thirds of the proceeds, the rest he kept for himself. On the drive home he thought that he must be out of his mind to give Irene two-thirds.

Fifty-fifty would have been fine! He shook his head thinking what a soft touch he was!

* * *

After almost a decade away from Asia in general and from Malaysia in particular, James found it difficult at first to come to grips with some peculiar and sometime disgusting habits of his countrymen and women had. Having temporarily forgotten about them while living in the West, they came back to him as a rude shock the morning after he had spent his first night at his new flat in Sungai Nibong. It was coincidental that the flat of his was not far from Penang International Airport. He was awaken one morning when a loud noise jolted him from his slumber. The sound apparently was coming from his living room.

Immediately alert, James opened his eyes and strained his ears and waited to see if the sound would reoccur, but when it didn't, he drifted back to sleep. Several minutes later he was awakened again, this time to the sound of loud repeated sneezing. He got out of bed and strode quickly into his living room where the sound seemed to be coming from, convinced that someone was in his flat.

James, in his muddy state of mind, had immediately thought of his landlord who may have let himself in with his spare key. He was furious because he was sure that there was nothing in their contract that would allow the landlord to walk into his flat whenever he liked. Surely he'd have the common sense to call first if he had wanted to inspect the premises or whatever. He then remembered that his phone hadn't been connected yet. Well, he could at least come at a decent time, he thought.

When James didn't find anyone in his living room, he did a thorough search of his flat. A few minutes later, although satisfied that no one was in his flat, he was nonetheless curious as to the source of the sound. Irritated at being awakened up so early in the morning, he dragged himself back to bed and tried to catch up with his sleep. Just as he was getting into his bed, he heard another sneeze. This time he pinpointed to where the noise was coming from. It came not from inside his flat, but from outside the window of his study. He jumped out of bed and went to open it, and when he peered out he saw an Old Man doing his slow movement exercise favoured by the Chinese right in front of his window. James asked him why he was doing his exercise in front of his window and instead of his own? He told James in a tone that matched his own rather sarcastic voice that since he was doing his exercises in a public corridor, it was no body's business except his where he chose to exercise. Before James could reply the Old Man turned his back on him.

Seething with anger, James closed the louvers of his window loudly and went to have a cold shower, changing his mind about going back to sleep, knowing fully well that it'll be just a waste of time. He knew he'll never get back to sleep.

With the exception of James, his brothers and sisters had their careers chosen for them by their iron-willed, civil servant father. James was the first-born among his nine brothers and sisters to have ventured out on his own doing things he had wanted to do. Despite the numerous setbacks he had encountered along the way, he knew it had been rewarding. James was certain too that there must have been a few shakes of the head and some sniffs of disapproval from his father as news of James's roller-coaster life reached his ears.

James had summed up his life over the last twenty years as something that hadn't gone that badly at all. In retrospective, he could have done some things differently, but all in all, he knew he had had a lot of fun doing all the things he had done during the last twenty years of his life.

He had travelled to many parts of the world others would only dream of, or read about. He had met and worked with all kinds of people of various cultures and backgrounds. And now he had finally arrived at the beginning of his Odyssey and not the end many had assumed. His long search, which took him from architecture, which he loathed because of the corruption involved, to doing all kinds of businesses, which he loved but were equally tainted, was finally over. He had at last found what he had wanted to do all these years and was looking forward to what the next twenty year will bring.

* * *

James have had on numerous occasions fines being imposed on him for late payments for one thing or another, such as failure to pay parking fees on time, or on one occasion he had walked into his flat only to find that the electricity had been disconnected due to his failure to pay his electricity bill. There was also the time when a friend had brought all her washings over to his flat hoping to do her washings because her own washing machine had broken down. She found to her exasperation that there was no water getting into the machine. Apparently James had forgotten to pay his water bill. James's occasional lapses with regards to paying his bills did not actually stem from irresponsibility on his part, but due to occasional forgetfulness. He had always made allocations for all his monthly payments, and he seemed to have no trouble in paying his bills, if only he didn't forget when to pay them.

James kept telling himself that he should keep a diary, or even write memos to himself - just like all the executives of those top 100 companies do. Writing in a diary or to write memos was no problem, it was just that sometimes he had forgotten where he had kept his diary or even the memos that he had written!

For his memos James used one of those stick-anywhere yellow memo pads that most executives in those big corporations use. On a few occasions he had to telephone some of his friends and asked whether they had received any of his memos by mistake; memos, which had accidentally got stuck to the letters that, he had sent them. On one occasion he had to call everybody that he had written to while he was in a supermarket and asked them whether any of them had received a shopping list which he had written which may have got stuck on the back of the letters he had sent them. Fortunately for him one of them did and he was able to read it back to James there and then. Can you imagine going to the supermarket without a shopping list? You'd end up buying everything in sight - what a frightening thought!

It must have been a week after the supermarket incident when James bumped into Mandy again. He was at the post office to buy some stamps and to pay his telephone and electricity bills when he saw her walk into the post office. Without turning left or right she had gone straight to stand in the queue at one of the stamp counters. After several minutes of waiting, disheartened that Mandy hadn't turned his way, James was tempted to leave his queue and walk over to her. The only thing that prevented him from doing that was his fear that Mandy might not remember him and didn't want to be embarrassed. He remembered how he had made a fool of himself the first time they had met. Heaven forbid! He couldn't bear to have that repeated.

Unfortunately for James, Mandy didn't even turn once in his direction. In a manner that was discrete, he tried every which way to attract her attention, but to no avail. No more than a few feet away from him stood Mandy, looking as beautiful as ever, staring stonily ahead of her, as she patiently waited for her turn to be served. As James inched forward in his line towards the counter in front of his line, he kept looking at Mandy hoping that she might look his way. Her concentration seemed to be directed at the lady behind the counter in her queue. James turned to look at the lady behind the counter to see if there was anything special about her - nothing! The lady, probably in her early thirties, wore her *tudung* in the old-fashion way making her look older than her age, was just a typical civil servant working for the post office before it became privatised recently. And now that it had, she, like thousands others like her, appeared to have changed little. Despite the long queue in front of her, she took her own sweet time weighing the letters one by one and writing the amount on each of them with a pencil. When she had done that she then began dispensing the stamps until she had gone through the bunch of letters the young man standing with elbow on the counter had given her.

It was obvious to James that the young man was probably an office boy on his early morning routine. James had recognised the logo of a well-known home-appliance manufacturer embroidered on the back of his shirt. He had bought one of its microwave oven not too long ago.

James smiled when he noticed, in the back left-hand pocket of the young man's pair of Jeans, a red comb was sticking out. Like the lady in front of him, the young man seemed unhurried. Nevertheless, despite the lady's leisurely ways, James could see that Mandy's line was moving while everyone in his seemed rooted to the floor.

James stretched his neck out to see what the hold-up was. Apart from the fact that another lady was in attendance in the counter in front of his queue, the hold-up seemed to be by an Old Man who looked like he was doing everybody in his neighbourhood a favour by paying their bills for them. He had this stack of all manners of bills in one hand and a wad of notes in the other, and like the office boy in Mandy's line, he too seemed to be in no hurry. James could see him handing the bills one at a time to the lady behind the counter. By this time James was so afraid that he might not have the chance to say hello to Mandy. It occurred to him that none of the people in that crowded post office would have any qualms about calling out across the room at the top of his or her voice to attract their friends' attention. James, on the other hand, couldn't bring himself to do that kind of thing, instead, he just stood there cursing himself silently for his upbringing.

Now that the office boy was gone, Mandy's line seemed to be moving faster than usual, James noticed that she was next behind an elderly lady who was being attended to, while James was still far away from the paying counter. Many times he felt like abandoning paying his bills altogether that day and go to Mandy instead.

He would have done that if not for the fact that if he didn't pay his telephone bill that very day it might get disconnected. It seemed that the one thing he cannot afford to be without, was a phone because of his phobia about missing phone calls. What do they call such phobia? *No-phono-phobia*? Well, anyway, he stayed put and hoped that Mandy would still be around when he had finished paying his bills.

Finally when he reached the counter, he looked up in Mandy's direction, he was relieved to see that Mandy was still there. James had made sure that he had the exact change so that there wouldn't be any delays, and there wasn't. To her credit, the lady behind his counter was most efficient, but unfortunately Mandy had already left the post office by the time he turned around to look.

James tried to look for Mandy among the crowd but she was nowhere in sight. He rushed outside to see if she could still be around but to no avail. James couldn't explain it, but he felt so shattered for having missed her and for several days later he was still thinking of her. He couldn't recall of anyone having that effect on him before.

ᚾᚱᚾᚱᚾᚱ

CHAPTER ELEVEN

As fate would have it, James met with Mandy again several months later. This time he was in the book section at the Yaohan Departmental Store when he saw her browsing at the magazine stand. Acutely aware that his heart was beginning to pound, he went over to her and said hello. He was both relieved and elated when she smiled when she saw him.

"Hello, nice to see you again," she said. She had said those words as if she had meant them. A couple of men who were standing close by turned their heads to look at her and then at James. It was obvious that they were being scrutinised and James felt as if he were ten feet tall because of the envious looks the two men were giving him. He could also see that they were very curious about the relationship between the two of them. It was obvious to anyone that James and Mandy were not related or anything like that. Obvious too was their age difference. Even though James's forty-ninth birthday was still some months away, he wasn't exactly over the hill, not by a long shot. But anyone watching Mandy and him would not fail to notice the age gap, and that, if nothing else, called for some speculations among the onlookers.

All of a sudden James became very conscious but managed to quickly put it out of his mind. After all, he was in the company of a beautiful young woman on that floor, if not the whole building, he proudly told himself, you guys can eat your hearts out!

James really felt like he was ten feet tall instead of just being slightly over five feet ten. He could smell Mandy's perfume as they stood close to one another. He wanted to ask her what it was but had changed his mind when he thought that it wasn't the right time. As they stood side by side James noticed for the first time that Mandy was as tall as he was, perhaps an inch or two shorter than he was, and he had liked that.

Mandy, on that day, wore a skirt and a blouse. Her hair had grown since he last saw her, and had it cascading on her shoulders. The overall effect was that it made her look very beautiful, very matured, and very sexy indeed. They talked a bit about books and each other's reading habits as they strolled around the bookshop, browsing as they went along.

James had originally gone there to get a copy of Jeffrey Archer's book entitled, *'As The Crow Flies'*. She told him that she had come for the latest copy of the Tattler magazine. When both had found what they ha come for, James asked her whether she would like to go somewhere for a drink. He was delighted when she had said yes.

They took the escalator, which was located right in front of the bookstore, and rode it down to the ground floor. They exited the department store by its side entrance and crossed the narrow lane before heading for the parking lot where James had parked his car that day. It wasn't his usual place for parking his car, but it was just a vacant lot that had been temporarily used as a car park and he found it convenient. He rarely use the car park because the area hadn't been properly levelled, it was strewn with rocks and pebbles. He warned Mandy of it and told her to be careful lest she'd fall. Almost as soon as he had uttered the warning, he himself accidentally stepped on a piece of rock and had stumbled. He would have fallen to the ground if Mandy hadn't grabbed his arm, and in the process, almost pulling her down to the ground. Fortunately for the both of them she'd reacted quickly and had managed to stay put, thus prevented a minor disaster, which could turn out to be a major embarrassment. James's foot had sunk into the ground, which was soft from the previous night's rain, and when he pulled it out of the mud, Mandy let out a shriek of laughter, pointing to his feet. James looked down and immediately saw the reason of her mirth. A heel from one of his shoes was missing. It must have broken off when he stumbled on the piece of rock and was still embedded somewhere in the mud. James asked Mandy if she would mind if they went to his place first so that he could change his shoes. She had said she wouldn't mind. When they reached James's flat Mandy was hesitant at first to come up, saying that she'll wait for him in the car. When he assured her that changing his shoes was all he had in my mind, she wrinkled her nose and smiled.

On entering the flat James suggested to her to make herself at home whereby she promptly kicked off her shoes and sat with her feet underneath her on the sofa and said, "Okay." It was an amazing display of nonchalance he had ever seen, a complete reversal to the shy, hesitant Mandy only moments ago.

It had three bedrooms when James had first moved into the flat about three years ago, but he had turned it into a two-bedroom one when he converted the smaller of the three bedrooms into a cosy dining room.

Once, not too long ago, it had a good view of the KOMTAR tower some twelve kilometres away, but unfortunately a recently-built blocks of flats had obliterated it from view. There was, however, another famous landmark that could still be seen from his dining room, provided of course one stood on the ledge just outside the window of the dining room. The view, of course, was of the famous Penang Bridge, touted by almost everyone on the island as the third longest bridge in the world.

Although to some people, Sungai Nibong, a suburb some eleven kilometres away from George

Town, was too far away from the city, James liked it because it was quiet, and besides, it was as close as he could get to being in the countryside without leaving the island itself. He adored the countryside as much as he detested the city, any city.

He remembered how one day Dr. Mahathir Mohammed, the Prime Minister, had singled out Penang as the rubbish bin of the orient. However since then things have improved slightly, although one must confess that Penang was still dirty and probably will always remained so because of its people's slothful attitude towards cleanliness.

Mandy had said to James that she had liked his flat very much and it pleased him greatly. To his credit, he did try to make it as comfortable as he possibly could by having it furnished with a good many pieces of furniture he could afford to buy.

After a quick tour of the flat, James offered Mandy some wine as they sat in the living room listening to some classical music which Mandy had selected from a collection James had brought back from overseas. The record she chose was the Romeo and Juliet Overture by *Peter Ilich Tchaikovsky*, one of James's favourites. He couldn't help wondering whether or not Mandy really knew what she was choosing, or was she only attracted to the title.

Mandy took a sip of her wine before leaning back against the sofa. She caught James looking at her. With a subtlety that belied her tender age she told him that she liked the wine, thus saving James from embarrassment, for he wasn't just looking, he was staring at her. Mandy looked so beautiful with her fair complexion, and apart from a tiny scar on her left chin, her face and her skin looked as if it was translucent. James couldn't help admiring Mandy's lack of pretension. Other women would have asked what wine it was irrespective of their knowledge on the subject. Mandy was different, she was simply telling James that she was enjoying the wine, that was all.

It was the same with the music. At first James thought she was trying to impress when she had asked Tchaikovsky to be put on, but as they talked, it became apparent to him that music, paintings, poetry and books were things she had liked. She had no talent for any of them but that didn't stop her from appreciating them. James couldn't help admiring that kind of simplicity in her. They spent the rest of the afternoon listening to classical music.

That night they went to a Thai food place for dinner, and since it was considered their 'first date' James had wanted to make an impression on her, he inadvertently ordered too much. But as soon as the waitress was out of their hearing distance, Mandy gently reminded him that there was no way that the two of them could finish all the food that he'd ordered and suggested that he should cancel a dish. How right she was, They were practically struggling trying to finish the food in the end, and that was despite the dish they had cancelled as suggested by her. Once again James couldn't help marvelling at the sensibility of someone as young as her.

Right through dinner, Mandy seemed to be enjoying herself and full of *joie de vivre*. After dinner he had asked her whether she would like to hear some music at one of the hotels along Ferringhi Beach. She had declined. She asked him if he would send her home instead. James felt shattered and must have shown it on his face because the next moment she looked up at him and said, "We could go out again next week, if you like."

"I'd like that very much," replied James.

"Why don't you call me Monday night."

James telephoned Mandy on that Monday night as she had suggested but was told by a young man's voice that Mandy wasn't home. James called again the next day and when he was told the same thing, he left his number with the same young man who had answered him the previous day. The next day, James debated whether he should call Mandy again, but when he did and was told the same thing, he concluded that he had been given the brush off. He tried to convince himself that it was all for the best, after all he knew that their relationship would go nowhere; the best they could ever be was being friends - good friends even - that will be all. However, three days later he was surprised to receive a telephone call from Mandy asking him whether he might be free that night. Unable to conceal his excitement, James told her that he would be. It took him a while before it sank in that a woman was asking him out – a beautiful woman at that!

When James went to pick her up at her house that evening, Mandy made no apologies about not returning his calls nor did she mention them; it was as if that episode didn't happen. James took her to a steak house that had made a name for itself during the time when the Royal Australian Air Force personnel and their families were living in Penang.

It was during the time when the RAAF had their base in Butterworth, just across the water on the mainland. Coffee and steak houses, as well as the ubiquitous bars and dance halls, were mushrooming all over the island then, catering mainly to the air force personnel and their families. Inevitably, most of them closed down when the RAAF packed up and left Butterworth some years later. But one restaurant in particular had made a name for itself, even among the locals. It not only remained in business, despite the loss of their Australian clientele, it prospered and expanded nationally. And now you can find *Eden Steak and Seafood Restaurants* all over the country. It was in their Hutton Lane restaurant that James and Mandy had dinner that night. He had chosen it not only because of its old world ambience but for its renown Beef Wellington that Mandy had indicated that she would like to try.

While they were having their coffee after a delicious meal, Mandy told James about a restaurant job she had been offered in Singapore. She seemed vague about her duties, but told him that it would be in a supervisory capacity. The restaurant, she said, was owned by a horse-owner she had met while at work. At that time Mandy was working as a sales assistant selling pewter wares in a shop in one of the leading hotels on Penang's famed Batu Ferringhi beach.

James casually mentioned to Mandy that living in Singapore could be very expensive. She said she knew that, she had heard it from a friend, but the important thing about the job she said, was that it would provide her with a place to stay. She wasn't sure but she thought that they were going to let her eat all her meals at the restaurant too, and to provide transportation to take her home whenever she worked the night shift. On the surface it seemed all right to James and he told her so. Mandy seemed relieved.

He pondered on what she had said about her job offer and he couldn't help thinking that maybe this particular horse-owner had other designs on her beside having her work in his restaurant. After all, Mandy had admitted that she had no experience whatsoever working in a restaurant before. He had pressed her about what her duties would be. She told James that she had no idea. James found it incredulous that anyone would want to take a job without knowing all the details beforehand. James thought to himself that perhaps at his age he was getting to be cynical, or was he judging others by his own standard? Still, it stank like hell as far as he was concerned, but then again, he could be wrong. Finally James asked Mandy what her parents thought about her job offer.

"My mom said I can take the job if I want to," she replied.

"What about your dad, what did he say?"

"My dad said nothing! He hasn't been around since I was six years old!" She practically spat the words out.

For a split-second James thought he saw a look of smouldering anger in her eyes, but it evaporated almost as soon as it appeared on her beautiful face.

It occurred to James that if her father had left them when Mandy was only six years of age, and since she had said that she had two other younger brothers, then the youngest of the two couldn't be more than a baby when her father had left them. He wondered what kind of a man would do that?

For the next thirty minutes or so Mandy talked about her family - her mother mostly - how she had managed to bring them up almost single-handed.

As a result of a gentle prodding from James, Mandy relented a bit and began talking about her father.

"My father was a very handsome," she said. "He gave the impression to my mother that he was a bachelor when they first met. My mother fell in love with him and they got married soon after. The truth of the matter was that he had two other families including two children with one and three with the other, and both of these wives were supporting him by giving him money from their meagre pay." What he didn't divulge was where these two families were living - in Thailand apparently. Mandy told James how for six years her mother had to work to support all of them including her father.

"My mother didn't know about the existence of the other two families until much later. He told her when she was carrying my second brother."

"What could she have done?" she said angrily. "Nothing, except to accept the fact and had gone on living the way had been living. And all she had in her life was my baby brother and me, and of course the baby in her belly."

It seemed that when Mandy's mother first met her father, he had told her that he was a travelling salesman, which entailed a lot of travelling on his part. At that time her mother was working as a seamstress at a factory not far from the fishing village where they lived. Three generations of her family had lived there, right from the time her grandfather had come down from China and decided to settle in Penang.

In the beginning her father had given her mother money every month but the role was reversed not long after she was born when her father started telling her mother of their need to put aside some money for a business he was contemplating of going into once they had enough capital. Every month as soon as her mother received her pay she would give him part of it to her father. The rest, which didn't come to very much, was used to clothe and feed all of them. While her mother worked, her grandmother was looking after her and her baby brother. Her father didn't even see the birth of her second brother. By the time her mother had given birth to him her father had already left their mother and was never seen again.

James couldn't help thinking about her situation now where history was about to repeat itself; like a remake of a movie or a television show, with her cast in the leading role not un-similar to the role that her mother had played in real life. Mandy was then supporting the family then.

He was thinking about the horse-owner and his designs on her. Sensing that being his mistress might be in store for her, James told her of his concern, perhaps in a round about way since he didn't want to grate on her sensitivity. He reminded her to be wary about whom she should trust and what she should look out for in a foreign country. He gave her his telephone number telling her that she was at liberty to call him whenever she felt like calling.

As he drove Mandy home that night, James pondered on why was he so concerned about a young woman, albeit, a very pretty young woman whom he had hardly known. What she should or shouldn't do with her life, was her own business. To be brutally honest James hadn't the faintest idea why he was so concerned. He stole a glance at Mandy who seemed to be deep in thoughts. At that angle, and for a split-second, she looked like a child and vulnerable. Mandy turned her head to look at him and gave him a weak smile. At that moment James felt a sudden overwhelming desire to protect her from everything that was hash and cruel in the world.

CHAPTER TWELVE

"James, I've known you ever since you came to Penang - how long has it been...?" asked Eddy.

"Almost five years," replied James.

"Right! And during all this time I've never known you to be so concerned about any of the women you've gone out with. Why is this Mandy so special?"

"My ex-mother-in-law was a mistress of a rich Singapore Chinese businessman," replied James. "So I have some idea as to how she had lived being the mistress of a man who had other mistresses."

Eddy looked at his friend and said, "I didn't know your ex-mother-in-law was someone else's mistress. She must be beautiful then?"

"She was when she was young, but in her later years she had put on a lot of weight and suffered from high blood pressure," replied James.

James was sitting in the Eddy's coffee shop as he retold Mandy's life story, the part he knew, and about his concern for her with regards to her job offer in Singapore. They were sitting at their usual table looking at the growing crowd that thronged KOMTAR's main concourse area.

Years ago when James had just taken the food franchise in the nearby food court, he had come to

Eddy's shop because it had served good cappuccino beside giving an excellent view of teeming crowd who had passed by. Drinking cappuccino at that table during that time of the morning had become the two friend's ritual for the last five years.

"Life was never a bed of roses as far as she was concerned," James was saying. "In times of trouble, the official family got taken care of first while she had to fend for herself and her family anyway she could. I remember how she had suffered when she did not receive any money from the office of her 'husband' for many months because he had been ill and was hospitalised. As payments to mistresses had to be initiated personally by the master normally, his incapacitation had caused all payments to her to be put on hold. She was in such dire strait and for such a long time but there nothing I could do to help. I had a family of my own including my three-year-old son and another on the way to look after. Without any other options my ex-mother-in-law sold or pawned everything she owned that was worth something. At that time she had to support six of her seven children, most of whom were still schooling." James paused to take a sip of his cold cappuccino before continuing.

"I had married her eldest daughter about five years earlier. My wife and I contributed whatever we could, which wasn't much as she was carrying our second child then, and as an architect I wasn't paid all that well." James took a couple more sips of his coffee and was about to continue with his story when a sound of laughter at the entrance of the crowded coffee house caused him to turn his head in that direction. Seeing it was just a group of people who had just walked in, he turned to his friend and continued.

"By choice, our wedding was a simple affair with only a few friends attending. My wife was an offspring of her marriage, her only marriage, to a Korean, who mysteriously disappeared just before my wife was born. He was never seen or heard of again. Speculation about him was rife then, that he was a Japanese spy during the war and when Japan had surrendered about six months earlier he had married my ex-wife's mother in order to avoid detection. Something must have gone wrong for him to have disappeared the way he did." James drained the remnant of his cappuccino and ordered another.

"My mother-in-law was number three or number four, I forget which, of the five wives this tycoon had. From what I heard this Cantonese, who never went to school and could only sign his name with an "X", had made his money from rubber and other dubious means. He had children that could fill a bus; assuredly he was a man of tremendous ego. In fact, he not only took in my mother-in-law but her younger sister as well, and between them he fathered fourteen children. Unfortunately or fortunately for my mother-in-law, depending on which way you look at it, he never recovered from his illness. He died several months later in a Hong Kong hospital despite the string of specialists from China, his number two wife had insisted in bringing in, to assist the local doctors there." James shook his head when his friend offered him a cigarette but waited until his friend had lighted his cigarette before continuing.

"Ironically, it was during the funeral held at his main residence just behind Orchard Road, the main thoroughfare of Singapore, that brought all his far-flung families together for the first time. Believe me, it was a great shock to the official wife when she found out that so many 'outsiders' outnumbered her family members. The old man had left his first wife and several children in China when he fled with the Kuomintang to Taiwan and finally to Malaysia. During the unsettled days soon after the communist takeover, his wife died and his children who were inducted by the cadres of the communist party, were never heard of again.

At the tycoon's funeral, my brothers-in-law, my sisters-in-law and my mother-in-law came; in their wake was my mother-in-law's younger sister and her seven children. I had suspected that their appearance was not so much as to pay homage and last respect to the dead Patriarch, but understandably out of concern for their own future being, and had wanted to be counted.

Far from being mercenary or anything like that, they were just being practical. It was apparent that there was no love lost as far as they were concerned, hardly a tear was shed at first until their mothers began to cry. Then, as if on cue, everyone cried as if their lives had depended on it. In a way it probably did, because soon after that, the official wife, putting aside her hostility, came forward and shook the hands of the two mothers and nodded her welcome to the others including my wife and myself; after she had scrutinized me for a second or two she offered hand which I shook. The children hardly knew their father, he only visited them whenever he wanted to plant his seeds in their mothers. It was there at the funeral where my mother-in-law and her sister made their, and their children's presence known to all and sundry." James paused to take another sip of his coffee while his friend Eddy stroked, in a contemplative manner, the hair that had sprouted from a mole on his chin.

"Your mother-in-law and her sister, were they friendly with one another?" Eddy asked.

"Sure. And all their children too," replied James. "They knew everything, they acted like normal siblings would to one another, and with great respect, I might add."

"Like brothers and sisters, and not cousins?" Eddy interjected.

"Yes, like brothers and sisters," replied James. He paused when a waiter and replaced the ashtray on their table. Eddy, in deference to James who was a non-smoker, had kept asking his waiter to clear the ashtray whenever it was half-full. As a chain smoker, it never took him long to fill up an ashtray.

"My mother-in-law is dead now, but I guess I will always remember her with fond memories because she had always treated me no differently than all her other sons-in-law even though I am a Malay. Not once did she remind me that I was any different, except when it came to food.

As a Muslim I am forbidden from eat anything from the flesh of swine and those not considered halal, my mother-in-law made sure that all the food her household served were halal. I found out later on that she took pains to ensure that everything was strictly followed - from the cooking utensils to the china used. Later on when her fortunes had changed for the better, and when all her other children had grown up and had got careers of their own, and after she and the other wives had demanded and received compensations from the tycoon's estate, she made sure my family and I got the same treatment as before - halal food all round when we came to visit.

Even after we had left Singapore and had gone to live in Kuala Lumpur, we made it point to visit her every year during the Chinese new Year. At the Chinese New Year's eve dinner she would make sure that all the food served were halal. In the beginning when she saw that I was discomfited by the special attention given by her to my family, she quickly assured me that it was no big thing because her whole family seldom eat pork anyway. In any case, she said, dietary differences among her large family were prevalent, and therefore having to cook different food for different members of her family was quite normal. At that time they had two lived-in Filipino maids so it was really no trouble at all, she added. I stopped feeling bad about it after that."

James suddenly stopped talking when he saw a smile playing on Eddy's face.

"Do you really believe that all the plates and the other utensils used in the preparation of the food were halal? How do you know they were?"

"Well, you have to trust that they were, that's all," replied James. Eddy raised both hands in a mock surrender, but said nothing.

James gave his friend a suspicious took before taking another sip of his coffee. He made a face when the coffee, which was getting cold by now, reached his throat. Eddy signalled to one of his waiters and asked for a refill for the both of them.

"I'm sorry for the interruption," said Eddy. "Please continue with your story, the coffee that's coming is on me."

"I believe it is true to some extent that mistresses tend to get better treatment from their partners than wives do, but it was also said that they had to connive and cajole for every penny they get. In emergencies for example, they seldom could count on their partners to be where they want them to be. And what about those festive holidays like Chinese New Year, Christmas and Thanksgiving and the likes, don't count on them to be there with you. But the ones that really get hurt the most are the children of these liaisons. While the other kids were bragging about what they and their fathers did over the weekends, the holidays or whatever, these pitiful ones just look at their mates with envy and in silence." James paused when the waiter returned with a carafe and topped up their coffee cups.

"The trouble with men who tend to have mistresses, they also tend procreate more. It has something to do their egos, among other things. They have this compelling need to prove their manliness to themselves and to others. So far, they seemed to stop short of advertising that fact to the world while they were still alive, but some managed to get it done for them after they are dead in the form of obituaries, whereby their wives and numerous children and grandchildren will be mentioned. Their Western counterparts may not be as daring as those in the East, but nevertheless, even if their methods may differ, their objectives remained the same.

In the East some of the men seemed to have gone overboard with this manic desire to having to constantly try to prove to themselves that they were still capable. Thousands of wild and exotic animals were slaughtered every year all over the world for their horns, which the Asians mainly, believe to be an aphrodisiac. Scientifically speaking these ground rhinoceroses horns are no more an aphrodisiac than ground nail clippings. One may wonder: How many unscrupulous *sin-sehs or medicine men* have been selling these nail clippings to these poor sods? Imagine having a teaspoonful of ground toenail clippings in a glass mixed with a raw egg and a generous lashing of Martell VSOP cognac - delicious! To be sure, like everything else in life, there are always exceptions, like for example there may be certain mitigating circumstances as to why a person may have to have a mistress and why the need to breed children out of wedlock, and so on, but we won't go into that now."

"So, you think this Mandy will end up as someone's mistress, is that it?"

"I don't know...I think so. She's so young and naive, I'm afraid that she might get hurt."

"What can you do about it?" Eddy asked quietly. He had never known James to feel this way about anyone before except for his two sons of whom he never stopped talking about. He sometimes felt that he'd recognize his friend's sons if ever he bumped into them in a crowded street despite the fact that they've never met. James had described them to him so many times during the past five years, he felt as if he had known them all his life.

"What can I do? Nothing, I guess," replied James. "Listen, Eddy, it's almost lunch time. I'd better pop over to my place to see if everything is ready for the hungry horde which should be due any minute now."

* * *

It seemed like a week of strange phone calls for James. It began on Monday morning at 3.30 AM when he was awakened with a start by the ringing of the telephone on his bedside table. He picked it up just in time to hear it being disconnected. The next day the telephone rang at three in the afternoon, the same thing happened, as soon as he picked it up he could hear it being disconnected. The same ritual was repeated the following day, this time it was around 11.00 o'clock in the morning. By this time, he was not only getting annoyed at whoever was playing these silly games, he was also very wary about picking up the phone whenever it rang.

So when the telephone did start to ring again at around 10.30 that night, James was naturally in no hurry to answer it. As a matter of fact he let it ring until it stopped, but a few moments later it began to ring again. This time, however, all kinds of wild thoughts came rushing to his head, with scenes of impending disasters in brilliant Technicolor being played on the built-in screen somewhere deep in his skull. He quickly rushed to pick it up and spoke anxiously into the mouthpiece. All he heard was an anxious voice saying hello over and over again. At that point James became anxious himself, thinking that something untoward must be happening to someone close to him. "Oh my God!" he uttered.

James quickly pressed the receiver against his ear, and with his heart pounding as if it was doing a 100-meter dash, he finally heard a voice saying, "Hello, hello, is that you James?"

"Hello! Yes this is James. Who is this?" he cautiously asked, as he held his breath.

"This is Mandy. I'm ringing from Singapore."

"Oh, hello Mandy," said James, feeling suddenly relieved and, at the same time, weak at the knees. He quickly plonked himself down on the sofa before continuing. "How are you and how is your new job?"

James had detected a moment's hesitation before she replied, "Ok."

"Are you coming back for the Chinese New Year?" James asked, anxious to keep the conversation going when he somehow sensed a lull coming, afraid that she might change her mind about talking to him. He was convinced that it must have been Mandy who'd been making all those recent unconnected calls to him and he didn't want to frighten her.

"Yes, I am," Mandy replied, and after a moment's silence, she said, "I am calling to tell you that I'm coming home for a few days, so if that offer of yours to have some classical music taped for me still stands, I'll come over to your place and choose from your collection."

"Mandy, you are most welcome, anytime. Call me whenever you want, even just to talk, okay?"

"All right. I'll call you when I arrived in Penang. Bye for now." She hung up.

James, unable to contain his excitement, went to his kitchen to make a cup of coffee to soothe his nerves. He couldn't believe it that after nearly a year he'd hear from Mandy again.

CHAPTER THIRTEEN

Three days later Mandy telephoned James telling she was back in Penang. He asked whether she had eaten yet, since it was almost dinner time, and he hadn't eaten yet. When she replied that she hadn't, he asked her whether she'd like to have dinner with him. After a slight pause, she had said yes.

During the short conversation over the telephone James had detected something in her tone which didn't seem quite right. He shrugged his shoulders and told himself that whatever it was that was troubling her, he'll know soon enough.

The moon was out when James arrived at Mandy's place. He saw her waiting by the light-post in front of the small wooden bridge that spanned the stream not far from her house. The last time James had sent her home, Mandy pointed out her house to him.

Hers was one of the three zinc-roofed wooden houses that formed a cluster in one big compound, which seemed to be separated from the rest of the houses in the village. James could see lights emitting from her house, as well as from the other two Mandy had said belonged to her relatives.

James saw Mandy crossed the wooden bridge before disappearing only to emerge again as she walked up the slight incline. He got out of his car to open the door for her.

The smile she gave him as she slid into the front seat looked as if she was pleased to see him, and he was glad. Despite the dimness of the car's courtesy light, James held his breath when he saw how beautiful she had looked. He saw something else too; she had a look of serenity that he hadn't seen in her before.

James chose a well-known hotel along Batu Ferringhi, one of many that dotted the famed beach, and at Mandy's suggestion, went to their coffee house instead of the Italian restaurant he had planned on taking her to. Whilst walking from the car park towards the hotel, James looked up at the sky and was disappointed to see that the moon, which was shining so gloriously earlier that evening, had disappeared completely behind some thick clouds. His plan to ask Mandy to take a stroll on the beach after dinner may have to be put on hold until another time, should there be another time.

After they had exhausted their basic enquiries on how they both had been, they finished their dinner in silence. They ordered coffee after their dinner. By this time Mandy, who appeared a bit more relaxed and had displayed the occasional sparks of animation, kept looking out of the window as she talked. Her main attraction seemed to be a pair of pink flamingos and some ducks feeding in the artificial stream outside the coffee house. It was obvious to James that Mandy was trying to get something off her chest but seemed to be in two minds about it.

In order to keep the conversation going, James talked about flamingos whereby he related to Mandy about a trip that he'd made to Florida not too long ago. He told her about a park he had been to where he saw an incredible sights he hadn't seen anywhere before.

He told her about seeing hundreds, maybe thousands, of the same pink birds feeding in one massive gathering. The scene, he told candy, looked like a painting whereby the painter had run out of all the other colours except pink, and he had decided to paint the middle of the landscape with it. And from afar it looked like a big squirming blob of pink on the water.

"It was quite a sight, believe me," he said.

Mandy looked at him and smiled. The smile was the carefree smile that James had seen before when she was at his place the first time. The image of her sitting on his sofa with her legs daintily tucked underneath her, sipping her glass of *Mateo Rose*, was still vivid in his mind. He remembered that they were listening to the music of Tchaikovsky that she had selected. She had looked so relaxed then, a far cry from the Mandy who was sitting in front of him then. A while ago Mandy was toying with her food like she had been doing when he first saw her in that pizza parlour several years ago. He suddenly wondered whether there was any correlation with that habit with something that may be troubling her?

"You know, the job I told you about in Singapore?" she said suddenly without looking at James. He looked at her and waited for her to continue, but instead, she rubbed, in an absentminded way, the rim of her coffee cup with a finger.

"Yes, I remember," James replied after a short while, trying to encourage her to continue. He could see that she was still undecided about letting him in on what was bothering her. He waited with extreme patience for her to continue.

After several minutes of what was obviously an intense struggle within herself, Mandy raised her head to look at him.

"The horse-owner I told you about...," she began. "The one who offered me a job in his restaurant?"...a pause..."Well, he lied to me. There was no job waiting for me when I got there." She paused again, longer this time.

"In fact he never even own a restaurant. When I reached Singapore, Wong, that's his name, was waiting for me at the airport. In the car he told me that as a temporary measure, until he got my accommodation sorted out, I was to stay in an flat, which according to him, belonged to one of his friends who had gone overseas for a holiday.

I suspect he is the actual owner of the place but didn't want admit it for some reason. He asked me whether I'd mind that, I said no. We then drove to this flat on *Bukit Timah Road*, not far from the Equatorial Hotel, which I recognised from my trips to Singapore.

"Nice flat, well furnished, had a modern kitchen," Mandy had said. "The living room had all that hi-fi stuff and a bar. It was full with beer, whiskey, brandy and everything." Mandy took a sip of water before continuing.

"We sat in the living room and talked for a while. He asked me whether I'd care for a drink, I said no at first but when he insisted, I said yes. He went to the bar to make the drinks. After we finished our drinks I told him that I was feeling rather tired and like to go to bed early. Like a gentleman, he got up, shook my hand and then left.

The next morning Wong came and took my passport telling me that he would be needing it so that he can arrange for a work permit for me. I was happy when he said that, it sounded so...official." Mandy flashed James a smile, but it was so fleeting, he hardly recognised it.

Outside, the two flamingos were coming closer to the window and they immediately caught Mandy's attention. She turned her head towards them and tried to attract their attention by tapping on the plate glass with the nails of her fingers. One of them momentarily turned up its head and looked in their direction before continuing with its pursuit of insects and other goodies among the weeds that lined the man-made stream. Whoever had looked after the grounds at the hotel had done a great job of creating a small jungle by the side of the coffee house. It not only looked wild, but exotic too. The headwaiter informed them that during some days they could occasionally spot birds from distant lands in the trees that surrounded the hotel.

"The next evening Wong came and took me to a night club and introduced me to a jockey. He ordered drinks for the three of us, but as soon the drinks came he took a sip of his and left, telling me that he had a urgent phone call to make, but he'll be back, he had said.

He never did come back that night, so the jockey took me back to the flat just after midnight. The jockey, a pimply young man about twenty-five, wanted to come up but I told him I was not feeling very well, so he left.

The next day Wong came to the flat around nine in the morning, and without so much as an apology for not coming back for me the night before, stormed past me, and sat himself on the sofa. He looked angry, but I didn't know why or with whom he was angry with, so I just stood there and looked at him. I thought that perhaps he was angry with some immigration officials regarding my work permit application...you know, like here, they always ask for this and that...just to give you hell!" Mandy paused to take a sip of her coffee.

"After a few moments he got up from the sofa and went to the bar. He poured himself a small brandy and drank it in one gulp. After a while he put down the empty glass on the bar top and turned to look at me. By this time I was beginning to get frightened. I backed away from him when he strode towards me, but instead of coming to me, he walked past me and took the easy chair nearby. He then beckoned me to sit opposite him.

As soon as I sat down he began telling me how easy it would be for me to make lots of money. All I had to do, he said, was to give him my full cooperation. I asked him what he meant by that. He didn't answer me, instead he took out some money from his wallet and handed it to me. A thousand Singapore dollars, he said. James, I've never had a thousand ringgit in my hand before."

Mandy looked at James with rounded eyes as if she was silently pleading for understanding. "At first he told me that all he wanted me to do was to escort some jockeys around the night clubs and restaurants - that was all. He then bought me some clothes and a couple of pairs of shoes too." Mandy took another sip of water without looking in James's direction.

"He even volunteered to buy my underwear for me. He had the cheek to ask for one of mine as a sample, I refused. I told him that I'll buy them myself." Mandy took another sip of her water before continuing, this time she avoided looking at James but began wringing her hands nervously instead.

"I enjoyed it at first," she said. "I went out every night during the next ten days, mostly with different jockeys, except on two occasions when I went out with two I had gone out with before. On the first occasion the jockey had tried to be funny with me when he dropped me home, but had immediately left when I threatened to call the police. The next day I called Wong and told him about the incident. He came by and gave me some more money with a promise to tell his jockeys to behave.

The second incident was more serious than the first time. This particular jockey whom I was going out for the second time, instead of sending me back to the flat, drove to a quiet spot, locked all the car doors and began forcing himself on me. I struggled..." Mandy stopped suddenly and began to dig into her handbag for a handkerchief and began wiping her nose with it. James saw that she had tears in her eyes but before he could say anything, she went on with her story. "...but despite his pint-size body, he was strong. He managed to pin me down on the car seat and ripped off my panties before I knew what was happening. I only managed to escape when he relaxed his grip in order to get his pants down. I unlocked the door nearest to me that set off the alarm. He released me the moment he heard the car alarm go off. As he bend over trying to turn it off, I kicked him hard in the groin, which must have hurt. He gave out a really loud yell. I quickly scrambled out of the car and ran towards a passing car, which barely missed hitting me when it went out of control when the driver braked suddenly. By the time I explained what happened to the startled driver, the jockey had driven off in the dark and escaped."

The driver, a kindly middle-aged Malay man, offered to drive me to the nearest police station so that I could make a police report, but I told that I'd appreciated it very much if he could drop me off at the flat instead. As soon as I reached the flat I immediately telephoned Wong and told him what had happened and demanded that he come immediately with my passport. I told him that I was going home. He tried to talk me out of it until I threatened to call the police and make a report. That brought a rather quick response from him - he agreed to come straight away.

"I waited for him in the lobby, right in front of the security guard's desk, which didn't please him one bit. The moment he saw me he tried to get me to go upstairs to the flat so that we could talk, he said, but I refused and demanded for my passport. Not wanting to make a scene in front of the security guard, he relented and handed me my passport. I asked the security guard to call a taxi for me and drove to the airport where I managed to get the last flight back to Penang." Mandy stopped talking when a waiter came to our table with a coffee pot in one hand. He asked us whether we would like to have our coffee cups refilled.

"Yes, please," Mandy said, nodding her head. As soon as their cups had been refilled, Mandy picked up her handbag and began rummaging inside it and came up with a crumpled packet of Salem. She took out a stick and began straightening it. After it was more or less straight she put it in her mouth and began rummaging in her handbag again, this time for a book of matches. James took it from her and lighted her cigarette. It was the first time he had seen Mandy smoke.

"I wanted to call you when I returned from Singapore, but I was afraid."

"Afraid? Of me? Why should you be afraid?" James asked.

"Because I didn't heed your warning," replied Mandy. "I should have been more careful whom I should trust. I didn't really know Wong but I was excited about the prospect of working and living in Singapore, so I went anyway. I've been hearing so much about Singapore from friends who had been there. They tell me everything is very modern over there. Not like in Penang," she said, making a face. "Here everything is so old and drab, and the people are so dull." James gave her a smile. "Oh, but you are not one of them," she quickly added.

"Several months ago my grandmother died...I forgot to tell you that when I came back from Singapore I managed to get my old job back. I was lucky because they hadn't got around to getting my replacement yet, and they even gave me a slight raise. I was happy and I worked very hard. I even managed to save some money.

Unfortunately, when my grandmother died, all that my family managed to come up with was a few hundred ringgit. It wasn't nearly enough for a decent funeral."

Mandy looked intensely at James and said. "I had no choice...we needed the money... so I called Wong and asked him whether he could lend me some money for the funeral. He asked me how much I wanted and I told him. He said he'd send the money immediately provided I'd work for him again. I had said yes, I'd do anything. The day after the funeral I left for Singapore."

As she talked she kept flicking her cigarette ash into the ashtray in a measured, preoccupied way that people do when they had something on their mind. James was going to interrupt her to tell her how sorry he was to hear about her grandmother but had decided to remain silent and waited for Mandy to continue.

"Like the first time I went there, Wong was already waiting for me at the airport. He drove me to the same flat he put me up before. And like the first time, he left as soon as he saw that I was settled. That night I was in bed by eleven o'clock and must have dozed off almost immediately. Sometime around 1.00 a.m. I was awakened when I felt a constriction in my chest, like I was drowning and struggling for air. As soon as I opened my eyes, I was horrified to find Wong on the top of me. I tried to scream but he cupped his hand on my mouth. I struggled and tried to get away from him, but he was strong, so I stopped struggling and waited for him to finish..."

Mandy stopped abruptly and began rummaging in her handbag again, this time she took out a tissue to wipe her tears. James tried to comfort her, but as soon as his hand touched hers, she jerked it away as if she had been stung, and in the process tipped over her glass of water.

Several minutes were to pass before she spoke again. James refrained from asking her any questions because he could see that she wasn't through telling him her story yet. In the meantime the waiter had tidied up their table and had brought her another glass of water and had their coffee cups refilled.

"...and as soon as he was through with me, he got dressed, but before he walked out of the door, he placed some money on the dressing table. I wanted to call the police but I was afraid, so I didn't." Mandy took a puff a from her cigarette before continuing.

"The next day when he came in, behaving as if nothing had happened, and began briefing me again what my duties were, which were to go out with his jockeys, and which included, he reminded me, sex with him whenever he wanted.

Before he left he told me to be ready by seven-thirty. That night a jockey whom I have not met before came around eight o'clock to pick me up. We went to a Chinese restaurant for dinner and then to a night club afterwards. Around 1.00 AM he sent me back to the flat where Wong was already waiting for me. We had sex again that night and practically every night after that. We only stop making love when I had my periods. He was so suspicious that I'd lie to him about that, he even asked me to remove my *Tampax* so he could examine it. And almost every night I had to go out with one of his jockeys. Going out with them was all right, one or two would try to be funny with me after they had too much to drink, but I always managed to control them.

About a month ago Wong came to the flat at the usual time. I could see that he had been drinking by the look of his red face. He came to me and grabbed both my wrists and practically dragged me into the bedroom. When he finished he told me that from now on I was also to have sex with his jockeys if they want to. He said he'll let me know before hand, before I could say anything, he slammed the door shut and left.

The next night the jockey that picked me up was the one that I didn't particularly like. Every time we went out he tried to be funny with me. That night, instead of sending me home, he took me to his flat, telling that he had to pick up something first. I was at once suspicious, but I thought I'd wait and see. When we got to his flat, he asked me to come up, but I told that I'll wait for him in the car. He kept trying to get me up to his flat with him, telling me that it wasn't safe down at the car park and all that. Finally he became angry, telling me that Wong had given him his word that I'd sleep with him. I was afraid of what he might do to me, so I told him in as-a-matter-of-fact tone that Wong hadn't told me anything. Without another word he drove me back to the flat.

I was relieved to be back at the flat even though I know that all that I had gain was some time. I was sure that he would have telephoned Wong by now and had told him about my reluctance to have sex with him.

Sure enough, within thirty minutes or so, Wong came to the flat and began abusing me verbally for not allowing that jockey to have sex with me. I told him that wasn't part of the deal. In fact, I told him, from now on if he ever lay a finger on me I'll call the police. Suddenly he became very violent and began slapping me around and finally after ripping all my clothes off he raped me."

Mandy began to sob uncontrollably but James didn't know how to comfort her for fear of invoking another bad reaction from her. He offered her a glass of water instead. She took it and drank from it. She took another cigarette from her packet on the table and a passing waiter quickly lit it for her. She nodded her silent thank to him. After a couple of puffs she began again with her incredible story.

"I called the police as soon as he had left, and when they arrived about twenty minutes later, I told them everything. They took me to the Kandang Kerbau Hospital where they examined me."

"Did they arrest Wong?" James asked.

She nodded her head. "The next morning at his office."

"Mandy, I'm really sorry," said James. "Try to put all this behind you and look towards the future. You're young, you can do anything."

She didn't say anything for several moments. After a while she took a sip of her coffee before she finally looked at him and said, "I can't put it all behind me because I'm pregnant."

"How far gone are you?"

"Not long, about three weeks. I know I am because I'm always punctual."

"What do you plan on doing?"

"I don't know. I just don't know." Her tears were beginning to flow again.

"Listen, Mandy. I want to ask you something."

She tilted her head and looked at him. "Sure, go ahead."

"Do you like me?"

Her expressions changed and she asked rather cheekily. "Are you fishing for a compliment?"

James smiled at her but said nothing.

"Well, you're one of the nicest man I've ever met," she continued. "You are kind and gentle, and I think you care about other people. Not like some of the jerks I've gone out with. I felt that I could talk to you. That's why I called you. I needed to talk to someone."

"Good," James said. "Now that you've answered my question, here is my proposition. I do care about you, very much. And I'd like to suggest something if I may. I'd like to suggest that you marry me. You must never allow your kid to be born without a father. You know what that was like, and I hope you are not thinking of having an abortion".

James paused to see Mandy's reaction, but she just sat there looking thoughtfully at him.

"After the baby is born, we'll both look after it," he continued. "As for giving up the kid for adoption, I don't think it'll be fair to him or her, and to you. I'll be a good father, I promise. I know it was a marriage of convenience, a marriage in name only. There's no obligation on your part whatsoever. If at, later a stage you want to be free,

I won't try to stop you. Until that time comes, I'll try hard to make you as happy as best as I can."

She looked at him with eyes bubbling in tears. "James, that's the nicest thing anybody have tried to do for me. I don't know what to say."

"Well, you could say yes that you'll marry me."

"Yes." She sobbed, "I'll marry you."

ᚾᚸᚾᚸᚾᚸ

CHAPTER FOURTEEN

The marriage was a simple affair witnessed by a few friends, followed by lunch at the same Thai restaurant where they went to on their first date. It was Mandy who had suggested it.

In the car after the ceremony, James said to Mandy, "That wasn't the kind of wedding or marriage that I would like to have for you. I feel that I'm robbing you of what should be a very special day in your life. Even though the cause is good and my motive honourable, but it was a poor substitute to what you should be having."

"James, It was a beautiful wedding, thank you very much."

"You're most welcome."

Mandy looked at him and smiled.

In Singapore, on the day that James and Mandy got married, Wong began serving his six years imprisonment. And while the newlyweds were spending their honeymoon in *Pulau Langkawi*, Sally, Wong's wife was on a verge of a nervous breakdown. The arrest of her husband, the trial, and finally his imprisonment, became too much for her to bear. To make things worse, they had no money left. To those living in a city state like Singapore, to be without money, spelt disaster.

Sally's immediate reaction was to think of all the curses she could think of so that she could heap them on her husband the moment she was allowed to visit him in prison.

It seemed that in a typical fashion, Wong had been operating his business solo. There was a manager, assistants and clerks to be sure, but none of them really knew the ins and outs of his business. Most of Wong's businesses were done on an ad hoc basis, with lots of palms being greased along the way, with him as the grease monkey. There was no such thing as long term projections, not even short term ones for that matter, and of course no budgets were ever prepared. Every business transaction was done on a personal basis. The whole company seemed to have rested on his shoulders, so it was no surprise to anyone except to his own family that by the time the following Chinese New Year came not long after Wong was incarcerated, the company was in such a poor state that even the employees could not be paid. Since no one in his company, not even his wife, for that matter, knew very much about racing or race horses, Wong stable of four prize horses was sold for a song. They were sold to the trainer in lieu of accumulated fees owed to him.

Sally Wong, on the other hand, had been a typical empty-headed housewife whose claim to fame among the likes of her, would be that she was clever to spend money, who'd spend endless hours either at her hair-dressers or playing *Mahjong* or visiting numerous friends' house for coffee mornings; or she would go to the club where they were members there for more chit-chats.

She had a rude shock when one day some gangster-like characters approached her as she was dropping her son off at his school. It seemed that they were there to repossess her car because her husband's company had failed to keep up the payments.

Sally flew into a rage and demanded an explanation from her brother-in-law as to why she was subjected to such humiliation in front of so many people, especially her son's classmates' mothers. Her brother-in-law, who had the title of manager in her husband's firm, had in reality very little to do if any, with managing the company. He was there merely as a watchdog for his older brother. He wasn't very intelligent, of course, otherwise his brother would be hard put to trust him.

At her husband's office Sally was surprised to find so many empty desks in the outer office, and the atmosphere there seemed almost funereal. Shocked at her brother-in-law's revelation as to the state of the company's financial health, and bewildered at her stupidity of not having been the least interested in its operation before, she found herself walking in a daze out of her husband's office presently occupied by her brother-in-law. She couldn't understand how things could be so bad when all the time she thought that they were rich.

After walking aimlessly around the vicinity of her husband's office for nearly an hour, Sally finally hailed a taxi and went home. As she got out of the taxi, she was shocked to see someone driving off with her husband's Mercedes-Benz. It seemed that it too had been repossessed by the same finance company that had financed her Honda Accord.

Ironically, her brother-in-law's car, an older Mercedes-Benz, also belonging to the company, was not touched by the financed company because it seemed that it had already been paid for, and under the terms of his employment, her brother-in-law had the right to purchase it for a token sum of one dollar when he reached fifty years old.

The auspicious day it seemed, was on the very day Sally's car was being repossessed. On that day her brother-in-law turned fifty, and since Sally happened to be in the office on that day, he made her as an official witness to the whole transaction including his token payment of one Singapore dollar to the company's cashier, who happened to be her husband's youngest sister. Sally watched with hatred in her heart as her brother-in-law took legal possession of the car.

Sally, who had known about the deal before and was quite happy about it then, had demanded to see the contract. Her brother-in-law, who seemed to be expecting such request from her, casually picked it up from his desk and handed it to her. Sally snatched it from his out-stretched hand began to read. When she finished, she tossed it back in her brother-in-law's face, her own was twisted in anger. She picked up her handbag from his desk and strode towards the door.

"Wait, you have forgotten to sign as a witness," she heard her brother-in-law called out after her. Sally quickly scribbled her signature on the document and stormed out of the office.

It was all too much for Sally. Finding out that her husband had been keeping a flat, which obviously was to cater to his extra-marital sex, wasn't too bad as far as she was concerned. She could relate to that because her own father had kept a mistress and so did a number of other Chinese businessmen, but to get caught for raping a young girl was a bit much. And now to find out that she was left with nothing was something she found most intolerable.

"After all, I only married him for his money," she had said to her mother over the phone. "Without that what use is he to me? I was so stupid not to be interested in the business before, if I had, his brother wouldn't dare cheat me of my money," she added forlornly.

One by one the rest of the staff at her husband's company began leaving, by the end of three months only three people were left out of a total of twenty. Sally, who hadn't received a penny from her brother-in-law for three months, was getting desperate. Unlike their former workers who had found jobs elsewhere, Sally who had barely passed high school and untrained for any trade or occupation, racked her brain for some ideas to make money, she came up with nothing except a splitting headache.

According to Chen, the account clerk who had agreed to stay on account of Sally who had found him the job, there was some money due to the company but collections had been difficult ever since her husband had been in jail. He gave her his word that he'd keep trying to make the collections. Sally implored him to do better than that, promising his extra bonus. He said he'd try!

Sally had already hocked most of her jewellery to pay Ah Hin, her servant, the money she owed. She had borrowed some money from her servant thinking that she'd pay her back as soon as she got some money from her brother-in-law, but unfortunately that didn't happen.

Ah Hin, who had been her amah when she was a young girl at her parents' house, was happy to come to work for her when she and Wong got married. She soon smelled the wind of change that had pervaded the household during recent months. Her instinct told her that it didn't augur well for her future or whatever left of it, to stay around.

Ah Hin, already in her sixties, was in a dilemma, she knew that her prospect for a new employment at her age was next to impossible. But she also knew that if she stayed on, her chances of getting paid wouldn't be that hot either.

Ah Hin may be old but her mind was still sharp especially when it came to money. After she had carefully weighed Sally's financial situation, she thought that perhaps under the present circumstances, she'd better keep her jewellery somewhere else instead of in the house. She figured that it might not be safe, and even if she decided to stay, she wouldn't want to keep any valuables in the house.

While Sally was racking her brains for some ideas to make some money, Ah Hin was at a quandary as to what she should do. If she stayed on, she was afraid she might may end up lending Sally more money again. This time she may not be so lucky like the last time. This time she may not get a single cent back.

She remembered all too well the last time she had loaned Sally money and Sally ended up paying her back late, and when she eventually did pay her, it was minus the interest. Ah Hin was livid and became so worried she almost became ill. She really thought that she was not getting the ten percent interest per month that Sally had agreed upon. Ah Hin didn't want that to happen again, fearing that her heart may not be able to withstand the pressure this time. Sally on that occasion was so strapped for cash she had only paid Ah Hin the principal sum with a promise to pay the interest within a week. When the week came and went and Sally still hadn't paid her, Ah Hin went berserk. She was eventually mollified when Sally promised her an additional interest on the outstanding amount. Ah Hin made sure that Sally signed new notes to that effect.

Despite their new agreement, Ah Hin made her displeasure known to Sally by neglecting all her duties, leaving the household chores left undone and her children unfed. Ah Hin was in that mode until the loan was settled in full. The score was zero for loyalty and compassion, and one for crusty old crone who wanted to be buried with her money and all her jewellery.

A week later Sally pawned her last piece of jewellery that was of any value and with the money she paid Ah Hin back in full: including all accumulated interests which was carefully computed by an equally crusty Old Man who came to the house at the invitation of Ah Hin. That night, Ah Hin, happy with the money she had received, was back to her normal self. She even prepared a special dinner for the whole family. Sally's children, having been deprived of decent food for so long, had two helpings of rice at dinner. Sally, her bowl untouched, smiled at them and told them to eat slowly. Sally was thinking that all she had left, that was of any value, was the pendant that her mother had given her when she married Wong. Her mother told Sally that the pendant was the family heirloom that had been passed down from mother to daughter. Her own mother had given it to her on her own wedding day. Sally herself had planned to give it to her daughter Lucy for her wedding. She was hoping...no... she was praying that she wouldn't have to sell it in order to survive.

Ah Hin by that time had already got quite a clear picture of her mistress's financial situation based on feedback she had received from her various informers. She knew that Sally had hocked most of her jewellery and had sold most, if not all, of the inexpensive ones. She knew that all she had left that was of some value was the pendant her mother had given her which she wore all the time. She also knew that Sally so far, hadn't touched any of the jewellery that belonged to her two children. She reckoned that it could be worth a fair bit, knowing the family's tradition of holding birthday parties for the two of them in which Wong's business associates were discretely told that presents in the form of jewellery would be more appropriate than toys or other presents. Ah Hin's sources had kept her well informed on the movements of all her mistress's jewellery. She had a complete picture as to which of her jewellery had been hocked and which had been sold. In her assessment Sally's present predicament looked even bleaker.

On the day Sally paid her the outstanding amount owed, Ah Hin was debating whether to stay on or move to an old folks' home. On one the hand if she stayed she would at least have a roof over her head and three meals a day, and on the other her chances of getting paid looked slim. In the end it was Sally's two children, who had cried non-stop and had refused to eat when told that she was going away, that had made her decide to stay on.

"The silly kids, why do they have to love me for?" Ah Hin said to herself. "Ah well, I guess it's much better than staying in an old folks' home with nothing to do except to wait for death".

Sally had no idea that Ah Hin had known the combination of her wall safe ever since she stumbled upon it in Sally's note book. Ah Hin had kept a constant check on its content whenever she was alone in the house. She had known about the children's jewellery because she had seen them in the safe often enough. That morning while Sally was out, she had opened the wall safe and was satisfied that the children's jewellery were still there but she couldn't find any of Sally's. She figured Sally must have taken whatever that was left with her. She felt a little apprehensive about that, fearing that Sally might do the same with her children's jewellery. Ah Hin was tempted to take them out of the safe there and then, but that would be stealing and she didn't want to do that. Finally she left them where they were and closed back the safe. "I'll do a daily check on them just to be on the same side," she told herself. "I'm out of here with them in my pocket the moment I don't get paid. I'm sure they are worth more than a couple of month's pay."

Ah Hin was one of those dying breed of '*Black & White*' amah who started coming to Malaya and Singapore from China at the turn of the century to find work as coolies or as servants of the lucky Chinese traders who had made it big.

The exodus of mainly men and a sprinkling of women, was at its height soon after the communists began to tighten their grip on the Middle Kingdom. Life was difficult in the beginning when all they ever got for their labour was food and shelter. In most cases the kitchen floor was the only place where they could lay their tired bones on after having been on their feet all day long, and perhaps, most of the night.

The lucky ones might end up with some money in their pockets at the end of the month given to them by their generous masters or mistresses. They would then save these pittance until they have enough to buy such things as cooking oil, soap, some dried food stuff and maybe a few yards of cloth to send home to China.

Those who weren't so lucky may not even have the kitchen floor to sleep on - like the coolies that worked the rice fields or the tin mines, or even those working in rubber plantations - more often than not, the dirt floor of the *kongsi* house awaited them each night. Some may not dare to close their eyes for fear of being raped by their male co-workers in the middle of the night. Many, especially those with a bit of looks and a good body, were abducted and sold as prostitutes.

Over the years the *black & white* amah began to recognize the society's need for the services that they had provided and started to form loose associations among themselves. There was nothing formal, no article of association or anything like that, or even a name, for that matter, but that didn't deter them from their determination to try to protect themselves.

They'd have meetings now and then to listen to each other's problems and grouses. Occasionally some of their senior members would be asked to mediate when disputes arose among their ranks, or even between them and the people they worked for. Some of their chapters even provided accommodations to those who had been dismissed for some misdeeds, whether real or imaginary, by their sometimes insecure and capricious mistresses.

Things have indeed changed considerably for their lot over the years. Some had demanded and got rooms of their own, while some were given television sets by their generous masters or mistresses. Normally, those who look after little children share rooms with their charges for convenience's sake. Nowadays they are given a day off each week to do whatever they fancy, without worrying about their little brats. They were only conspicuous by the uniform they wear: a white *samfoo* - a blouse like top with a Chinese collar, and black silky baggy pants. Most have their hair in long ponytail, some meticulously groomed and oiled. Nowadays, their employers treated many just like members of the family.

However, some like Ah Hin, could become quite mercenary and heartless. When Sally couldn't raise the money to pay her at the end of the month she bolted with the children's jewellery and was never seen or heard of again.

One would like to think that Ah Hin was the exception rather than the rule, because there were those who had become quite attached to the family they had worked for. Many have known of cases where the families themselves tend to look after their old servants by allowing them to stay on, giving them only light work to do, and when they die they were given decent funerals.

CHAPTER FIFTEEN

As her pregnancy progressed, Mandy was showing signs of hatred towards the baby in her stomach and it worried James. She would hardly talk about her pregnancy nor about the baby she was carrying, pretending as if it didn't exist. She'd clammed up whenever James tried to get her to talk about it, slightly peeved at him for bring up the subject. It was obvious that she hated being reminded that she was pregnant due to rape.

Even though he didn't know much about psychiatry, James was certain that what candy was doing wasn't very healthy for her. So he tried with varying degrees of subtleness that he could muster to try to get her to come to terms with her pregnancy and to get her to be interested in the wonderful thing that was growing inside her. The regular visits to the doctor were done with great reluctance on Mandy's part. She'd come up with all kinds of excuses not to go and James practically had to drag her there every time. Finally in the third month of her pregnancy, Mandy was beginning to show signs that she cared about the baby in her stomach. James's persistence in bring up the subject of the baby whenever the opportunity arose seemed to have worked. It eventually made Mandy turn around and began, with reluctance at first, to accept the fact that the baby was hers, her flesh and blood as much as Wong's.

"More so," James said to her. "Because you are carrying it, and nurturing it twenty-four hours a day for nine months. Don't hate it because now it's ours; you and I are going to give it all the love and care that it deserved."

Mandy, after that initial dark period of trying to come to grips with her pregnancy, endured pregnancy quite well. She never once complained about morning sickness, or made unrealistic demands for exotic foods and such. In fact she was a perfect mother-to-be, following the doctor's advice about eating a well-balance diet as well as certain vitamin supplements she should take. Mandy even followed the mild exercise routine that the doctor had recommended. James who had been very worried, was relived at Mandy's change of heart. To keep her from dwelling on her pregnancy, he planned various trips for themselves, like visiting the parks, a couple of kindergartens, to the theatres and even to Cameron Highland resort for a few days.

For relaxation, Mandy and James would listen to classical music or go for walks, usually in the evenings, when it was cooler. Mandy's recent interest had been in reading - something she hadn't done since she left school. Initially she would pick a couple of romantic novels from a nearby book shop, but when she got to the stage whereby she was reading a novel every fortnight Mandy decided to join the library at *Sri Pinang*. She wanted to expand her knowledge in everything, she had told James.

In the beginning Mandy found it tough going due to her limited vocabulary, so whenever she came across any word she didn't know she'd ask James to explain. James humoured her for a couple of weeks, but when she began to ask for the meaning of the same words over and over again, he knew then she wasn't learning anything. James decided to stop being a walking dictionary for Mandy by handing her a dictionary for her to look up the words herself instead of shouting across the room, the kitchen, the bedroom, or wherever he happened to be, for the meaning of the word or words she may be looking for.

Mandy tried it for a while but soon found the effort too much so she decided to cut down on her reading. Sometimes she would behave like a child by telling James that she didn't want to read anymore until he'd told her the meaning of the word she had asked. And at other times she would sulk, and without saying a word, would storm out of the room with her book. James shook his head and tried not to be angry with her. He consoled himself by telling himself that maturity would come with age.

Several weeks later, James was awakened during a thunderstorm in the early hours of the morning and found Mandy missing from bed. Thinking that she had probably gone to the kitchen for a glass of water, he slumbered out of bed and went to look for her. He found Mandy curled up on the living room sofa reading while munching on potato crisps. Next to the packet of crisps lay the thickest, heaviest, dictionary they had in the house.

Mandy looked up and smiled at James as soon as she saw him approaching. He smiled when he saw that his occasional nagging had finally paid off. From that moment onwards, Mandy would seldom be without a dictionary by her side whenever she was reading, be it a book, a magazine or whatever. And by that time too, they had already accumulated a number of dictionaries of various shapes, sizes and colours. It had been Mandy's new hobby - collecting dictionaries.

"Hi, come and sit down," she said. "Have some crisps." Without waiting for his reply, she went on, "This lady sure can write." James reached into Mandy's opened packet of crisps and sat down next to her. He twisted his head to look at the title of the book Mandy was reading and saw that it was Jane Austen's Emma.

"She was an enigma, wasn't she?" asked James.

"No, silly," she replied. "Emma."

Enigma, now that was some word, wasn't it? It seemed to James that description would fit Mandy more than it did Emma.

James looked fondly at his young bride as she sat there with her book on her lap and her jaws moving constantly. The familiar sound of the crunching of crisps, although muffled, could still be heard coming from her mouth. He was glad that she was, at last, beginning to come to terms with her pregnancy.

James noticed that since Mandy had put on some weight, the scar on her chin seemed more prominent, and even though her hair was tied in an untidy pony-tail, to him she still looked beautiful. James knew deep down in his heart that he had never loved anyone before as he had loved Mandy. He hadn't forgotten the promise he had made to her when he had proposed marriage, he was just hoping that she will not hold him to that promise. He couldn't bear the thought of losing her - not then, not ever. While others may fall out of love as the years go by, in his case his love for Mandy got stronger as each day comes along.

James awoke the next day with his head resting on Mandy's lap. A bleary-eyed glance at the *Selangor Pewter* clock on the sideboard told him that it was almost 8.00 a.m. and it looked as if Mandy had been up all night reading. She put down her book when she sensed James looking at her.

"Good morning," she said cheerfully. "You snored last night." James looks up at her trying to read into her statement. There was none to read, she was just telling him a fact that was known to him, and he did snore at times.

"Sorry," he said, as he reluctantly got off her warm lap, aware that something was beginning stir in his groin. She must have read his mind because the next thing she said was, "Let's go to bed."

Mandy, the instant decisions maker and instant change-of-mind. However, the decision she made that morning was not only good, but exhaustingly nice for both of them. The intimacy that both had shared that morning, unfortunately would not be repeated for another ten months. It was not due lack of trying on James's part, but each time he tried to be intimate, he sensed Mandy's nervousness and he backed away.

Sometimes James tried hard not to think about the thirty years difference in age between them, but Mandy's constant reluctance made it difficult for him to forget. Somewhere in the back of his mind he sometime hadn't held much hope that this marriage of theirs would last. However, his desire to make it last was all consuming. He knew he was being used but he didn't care, he really loved her and cared for her. For all he knew she might take up her option and leave as soon as was able to, after all, that was what he had promised her: "You can leave whenever you want to, I will not try to stop you."

As the birth of the baby was getting closer, Mandy began to talk more and more about it, telling James that it had kicked or that it had moved, and it was obvious from the expressions on her face that she was at last tickled pink with motherhood. One day James asked her about what they should call the baby.

"If it's a girl," she said, "how about calling her Samantha?"

"Samantha, eh!" James said, "I like it. And what if it's a boy?"

"Then, you name him," she had replied.

"All right. How about Alexander, after Alexander The great."

She looked at him and smiled. "Yes, Alexander would be nice."

The birth of Alexander was obviously painful to Mandy as forceps had to be used. The doctor told James that he had to use forceps to assist in the delivery because it turned out that he was a nine pound baby.

Although James and Mandy had earlier agreed that he, James, would be in the delivery room with her during the delivery, James became so nervous as they wheeled her into the delivery room, Mandy took pity on him and told him gently to wait outside. Not to hurt his feelings, she told him that she'd probably scream louder if he were in the room with her.

Twelve hours after Mandy was admitted in, Alexander let out a scream on his own as he emerged from of his mother's womb, beating the doctor of the traditional slap on the bottom (the baby's and not his). The forceps, which were used to pull him out, made Alexander's head look so grotesquely elongated when he emerged. Mandy turned her head away in consternation the moment she saw him. It was only after the doctor had assured her that Alexander's head would turn to normal in no time at all, the look on her face began to lose its anxiousness.

Two days later James brought Mandy and baby Alexander home to the flat. It was Mandy who had suggested that perhaps it would be better if she and the baby stayed in the spare room during the confinement month. She said it would make it easier for her to look after the baby, and it would also be easier for James to work in their bedroom without being disturbed. James saw the logic in what she had said and had readily agreed.

The doctor was right about what he had said about Alex's head. Looking at how well-formed it turned out to be, one can't believe how misshapen it was when he first emerged into this world.

A few days later, Mandy, with her family's help, managed to get a baby amah, simply known as Ah Kam, to help out. She came highly recommended by Mandy's grandfather who had warned Mandy that Ah Kam would only look after new-born babies and wouldn't stay longer than a year at the most. That it seemed was the rule she had followed without fail. She felt that once the baby was about ten, eleven months old, it was time for her to leave. Ah Kam had been known to refuse to stay once her charges had reached a ripe old age of one year. Unlike the rest of her counterparts, she could not be bribed to stay on. She had even rejected offers to double or even triple her salary.

Mandy seemed really engrossed with Alex as well as being a mother. She found the whole experience totally acceptable, and seemed to wear it like a crown.

James had tOld Mandy that now they had Ah Kam, she could move back to their bedroom. Mandy had replied that it would be better if she stayed put at least until the confinement was over. James didn't argue the point because for the first time in his life he was happy. He looked forward to each coming day with relish.

When her confinement was over and Mandy hadn't made any plans to move back to their bedroom, James debated whether to ask her or waited for her to make the move herself. Two weeks later when he asked her, she had told him that she'd wait a week or two longer, but when that two weeks had passed, James decided not to pursue the subject any more. He'd let it be her decision to make the move. Mandy, who had looked so hideous while she was pregnant, reverted to her beautiful self once she had lost some weight.

She started with her exercises as soon as her confinement period was over.

James who had watched Mandy's effort to lose weight with admiration at first, but became alarmed at her single-mindedness to become slim. And when she became as slim as she was when they first met, he wondered whether leaving him was her next plan.

James had never known happiness like this before and he was terrified at the prospect of her leaving. He knew he would be devastated because by then the baby too had stolen his heart. How he wished that everything would remain as it were. Mandy and the baby being part of his life, was something he had cherished. He was hoping that Mandy too was happy although he had no way of knowing. He didn't dare ask her for fear of reminding her of his earlier promise to her.

James found working at home advantageous because whenever he had the inclination, which was often, he would sneak into little Alex's bedroom to play with him. More often than not, he would invariably find Mandy had already beaten him to be with Alex. Even though he wasn't much better, James noticed that Mandy tended to fuss over Alexander quite a lot, so much so that he was afraid that the little rascal might ended up like one of the 'Little Emperors of China' - spoilt through and through. He noticed how Mandy would drop everything and fly to his side whenever he cried and the little rascal would inevitably ended up in his mother's arms. James reminded Mandy not to over-indulged the baby otherwise he might end up being spoilt. She agreed readily with him but would soon forget.

❧❧❧❧❧❧

CHAPTER SIXTEEN

Except for the tea ceremony that they had for Mandy's mother and her close relations soon after they were married, James and Mandy had very little contact with any of them again after that. However, a month after Alex was born he received a telephone call from her brother Mark, asking them to collect something from their house. And since James didn't want Mandy to exert herself, he went alone.

Although once married to a Chinese before, James had forgotten that most Chinese families take their dinner rather early. When he arrived at their place, Mandy's mother and her two brothers were about to eat. He apologised for the intrusion. Mandy's mother asked him to join them, but James declined as politely, telling them that Mandy was expecting him home for dinner.

James knew that Mandy hadn't come from a rich family, but he was quite unprepared when he witnessed the austerity of their lives as demonstrated by the dinner that they were about to partake. It consisted of two dishes, one of which was a salted egg cut into tiny pieces, and the other was a plate of vegetables. Not even a whole fish was included! It looked as if they were just eating boiled rice. Despite that, he could see that they were anxious to get on with dinner. Mandy's mother, who had gone into her bedroom, came out holding a small packet and handed it to James.

"This is for young Alex for his one month," she said. He thanked her and bid her good night as well as to Mark and Luke - the latter being Mandy's youngest brother.

When James handed Mandy the packet on returning home, she immediately opened it and exclaimed, "It's beautiful. I must ring her and thank her."

James agreed with her, the gold chain was beautiful. It must have cost her mother a great deal of money. He couldn't help wondering what they had to do without just to be able to buy Alexander this beautiful gift.

"It's so lovely," Mandy repeated, but she looked thoughtful as she gazed at James. He couldn't tell what was on her mind. She reached for telephone and began to punch some numbers. Moments later James heard her speak to her mother in *Hokkien*, a language he regretfully had never bothered to learn despite the fact that nearly fifty percent of the population of Penang spoke that dialect.

Occasionally, people had mistaken him for a Chinese probably due his slightly fairer skin, and they would speak to him in Hokkien. He had often thought how nice it would be if only he could speak the language. He made a mental note to try to find out where to learn it properly: classes, text books and all.

The ensuing months were quite productive for James with two articles complete which he managed to sell to a magazine. Encouraged, he started working on the novel he had been toying with in his head for several years now, but didn't have the nerve to kick it off. James was happy working at home, playing with Alexander whenever he wanted, but most important of all he was happy because for the first time in his life he felt he was in love.

"I must be," he said to himself, "because everything seemed so wonderful. Even the colours around me seemed to have an enhanced tinge about them or perhaps they are like the aurora borealis, only better."

In the beginning their relationship was cordial but correct. Despite sharing the same bed, they never made love except the one and only time. After she had given birth Mandy and the baby had moved to the spare bedroom, Ah Kam joined them a few days later. It wasn't until Alexander was about four months' old before the consummation of their marriage was repeated again.

One day Mandy had come into James's bedroom after the amah had put little Alex to bed. He was in bed at that time reading a book when he heard Mandy knock on the door. Since he never lock my door he asked her to come in. Mandy said that she wanted to hang up some of his clothes which had been ironed in the wardrobe.

James had often looked at Mandy whenever she wasn't looking and he had always admired her beauty, but when she walked into his room that night, and even though she was only in her house coat, she had never looked more radiant to him. He felt as if his heart had skipped a beat. And worse still, he felt as if he had a lump of coal in his throat that prevented him from making even the smallest of small talks.

After Mandy had hung up his shirts and trousers on the rack and had put the socks and underwear in the drawers, Mandy turned to James and asked him if he'd mind turning off his reading light. Momentarily taken aback by her request, James looked at her for several seconds before comprehension sank in, he quickly turned off his light.

In the dark he could hear the bedroom door being shut, followed by a sound of rustling clothes near him. Moments later he felt a movement on the bed, and Mandy's warm body next to his. They kissed, slowly, tentatively at first, and then with increasing warmth.

James had been looking forward to this for such a long time but when it came, it came as a shock to him and was terribly embarrassed when he came rather prematurely.

Their second attempt, however, was much better, thus averting what could have been his total humiliation.

The next morning Ah Kam gave them what looked like a smile, although James couldn't be sure; he had never seen her smile before. It could be a smile - happy perhaps to see Mandy and him behaving like a husband and wife at long last. Or could it be because now she thought she needn't have to share the bedroom with her mistress any longer, that had brought out the smile? However, she'd still be sharing it with baby Alex and his cobalt-blue crib which stood at the foot of her bed.

The crib was the source of consternation to Ah Kam in the beginning. In fact she once told Mandy that children's bed were either painted white or magnolia.

Alex's bedroom used to be James's office-cum-study. It also doubled as a guest room whenever he had guests. The room was the same size as their bedroom but it had two single beds in it instead of a Queen-Size bed like they had. Mandy and Baby Alex had occupied it when she returned from the hospital. When Ah Kam joined the household, she occupied the other bed.

Now that Mandy had decided to re-join him, he thought of taking out one bed so that there'll be plenty of space for Alex and Ah Kam but he changed his mind. He didn't want to make it look as if he was forcing Mandy to move in with him.

He was glad that it was Mandy herself who had suggested that the bed should be removed. James had wanted Mandy to come to him on her own free will and at the same time giving her a clear signal that she was also equally free to return to her own bed if she wanted to. He couldn't hide his happiness as he dismantled the single bed and had it stored away.

For the first time since Mandy came into his life James felt that at last he had everything that he could ever want. He had Mandy whom he loved and adored, and as for baby Alex, one will have to have a heart of stone not to love and adore him. The little devil, despite his tender age, seemed to recognize James whenever he came near him. He would be making gurgling sound, kicking and jabbing the air with his hands and legs like an overturned turtle. Invariably he would end up in James's arms, much to the consternation of Ah Kam who didn't approve of such method of bringing up children. She subscribed to the theory that too much cuddling is bad for the child. Not wanting to upset her, James pretended to agree with her and reluctantly handed Alex to her.

Like his mother, Alex was healthy as a horse. His weight had gone steadily up and he seemed to be bursting with energy. James wasn't sure whether Ah Kam, who was in her late fifties, would be able to keep up with him. James tried not to interfere with Ah Kam's routine as far as possible, but he did however put his foot down when he saw her feed little Alex with some fried *kway teow* that Mandy had bought for Ah Kam. And on another occasion he saw her spoon some of her coffee into his mouth.

James was about to have a word with her about not feeding Alex coffee, kway teow and stuffs like that, when a telephone call prevented him from doing so that day. But a few days later, as he was going to the kitchen, James saw Ah Kam do the same thing again. He lost control and began telling her that under no circumstances should she feed Alex any junk food, and that included coffee or tea. He told her Alex was too young for that kind of food or drink.

Ah Kam gave James a fixed and challenging stare, her face was slowly turning dark with anger. And as soon as she saw Mandy, who had just come into the room, she began her tirade in Hokkien. James left the room soon after because he was beginning to get hot under the collar himself. Despite his lack of comprehension in the language, it wasn't hard for him to deduce what was being said, and he came to a conclusion that he was witnessing the ugly side of Ah Kam: her display of arrogance and blind pride. To cool down, James had gone to his study to try to do a bit of work. About twenty minutes later he heard loud voices in the living room. He walked in just as Mandy was shutting the front door rather forcefully. When she turn around James asked her what was happening.

"I just fired Ah Kam," she replied. "She was rude to you and I can't have that."

It was the first time Ah Kam had ever been fired. All the while she had told that she was a perfect baby amah and it had always been her who dictate what should and shouldn't be done as far as her charges were concerned. To be told off by a *Malai Kwai* was too much for her, and she had never been fired before. It was so humiliating for her and she didn't take it kindly. Her loud tirade reverberated throughout the flat block as she waited for the lift to arrive. And when it did arrive, she kept its door open for quite some time and continued by shouting at the empty corridor how ungrateful Mandy and James were, despite all she had done for them.

Ah Kam kept at it while she was in the lift and continued even after she came out of the lift on the ground floor. Despite being five floors up, Mandy and James could still hear Ah Kam told a few curious residents who had come out to see what all the commotion was all about. Ah Kam kept repeating to them how she did us a favour by coming to work for us instead of working for some rich Chinese *Towkay* as she had originally intended.

Finally the noise stopped and out of curiosity Mandy took a peek through the curtains and watched as Ah Kam emerged into the inner car park. Mandy saw her looking up in the direction of their flat. She saw the old amah, her face twisted in anger, put her bag down and then began spitting vigorously onto the car park's asphalt surface. James, relieved by the silence, had assumed that Ah Kam's lift must have arrived and that she was on her way and that, he thought, would be the end of that. How wrong he was! As soon as Ah Kam saw a family emerge from their car, Ah Kam began to relate to them her tale of woe all over again. Mandy who was in the living room, and James at his desk in the bedroom, could hear Ah Kam all the way up on the fifth floor; there was no doubt that she was loud.

James came out of his room and saw that Ah Kam's renewed noise was making Mandy very angry. She stormed out of their flat and marched towards the lift. James managed to catch up with her and persuaded her to ignore Ah Kam and to return to the flat with him.

James had never seen Mandy so angry before, and it took a considerable effort on his part to get her to come back with him to their flat. He shuddered at the thought what could happen if Mandy had caught up with Ah Kam. Vivid images of Ah Kam's face being slapped and her hair being pulled seemed to appear before his eyes, and they weren't very pretty sight. On the other hand, would she really hit an old woman? Even a nasty one like

Ah Kam? James dismissed the thought from his mind and held her tight in his arms. She sought his lips and they kissed.

"I'll never allow anyone say bad things about you...never!"

❈❈❈❈❈❈

CHAPTER SEVENTEEN

Life without Ah Kam was in disarray for a while. Alex, with his energetic kicks, kept making his nappies slide to his feet, when only moments ago Mandy had spent a considerable time and effort putting it on him. And on one occasion Mandy had even forgotten to dispose of Alex's stool from his nappies before putting them in the washing machine. She had never forgotten it again after she saw what it did to their washing machine - not to mention their clothes.

Mandy, tired of seeing James go out to buy food for their meals, tried to solve the problem by having all of their meals, with the exception of breakfast, delivered to them by a man on his motorcycle. He had them delivered in stainless steel multi-compartmental containers. Each day, just before lunch and dinner, he would hang these containers on to their collapsible gate using a special hook he had provided,

It reminded James of his bachelor days when he and his three other flatmates had done the same thing while living in their Moulmein Road flat in Singapore. Back then having their meals sent by similar *'tin-can man'* was how they solved their cooking problem.

James could still remember how difficult it was for him to swallow the food the first time Mandy had served him. "I shouldn't complain," he said to himself, "A lot of people who have had a steady diet of this kind of food are still alive today."

Mandy for some reason didn't want to find a replacement for Ah Kam, at least not yet she told James. She said that she wanted to find out whether she was capable of being a good mother and a wife and had asked James to be patient with her.

He told her that he will try, provided she wouldn't force him to eat the food from the *'tin-can-man'*. He solved their food problems by cooking a variety of spaghetti sauces during the week ends and kept them in the refrigerator. That way they'd have spaghetti for all their meals - only their sauces were different.

Mandy in the meantime tried her hand at cooking, which resulted in inedible meals in the beginning, to almost edible meals several weeks later. Their social life was almost non-existent because Mandy refused to allow baby-sitters to look after Alexander. They did manage to entertain at home on a few occasions by having some friends over, either to watch some movies on TV or to play scrabble, which Mandy took to with a vengeance after James had introduced it to her earlier on in their marriage. It was a neat trick to get her to be interested to look up words in the dictionary.

Several months were to pass before Mandy risked inviting those same friends for dinner at their place. It was done with a lot of trepidation on her part. She needn't have worried really, for in the end it turned out to be quite a success. After that, they had friends for dinner at least twice a month, unfortunately they themselves could not accept any invitation due to Alex and Mandy's unwillingness to let baby-sitters look after him. It seemed to James that he and Mandy were fast becoming the typical suburban married couple in which he was quick to relate to - after all he had been there before. The exception being, this time around he was happy, and he was hoping that Mandy was too. But he had an uneasy feeling that she wasn't all that happy that she made out others to believe. Whenever James asked her, she would say yes in a manner that seem to suggest that she was trying to convince herself more than anything else. He tried not to read too much into it, and with difficulty, he tried to dismiss it out of his mind. One day while James was working on a paper a university had asked him to contribute, Mandy came into the room where he had been working and said, "James, I would like to have another baby." She was looking at him in a way he had never seen her look before. It was as if she was imploring him to agree with her.

James was a bit puzzled as to why she thought that he would deny her that, or anything for that matter. Three years had passed since she came into his life and filled it with happiness where once only loneliness was in permanent residence, with despair coming to visit on occasion. And now, to have a baby of their own, their own flesh and blood, was more than James had hoped for; he was thrilled. Mandy didn't have the penchant for any exotic food when she was carrying Alexander. But this time around, as she approached her third month, durian was in season, and her love-affair with the King of Fruits became all-consuming. Her appetite for it was of a gigantic proportion - something that had to be seen to believe. She would eat the fruit practically every day, consuming two, sometimes three fruits a day. At the weekends she would suggest to James that they went up to *Balik Pulau*, where most of the island's durians were grown, and seek out the pungent smelling fruit. On reaching there, she would make James stop at practically at every fruit stall along the way and there were many such stalls on these hills. The road to Balik Pulau was very narrow, and so these stalls had to be built on the slopes of these hills in order not to hinder the flow of traffic. The stalls, usually on stilts, would cling precariously on the hill slopes.

Tourists who weren't used to such sights held their breaths as they drove by, afraid that the extra gush of wind from their moving bus might cause the stalls to topple over the cliffs. They didn't seem convinced when their tour guide told them that it hadn't happened before.

Ironically these durian trees seemed to thrive on these slopes where there were plenty of rainfall and where the water retention was minimal. However, harvesting the fruits posed a bit of a problem. Since they were grown on the slopes of the hills, the fruits have a tendency to obey the law of gravity, and kept falling down the slopes until they reached the bottom of the hill. In the early days, the farmers themselves would build huts at the bottom of these ravines and would wait for the fruits to drop by. They would then haul the fruits in baskets up the slope by rope. Fortunately in those days there weren't that many traffic on the road. However, apart from the manpower and the energy required to haul the heavy fruits up the cliffs, many were damaged when they fell from the trees to the bottom of the hill. Invariably they were sold cheaply to confectioners to be made into durian cakes. Nowadays the farmers use nets just like the olive farmers in Europe do to prevent the fruits from falling into the ravines. As Mandy and James drove up the steep hill, their car engine screaming on first gear, Mandy would case every stall with a pair of binoculars while they were still some distance away. And whenever she saw a stall to her liking she would tell James to stop and they would go down to take a closer look. Not only Mandy would scrutinize practically every fruit on display there, but she would also check the carcasses or skins of the ones other customers had eaten for some tell-tale signs about them. James once asked Mandy why she bothered with the empty skins? She told him the one can tell a lot about the fruit just by looking at the skins such as infestations, age, size of each fruit, and so on.

Incidentally, some people would prefer eating them at the stalls to avoid contaminating the inside of their cars with its pungent smell, while others like Mandy would prefer to take them home and to eat them at leisure. Once home James would open all the car doors, including the boot, to air it. And once the fruit had been eaten, the carcasses and the seeds had to be disposed of quickly in order to avoid contaminating the inside of their flat.

A European once described durian as a fruit that smells like hell but tastes like heaven. He should know, he once owned one of the biggest durian plantation in the country. Most probably the only *Mat Salleh* who've ever done that. Of course he had to give up drinking his favourite scotch whisky if he had been eating the King of Fruits, otherwise, they say, he might suffer some body discomfort or some say even death. On the other hand, according to some, durian was also an aphrodisiac. Whatever the reason durian was certainly very popular from Hong Kong to Hanoi and from Saipan to Singapore.

In Malaysia, the Chinese never seemed to get enough of the fruit, despite the mountains of durians available during every season. The Malays, some of whom have durian orchards back in their kampongs, would make that special trip back during the durian season. It's well known that a number of sultans in the country have durian orchards of their own. No other fruits known to men seemed to have that kind euphoria surrounding them as durian does. It certainly is not only the King of Fruits, but the fruit for the kings.

Mandy seemed to know what she was looking for, but as far as James was concerned they all look the same to him. Many times they would leave this or that stall empty-handed and moved on to the next. She would tell him that they had nothing good, despite the mountain of durians there. James must admit that the ones that they did bring home seemed to taste better than some of the ones that he had eaten before he met Mandy. And on the top of that, James must admit that their sex life was more active during the durian season than at any other time, but he couldn't swear that it was due to all the durians that they had consumed.

Mandy's cravings for these King of Fruits continued until the end of the season by which time she was already in her eighth month of pregnancy. The once slim and beautiful Mandy looked like a walking tent with a head. Her face was round as a moon's, and she had once remarked to James that she had forgotten how her feet look like. Someone once said that some women during their pregnancy, look their best during pregnancy, while others, like Mandy, looked utterly hideous.

James wasn't worried about how she looks, but he was worried about her health, after having been brought up thinking that being overweight was unhealthy. He needn't have worried because during her check-up the following week, the doctor assured him that both she and the baby were as well as can be expected.

"What about the baby? Wouldn't it..."

"Like I said, the baby's fine." The doctor, who was about James's age, interrupted him and said in a rather condescending manner to James.

"That wasn't what I was going to say," replied James, feeling slightly annoyed at being patronised. "I was going to ask if the baby is going to be too big at delivery?"

The doctor looked at James and pondered over the question for a moment.

"Mmm" he replied.

He walked to his desk and fussed about with some papers on his desk looking for something. When he didn't find whatever he was looking for, he turned to Mandy and said, "Try not to go beyond your present weight, okay?"

While physically Mandy was healthy as a horse, she was however beginning to show symptoms of having depressions as her pregnancy progressed. It wasn't something that came out of the blue, but appeared gradually.

It became more evident as her delivery day was getting closer. James came home one evening and found her sitting on the bedroom floor with her back against the wall. She just sat there with her legs stretched out in front of her and seemed to be staring at her toes.

James asked her what she was doing. She just looked at him without saying a word. Moments later she started to cry. All of James's effort in trying to find out what the matter was, was in vain. Finally, in despair he sat next to her and gave her a light massage on her arms, her shoulders and her back but not before he brought a box of tissues and placed it near here. Her crying continued for several more minutes before it began to subside and then finally stopped. James could feel the tension dissipating from Mandy's body as they sat there staring at the blank wall in front of them. God, she was heavy, he thought, as he found himself struggling to try to pull her up. He gave up after a while.

They sat there for quite a long time. James was acutely aware of the pins and needles he was feeling around his bottom. His legs felt as if they had gone to sleep, and judging from the rhythm of

Mandy's breathing, she too seemed to have fallen asleep. James knew that if they had stayed in that position for another fifteen minutes or so, gangrene would probably have set in his legs. With considerable effort he managed to lift Mandy onto the bed. Looking back, James could remember with clarity how Mandy's mood could swing from gaiety one moment and to depression the next. These mood swings would continue on and off until just before the baby was born. When she was in her gaiety mode she would tell James funny stories about some of the people she had met. And sometimes while she worked in the kitchen, he could hear her singing in tune to the radio.

If she were in her dark moods, she would burst out crying for no apparent reason. Once, while she was in that mood, she told James how her mother had her chained like a dog because she had returned home late from an errand. He mother, according to Mandy, would beat her at the slightest provocation. Her legs and arms would be swollen and marked so badly after each beating, some days she could hardly go to school.

She hated that, she said; not for so much for the beating itself, but for not being able to go to school. Apparently she liked going to school very much. It seemed to symbolize a place where she could feel safe - her sanctuary. James had asked her how she did in school. Before answering, she ran to their bedroom and when she re-emerged a few minutes later, she held in her hand a tattered-looking brown envelope and handed it to James. Not knowing what it was he looked blankly at it.

Impatiently, Mandy snatched it back from him and took out something that looked like a folder before handing it to him. He looked at it and saw that it was her school report book. At her insistence he looked through it. He discovered that Mandy was a bright student, with "A's" and "B's" mostly. The only C seemed to consistently come from history. He looked at her with his eyebrows raised questioningly.

Mandy gave James a sheepish smile before replying. "I'm terrible with dates and names," she said.

However, when James read the headmaster's report, he was astonished to see the notation that said she had quit when she was in form four. He immediately recalled her telling him that when they first met. And he remembered how sad she had looked when she'd said that.

"So, you did quit like you said you would?"

"I had no choice. My mother ordered me to," she replied.

"But why?"

"She told me to go and look for a job so that she could stop working."

"And what work was that?"

"She was as a kitchen helper in one of the restaurants not far from our house."

Her mother who had worked at the restaurant from six in the morning till midnight, seven days a week, thought that it was time for Mandy, not only to earn her keep, but to support the rest of the family. She was hardly seventeen years old at the time.

Andrea was born at precisely 10.47 p.m. during a wet, stormy night at the Glendale Hospital. In attendance was Dr. Gunn and her team of dedicated nurses. Dr. Gunn had replaced Dr. Ismail as Mandy's doctor when she sensed that the latter was at times hostile towards James. With her usual bluntness she had told James that she did not like Dr. Ismail because he had, during more than two occasions, flirted with her, which she said she found insulting, not only to her, but to James as her husband. James had noticed that too during Mandy's second visit at his clinic but had brushed it aside, thinking that it was the doctor's style of bedside manner.

Mandy, however, had seen through the good doctor's facade and had immediately recognised him as a lecherous Old Man. His latent hostility towards James was nothing more than pure jealousy. Mandy was not a vain person by nature, but she knew that nature had bestowed her with a beauty, just like it had done to countless other women the world over. Perhaps nature had been a little bit more generous to her than to others, that was all. That attitude could explain why she had never taken her beauty seriously. To Dr. Ismail, Mandy was one of the most beautiful women he had ever met. And to one who had always fancied himself a ladies' man, he found Mandy's obvious lack of interest in him unnatural. He put the blame squarely on James's shoulders. He's the reason for her lack of interest, he told himself.

Outside, the atmosphere was thunderous and highly charged. Intermittent lightning flashes displayed their zigzag patterns across the dark ominous sky. Sometimes the sound of thunder seemed so close, people who had taken refuge in the outer corridor of the hospital, huddled in fear of being hit by the lightning. And in the delivery room, Mandy was being told to push as hard as she could by Dr. Gunn as she prepared herself to receive the baby whose head was clearly seen protruding out of Mandy's womb. A few minutes later when Andrea let out her first cry, the sky opened up and the downpour began.

ะ‌ะ‌ะ‌ะ‌ะ‌ะ

CHAPTER EIGHTEEN

James and Mandy decided to name their new baby Andrea and not Samantha as they had earlier planned. It happened one day while they were browsing in a record shop along the busy Penang Road when they came across a poster of the famous the British singer, Samantha Fox. Mandy took one look at the poster and told James she didn't like the name Samantha after all. Mandy being the instant decision maker decided on the spot that Samantha wouldn't be the name she would choose for their daughter if ever they had one. James took a second look at the poster but failed to see anything wrong with the name Samantha or the singer.

By the time Andrea was fed her milk the following morning, many parts of Penang island were under several feet of water. And the rain that came with her first cry had shown no sign of letting up as it continue to lay waste to many low-lying areas. Although the residents living in these areas were quite used to flash floods ever since the surrounding hills were made bare by the greedy developers in their mad drive to build as many condominiums as they could, they realised that this time it was different because of the amount of damaged it had caused in such a short period of time. They feared that if the rain were to continue for several more hours, these unfinished condominiums may topple on the top of them.

In several areas across the city, weary residents were seen clinging to their valuables, especially their documents, as they waded through the swirling, soupy water, to higher grounds.

Several roads to the city were already impassable to traffic. Villagers who lived along the island's many rivers, and whose homes had been threatened with inundation by the rising water, were told to move to various shelters the state government had provided for them. However those who had defied the government's directive and had stayed put hoping that the situation might improve, had perished when their homes were swept away by the fast rising waters.

Schools, churches, mosques and even some temples, were quickly turned into shelters to take in those who had lost their homes. Everyone, without exception, agreed that it was one of the state's worst floods in living memory, whereby, even some of the permanent shelters that the authorities had taken pains to erect in parts of the state that were known to be prone to flooding, were themselves inundated under several feet of water.

Reports about children being swept away by strong under-current while playing in the flood water, prompted the Federal Minister of information to make an announcement over the television advising parents not to allow their children to play in the flood water. But despite his plea, many more children had died under similar circumstances. Without warning many of them were swept away by strong current while they were playing in the water.

James was up all night, unable even to take the occasional forty winks. He kept ringing their flat to find out from Alice how little Alex was doing. Alice Cheah had volunteered to look after Alex while James was at the hospital. George and Alice Cheah was their neighbours from two floors below their flat and they had known them since Mandy and he got married. When James had first moved in his flat, George Cheah was the first person who had engaged him in conversation while James, one day, was washing his car underneath a cherry tree at the back of their block of flats. George pointed to James a proper spot to wash cars - at the end of their block of flats - which the developer built for the purpose. James was not only surprised but he was impressed too. He couldn't think of any single act by any developer that could be construed as humanitarian in nature. He had always thought that their philosophy was to make a fast buck anyway they can with scant regards to the consequences.

According to George, he and his wife, Alice, had decided to buy the flat of theirs when they saw the signboard being erected while one day they were on a lookout for a flat to buy. They were then renting a single-storey terrace house in *Glugor*, a suburb quite close to George Town.

Their decision weighed heavily on the fact that it was only about five minutes away from the electronic factory where they both work. The price at that time was only sixty thousand ringgit. It was considered a good buy for a three-bedroom, eight-hundred square-foot flat. And because of its close proximity to the *Bayan Lepas* Industrial Estate, the flats were very much sought after, especially by those working there.

It comprised of nine blocks of flats of four and five-storey high, with their block being the only one that was one storey higher than the rest.

Many of the original owners had seen their investment soared after just a few years. As a matter of fact the Cheahs had made a good appreciation on their property by the time James had moved there five years later. George told him that someone had offered him ninety thousand ringgit for their flat which he turned down.

In the beginning, James and George's relationship didn't go beyond a quick chat in the lift or whenever their paths crossed. It was only after he became a married man that their relationship began to get a bit more neighbourly. It was during one of the Chinese New Year when James and Mandy received an invitation card from the Cheahs. James and Mandy went over to their flat and spent a pleasant time getting to know their neighbours who were first to be nice to them.

Alice Cheah who adored children was childless, so when James asked her if she wouldn't mind looking after Alex while he went to the hospital with Mandy, she jumped at it. The prospect of being a mother to Alexander even for a few hours got her to burst into tears of joy. As it turned out, it was a forty-eight-hour bliss for her because James was delayed in returning home because of the flood.

Over the telephone Alice kept telling James that he needn't worry about baby Alex, he was perfectly all right. She'll look after him until he came home, she had said; no matter how long that'll be. She sounded so happy, James had a feeling that Alice might be the only happy person in the sea of despair and frustrations that had pervaded the whole island at that time, besides Mandy and him.

Thirty-six hours after Andrea's birth, the city of George Town was virtually inundated under several feet of water, and the worst, it seemed, was yet to come. Several roads in and around the city turned to rivers, which enabled the marine police to use their boats to rescue people from their roof tops.

Reports from the Meteorological Department, heard over the radio and television, predicted no let up for at least the next twenty-four hours. For a city that was prone to flooding during occasional showers, that bit of news spelt disaster.

Even though James and Mandy lived in an area that wasn't prone to flooding, they were still unable to get home until two days later. The only two roads leading to their area were under several feet of water. Like him, several other people who came to visit relatives in the hospital, were forced to sleep wherever they could find a place in the overcrowded hospital. People were sleeping in waiting rooms, along the corridors, and even in the overcrowded, chaotic, downstairs canteen, which was fast running out of food. Fortunately for the hospital, their suppliers, especially their food suppliers did not run out. They solved their delivery problems by hiring boats to bring in the food.

While many at the hospital were enduring some mild discomfort, many people elsewhere on the island were experiencing sufferings of catastrophic proportion with landslides causing massive destruction to properties and the death toll ever on the increase. A helicopter view shown on television indicated a number of houses and flat buildings along river Banks and on the hillside not far from the hospital were either swept away, toppled or badly damaged, leaving hundreds homeless.

That evening's news on television showed that Penang island was not the only place affected by the bad weather. It seemed that many parts of the country too was suffering from the same bad weather condition. An entire eleven-storey flat block built on a hillside in Kuala Lumpur was shown on the television screen resting grotesquely on its side and hundreds were feared dead, buried under tons of concrete. The occupants of the remaining three buildings nearby were told to evacuate by the authorities when it seemed certain the they too could follow the same fate. In the same news report the number of causalities throughout the nation seemed to be mounting and when the number of those who were reported missing were included, the total figure could be of a catastrophic proportion.

Ironically, there were still many who lived in condominiums that had been built precariously on hillsides who had refused to budge for fear of losing their valuables to possible looters. They clung to their belief that their condominiums were better built than those which had toppled over, so there was nothing to fear, they said to the news reporters. However, the death toll were high and those who were missing were feared dead. The authorities were curious as to why so many of these edifices were falling down likes house of cards all over the country. They had promised that they will carry out a full investigation into the allegations that shoddy workmanship and that sub-standard concrete mixtures used during the construction may have resulted in the structural failures which were obvious in two cases.

Certain quarters had even raised the possibility that misconduct by government officials, who may have given approval to certain projects when know they shouldn't, may have been another contributory factor. In a country where corruption hadn't really gone away, but had merely taken an occasional holiday, the possibility was very real.

At the end of two days, the country's death toll so far, according to the government report, was over three hundred, but it was feared that it may rise considerably due to the fact that a number of those who had been reported missing may be dead too.

Meanwhile at the hospital, when the rain finally stopped, the Matron had suggested that under the circumstances, it might be a good idea for James to take Mandy and their baby home.

Several hours earlier, the power supply from the *Tenaga Nasional* was suddenly disrupted and the hospital was running on their standby generators, and it was feared that it'll be several hours, if not days before full power could resume, and until then the air-conditioning would not be functioning and therefore it'd be most unbearable inside the hospital wards.

James was quite anxious about moving Mandy from the hospital, but once assured that there was no danger to either Mandy or the baby regarding their moving, he acted as quickly as he could to get the both of them home.

The drive home wasn't without difficulty. They had to stop several times at various places due to traffic jams, caused by cars which had broken down and had been abandoned by their owners during the flood, and were blocking the roads. James had telephoned Alice earlier to tell her that they were on their way home. She told him that she and Alexander will be waiting at their place, and to take it easy on the road.

* * *

During a dinner party at George and Alice's flat about two months after the flood, George was telling his guests comprising of Mandy, James and two other couples, how he and Alice were almost drowned when their car was swept off the road into the monsoon drain while driving home after a flood similar to the one they just had. According to them, had it not been for two young men, who risked their lives by jumping into the swollen water and had pulled them out, they certainly would not have made it.

They told James and Mandy that even though they were both strong swimmers, they had still found themselves helplessly stuck inside their car, which was then rapidly drawing in water. They couldn't get out because to their dismay they found their car doors were unexplainably stuck. They said that the moment they knew that death was imminent as their car was being sucked into the swirling muddy water towards the swollen river close by, their only thoughts were how fortunate they were they didn't have any children.

They were fortunate, not because they didn't have any children, but because some people saw their car took the plunge into what seemed like a shallow stream of water beside the road. Within minutes of their car sinking into the water, the two young men dove in and went after them. If they had waited even a moment longer, most probably George and Alice could not have been rescued. With their car totally submerged, George, with Alice who was in near panic but managed to calm down in time, took a deep breath and tried to push the car door open with all their might from inside. The two men, on reaching their car which was completely filled with water, tried with all their strength to open the car door from the outside. Precious moments were lost before George and Alice realised that both of them were trying to activate the door-opening mechanism at the same time. Their two rescuers managed to signal to them not to touch the levers but to push while they try to open the door from the outside.

Miraculously all of them managed to get the two front doors open after several agonising minutes. It wasn't a moment too soon, for their lungs were screaming for air. Alice and George scrambled through the open doors and with their rescuers close behind, they swam for dear life to the surface. Although at that moment they did not see it, their car did a half-turn before joining the fast-moving river seconds later. There was no doubt in their minds that the two strangers' quick and brave action saved their lives.

The two Samaritans, both in their thirties, were commended by the state's top cop, and their story dominated the front pages of most of the nation's newspapers the next day. And while the two men basked in the limelight which they rightly deserved, and while Alice and George owed them eternal gratitude for saving their lives, many people, while reading their newspapers, were privately thinking that what the duo did was not only dangerous but foolhardy. They just shrugged their shoulders indifferently before turning to their stock market report.

❧❧❧❧❧❧

CHAPTER NINETEEN

'Pearl of the Orient'- that was what they used to call Penang Island or *Pulau Pinang* in Bahasa Malaysia. The Malays who were the original inhabitants of this island, whose shape and outline slightly resembled that of France, used to call it *Tanjung*. As a matter of fact, some still do, especially the old-timers.

Once a beautiful and tranquil place, with fishing villages dotting the coast line of white sandy beaches where most of the five-star hotel were presently located. It was an ideal place to come to when you want to get away from the hustle and bustle of daily grind of big city life. A place to unwind, and to savour what nature had originally intended to bestow to the human race. A place for escapists who don't want to escape too far.

Unfortunately, the human race being the most destructive of all the species that walk this planet, bent on destroying all that is good and pure, and it seemed that nothing can stop its self-destructive goal, succeeded in making Penang into what the Prime Minister Mahathir Mohammad call the 'Dust Bin of the Orient'.

All over the world one reads about the destruction of the environment, historic monuments, works of art, and even of total annihilation of whole race. Even as this story was written, desperate battles were being fought in Bosnia-Herzegovina in which thousands of people had been killed and millions others were displaced due to ethnic cleansing cruelly perpetuated by its mainly Serbs population who were well-armed, against its weak, badly armed Muslims, and now, even the Croats had joined the feeding frenzy. Other desperate battles were also being fought in Somalia and Angola in Africa, Sri Lanka and Kashmir in the Indian sub-continent, as well as in numerous other areas in the former Soviet Union such as Georgia, Azerbaijan and Armenia - the list goes on. Although the people of Malaysia like to think that they have been spared all these turmoil and wanton destruction, they would only be deluding themselves if they thought that.

Not to be outdone, we Malaysians, knowingly or unknowingly, are on the verge of destroying ourselves - only our methods are more subtle. We do it by pollution: First we choke up our rivers by dumping into them anything we can think of, then we dump tons of raw sewage and other untreated effluents into rivers and our sea, some, ironically, by the five-star hotels themselves who were the loudest to complain when the tourists gave their hotels a miss and moved somewhere else. At the same time we indiscriminately destroy our forest by over logging, legal or otherwise. We cut down trees from hill slopes in order to build condominiums for those who, in the first place, were attracted to these places because of their forest.

From James's bedroom window where he once could gaze at green covered hills, earthworks have made parts of that same hills look like they have some festering wounds. Like in some mad race, piling works had been going on day and night. Soon, James wouldn't be able to see the hills - thanks to the get-rich-quick developers who cared for nothing except a healthy bank balance, tall buildings will obliterate the view. Some of the things we like to do best, and we're very good at it, is to dump our garbage whenever and wherever we feel like it. We're not choosy where we litter from - from high-rise tenement blocks to modern condominiums. From houses on stilts in the kampongs to the terraced-houses in the towns and cities, from the humble Proton Sagas or from the gleaming Mercedes-Benzes – we will continue to dump our rubbish wherever and whenever we can. And we're not particular either where we litter either – in buses, in gleaming supermarkets, in front of mosques, churches or temples, at the bus stands or even in front of our neighbours driveway. You'll notice that despite the differences in our level of affluence and education, littering is our common denominator. We do it regardless of who we are, from the CEO of public listed companies to the lowly peon on his Suzuki delivering letters, we just love to litter, it's something we do best.

What about the air we breathe in, we can't allow it to swirl around us unsullied, we must contaminate that too. The easiest way to do that of course is to discharge carbon monoxide in the atmosphere, and we do that easily from our cars, trucks, buses and our factories. If that's not enough, we can always rely on the good old fashion open burning of our rubbish and what-have-you. You can be rest assured that our creative minds will find other more high-tech ways to degrade our environment. Take the constant flooding that had beset Penang during the past decade or so, in the main it has been due to people clogging up the drains, streams and rivers when they indiscriminately dumped their rubbish in them.

Ironically, some of the greatest culprits are the people who suffered most from these flooding. Since they lived near the open drains themselves, they found it so convenient to dump all their rubbish into it. To call Penang island the 'Pearl of the Orient' now would be most inappropriate, the lustre it once had, had long gone, perhaps forever. Yet, despite its fall from grace, or because of it, it had been overrun by people from other states, buying up real estates and setting up shops all over the place. It brings to my mind a popular American song made famous by *"Ole Blue Eyes"* Frank

Sinatra. I think title was, "New York, New York", and in it there's a lyric that says..."if you can make it there, you can make it anywhere..." suggesting that if you can make it in New York, you can make it anywhere. Well, in the case of Penang, I think it should be "... if you can't make or do it anywhere else, you can make it or do in Penang."

For nearly a quarter of a century the people of Penang had been enjoying certain freedom which in most other states they wouldn't dream of having or even tolerated. Due to lackadaisical and laid-back attitude by the city fathers, its citizen had been flouting, bending, and even breaking the laws whenever it suited them, most will get away with it with impunity.

A lot of laws which had been created by men were done base on a lot of common sense. For example, if you live in a housing estate, you can't just convert your house into an car workshop, a second-hand car show room, a factory, or even a doctor's clinic. Even though doctors in other countries have been known to use private houses as clinics and consultation rooms, they first had to have permission before they can do so. In Penang, even though there are laws, some of which are similar to those in other countries, very few people bother going through the procedure of applying for and waiting for its approval before work can begin on the premise of their choice. They just go ahead and do whatever it is they wanted to do, hang the laws, and to hell with what the neighbours think. Some have no qualms about hanging up a big, bold signboards above the entrance of their premises. On the top of that, they may have it lit up all night long with fluorescent lights, robbing their neighbours, not only the aesthetic value of their surroundings, but their good night sleep as well.

It never occurred to them, or if they did they just don't give a hoot, that their neighbours would hardly find any peace nor tranquillity in the confines of their homes, while they may have found theirs since have already solved their problem of finding a suitable premises for their business. Well, that's exactly what's happening in Penang. Some people in Penang, devoid of basic common sense have been turning decent housing estates into ghettos almost as soon as they were completed. And if the government ever try to act on these unscrupulous operators, it'll find itself confronted by opposition members who will suddenly come out of the woodwork, falling all over themselves, to become champions of these lawbreakers; to protect their rights it seemed. Well then, who protects the rights of the law-abiding silent majority?

Throughout the journey home, James had been subjected to all these angry thoughts. He really couldn't help it as he witnessed the unnecessary degradation of their environment. Mandy who was sitting in the passenger's seat next to him was fading in and out of sleep, while baby Andrea was sound asleep in her basket on the backseat of the car, oblivious to the mental torments James was going through.

After about one hour of very careful driving on his part, James finally managed to get his family home safe and sound. As they got out of the lift, James saw someone who looked like a ragamuffin standing their door. He couldn't see the person's face as he had his back towards them. And the clothes he wore were so tattered and torn, James was apprehensive about letting Mandy and baby Andrea go any closer to him until he'd checked him out.

James told Mandy to wait near the lift while he found out what the stranger wanted. As soon as he heard footsteps behind him, the stranger turned around. Mandy who was carrying baby Andrea in her arms, let out an involuntary gasp the moment she recognised him as that of her brother Mark. He looked as if he had gone through hell: his face was badly bruised, his hair was caked in dried mud and his left hand, badly bandaged, was in a sling.

"Our house... destroyed...floated away," he uttered, sobbing uncontrollably as soon as he saw them. "I saw grandfather being swept away by the rushing water. I saw his head bobbing up and down in the water for few moments before he disappeared altogether. I tried to save him, but I couldn't reach him in time. The rest of us managed to get to safety. Mum and Luke are now at the shelter near our place. I tried to phone you but I couldn't get through, so I came here."

Mark's rapid-fire utterances stopped abruptly and all of a sudden he began howling liked a wounded animal. James quickly opened their door and gently led all of them in the flat. Seeing that Mark was wet and cold, James quickly guided him into the bathroom and turned on the hot shower and asked him to have as hot a shower he could stand. About ten minutes later, Mark, dressed in James's clothes, which was one size too big for him, but nevertheless looked little less like a ragamuffin, drank the coffee and ate the sandwiches that Mandy had made for him. After that Mandy made him lie down on the sofa and he fell asleep almost immediately.

James, in the meantime had gone to Alice's place to pick their son Alexander. He had rung earlier telling Alice that they were back and that he was on his way to pick up Alexander. Alice couldn't hide the disappointment in her voice on hearing the news, nevertheless she told James not to come down but she'll bring Alexander herself. She added that she was anxious to see Mandy and the baby. When Alice arrived with Alexander in tow, she saw Mark and the condition he was in lying on the sofa. She looked inquiringly at Mandy. Mandy filled her in as to what had happened and Alice became most sympathetic and asked whether there was anything she could do to help. James couldn't help thinking what a nice person Alice was, bringing to mind the dangers of creating racial stereotypes which some people seemed to have of her race - that they live a rather insular life and that they didn't give a damn about other people as well as other clichés pertaining to their loyalties to the country and so on. James doubted that there was a mean bone in Alice's body but he wasn't sure about the rest of her race, after all, his first wife was a Chinese too. All of a sudden a big question mark loomed high in his mind: What is it about the Chinese that seemed to attract him so much? Beside his two wives - past and present, most of his friends were Chinese!

Mark, after having slept for nearly twelve hours, woke up and asked James whether he could have something to drink. James asked him whether he'd care to eat something. Mark shook his head and said that he'll just have something to drink. James asked what he'd prefer, his immediate reply was for a cup of Milo, but he quickly changed his mind and asked for a glass of water instead. James went to the kitchen and made Mark a pot of Milo and he also brought him a glass of water. In a plate he also brought some cookies and some fruits. Mark ate the cookies and drank his Milo but left the fruits alone. When James related that fact to Mandy sometime later, Mandy told him that in their household, fruits were considered expensive, and Milo too, so they don't consume much of either.

James was first to get up the next morning, and when he took a peek in the living room and saw that Mark too was up, he quickly prepared breakfast comprising of orange juice, some toasts and coffee. After having been brought up on a steady diet of rice three time a day, James could understand why the toasts and jam did not light up Mark's face when he saw what was on the table. He looked up at his sister and grimaced when he saw her downed her glass of orange juice in one gulp.

"How can you drink orange juice early in the morning?" Mark asked, looking positively shocked. "It'll give you an upset stomach. You'll have to go to the toilet then!" Mandy, not too long ago, would have been just as shocked too. She had wanted to let her brother know that what he had just said was the general idea, but changed her mind. Instead, she asked him to tell them what had happened exactly, now that he had his rest.

Mark told them how he was awaken just before dawn yesterday morning by the sound of a loud scraping sound. It sounded strange and unfamiliar to him. It was as if someone was dragging an empty steel drums along the cement floor of their house. Mandy thought that the noise must have been very loud to wake Mark up as he was usually a heavy sleeper. Very rarely anything would disturb his sleep. She remembered fondly now, how she used to get so infuriated with him because she found it so difficult to wake him up for school.

Mark said he didn't think much of it at first and was about to close his eyes again when all of a sudden the wall opposite him started to buckle and bend towards him before collapsing. When he saw water gushing in, he rolled off his bed just as the roof above his head was about to fall on him. Seconds later he found himself being dragged down into the torrents of swirling muddy water. He was hit on the head by a bobbing wooden chest as he was being swept away into the swollen river in which the stream near their house had become. It was fortunate that he didn't pass out, he said, otherwise he certainly would have drowned. As he was being hurled in the fast moving water towards the sea, he somehow managed to grab with both hands the wooden chest that had floated by him - most probably the same wooden chest that had hit him on the head before, he said. He clung to it and somehow managed to stay above water as he bobbed up and down past ravaged houses and assorted debris towards the open sea.

With the buoyancy provided by the chest, Mark managed to stay afloat and miraculously it had saved his life. If he had gone under, it was unlikely he would have survived. Ahead of him he saw a couple of dead bodies. One of which, an old woman, bumped into him. It gave him such a fright, he almost let go of the wooden chest which would have meant certain death for him too. Mark was a good swimmer, but in the state of exhaustion he was in, without that wooden chest to keep him afloat, he certainly would have perished.

While Mark was still recovering from the shock of seeing the two dead bodies drifting away, he noticed in the distance, on his right, a man struggling to keep afloat by clinging to a branch of a partly-submerged tree. He could see that the branch that the man was holding on to was broken and that it was on the verge of parting away from its trunk. The man, unaware that the branch that he was clinging so desperately to was about to snap, had been trying for the last several minutes to get to the safety of the tree top, away from the swirling water that was sapping away whatever strength he had left. The effort was too much for him and felt that he could no longer hold on.

Mark saw what the man was trying to do and from the way he was holding on to that branch, he knew that the man would not be able to hold on much longer. For some reason, Mark was mentally trying to get the man to hold on, but it was obvious that he was very tired. Mark was afraid that the man might just let go and to let fate takes its course. The feeling was familiar to him , he had more than once wanted to do the same thing when tiredness began to take hold and to leave it to fate whether he live or die. I'm too young to die, he thought suddenly. With sheer determination, he clung on to the wooden chest as he continue to look in the distance at the Old Man who was still clinging on to the partially submerged branch.

Mark had rightly concluded what the Old Man was thinking. He could not hold much longer, his body was so racked with pain and he was so tired. Perhaps by letting go, he was thinking, he might still make it. Mark could only see the back of the man's head for he was looking towards the swirling water downstream. The Old Man was weighing his chances of survival if he were to swim with the flow of the tide. But when he saw the torrent of fast flowing water swished past him, he knew that his chances would be slim indeed. He turned his head to look up the tree top and decided to make one last attempt to pull himself up there. If he failed, he'll just have to leave it to fate by letting himself go. He'll try to swim downstream as best as he could, he knew he could not hold on much longer.

After a moment or two Mark saw the Old Man try to make another attempt to pull himself toward the tree trunk, when all of a sudden the branch snapped. Helplessly Mark watched the fast-flowing water drag the poor man to his watery death. He disappeared for several minutes before Mark saw a hand come up first, then his head. Even though it was only for a split-second, Mark, to his horror, recognised the man as his grandfather. Before he could react, his grandfather had disappeared into the water once more and he watched anxiously for any sign of him. He called out to his grandfather on the top of his voice, "*Akong!... Akong!... Akong!*".... He kept scanning the surface of the water to see if his grandfather had come up. He kept on calling until he felt his lungs were about to burst. Minutes later a member of the rescue team heard his shouts and alerted his crew by radio, who by that time, were circling the area in an inflated raft looking for survivors. Mark was rescued and brought to a Red Crescent centre where they attended to the cuts on his head and hand, which they also suspected may have been fractured. They gave him a number of injections to ensure that he was adequately protected from any disease that he may have picked from the dirty water. They were about to give him some dry clothes and some food when he decided to come to look for Mandy. He managed to hitch a ride part of the way, and walked the rest of the way.

Meanwhile in a separately development, their mother who was sleeping in another room, and Luke who shared the same bedroom with Mark but had narrowly escaped from being hit by the falling roof, were swept by fast moving water. Fortunately for them they managed to climb up an embankment of the river when he got entangled in a mangrove swamp along the river. They scrambled with all their might and managed get to a higher ground and found their way to the same Red Crescent centre in which Mark was brought to much later. As there were too many people there, they did not meet each other.

Soon after breakfast, Mandy and James, once again had to impose on Alice to look after Alexander and the baby while they went with Mark to look for Mandy's mother and her brother Luke. James had tried to make Mandy stay at home while he and Mark scoured the relief centres, but she had insisted on coming.

Fortunately for them, the roads, although muddy and in some places and strewn with stranded cars, were but impassable to traffic. After about an hour's search at various relief centres, they finally found them huddled together under a blanket in a corner of a local school's badminton hall the authorities had used to house those whose homes were either destroyed or were still inundated by the flood water. Even though the rain had stopped, the massive clean-up which had already begun could take some time, and to those people whose homes had been swept away or destroyed, they may have to stay at these relief centres for God knows how long!

Although they were reluctant at first, James and Mandy managed to persuade Mandy's mother and her two brothers to come and stay with them. But two days later and to their surprise, they decided to move out when they received a telephone call from one of their friends at the relief centre telling them of the rumours that had been going around at the relief centres that the authorities were going to distribute aids and other assistance to those who were presently staying there. And not wanting to miss out, Mandy's mother and her two brothers had wanted to move back to the Red Crescent relief centre to reclaim their place on the list.

James telephoned the relevant authorities and asked them about the authenticity of the rumours that had been spreading around and was told that it was just that - rumours. They emphasised that all those who had lost their homes regardless whether they were staying at the centres or with friends or relatives, provided of course they had registered, will receive aids from the government.

James tried to dissuade Mandy's mother from leaving by relating to her what the authorities had told him, but to no avail. She insisted that they should go back to the relief centre straight away. James and Mandy packed some food for them including some tins of sardine, soup, plus some money. He then drove them back to the relief centre.

Despite their good intentions, it took the authorities another week before they were able to provide proper accommodations for all the flood victims. Mandy's mother and her two brothers were put in a longhouse together with dozens of other families, who like themselves, had lost everything, including some who had also lost their loved ones. Mandy and James paid them a visit at their longhouse, leaving Alexander and Andrea with Alice to look after. James and Mandy tried their best to make her mother and her two brothers' stay there as comfortable as possible by providing all the essentials they thought they would need.

On the way home, James and Mandy stopped to look at what was left of her parents' devastated home - the house she was born in. They were not prepared at what they saw. Nothing of the old house could be seen except a pile of rubbish that had been left behind by the overflowing river which the stream had turned into. Its banks were now several feet high and its width had expanded to more than twice its original size. The site of the house had now become completely cut off from the main road. To rebuilt a house on the original site would require a costly bridge to be built in the first place, across what was originally a small stream. James doubted if the government would be willing to spend that kind of money. He wondered what'll they do if that happened. Will he have to offer them to live at their tiny flat? He shuddered at the thought and tried to put it out of his mind.

As they stood at the edge of the chasm and looked across to what once stood three houses, only the roof of her grandfather's house was visible at the bottom of the slope some distance away. It was wedged between an old banyan tree and another tree James could not recognize, and it was covered with debris. He had immediately recognised it when he spotted its shiny zinc roof among the debris. He remembered the time when Mandy's grandfather was replacing the old rusty zinc sheets with new ones. It was just before the last Chinese New Year while Mandy and he were on a visit there. He remembered thinking whether he could, when at the Old Man's age, be able to do what the Old Man was doing then.

James had assisted Khong, when was trying to reinstall his television antenna, by observing the reception on the television screen while he, the Old Man, was on the roof orienting it for the best possible reception. Even though his contribution to the Old Man's rebuilding effort was minuscule, he remembered it clearly nonetheless. Immediately he tried to look for the antenna. Although it was twisted out of shape, he saw it protruding out some twigs and dead woods. It stood proudly on the same sprocket which was screwed on the eaves.

James was about to point the antenna out to Mandy when he saw tears running down her cheeks. He cursed himself silently at what he thought of doing; he was thinking of making a flippant comment about the antenna. He quickly steered her away from the scene and started back towards their car.

Khong's body, together with dozens of others were found in the sea, several miles from where

Mark had seen him disappear. Due to the poor condition of the body, it was decided by Mandy's mother that the funeral should be held immediately. By the evening of the same day the Old Man was buried in a cemetery on the hill that overlooked the same part of the sea in which his body was found floating.

James couldn't help thinking that even though he and Mandy's grandfather hadn't had much contact with each other, the few times that they had met, he found himself liking the Old Man. He was a man of few words who chose his words very carefully, and was always to the point. He didn't seem to care for anything superfluous, and that seemed to apply to his body too; there wasn't an ounce of fat on it. And when he walked, he walked like a man twenty years younger - he was nearly eighty-two years old when he died!

CHAPTER TWENTY

When Khong's wife died several years ago when Mandy had just turned eighteen. While other girls her age would be in high school, she had to work from ten in the morning till ten at night selling trinkets to rich tourists. He was angry with his daughter for forcing Mandy to quit school so that she could stay at home and play Mahjong. He tried to talk her out of quitting her job at the nearby restaurant at least for another two years so that Mandy could finish high school so that with that she could at least get a better job instead of doing what she was doing earning a measly pay.

Khong became so angry with his daughter and her selfishness, he had decided at that moment that he will have nothing to do with her ever again. When his wife had died and Shirley had asked him to move in with them, he had refused suspecting that his daughter had only made that offer hoping that he would make a counter-offer by asking all of them to come and live with him instead. His house was bigger than theirs and had more rooms. However, if any of them were sick, he would be at their bedside in a flash. He would be there like a mother hen looking after them. It wasn't because he loved them less, it was that he loved his freedom more.

When his wife, who was as tough as he was, suddenly became ill, he had a premonition that same night that she wouldn't recover from her illness and it scared him. Although not the type to show affection, Khong had loved her very much and he couldn't bear the thought of losing her. He kept a nightly vigil over her, doing all he could to make her comfortable.

Mark, who was close to both his grandparents, was surprised to find his grandfather missing the next morning from his usual place by her bedside. Instead of hovering over her like a mother hen like he used to do whenever any member of the family became ill, Mark found his grandfather sitting on a tree stump in his small vegetable patch behind their house.

"Akong, is grandmother going to be all right?" Mark asked as he sat on the grass near his grandfather.

"She's very sick and she's also in a lot of pain," said the Old Man without looking at his grandson. He broke off a piece of dead twig from a tree near him and began poking it into the soft ground around his chilli plants in a preoccupied way. After a while, the Old Man stopped poking around in the dirt and turned to his grandson and said, "The doctor seemed unable to help her, I have to get help from another source." He did not elaborate. After a while he got up and went back to his wife's side while his grandson was called out to play by a neighbour's son who had poked his head over the rusted corrugated zinc fence when he heard voices from his side of the fence.

The next morning, after having slept fitfully all night, the Old Man prepared a bowl of porridge and placed it on the table next to his wife's bed. Next, he went to her sewing box which was beside her ancient hand-operated Singer sewing machine and began rummaging in it. He took out a pair of scissors and then after hesitating for a few moments, walked back to where his wife was lying. He pushed back the strands of hair that had covered her face with his left hand. He looked at her wrinkled face for the longest time, finally, he raised the scissors and brought it down towards her head and cut a few strands of her hair. After returning the scissors back into the sewing box, he dipped his hand into his pocket and took out a handkerchief and placed it on the table next to the sewing machine. Awkwardly with only one hand he tried to spread out the handkerchief flat on the surface of the table. After managing to finally do it with taps here and there with the palm of his hand, he put the strands of hair on it. And as if they were some precious objects, he then began to fold the handkerchief over the hair into a square before putting it in his hip-pocket.

The journey to Cameron Highlands took Khong several hours by bus through treacherous and narrow mountain road that wound up for nearly sixty kilometres. And when the bus finally reached the town of *Tanah Rata* he stopped at a coffee shop for a quick meal before continuing with the rest of his journey on foot. His destination was a small village located deep in the jungle where no vehicle, except for a four-wheel drive or a donkey, could make the last leg of his journey.

By nightfall he finally reached his destination - a thatch-roofed wooden structure built in a traditional style of a Malay house. It was built on a plot of land that had been levelled on the slope of a mountain. It was so desolate, Khong doubted if the old *bomoh* received many visitors.

"Pak Mat!" Khong called out as he approached the *anjung* of the house. When there was no reply, he called out once more and waited.

Just at the bottom of the wooden steps stood a big earthen jar filled almost to the brim with water. Khong bent down and dipped his hand into the jar and began feeling for the *tempurong* cup which he knew must be lying at the bottom somewhere. After groping in the water for a minute or two and wetting the sleeve of his shirt in the process, he finally found the well-worn coconut shell cup which he had looked for. He took a scoop of water and poured it onto his slippers and feet. He scooped out another cupful of water from the jar and began to wash his feet more thoroughly this time using his hand to scrub the dirt out. When his feet were done, he washed his hands starting from his elbows; finally he washed his face. He carefully counted the number of times he had to pour water on his feet, his hands, as well as his face. He wanted to make sure both his hands and feet got equal treatment.

When he finish, Khong called out once more. "Pak Mat! Pak Mat!" He was about to take a seat on the long wooden bench which was placed underneath the covered entrance in front of the bottom of the stairs when he heard a voice asking, *"Siapa_itu?"* coming from somewhere inside the house.

"Pak Mat, I'm Khong. I've come a long way to see you. I hope I'm not disturbing you."

"Oh, I'm sorry, have you been waiting long? I was performing my evening prayers," said the man as soon as he saw the stranger at the bottom of his staircase. *"Sila lah,"* he beckoned to Khong to come up.

Khong could not immediately determine the other man's age. He was obviously old, with not a hair on his head, but his beard was long and white. He stroked it with his left hand as they shook hands, whether consciously or not, Khong could not tell. He was dressed in a sarong and a faded white T-shirt which he had tucked in his sarong. Around his waist he wore a wide money-belt similar to those favoured by the *Mamaks* he had seen in Penang. He guessed the man must be around his own age, perhaps, one or two years older.

"I'm sorry if I have disturbed you," Khong said to the other as he walked up the wooden stairs and shook his host's hand. The Old Man ushered Khong into the *anjung*.

"Not at all," replied Pak Mat. "I had already finished the *asar* prayer some time ago. I was only reading the Koran".

Pak Mat told Khong that his hearing was not as good it once was and apologised if he had made Khong wait. Almost as soon as they had sat down on the *mengkuang* matted-floor, a young woman of Mandy's age wearing a *baju kurong* came in and placed a tray consisting two cups of tea and some Malay *kuih* in front of them. She looked at the Old Man, who nodded his head, and then at Khong. "*Silakan,*" she said before disappearing into the kitchen.

Khong took the proffered tea and accepted a piece of cake from the steady hand of his host. But before Khong could take a sip of his tea, the Old Man got up to fetch his cigarettes from the top of the book shelves a few feet away. Khong took the opportunity to take in the front room which was the part of the house that jutted out from the rest. It had windows on all the walls facing the front of the house. He noticed the neat little curtains above the windows as well as above the main door. They were hung and secured in place by tiny yellow ribbons and he thought that they looked nice. He made a mental note to try to get some made for his house as soon as his wife was well again. They'll cheer her up, you'll see, he was thinking.

Khong hadn't been in a Malay house before despite the fact that he lived not far from a Malay Kampong. As the matter of fact the area in which he was living in was once a Malay kampong. He had bought the piece of land from a Chinese owner who had previously acquired it from a Malay for a song.

During the forty years that Khong had lived there he had witnessed the expansion of his community from a handful of Chinese settlers in what was initially a corner of a Malay kampong, into a thriving one that left intact none of its original features. Finally the Chinese had bought all, but the heartland of the original kampong itself.

Khong had often felt the glow of pride in him at the thought of how many of his countrymen who had come to this country almost penniless, ended up owning large chunks of real estate all over the country, and they owe it all to their trusting and hospitable hosts.

Khong hadn't been in a Malay house before simply because he hadn't known any Malays that close before nor did he have the desire to be close to anyone. In all the years he had lived almost next door to a small Malay village, he hadn't made any attempts to know any of its inhabitants. He actually hadn't seen the need until now. Sure he had met a number of Malays after having lived in the country for so long. How could he not? Whenever he had to pay his utility bills he would invariably meet them over the counter, or at the Post Office and some other government offices in which he had some business with.

Ironically it was to the Malay kampong that Khong had turned to when he saw his wife's condition hadn't changed after doctors had treated her. He then went to the *sinsehs* and they too didn't do much for her. And now, in desperation, he decided to seek the help of a Malay bomoh.

He had often heard rumours that sometimes the Malay *bomohs* could cure ailments which others could not. Since he didn't know anyone in the Malay kampong, Khong had gone to see the *Ketua Kampong* and told him of his wife's illness. The village headman was most sympathetic and he immediately took Khong to see the kampong's bomoh.

This man was supposed to have had a reputation as being fearless. He had one day saved a young child from being dragged into the muddy nearby river by a large crocodile. Everybody in the village, as well as those outside, including Khong, have heard the stories of how the bomoh, who was already in his sixties at that time, had jumped into the murky water and after several agonising minutes of searching the muddy river bed, found the reptile. With his powerful hands, the Bomoh forced open the crocodile's jaws open to release the badly mangled six-year old girl's left thigh from its grip. Once relieved of its victim, the crocodile dove into the murky water and disappeared. The bomoh grabbed hold of the little girl and swam quickly to the river bank. With the help of some of the kampong folks he and the little Chinese girl were soon on the safe ground where he managed to resuscitate her back to life. From that day onwards the cold indifference that had existed between the two communities for generations began to take a different shape. For the first time in decades, the following Hari Raya and Chinese New Year saw the two communities exchange visits.

The Bomoh asked Khong to take him to his wife. After he had examined her, he made up some concoction and asked her to drink it. He also left behind some foul-smelling ointment and instructed Khong on how to apply it on her. When he returned the next day and saw that there wasn't any change in her condition, he told Khong that he had done all he could. "It's all in the hands of Allah now," he said.

When the bomoh saw how dejected Khong was at the news, he told him about Pak Mat - a well-known Bomoh who lived somewhere in the jungle of Cameron Highlands. "He was reported to have magical powers," he said. "Maybe he could save your wife."

The Malay bomoh told Khong where to find Pak Mat. Khong replied that he'll leave straight away. The other told him of the things he had to take with him. He also instructed Khong on the cleansing ritual he must follow before meeting with the *Bomoh*.

As they sat down to enjoy their tea and cakes, Khong couldn't help noticing the difference between his house and Pak Mat's. The thing that struck him most was how clean it was compared to his; one could literally eat off its floor. Whereas his would be littered with things his dog would have brought in and it would also be covered with sand and possibly mud, if it was raining. Being built above ground seemed to have a distinct advantage too - it was airy and therefore much cooler.

When he had drunk his tea and had eaten some of the *kuihs*, Khong told Pak Mat about his wife's sickness and the inability of the local doctors and the *sinsehs* to cure her. He also told him of the other Bomoh he had seen, and of his recommendation to come to see Pak Mat when he had observed no change in his wife's condition. All throughout Khong's narrative, Pak Mat sat cross-legged on the mat with his eyes closed as if he was asleep. Finally he opened his eyes and gave Khong such an intense look, it almost unnerved him.

"Have you brought something that belonged to your wife?" He asked finally.

"Yes. I was told that you may need this."

Khong took out a white handkerchief from the trousers pocket. And with the same care that he had exercised when wrapping it up, he unfolded the handkerchief and placed it on the mat in front of the Bomoh.

The Bomoh nodded his head when he saw the hair in the handkerchief. With agility that belied his age, he got up from his sitting position in a springy and fluid motion. He then went to fetch a tray and a brass *sireh* box from the top of a small wooden cabinet that was standing by the wall next to an open window. Khong noticed that the Old Man's walk was in a manner that was brisk. When he came back he took a sireh leaf from inside the box and spread it on the tray which he had placed in front of him. He then pick up a few strands of Khong's wife's hair from the handkerchief and placed them on the leaf. From one of three small jars inside the brass *sireh* box he took out a betel nut, and with a *pinang* cutter which also came out of the box, he began to cut a few slivers from a betel nut and placed the tiny pieces onto Khong's wife's hair. He stood up and disappeared through the door that lead to the rest of the house. When he returned out a few minutes later he had in his hand a strip of white cloth in which he wrapped the *sireh* leaf with the hair and strips of betel nut in it and made it into a shape of an amulet. He completed his job by tying the ends together with yellow thread. A few moments later the same young woman who brought them their refreshments earlier came in with a smoking incense burner in her hand. But instead of coming straight to where Khong and the Bomoh were sitting, she circled the room, thus engulfing the whole room with the pungent smelling smoke. With that done, she placed the incense burner near the Bomoh and then disappeared to whence she came from.

The Bomoh in the meantime was preparing another sireh leaf by first placing it on the palm of his hand, and from one of the three jars he dug out with his finger some *kapur* - a chalkish like substance and spread it onto the leaf Like he was spreading butter on a piece of toast. He then placed some strips of betel nut, which he had kept aside, and placed them onto the painted sireh leaf. He then added a clove and a small piece of *gambier* which he picked out from one of the jars. When he was satisfied that he had all the ingredients needed to make a proper sireh, he began folding the sireh leaf into a neat little square. Finally he placed the sireh on the tray next to the amulet he had made: the one containing the sireh leaf and Khong's wife's hair which was encapsulated in the white piece of cloth. Moments later he began reciting something in a voice so low he sounded as if he were just making some grunting sound in his throat.

After several minutes, Pak Mat stopped his chanting, or rather the noise he was making but had continued to remain seated with his eyes closed. Khong seemed fascinated by the whole procedure and believed by what he saw that the Bomoh must have made contact with his god, and that he had asked Him for help to cure his wife.

Khong couldn't help but felt anxious and nervous as the Bomoh continued to remain in his trance-like pose and appeared as if he had stopped breathing. This went on for several minutes and just as Khong was beginning to feel panic coming on, the Bomoh came out of his trance and began to appear normal again. The next thing the Bomoh did was to finish his cup of tea which Khong was sure must be quite cold. He noticed that in these hills it began to get nippy the moment the sun sets; he felt it in his hands and feet.

"Encik Khong," said the Bomoh at last. "I have this strong vibrations...a feeling, if you like, that your wife is resting peacefully. Go home now and take these things with you. I want you to tie this one on her right arm," he said, indicating to the amulet he had made. "But with this sireh you must first pound it into a paste, stir in a glass of water and after you have strained it, keep it aside. In the meantime you must do something first. You must make sure that you've removed everything from your house such as your altar, deities, joss sticks, water bowls and all other things that you use in your prayers. Please make sure you take them out of your house. You may return them to their original place after your wife is fully cured but not before. Do you understand?"

Nodding his head, Khong replied, "I understand."

The Bomoh gave Khong the amulet and the sireh which he had wrapped in a white sheet of paper.

"Thank you very much," Khong said to the Bomoh as he shook his hand. He then took out a ten-ringgit note out of his wallet and placed it in the *Bomoh's* hand. "For coffee," he said simply.

Khong took the same narrow jungle path he came through earlier and walked the two kilometres back to Cameron highlands' town of Tanah Rata. Although the moon was in full bloom, it was still dark due to the thick clouds. With some difficulty he managed to get to the main road which led him straight to the town centre. However, getting to his next destination proved to be more difficult than he had anticipated.

Although a pragmatic man, Khong was awed by things he did not understand, and to be sure there were many things in the in the world in which he had lived for over eight decades, he did not understand. He was awed by the Bomoh but at the same time he felt uneasy about what he had said about his wife. He couldn't help thinking of the worse when he interpreted what resting peacefully meant in Chinese was to him. He shook his head in an attempt to clear it from the bad thoughts that was beginning to dominate it.

He quickened his pace slightly and concentrated on the task on hand which was to get to the temple before it got too dark. Walking too quickly along the narrow path in the dark was not something that should have been taken lightly as Khong had discovered a few minutes later. His foot tripped on a protruding root of a tree which caused him to fall flat on his face. Fortunately for him nothing serious befell him. After picking himself up from the dirt-track and after flicking the dirt off his clothes, Khong took a slower pace and paid more attention to where he was going instead of thinking of wild thoughts.

Khong, like many of his fellow countrymen, was a very superstitious man who was contented to accept instead of questioning the logic of the numerous beliefs they've held dearly from time immemorial.

After he had found himself going practically in a circle, Khong approached a small hut on his right he had seen with its light on, and asked its occupant for the location of the temple. Its occupant, a kindly Old Man, who was about Khong's age, gave Khong the direction to the temple. Khong thanked him and was about to walk in the direction indicated when the Old Man suddenly asked him to wait. Khong waited as he watched the man disappear out of sight behind the open door. A few moments later he reappeared with a glass of water in his hand which he silently handed to Khong. Khong drank thirstily, emptying the glass in no time at all. He thanked the man once more as he handed him the empty glass.

And after having walked for nearly thirty minutes through a gully covered with bracken on either side of the path and then up a steep slope until he reached a clearing, and, like the Old Man had said, he finally sighted the temple's lights in the distance.

Khong had to walk for nearly thirty minutes more before the temple's roof line became visible. And even though he was tired and hungry, his spirit was somehow uplifted by its sight.

Seeing that he had almost reached his destination Khong decided to take a short break before continuing. As he sat on the hard ground, the faint twinkling lights in the distance had a mesmerising effect on him; they seemed to beckon to him. Khong decided to cut short his rest and began to walk briskly towards the temple. A few minutes later the faint outline of the temple's traditional roof loomed against the now clear moonlit sky, he knew he had arrived. Nothing could be so welcoming to him or so familiar.

Khong stopped momentarily at the bottom of the temple's steps to catch his breath. He had never felt so tired and so hungry before. He felt as if he could eat a whole hog all by himself. He cursed himself for not thinking of getting something to eat while he was in the town. And now seeing how late it was, he had grave doubts about his luck at getting anything to eat in the temple at this hour.

Khong walked up the steps toward the entrance hall and tried the door and was relieved to find it unlocked. Once inside, he was assailed by the familiar smell of burning joss sticks and the dankness synonymous with temples in general. The generally busy main hall was empty at that hour as he had expected, not even a caretaker was in sight. He put some coins in the box and took out some joss sticks from the tin next to it and began lighting them. He place them in an empty spot in front of the altar and began to pray. He prayed for the recovery of his wife and for a good fortune to befall them.

Khong couldn't help thinking about what the Bomoh had said about the feeling he had had about his wife resting peacefully. Khong wanted to interpret it as a good omen and that she was getting better. Still, the uneasy feeling had persisted.

Khong was momentarily startled by a rustling sound behind him. He quickly turned around and found himself face to face with a priest whose shaven head glistened under the single overhead electric lantern.

Khong flinched involuntarily when his eyes began to focus on the priest's entire face. He was young, perhaps in his late-twenties, but in all Khong's life he had never seen a harelip that severe on a person before. It looked as if the young priest's lower part of the face had been torn in half. The effect the resultant shadows the overhead light gave, compounded by the temple's grim surrounding, gave the young priest a look that was quite frightening indeed. To those who had a weak heart, the shock of being confronted by such a sight might be fatal.

"Please forgive me if I'm intruding," Khong said. He gave a slight bow to the young priest hoping that by doing so the other would forgive him for his unintended rudeness by staring.

The priest looked at him but said nothing. The overhead lantern projected bizarre patterns around the two men and on the cement floor, as it swayed slowly in the breeze.

"I realize it is late," Khong continued, "but would it be possible for me to spend the night here?"

"Certainly," said the young priest, lisping pronouncedly. "Please follow me."

Without further ado he strode out of the main hall followed by Khong. As they walked towards the back of the temple, he couldn't help noticing the young priest's gait. If he hadn't seen the priest at close range, he could've sworn that the young priest was a woman.

The room he was taken to had no other furniture except for a raised wooden platform which was placed in a corner. There was no mattress on it, but a pillow was placed at the top end against the wall. Down by its foot was a folded blood-red blanket. The Old Man was in two minds about asking the young priest for some food, thinking that it would be a bit much to impose further on the temple's generosity. In the end he decided against it and began to prepare for bed.

As soon as the young priest had left, Khong, not wanting his shirt and trousers creased, removed them and hung them on nails that studded the unpainted cement walls. Wearing only his singlet and underwear, he laid underneath the blanket on the wooden platform, acutely aware how cold it was. Even though the blanket felt rough to his skin, and its smell none too kind to his nostrils, he was nevertheless grateful for it. He had never been up these mountains before, he didn't know that the temperatures could plunge several degrees at night. Despite the blanket, he could still feel the cold in his bones. He wanted to put his clothes back on in order to keep warm but that would mean that he'd have to wear them crumpled the next day and that would be something he'd hate, so he didn't.

The British, who colonised the country before it gained its independence on 31st August 1957, had houses built up on these hills complete with fireplaces in them. And in some cases their architecture resembled those they had in England.

One can imagine the master of the house, attired in his smoking jacket, sitting in his winged chair, puffing away at a pipe while reading an old copy of *The Times*. On the wine table next to him, probably, was a glass of his favourite sherry. His wife, also attired in the current fashion of the day and similarly with a glass of sherry next to her, sat opposite her husband near the fireplace, probably knitting a jumper. A son and a daughter would probably occupy a room each upstairs, while their amah would lie in her cot, shivering slightly, in a back room behind their kitchen. Her husband - the family's chauffeur and gardener - would lie next to her and he too would be shivering slightly. All they had for blanket was their traditional sarongs - not quite suitable for chilly nights on these hills.

Despite hunger gnawing at his stomach, Khong, after tossing and turning several times in a futile attempt to try to make himself comfortable, fell into a deep sleep: the resultant effect of the ravages of a long hard day on his tired old body.

The next day Khong, up at the crack of dawn, anxious to have an early start, was surprised to find at least half a dozen men ahead of him in a queue in front of the solitary bathroom. Breakfast consisting of porridge and some vegetables were served. It was cheap compared to outside according to Khong's reckoning, and he was wondering how they had managed to do that. As if reading his thoughts, the young priest with the harelip, who was making his rounds, stopped at Khong's table. "We grow all that we eat, except for the rice," he said. "Rice don't seem to grow well at this altitude." He faced cracked wide open in his attempt to smile. Khong who remembered his mistake last night, smiled in return.

"The food is very good," he said. "And thank you for letting me stay here last night."

"You are most welcome," said the priest. "Well I must continue with my work, enjoy your stay."

"I must leave for home this morning, my wife is very ill. I came here to seek the help of a Bomoh who was recommended to me and he had given me something for my wife. I must get home as quickly as I can."

"A Malay Bomoh?" asked the priest, lisping more pronouncedly.

Khong, although taken aback by the severity of the of the manner the other had asked the question, replied calmly,

"Yes, a Malay Bomoh."

"Do you believe in all that mumbo-jumbo?"

"I think they might think the same of our medicine-men....I don't know," said Khong. "But I'd like to believe that this particular Bomoh can cure my wife. He had been highly recommended to me, our traditional medicine men can't seem to cure her, nor did any of the regular doctors."

"Well, good luck to you then!" Without saying another word, the priest stormed out of the tiny dining room leaving Khong utterly confused.

ᚾᚲᚾᚲᚾᚲ

CHAPTER
TWENTY-ONE

Khong knew something was wrong as soon as he got off at the bus-stop not far from his house. People he knew, as well those he didn't, kept staring at him as he walked towards his house. He wanted to ask them what was the matter, but something in the manner they had looked at him held him back. As he walked past them, some inexplicable fear began to permeate through his whole body, he quickened his pace. On reaching the top of the slope which overlooked his house, he was shocked to see a number of people gathering about in his front porch. Without realizing it he found himself running down the sloping path. He nearly stumbled when he stepped on a slippery algae which had formed on the mud track. He averted what could have been an embarrassing sight by grabbing on to the wooden railing he had erected just for the purpose. Having recovered quickly, Khong walked briskly over the small bridge towards the sombre-looking group of people who were standing awkwardly outside his front door.

Inside his living room he found more people but no one spoke to him. They averted their eyes whenever he looked in their direction. He knew then that his worst fears were realised. He knew that his wife was already dead. All of a sudden he remembered the words of the Bomoh..."I felt that your wife is resting peacefully". Khong, his feet felt as if they were suddenly made of lead, walked slowly towards their bedroom. Mandy, who was bending over her grandmother's inert body, turned her head when she heard whisperings behind her. When she heard someone mentioned her grandfather's name, she ran towards the door him and into his arms, sobbing uncontrollably.

Crying was something Mandy had rarely done, even as a child, but at that moment all her inhibition seemed to have abandoned her and she was wailing like a child. At that moment, even her grandfather was startled by the intensity of her crying. He, like the rest of his family, had never seen Mandy cry before. It seemed that the floodgate had opened up and all Mandy's pent-up emotion came gushing out by the loss of her grandmother whom she really adored.

Khong could still remember the day when his daughter had gone berserk and began beating Mandy with a bamboo pole until it split into two. He was working in his garden at the time when he heard his daughter screaming at Mandy. When he reached the scene, he was fortunately in time to stop his daughter from hitting Mandy with a piece of the split bamboo pole, which would have caused

Mandy great injury and maybe her death. He had no doubt that the sharp edges of the bamboo would've have cut into her like a knife. Seeing what his own daughter was about to do to Mandy, Khong, for the first time in his life, hit his daughter. The blow on the side of her head had rendered her unconscious. But before she passed out he saw for a split-second, the surprise look on his daughter's face. Mandy on the other hand showed no emotion at all, and despite the horrific beating she had received from her mother, she'd refused to shed even a tear.

One or two people who had been crowding near the bed moved quietly back to make way for Mandy and her grandfather as they approached. Khong had asked when his wife had died. Ah Meng, his closest friend, told him that his wife probably had died in her sleep sometime between five and five-thirty yesterday afternoon. Khong figured that it was approximately the time he arrived in Cameron Highlands.

As he gazed at her inert body on their bed, Khong couldn't help wondering whether the Bomoh had known that his wife was already dead when he made that remark about her resting peacefully.

According to his grandson Mark, he saw her still alive at five when he went in to check on her, but when he went back at about half-an-hour later, he saw her arm dangling lifelessly from her bed and onto the floor. Sensing that something was wrong, he went to the kitchen to call his mother, moments later her loud wail brought in their closest neighbours.

The ensuing commotion told Mark what he didn't want to know, that his grandmother was dead. He had never seen anyone die before and he didn't know what to do. The feeling he felt was something alien to him. It felt like someone had just dealt a heavy blow to his insides with a sledgehammer; it wasn't as if he was hurt or anything, but the pain was there all the same. Unlike Mandy, Mark was known as a cry baby. At that moment the tears seemed to come in torrents.

Although crying was not a new experience to him - he remembered doing that all the time, and he knew about the nickname they had given him, what he couldn't explain was the intangible loss he suddenly felt before the tears came. Mandy's youngest brother, Luke, was in school when he heard the news. He too had cried shamelessly when told by his sports teacher that his grandmother had passed away. It was during his badminton practice when the teacher gave him the bad news. Mumbling his request to be excused, and still in his badminton outfit, Luke ran all the way home. Like his brother Mark, he too was crying uncontrollably, but unlike his brother he didn't cry easily.

Luke tried to console himself by repeating over and over again that his grandmother had died because she was already quite old. "Death is inevitable," he mumbled to himself, repeating what his best friend had said to him "Everyone dies, it was just a matter of time, something that can't be avoided, so what was the point of grieving unnecessarily," his friend had added. That cool logic made Luke stop crying rather abruptly but not his determination to get home as quickly as possible. The funeral was a grand affair complete with a band, and it had a long procession including a dozen or so hired mourners. And following the cortege were a number of cars filled with people suitably attired for the occasion. In front of the gleaming hearse, which belonged to the nearby funeral parlour, were people directing traffic while behind them walked sombre-looking men in white robes, pushing carts of effigies, lanterns, and other paraphernalia deemed necessary for the deceased's own use in the next world.

As the hearse meandered through the winding hill towards the cemetery, its occupants, with the exception of Ah Chew their next-door neighbour, consisted of only the immediate family. Mandy sat next to her grandfather on his right, while Ah Chew sat next to her. On the bench seat opposite her sat her mother and her two brothers. None of them spoke, all they did was to stare unseeingly at the coffin in front of them, and with the exception of Khong, all were sobbing incessantly. Although he have loved his wife, Khong refused to cry for her. He felt that under the circumstances he should show some strength.

For some inexplicable reason, and as if on cue, all those who were crying suddenly stopped their crying when the hearse came to a stop at the gate of the cemetery. But as soon at the coffin was lowed onto the shoulders of the waiting pall-bearers, the crying by the immediate family immediately resumed, this time they were joined by the paid criers, as they followed the coffin on foot to the grave site.

At that time, apart from her brother Mark, who worked as a part-time waiter at a restaurant near their house, Mandy was main breadwinner for the whole family. She had worked as a Sales Assistant in one of the hotels along Penang's famed Batu Ferringhi coast. Her take-home pay then was three hundred and fifty ringgit per month.

Despite the Malaysian government's brave efforts to try to curb inflation with their on-going zero inflation campaign, three hundred and fifty ringgit per month, after deducting her own expenses such as lunch and bus fares, weren't nearly enough to feed and to clothe her mother and her two brothers.

Khong, determined not to let Mandy shoulder the burden of trying to support the family on her own, managed to contribute something by growing some vegetables and rearing some chicken for their eggs and meat. He would sell the eggs and vegetables and with the occasionally live chicken or two, to the same provision shop his family buy their foodstuff from. Each month Khong managed to get approximately the same amount Mandy earned as a salesgirl.

Although small in size, the plot of land behind their two houses was utilised at its optimum. The chicken droppings provided Khong all the manure he needed for his vegetables, while the scraps from the kitchen mixed with some cereals he purchased from the same provision shop, provided food for the chicken. Occasionally he'd let his family have a chicken or two, especially during the festive season. Most days rice with some eggs and vegetables with an occasional fish would be their staple diet.

During the time Mandy worked at that hotel's shop, she had met a number of people who passed through the shop. Most of those who came to her shop were foreign tourists who came either to buy souvenirs. Some who came were rich while some were neither rich nor poor; most will not return to her shop again because next year they would probably be somewhere else or at home dreaming of another vacation in not a too distant future.

There was one exception however. His name was Wong and he wasn't a tourist. And he had always made a point of coming in to see Mandy whenever he was in Penang which was often, and according to him he always stay at the hotel. Each time he came to stay at the hotel he always made a point of looking up Mandy. The first time they met, he had introduced himself as a businessman from Singapore. On that day he had asked for Mandy's recommendation on a present he intended to buy for a client of his. Mandy asked him a few pertinent questions about his client's taste and so on. Finally she showed him a few items which she thought would be ideal for the person and for the occasion he had mentioned. After spending a small fortune on the items he had finally chosen, Wong left looking quite pleased with what he had purchased while Mandy was extremely pleased with her commission. On his second visit the following week, Wong gave her a small present saying that it was a token of his appreciation for Mandy for helping him choose the presents his clients really like.

When Wong came for the third time a month later, he asked Mandy to have dinner with him. Mandy politely refused him by saying that she had to work nights all that week. Undeterred, during his next visit to Penang Wong asked her out again, and like before Mandy had declined his invitation by giving him another excuse.

After numerous attempts to get Mandy to go out with him had failed, Wong finally decided to give up on her. However, on his next trip to Penang and as soon he saw Mandy walking in the hotel lobby, his resolve not to see her again suddenly disappeared. He told himself that this will be the last time. Perhaps what he meant to say was that it'll be the last time he was going to humiliate himself and to be rebuffed, but to his surprise Mandy agreed to have dinner with him.

Over dinner Wong told Mandy that he owned a number of race horses and whenever the Penang races were on, he normally would have one or more of his horses racing in them, thus the reason for his frequent trips to Penang. He added that not only he raced his horses in Penang but also in the other parts of the country too, and of course in Singapore, where he came from. That night he told her a little bit about the horse racing business.

"That's right," he told Mandy. "Horse racing is not a sport, but a business. And like any other business, I have to look after every aspect of it. But sometimes I personally can't look after everything, so I hire people to do all kinds of things for me. I pay them of course, and handsomely, I might add. Take the jockeys for instance, I pay them to ride my horses and if they win, they get a percentage of the prize-money. The horses and the jockeys, being animals and not machines, tend to perform depending of their forms, moods, bio-rhythms and what have you. As far as the horses are concerned, I let my syce exercise, groom and feed them. On the top of that, I also have vets to check on their health. However, when it comes to the jockeys, I find that it's a different kettle of fish altogether. I have very little control of, and those are the jockeys. I'm not saying that all jockeys are the same, but there those that require to be taken care of in a special way before they can function at their optimum. They need nurse maids so to speak, to pamper their egos, laugh at their jokes, and most important of all to keep them company prior to the races, out of harm's way from over-anxious or over-zealous punters or bookies. So, I have a proposition for you - how would you like working for me. I'll pay you two thousand ringgit per month plus bonuses if the horses win. All you have to do is to look after my jockeys for me. I'll pay for the plane tickets, the hotel bills and other expenses, all you have to do is to keep my jockeys company. You like to go to discos, don't you? and you like to eat in fancy restaurants? Well, I assure you, you'll like this job."

"Do I have to sleep with them too?" Mandy asked, jokingly.

"No, not necessarily," replied Wong, his tone was serious. "Some of the jockeys are libidinous people and maybe, just maybe, you may have to, sometimes. Although most of them will refrain from having sex prior to the races, believing that it might hamper their performance during the race."

"Thank you very much for dinner," replied Mandy. "But no thanks for your other offer." Before they parted company, Wong gave her his business card and this parting shot. "Call me if you change your mind."

On the day of her grandmother's death, little did she realize that she would be forced to embark on a journey that will take her into the heart of the sordid world of horse racing when she picked up the telephone to call Wong. Mandy asked him whether his offer of a job still stood. He had quickly replied that the job was hers if she wanted it. She told him that she'll take up his offer provided he would send her some money immediately. She told him of her grandmother's death and that she needed the money for her funeral. Although she didn't specify the amount she needed, she was amazed to find six thousand ringgit in her savings bank account less than three hours later. She telephoned to say that the money had arrived and to thank him. He replied by saying that he expected her in Singapore soon and hung up. Mandy stared at the dead receiver filled with foreboding.

Needless to say, an appropriate amount of money in the hands of the funeral directors went a long way to make Mandy's grandmother's funeral one that their small community wouldn't soon forget. At the end of the day, everyone without exception agreed that it was a beautiful funeral.

Two days after the funeral, a courier came to Mandy's place of work and handed her an envelope containing an air-ticket, some money and a note from Wong telling her to come to Singapore the following day. The same night she told her family that she had been offered a job to work in a restaurant in Singapore and that she'll be leaving the next day.

Mandy didn't care one way or another about lying to her mother nor to her two brothers, but she felt very badly when she had to lie to her grandfather. She had always respected him and had never failed to be there for her when she had needed him. He had been her pillar of strength, someone she had looked up to and someone to go to whenever she was troubled. And now more than ever she had wanted to tell her grandfather the deal she had made with Wong and the bad feelings she had not only about the job but about Wong too. She could always remember that during the bleak days when she was younger, when her mother used to think that she was nothing but a nuisance, just another mouth to feed, Khong had assured her she wasn't a nuisance but someone special.

Mandy had found her grandfather a source of comfort. Her cares as well as her pain seemed to disappear at the stroke of his touch. She could count on him to be there to apply some soothing balm on her bruises whether she got a beating from her mother, or when she had hurt herself falling off her bicycle. He was a man of few words but his actions spoke volumes of his affection for her.

She could remember the time when her mother, in one of her darkest moods, had her chained up like a dog, and even though her grandfather didn't dare go against his high-strung daughter, he would hover around her, smuggling bits of food and drink to her.

Even when she was growing up, she would have nightmares of being all chained up and rats were running all around her, some gnawing at her toes and flesh. She would wake up screaming, loud enough for her grandfather, who lived next door, to come running to her bedside to comfort her until she fell asleep again while her mother who was sleeping in the room next to hers slept unperturbed.

Mandy was thankful not only for the comfort her grandfather had given her but his presence had many times prevented further abuse from her mother for the slightest mischief. Mandy could never forget nor forgive her mother for what she had done to her, and that it only her grandfather's presence that had made it bearable for her. Mandy felt terribly sad because she couldn't tell her grandfather that she wasn't really going to Singapore to work in a restaurant but to work for a rich horse-owner to baby-sit his many jockeys.

CHAPTER TWENTY-TWO

On the plane Mandy's most inner thoughts seemed to emanate from what someone sitting in the seat in front of her had said. It was exactly what James had said to her a few days ago when she went to see him even though she had made it look like a chance meeting at the Yaohan Book Store. She had gone to see him at his food stall, but having been told by his workers that he had just left, she looked for him among the crowd in the concourse area. After a fruitless search that took her to the other end of the building, she saw him walking towards the book store. She walked as fast as she could without causing any attention until she overtook him without him seeing her. When she was sure he was going into the book shop, she went in and pretended to look at some books near to where James was standing. Mandy had wanted to ask him about Singapore since she remembered him telling her that he had lived there for a number of years. Her real reason for seeing him was to ask his opinion about what she should look out for when dealing with people like Wong.

Even though she hardly knew James, Mandy felt that she could trust him, besides, she had no one else she could confide in except her grandfather. She didn't want her grandfather to know what she was planning on doing, it would only upset him.

Outside the plane's window, the clouds seemed to be dispersing, giving Mandy a clear view of the coastline of Peninsular Malaysia and the Straits of Malacca. She dug into the back-pocket of the seat in front of her for the airline's in-flight magazine and quickly turned to the map of Malaysia. She looked at the map and then at the coastline down below, to see whether she could locate where they were. Unfortunately the plane flew into a rather thick cloud and the view below was obliterated completely. Mandy waited to see if would clear but an announcement heard over the overhead speaker system told everyone that the plane was about to encounter a slight turbulence and had asked everyone to return to their seat and to fasten their seat belt. Moments later Mandy felt a swaying of the plane followed by some bumpiness which lasted for several minutes. Although she had never flown in an aeroplane before and had never known what an air turbulence was, Mandy felt not the least afraid, while the passenger next to her looked to her as if she was in a state of panic.

"What's happening?...What's happening?" she uttered, looking at Mandy, panic was written all over her face.

Mandy tried to comfort her by telling that everything was going to be all right. The woman, who may be about thirty-something years old, suddenly grabbed hold of Mandy's left hand and held on to it until the plane finally flew normally again about a minute or two later. When the woman realised that, she let go of Mandy's hands as if she has accidentally touched some nasty thing. "Sorry," she said, retreating to her seat.

Mandy simply nodded at her and return to look outside her window as her thoughts took her back to the wonderful day she and James had spent together. Despite their age difference she had found him interesting to be with. She had enjoyed the afternoon they spent at his flat listening to his large collection of classical music and the conversation they had.

He remembered that she was quite apprehensive at first when he said that he had to go his flat first to change his shoes. The heel of one of his shoes had broken off when he accidentally stepped and slipped on a rock while they were walking towards his car in the car park.

When they arrived there she suddenly became afraid to go up with him to his flat. James must have noticed that she was hesitant because she remembered him telling her that all he wanted to do was to change his pair of shoes and he didn't want to leave her alone in the car in the car park that was quite deserted during that time of the day.

She relented and went up to his flat with him. Her fears were soon dispelled when she found him to be a perfect gentleman.

That afternoon as they sat listening to music and talked, she felt comfortable with him. Unlike the boys she had gone out with, James didn't try to get fresh with her.

That night they had dinner together at a Thai restaurant and when James sent her home, he didn't look disappointed or surprised to see that her house was nothing more than a wooden shack with corrugated zinc roof.

Mandy's reverie was interrupted when she suddenly became aware that someone was staring at her. She turned her head from the window just as a man resembling her uncle Eddy walked briskly away towards the rear of the aircraft. Even though Mandy only managed to see the back of the man's head, she was sure it her uncle she had seen and she began to tremble uncontrollably. This time it was the woman sitting next to her who held her hands and tried to calm her down.

A flash-back took her to that horrible day, when she was about fourteen years old, when she woke up from a nap and found her uncle sitting on her bed. He was her mother's older brother by about two years and he was fanning her face with what looked like a small shopping bag. She sleepily rubbed her eyes, trying to get them to focus. When she opened them again, she saw him smiling at her.

As soon as he saw that she was fully awake, he dug into the shopping bag and took out a number of different coloured, skimpiest panties she had ever seen. He handed them to her one at a time, telling her that they were presents from him. He then suggested to her to try them on for size.

Still groggy from sleep Mandy could only stare at her uncle, feeling quite confused as what she should do. She had always liked this uncle of hers - her only one - and had on a number of occasions rough-horsed it with him in mock wrestling matches, or had played catching with him when she was little. She remembered when she was about twelve years old when she stopped playing with him because he always ended up on the top of her, or his hands would end up between her legs. And whenever he saw an opportunity during these games, he would give her kisses on her cheeks. At first she didn't mind it very much, but when he started to kiss her on the mouth, or when his hands began ending up under her panties, she stopped playing with him altogether. When on his next visit to their house he somehow managed to cajole Mandy into playing what she thought was a silly game of hide-and-seek. And Mandy wasn't really in the mood to play the game properly so she deliberately allowed herself to be caught, thinking that by doing so she could go on with what she was doing before her uncle so rudely interrupted her.

Mandy got a shock of her life when he suddenly grabbed her by the shoulders and planted his lips on hers. Caught by surprise Mandy could do nothing except to try to fight him off, but he was strong. Helplessly she endured it. When he finally let her go, she shouted abuses at him and threatened to tell her mother about what he had just done. He quickly left the house and from that day onwards he never came near her again.

Now facing him again, all alone in her bedroom, Mandy was more frightened than she had ever been. She tried to get out of bed but before she could do anything he put both hands on her shoulders and forced her back on the bed.

"Go on. Try them on," he said, referring to the panties. When he saw that Mandy was not making any move, he lifted up her night dress and with both hands began to tug at the elastic band of her briefs. She tried to stop him, but his action was quick, and before she realised it, he had deftly removed her panties and was picking up one of the new ones lying on the bed and held them up one by one for her to see.

"Here! Try this one on first," he said. He handed her a red-coloured one. Hesitantly Mandy took it from his hand and was about to put it on when she felt her sex was being spread apart, and to her horror she saw her uncle was kissing her there. She screamed on the top of her voice, and tried to kick him off her with both legs. Being almost twice her size, once again she felt helpless. She screamed on the top of her voice for her mother but no one came. She couldn't understand why her mother wouldn't come to her aid! She knew that her mother was home before she decided to take her nap. "Help mother! Help!" she kept on screaming.

Unknown to Mandy, her mother had earlier consented to her brother's request to have sex with Mandy for five hundred ringgit, and had made sure that they'll both be alone! She had deliberately gone to play Mahjong in one of the neighbour's house. Although the house was some distance away she could still hear her daughter's muffled voice call out for her. She pretended not to hear her and went on with her game. After a few moments she felt relieved when she heard no more cries from her house.

Meanwhile in their house her brother had managed to stop Mandy from crying out by clamping his hand on her mouth. During the struggle, the clasp from the strap of his stainless steel watch cut deeply into Mandy's right cheekbone. Despite the bleeding and the pain he must have known he was inflicting on his niece, he roughly rammed his member into her without mercy, avoiding looking into her terrified eyes. Determined to get his five hundred ringgit's worth, he plunged in and out of her relentlessly, ceasing only after he had unloaded his sperm in her. After a while he got off Mandy to put his pants on and left, leaving her sobbing and bleeding on the bed.

The hurt she felt was not only physical but mentally as well, unable to comprehend what was happening. She couldn't understand why her uncle, who had been like a father to her, could do such a horrible thing to her.

When Mandy finally managed to drag herself to Ah Chew's house next to theirs, she found her mother playing Mahjong with Ah Chew and two other ladies from their neighbourhood. Her mother, who had a cigarette in her mouth, was busy rearranging her Mahjong tiles together with the other ladies. Since she had her back towards the door, she could not see her daughter when she stumbled into the room.

Ah Chew, who was sitting facing the door, gave out an involuntary gasp the moment she saw Mandy. The other two ladies too turned their heads and were horrified to see Mandy in such a bloody mess. Blood was trickling down from the wound on her chin and her night dress, torn in places, was soaked in blood. Mandy's mother on the other hand seemed unperturbed by what was happening and seemed to be in deep concentration with the task of arranging her Mahjong tiles.

"Ma! *Kow Foo* did something bad to me!" Mandy told her mother and her three Mahjong companions. Ah Chew had rushed towards Mandy and led her to her sofa. She asked one of the two other ladies to go to her kitchen to bring her a bowl of water while the other was told to look for a small towel in her cupboard in her bedroom. When she had cleaned Mandy up, Chew asked her to tell them what had happened. Mandy, by this time had stopped crying, related to them how her uncle had raped her.

When she finished telling them, Mandy couldn't believe her ears when all her mother said to her was, "Don't be such a baby, these things happen to women." She seemed not to notice that her daughter was still bleeding from her cheek and that her white night dress was bloodied. Even if she did, she chose to ignore it and kept on rearranging the position of her Mahjong tiles.

Ah Chew told one of the two ladies to fetch fresh clothes for Mandy to wear from her house while she led Mandy to her bathroom to clean bathe her. When they finally came out of the bathroom, Ah Chew gave Mandy's mother such a hard stare. Shirley quickly turned her head away and pretended to concentrate on her Mahjong tiles in front of her. Ah Chew's other friend suggested calling the police but had immediately clamped up when Mandy's mother gave her a cold stare. The mere mention of the police made everybody in the room look at each other uncomfortably. Even Ah Chew avoided looking at Mandy again or her mother. All of a sudden everyone seemed anxious to continue with their game of Mahjong.

Mandy stood there and stared at the people she had known all her life, expecting some kind of action or at least some words of sympathy. Instead, all of them turned their backs on her, and, in an embarrassed silence look at the piles of Mahjong tiles in front of them and pretending as if nothing had happened. Mandy turned her back towards them and shuffled towards the door. As she stepped out of it, she heard her mother called out to her to put a plaster on the cut on her chin. Moments later and amidst the familiar sound of Mahjong tiles being shuffled, Mandy, with tears streaming down her face, staggered back to her house.

Back in the house, and while searching for some piece of plaster to put on the cut on her chin, Mandy saw what looked like new notes sticking out of her mother's purse. Out of curiosity she opened it and was surprised to find five crispy hundred-ringgit notes in it. Five hundred ringgit! Where did they come from? She knew the money wasn't there the night before. She remembered that she had gone to get some money for her mother last night and was sure that the money wasn't there. All her mother had then was about forty-three ringgit and some loose change. She remembered taking the three ringgit to give the bread-man for the loaf of bread her mother had bought and had pocketed the seventy-cent change.

Mandy quickly dug into her mother's purse. All she could find was some coins but the forty ringgit was gone. She reckoned that her mother must have taken that this morning to play Mahjong with. So where did the five hundred ringgit come from?

Mandy slumped onto her bed when realization hit her. The money could only have come from her uncle and no one else! He must have given the money to her this morning. She knew then that her mother had sold her virginity to her uncle. That could've explained why he wasn't the least bit afraid when he raped her; he had his sister's consent. What's more, he had paid her with hard cash.

Mandy slumped onto her bed and began to sob uncontrollably.

"Akong! *Po-Po!* Come help me!" she wailed, but she knew that they will not come to her aid. Early yesterday morning her grandfather and grandmother had left for Medan in Indonesia to visit some relatives there. She was sure that, had they been around, neither her mother nor her uncle would have dared do what they done to her.

After patching up her chin as best as she could, Mandy decided to take a bath. On returning to her bedroom she was startled to find her mother sitting on the edge of her bed. Apparently she had come in while Mandy was in the bathroom and had made up the bed - something she hadn't done for Mandy for a long time.

She looked nervous and avoided her daughter's eyes. She cowered slightly in her seat when Mandy strode towards the bedside table near her to pick out a pair of her own panties. The panties that her uncle had brought her seemed to have been neatly folded and were placed on her dressing table in the corner of her bedroom. Her mother stood up and moved out of Mandy's way when Mandy angrily yanked out the drawer and spilled its content onto the floor.

"I've taken only one hundred ringgit from the drawer, the four hundred is for you," her mother said, hoping that the money would smooth things over. "Your uncle told me how the metal strap of his watch cut your chin....he said he's sorry about it."

"He's sorry for the cut on my chin, mother? Or is he sorry for raping me?" Mandy screamed at her mother who was beginning to lose some of her self-assurance. Mandy, who had all her life been intimidated by her mother, suddenly felt, for the first time, unafraid of her.

"Come on! What's the big deal?" Her mother had replied. You have to lose your virginity some time anyway! Why not give it to someone you know. Someone who loves you."

"Someone who loves me?" Mandy lunged at her mother who toppled back onto the bed. "You called a man who raped you...cut up your face...terrorised you, someone who acted with love in his heart? He's worse than an animal, mother, and you know the sad part about it? He is your flesh and blood, which disgustingly made it mine too! I wish I can drain all my blood and replace it with someone else's. I feel dirty and contaminated."

"Don't say that!" Her mother responded needlessly. "He has been good to all of us. He has help us financially all these years." She looked at Mandy, her eyes imploring for understanding. Mandy glared at her.

"It hasn't been easy for me, you know... bringing up three children all by myself.... Your no good father had never lifted a finger to help us. Your uncle was the one who has helped us all these years. So when he asked me whether he could have sex with you, I gave him a tight slap. But he told me all he wanted was your virginity, that's all...one time. He believes that virgins could make him young again...."

Mandy looked at the pathetic figure of her mother and said, "So, it was payback time, was it? And you sacrificed me. How kind of you, mother."

"Come on! Please don't say that.," her mother implored. Her composure gone, she was practically begging for her daughter's understanding as she watched Mandy dress and pack at the same time, tossing whatever meagre clothes that she had into a small plastic bag.

Once dressed, Mandy looked down at her mother with disgust. She stuck out her hand and demanded, "Hand me the other hundred ringgit. It was my virginity that he took from me, so I've earned every penny of it". Judging from the angry look on her daughter's face, she quickly dipped her hand into the pocket of her samfoo and took out the hundred-ringgit note and handed it to Mandy.

"From now on, mother, you can ask your precious brother to look after you. Unfortunately you are no longer a virgin so you have nothing to bargain with." Mandy picked up her plastic bag and stormed out of the room.

"Mandy, where are you going? Please come back...let's talk...." Her mother ran after her but stopped abruptly when Many stopped at the front door and turned to look at her. The look she gave her mother spoke volumes of her hatred for her.

Mandy spent that night in a friend's house, but unfortunately she had to leave the very next day, when her friend and her parents left for their vacation.

Mandy telephoned another school friend and asked her whether she could come and visit. Her friend who had found the school holiday a bit boring was delighted that Mandy had called and invited her over to stay the night. Mandy told her friend what had happened. She asked Mandy to repeat what she had told her to her grandmother with whom she was staying. Both her parents had died tragically in an automobile accident about a year earlier.

Mandy's friend's grandmother who had always liked Mandy, was happy to have her over for a few days, provided Mandy allowed her to speak with her mother. Mandy told her that they didn't have a phone but gave Ah Chew's number. A few minutes later the kind old lady, who was in her early seventies, informed Mandy that her mother had given her permission to spend a few days with them.

Unknown to Mandy, her friend's grandmother, who been a magistrate before she retired, had demanded and got the truth out of Mandy's mother. Shirley, evasive at first but like most bullies, she had decided to come clean when the old lady threatened to make a police report. In reality, the old lady had not been successful in persuading Mandy to make a police report. Initially she had agreed but had balked at the idea, saying that it would only bring disgrace to her whole family, including her grandparents whom she loved and adored. However, the former magistrate had persisted with the idea since a heinous crime had been committed. In exasperation, she finally told Mandy that she felt duty-bound to make the police report herself even if Mandy didn't want to.

Mandy felt that since she was staying with them, the least she could do was to give the idea some thought. She told her friend and her grandmother that she would give her decision after she had spoken with her grandparents when they return in a day or two.

Mandy spent the two weeks, till the end of her school holiday, with her friend and her grandmother. The former magistrate, together with her granddaughter, had accompanied Mandy home in order to let Mandy's mother know that her daughter was not alone and that she had her as a friend. She warned Mandy's mother that should anything else untoward were to happen to Mandy, she will have her to reckoned with. Mandy's mother was terrified at the prospect of spending some time in jail and had promised the former magistrate that she would take good care of Mandy from now on. Unfortunately about three years later, the old lady had suddenly died of a heart failure.

Mandy's mother, who had read about the former magistrate's untimely death in the Chinese newspaper, smiled gleefully to herself. That very night over dinner, she announced her plan about quitting her job so that she could take it easy at home. She told Mandy to quit school and to go to work. "It's about time that you support the family," she added.

Mandy had planned to tell her grandparents about the rape incident when they returned, but had changed her mind when her uncle had died in a car crash on the very day they returned home. In retrospect, what her mother and her uncle had committed was detestable, but she also realised that by telling her grandparents what they had done would not have lessened the hurt, the anger, and the humiliation that she had felt. Besides, she told herself, her uncle had already died so what was the point of telling them.

"God had punished him for what he had done to me," she said to her friend while her friend's grandmother looked at her without comment. The former magistrate was thinking about the police report regarding the accident in which an express bus had purportedly rammed into the back of Mandy's uncle's car and it had caught fire in which the body was burnt beyond recognition. Identification was made based on the car's registration number which was barely recognizable.

"Mandy, I want you to know that you are welcome to stay here whenever you want. My granddaughter Jade and I would like to ask you whether you'd like to join us on a holiday during the next school break."

"Oh, I'd like that very much. Thank you," Mandy replied excitedly. During the following three year until the old lady's death, Mandy had spent many wonderful time with Jade and her grandmother, visiting many places, not only in Malaysia but to Thailand as well. Whenever she felt like it, Mandy would spend the week-ends at their home. She'd bring her school work with her where she and Jade would complete it together.

In the beginning Mandy found their way of life alien compared to her own, but with the help of her best friend and her grandmother, she slowly began to adapt to it and was able to hold her own even among the cream of the society in which Jade's grandmother belonged to. The cut on Mandy's cheekbone left a permanent scar. Many years later James had asked her whether it bothered her and whether she'd want to have plastic surgery done to it.

"Does it bother you?" She had asked him.

"No. It doesn't bother me at all," James assured her. She gave him a searching look, her face looked grave. After a moment or two it began to soften again. Whatever she saw in his face must have convinced her that he must have meant what he had said.

"Excuse me, miss," said the air-hostess. "Will you please bring your seat back to its original upright position for the landing?"

Momentarily startled, Mandy looked at her blankly. The air-hostess repeated what she had said and even helped her to put her seat upright. Back to reality, Mandy found herself dreading the moment the plane landed. It wasn't so much the landing itself, although a week earlier she had read about a plane that had crash-landed in a fog somewhere in Tibet, it was the thought of what lies in store for her after they had landed that had caused her a great amount of anxiety and fear.

Suddenly she wished that the MAS plane she was on would crash too.

Curiously, as the plane was making its decent towards Changi Airport, Mandy suddenly thought of James and his concern when she had told him that she was going to Singapore to work in a restaurant for Wong. She had never thought that after her narrow escape from Wong's clutches, she ended up running back to him. Mandy had a dreadful feeling that she wasn't going to get away scot-free this time. She could only imagine what was in store for her but there was nothing she could do about it, she was there to fulfil an agreement she had made.

Wong was at the airport to meet her, and after he had checked her into the flat, he began to give her the rundown of what her duties were. That night he took her out to dinner after which they came to the flat and he spent the night with her. The following evening he introduced Mandy to the first of three jockeys - her charges for the duration of the Singapore Turf Club meet.

At first her job was to escort them to dinners, night-clubs or discotheques after which they would send her back to the flat where Wong was already waiting for her. After the second or the third time they had gone out, one by one they would demand sex from her. Mandy had managed to avoid having sex with any of them by telling them that she had contracted VD when she was raped at the age of fourteen. The VD part was something she'd cooked up to frighten them, but as far as Wong was concerned he always use a condom whenever he made love to her.

One day, three months later, Mandy was alone at the flat because Wong and his wife were celebrating their wedding anniversary and wasn't expected to turn up that night. She rarely had the opportunity to sleep alone except when she had her periods. Even then he wouldn't hesitate to check her himself to see if she was telling the truth. She was awaken sometime early the next morning and found Wong on the top of her. It was obvious to Mandy that he had been drinking rather heavily. When it was over she was shocked to find that he hadn't used a condom. The next day she had screamed at him and told him what he had done. For the first time Mandy saw Wong had lost his composure and had looked worried. It began to dawn on Mandy that perhaps this was the break she had been waiting for. She hurriedly put a dress on and took a taxi to the nearest police station and made a report charging Wong for rape. She knew it was risky, but for the first time she had Wong's sperm in her as prove, and as fate would have it, Wong, in an attempt to penetrate her while she was asleep, bruised her vagina. The police took her to Kandang Kerbau Hospital and gave her a thorough examination. That morning the police arrested Wong at his office and charged him with rape. He pleaded innocent and was advised by his lawyer not to pursue his line of defence when he tried to give the police his side of the story by telling them that Mandy was his mistress, implying that he had a right to what he did to her. His lawyer warned him against that kind of thinking by telling that it wouldn't wash because his jockeys would testify under oath that they were made to believe that Mandy was employed by Wong to escort them to dinners and such, and nothing more and none of them had ever slept with her. Wong had no choice but to abandon the idea and pleaded for leniency.

CHAPTER
TWENTY-THREE

TWENTY YEARS LATER

It was dusk when Elizabeth Wong walked out of the entrance of the Royal Melbourne Institute of Technology. The rain which had been falling ceaselessly for the past half-an-hour was now pouring down in torrents. She paused at the corner of LaTrobe and Swanston and craned her neck out to see if any trams were coming.

Determined not to get soaked more than necessary, Elizabeth decided to wait for her tram by standing on the on the kerb just in front of the RMIT's book shop, away from the onslaught of the rain and biting cold wind. It seemed that she wasn't alone in refusing to stand at the usual tram stop in the middle of the road and got soaked, there seemed to be others who shared the same thoughts with her.

There were of course those who had braved the elements and had stood their ground at the normal tram stop and got soaked to the skin for their trouble. Elizabeth wasn't sure whether to admire them or pity them. Five minutes later she craned her neck out in the rain once more, still no sign of her tram. A passing car, with no regards for anyone, drove through the puddle of water near the kerb and drenched everyone there. Within seconds Elizabeth felt the cold water on her legs and in her shoes and socks. She deplored having water in her shoes most; found the noise her water-logged shoes tend to make most annoying.

Elizabeth was thinking how useless the shoes from home were. They had looked so nice and stylish back home in Singapore but utterly useless in a weather like they were having in Melbourne. Her umbrella too was quite useless in the strong wind. Her small frame felt as if it was being lifted up in the air whenever a strong gust of wind blew.

Elizabeth was fiddling with her umbrella for the third time after the wind had caused it to be unfolded inside out when she realised that her tram had arrived and was about to move off. Incensed, she threw down her umbrella in the gutter and made a run for her tram, managing to catch it as it was pulling away.

Inside the tram it was crowded as usual with not a vacant seat in sight. Elizabeth moved to the centre, and as she held on to the leather strap, she glanced down at her shoes and the condition they were in. She shook her head in disgust but her thoughts were really on the umbrella she had left behind. She felt angry with herself for throwing away not some cheap imitation made in some backyard somewhere in Asia but an expensive

Australian-made umbrella she had recently bought at Myers Emporium!

It was Elizabeth Wong's first taste of winter ever, after having arrived not too long ago from a tropical Island-state Singapore. Unfortunately for her Melbourne was then experiencing one of the coldest winters on record, and the clothes that she had brought with her were not suitable for an arctic-type weather.

Elizabeth glanced at her watch, it was almost 8.00 o'clock and they were still a long way from Toorak Road. She let out an expletive in Hokkien. Realising at once what she had just uttered, Elizabeth turned around to see if anyone had heard her. Relieved to see that no one had, she moved on to the back of the tram where she found a vacant seat in the back row. She excused herself to the man sitting by the aisle and slid in and sat by the window.

Elizabeth knew that she was very late but she was hoping that her flatmate, Jennifer, would be home by now. Both she and Jennifer were expecting a new arrival from Penang whom they were hoping would take up the spare room in their three-bedroom flat. It was someone whom Jennifer's mother had recommended. They were hoping that it would be someone sensible this time and not someone like Ruby.

Ruby, who was their former flatmate, began as a diamond but turned out to be a worthless glass in the end.

They lived in a three-bedroom flat on a tree-lined street just off Toorak Road. Mrs. Ashburner, their kindly landlady, although in her sixties, was a celebrity of sorts in her neighbourhood. It happened one night when she confronted a young man who had broken into her house through her kitchen. As the story went, she had rendered the intruder unconscious by applying her combined knowledge of judo and karate on the unsuspecting young man. It seemed that when the police arrived not long after they received a call from her, they found intruder tied to a chair being fed some biscuits and coffee. Mrs. Ashburner, elegantly dressed despite the lateness of the hour, was sitting opposite him and was feeding the hapless youth biscuits and coffee like a person would to an invalid. And according to newspaper report that carried the story next day, she had just turned sixty. Mrs. Asburner had been renting out that flat of hers ever since she and her late husband bought it some thirty years earlier. Her tenants had always been Asian students who had come to Australia to study. She had often said to her family and friends that she had been lucky with them for she never had to place an advertisement whenever it became vacant. The students themselves would find their own replacements whenever they wanted to leave. It seemed that they had been doing that for over thirty years. Over the years she had befriended many of them as evidenced by the number of birthday and Christmas cards she had received. Many had paid her a visit whenever they were back in the country either on business or for pleasure. Sometimes they came on their own and at other times they'd come with their families. Most of the students considered her "Mum away from home" and to her, they'll always be her "children".

Elizabeth and Jennifer themselves had taken over the flat from two departing Malaysian students, one of whom was reading economics, while the other was doing an accountancy course. Their former flatmate, Ruby, came from Malaysia and was doing a computer science course. She was senior among the three of them as she was already there when Elizabeth and Jennifer moved in.

Both of them were fond of Ruby when they first moved into the flat. She was kind and considerate, and acted more like a big sister to them, that was before Jason had destroyed everything that was good and decent in her. Not long after their short-lived love affair broke up, Ruby became someone whose personality went through a dramatic change. She became a person neither Elizabeth nor Jennifer could live with.

One day, having met each other on the same tram home, Elizabeth and Jennifer found themselves assailed by a loud music as soon as they opened their front door. The music, as they had expected, came from Ruby's bedroom. Jennifer, who had recently found Ruby's behaviour irksome, strode quickly towards the offending bedroom but found it empty. However as she walked past their bathroom, whose door was opened, she saw a hand dangling outside the bath tub.

Gingerly, Jennifer walked in and found a stark-naked Ruby lying in the bath tub with the water up to her chin. By the look of her Jennifer was sure that Ruby was stoned out of her mind. She called out to Elizabeth who came running into the bathroom. Both tried to revive Ruby but failed, so they decided to carry their unconscious flatmate to her bedroom. Fortunately for them, Ruby, who was once quite chubby, had lost so much weight, so lifting her out of the bath tub was no trouble at all.

On reaching Ruby's bedroom they almost dropped her on the floor when they saw Mario, Ruby's current boyfriend, also in his birthday suit, doing kickboxing to the latest tune from `The New Kids On The Block'. Against the background of loud music coming from Ruby's powerful hi-fi system, Mario suddenly stopped with his kickboxing and began doing an impromptu minuet rather unsteadily with an invisible partner. Despite the fact that Elizabeth was holding Ruby by her armpits and Jennifer by her ankles, and with Ruby naked as the day she was born, Mario didn't appear to notice them at all. Unlike Ruby, he was still on his feet, but it was obvious to the two young women that he was high for he hardly paid them any attention. All he did when they brought Ruby in the room was to give them a glassy-eyed look before continuing with his mixture of kickboxing, kicking the air around him, and the minuet. Elizabeth and Jennifer however, stopped in their tracks and gawked at Mario.

Elizabeth was first to recover when she realised that Ruby's bottom was dragging on the floor. She called out to Jennifer to move on, but Jennifer seemed mesmerised by Marie's semi-erect member and didn't hear her. Elizabeth called out to Jennifer to lift Ruby up. But Jennifer, whose mouth was wide opened and still brazenly eyeballing Mario's prancing prick, only moved a few steps before stopping again. She couldn't imagine how Ruby could ever accommodate such a thing!

Jennifer who had openly admired Mario moments earlier, suddenly became uncharacteristically aggressive by telling Mario to turn off the music and to go home. Mario simply ignored them and continued with his prancing.

Despite the distraction, the duo somehow managed to get Ruby onto her bed. Angrily Jennifer strode towards the hi-fi set and turned it off. Expecting some kind of reaction from Mario, she was surprised to find him still doing his minuet with his invisible partner. His unkempt hair hung about his rather sallow face as he continued with his ridiculous dance routine, oblivious to the fact that the music had been turned off. It was obvious to Elizabeth and Jennifer that he too was stoned like Ruby, his glassy-eyed look confirmed that.

Elizabeth couldn't help examining the young man who was perhaps in his late twenties with fair complexion, tall but skinny as a rake handle, whose long blond but unkempt hair, swirled about his bearded face. Despite herself, Elizabeth's eyes kept zeroing in on his well-endowed, partially-erect member, which bounced about erotically as he moved around the room. She also noticed that he was sweating profusely, and at times his movements seemed jerky and uncoordinated.

Jennifer strode towards Mario and was about to tell him once again to go home when he suddenly keeled over and laid crumpled on the bedroom floor like a wet rag. Elizabeth who had been unashamedly ogling at Mario, let out a cry. Jennifer rushed to his side and after a glance at Mario's frightening parlour she telephoned for an ambulance.

Despite the quick arrival of the ambulance and the attempts by the paramedics to save the young man's life, Mario was pronounced dead on arrival at the hospital. Miraculously they somehow managed to save Ruby's life.

Needless to say Mrs. Ashburner, their next door neighbour and landlady was not too happy about the loud music coming from their flat. She had been ringing their telephone without success and was about to go out and tell them off when she saw Elizabeth and Jennifer walked up the path towards the main entrance of the flat block. When the music finally stopped, Mrs. Ashburner decided against confronting them this time but made a mental note to talk to them about it the next time they come to pay her their rent. Most of the time she left her tenants alone, intruding only when absolutely necessary. This time she knew she must put her foot down and talk to them about the loud music and the going-on in the flat. Other tenants in the same block of flats had already complained to her about it the noise and the loud music, and not for the first time either.

These occurrences, observed Mrs. Ashburner, seemed to happen whenever Ruby had one of her many boyfriends over. She wasn't a snoop or anything like that, but from her living room she could see clearly whoever walked past the corridor towards the girls' flat. She didn't approve of any men staying overnight in the girls' flat and she had made sure it was stipulated in their tenancy agreement.

Mrs. Ashburner didn't really want to throw all of them out of her flat because she knew that Elizabeth and Jennifer were sensible girls. As a matter fact, so was Ruby at one time before the unfortunate thing happened to her. She could still remember how well-mannered and quiet Ruby was when she first moved in. Like Elizabeth and Jennifer, she couldn't understand how a quiet, and supposedly well-brought up young lady like Ruby, who came from a well-to-do family of high-achievers, can become what she had become - a low life. In the beginning Elizabeth and Jennifer found Ruby to be a perfect flatmate. She was a quiet and studious person who did her share of the work around the flat meticulously. The three of them had prepared a workable roster in which each of them had to do their fair share of the work around the place. Ruby was the most fastidious among the three of them. For example she'd insist that each one of them should tidy up after every use of the toilet or the bathroom. To make sure nobody forgets, she taped a neatly typed reminder on the wall just above the cistern. There were other reminders, just as neatly typed, placed strategically all over the flat.

During the weekends Ruby could be seen puttering around the garden planting or replanting, or whatever people do in their gardens. Her room was as immaculate as a showroom exhibiting some *objet d'art* at Myers Emporium. She would hardly go out except with her two flatmates, either to the supermarket or for dinner in some Chinese restaurant they'd take turns in choosing.

Ruby, despised the fact that she came from a well-to-do family, was thrifty. She never fail to point out to them that it was always cheaper to eat in a group and much more fun too, than eating alone, especially in a Chinese restaurant. She would insist that each of them order a dish that they especially like with one or two other dishes extra. They'd eat all that together with rice. Occasionally if their schedule permitted, or if Elizabeth or Jennifer didn't have a date, the three of them would go to the movies together. Since Ruby had no boyfriends, she rarely went out on dates and would wait up on either Elizabeth or Jennifer if they went out on dates.

Ruby did go out once to see a play with a cousin who had stopped over on his way back to Adelaide. He was a student reading law at a university there. He had been home in Malaysia during the summer holidays and apparently was only doing his duty by dropping off some foodstuffs to Ruby given to him by Ruby's mother - his Aunt Pinkie. Due to a mixed-up travel arrangement he found himself having to spend a night in Melbourne. The three girls insisted that he'd stay the night at their place and not waste his money on a hotel bill. It seemed that his connecting flight to Adelaide was for the next morning instead of that night and unfortunately for him all other flights that day to Adelaide were fully booked.

Ruby had always liked this cousin of hers but was always too shy to make her feelings known to him. Thinking that this was an opportunity she shouldn't miss, she had asked him whether he would like to see a play with her that night. She made up a story about a girlfriend, whom she was supposed to have gone out to see the play with, who had gone down with the flu, and so she was left with an extra ticket.

Ruby was elated when he had said yes. After the show they had gone to a coffee house for supper and finally when they returned home both of them ended up in her bedroom.

After the second time they had made love, Ruby tried to persuade her cousin Jason to postpone his trip back to Adelaide. Jason told her he couldn't on account that he had already made an appointment to look at a place he was going to move to once he got back to Adelaide. "Besides, I don't have their phone number to change the appointment," he added.

Jason also told Ruby he had to move out of his old place soon because the owner had already sold it and the new owner was going to take possession of it soon.

"But don't worry," He gave her the grin that used to melt her heart. "I'll be back."

Ruby felt so happy; for the first time in her lifer she was really in love. She clung to every word Jason uttered with joy, remembering his promise to return soon. To her that was all that matters to her.

The next day, being Sunday, Jason had left before Ruby or any of the other girls were up. She felt a little hurt, but most of all, she was angry with herself for not making sure she was up early that morning.

The couple of weeks that followed transformed Ruby so much so, even her two flatmates could hardly recognize the old Ruby. "I don't believe it. She has become a completely different person. She's more cheerful, more tolerant, in fact she became more human. I think she's in love!" Jennifer told Elizabeth.

"Jason must have pushed all the right buttons!" Elizabeth said and they both sniggered.

Ruby who was in the kitchen overheard what her two flatmates had said about her but she didn't care. They are right about one thing: for the first time in her life she was in love. Jason, whom she had admired for so long was finally hers. She remembered all too clearly now how much a crush she had on him as far as she can remember. As a young girl she would dog him everywhere he went. She would volunteer, at every opportunity, to do errands for him just to be on his good side, and of course to be with him. Jason was very popular with the other girls, Ruby, being plain and slightly on the plump side, had to fight harder than the rest of them for his attention. In the end she always ended up doing all the donkey work while all the other girls were getting all his attention.

"Well, now, girls, eat your hearts out, I now have Jason all to myself and I think he loved every minute of it." Ruby looked at herself in the bathroom mirror and smiled.

Jason had telephoned soon after his arrival in Adelaide. The following weekend he had called again and they had talked for several minutes. Ruby had wanted to tell him that she loved him but held back when he kept on rambling about what a nice place his new dig was.

Ruby pressed the telephone hard against her ear so as not to miss out what Jason had to say. She would have much preferred him talk about how they had spent the wonderful evening together instead of about his new place. On the other hand, she had always loved listening to his voice, it sounded so melodious to her ears.

According to Jason his new place was a house owned by a lady and her daughter. He described how his room, which was on the first floor, overlooked a beautiful garden complete with a gazebo in it. Beside the view, the bedroom itself was enormous in size, with loads of room for him to put his hi-fi equipment and large collection of records and tapes. A far cry from the last place he had been lodging in, he had told her. He reiterated the reason why he had to leave his former place. "It was because the owner had sold it to a developer," he told Ruby. "A five-storey block of flats had been earmarked for the site," he added.

About a month later while the three flatmates were having a late supper in their kitchen, Ruby quietly told them that she was pregnant.

"My God! Ruby, are you sure?" Jennifer asked, looking at her friend across the table. An expression of shock and sheer incredulity written on her face. Elizabeth who was sitting next to her, the youngest among the three of them, said nothing as she absorbed Ruby's quiet declaration. Ruby nodded her head. "Yes, I'm sure. I'm about two weeks overdue now."

"Oh, my God!" Jennifer repeated. "What are you going to do? Do you know who the father is?" To her the last question was the most natural one to ask. She couldn't understand why her two friends looked so annoyed with her, then finally it dawned on her. "Jason, huh?" Elizabeth rolled her eyes to the ceiling.

"I don't know what to do," cried Ruby. "I told Jason about it yesterday, he said he'll think of something and had promised to call back but he never did. This morning I called him again, his landlady said he had already gone out. I left a message for him to return my call...." She began to sob uncontrollably. She took out a soggy handkerchief out of her pyjama top and blew her nose loudly.

Jennifer couldn't help thinking how anyone in this day and age could be so naive about something as old as sex. Haven't they heard of safe sex? Being the most promiscuous of the three, Jennifer would never dream of allowing any man to touch her until she was sure he was well-equipped in every sense of the word. And for her, like the old boy scout motto says, to 'Be prepared' can make love-making so much more fun; after all, she reasoned - isn't having sex a normal human function?

CHAPTER TWENTY-FOUR

Jason, as it turned out was a spineless son-of-a-bitch, who, by that time, were already being seduced not only by his good-looking but rather plump forty-two-year old landlady, but he was also servicing her eighteen-year-old daughter on the side. When Ruby told him that she was pregnant, his first thoughts were to ignore her, hoping that she and her problems will go away.

Jason told his older lover about the mess he got himself into and had asked her what should he do. She told him she would handle it and had asked him not to worry.

When Ruby telephoned again, Jason's landlady answered the phone and told Ruby that since she got herself into this mess she should get herself out of it without involving Jason. She also told Ruby not to call again as Jason was about to take his examinations soon.

Ruby, with the support of Elizabeth and her calm efficiency, combined with Jennifer's resourcefulness, managed to get her through her abortion without much difficulty. Both Elizabeth and Jennifer, with a bit of juggling on their part with regards to their tutorials and their lectures, managed to look after Ruby as best as they could.

Almost as soon as they brought Ruby home, she became morose and withdrawn. As the days went by, she became more uncommunicative, never made any demands on them nor did she ever complain. When she wasn't resting in her room, she would sit by the fire in the lounge reading or she would watch the television. She didn't seem to care very much what she was watching as long there was something on. As she began to recuperate under the care of her two friends, a change was beginning to take place in her. She had been thinking a lot of Jason lately - not the way she used to think of him, but with loathing and contempt. She felt so humiliated when she recalled how she had thrown herself at him. "It must have made me look cheap, no wonder he couldn't be bothered with me," she thought. "Well, cousin Jason, you ain't seen nothing yet!" Ruby screamed at the empty room. The first thing she did when she was up and about again was to get her long hair cut and styled by a well-known hair-stylist in the city. The next thing she did was to go shopping for the latest trend in clothing including half-a-dozen pairs of imported shoes. During the ensuing weeks, whenever Elizabeth and Jennifer came home to their flat, they were treated to not only the sights but the sounds of the new Ruby. Each day they would invariably be assailed by the loud music of

Heavy Metal coming out of her high-powered hi-fi set. Upon entering they would be struck with envy by the new clothes Ruby would be wearing. Sometimes she would parade for them one by one all her purchases, as if she were a model from the House of Dior.

Then came the men, ranging in ages from as young as eighteen, to a man who must be at least forty-five by the look of his hair, or rather lack of it. Those who came to pick her up would invariably end up staying the night. Either she was unaware or just didn't care, Ruby seemed to be oblivious to her friends' concern at her new life-style. Weekend after weekend she would have these strange creatures shacking up with her. Once her bedroom was a joy for anyone to see, now it looked like a store during its annual jumble sale - she had clothes and shoes piled up everywhere. Dirty underwear and stockings hung on the back of chairs, and wrapping papers gathered in one corner of her room and growing.

Elizabeth and Jennifer tried their best to accommodate the new Ruby hoping that it'd be just something that was temporary and in time it'd go away until one day Elizabeth had a fright of her life when one of Ruby's beau had walked into her room and tried to force himself on her. He had retreated only after she had screamed, causing both Ruby and Jennifer to rush to her aid. The man had pleaded that he had made a mistake regarding the room, which was most unlikely since Ruby's room and her room were at was at opposite end to each other. And on another occasion, it was Jennifer who felt that she was being spied on while she was in the toilet. The toilet was actually part of the bathroom divided by a wall, anybody in the bathroom next door could easily climb on the sink and peeked in the toilet. Jennifer rushed out as quickly as she possibly could and in the corridor she caught sight of Ruby's bald-headed friend as he was about to enter Ruby's bedroom.

The next day, after her beau had left the house, they dragged Ruby into the kitchen and had it out with her - no more men in the flat or out she goes! For nearly a month, their flat was like what it used to be, except that Ruby had kept herself to herself with little or no contact with either Elizabeth or Jennifer.

The only time either of them ever saw Ruby was they had to pass each other on the way to the bathroom or to bump into her in the lounge or in the kitchen. And each time she would act as if neither Elizabeth nor Jennifer were there. Nevertheless, since the place was quite small, avoiding each other completely was impossible. And so each day they would go through their silent routine of avoiding each other.

However with each passing day, Ruby's attitude towards Elizabeth and Jennifer seemed to become less and less hostile, and finally one Sunday morning she made the first move at breaking the impasse by preparing breakfast for all of them. Her two flatmates, who were her friends and had always been their friend, responded positively by cracking jokes and by behaving with jocularity like they used to do. The atmosphere in their flat became, more or less, back to normal for several weeks after that, until now....

Elizabeth reminded Jennifer what they had promised to do should Ruby reverted to her old ways again. As they struggled to lift Ruby out of the bath tub, they remained resolute in their determination to ask Ruby to leave the flat as soon as possible.

Elizabeth had for some time suspected that Ruby must be on some drugs when she saw puncture marks on her friend's arms. At first she thought that perhaps they could be just mosquito bites and had casually asked Ruby about them. Ruby snapped at her and told her to mind her own business. A few days later, as she was cleaning out their bathroom trash bin, she came across a used syringe. She told Jennifer about her find and about the conversation she had with Ruby regarding the marks she noticed on her forearms.

"I have a feeling, Jen, that Ruby may be on dope." Elizabeth said, as she showed her friend the syringe that she had found in their bathroom. "This is what I found when I cleaned out the toilet's trash bin this morning. Ruby is not diabetic or anything like that, why would she need this? Have you seen this before?"

Jennifer picked the syringe up from Elizabeth's open palm and became very alarmed. "We must confront Ruby with this syringe, Beth, and we must get to the bottom of it," she said. "If she is on dope, we must try to get her to stop using it before it's too late."

They both agreed that they have no other alternative but to confront Ruby the moment she walked in the door. If their suspicion had proved correct, then they must try to make her stop using it by resorting to desperate measures if necessary - by informing her parents.

That evening Ruby readily admitted to both of them that she was on heroin had promised that she would stop using it immediately. But like all drug users, saying they were going to kick the habit was one thing, to have the strength, and the commitment, to do it was another.

A few days later, Jennifer, who was always home before Elizabeth, found Ruby stoned out of her mind on the living room floor. Both Elizabeth and Jennifer had it out with once again, and like before Ruby gave them her solemn promise that it would never happen again. To prove her sincerity she even handed them a small sachet of white powder which Elizabeth promptly flushed down the toilet.

And now as they were witnessing more or less the repeat of Ruby's last act, they knew that it was the last straw.

The incident finally snapped the patience of their kindly landlady who felt that she had no choice but to ask the three of them to leave. However, she decided to wait until Ruby was back on her feet before taking any action. And despite her annoyance with Ruby, Mrs. Ashburner was quite glad to see that she was recovering quite well and was being well taken care of by her two friends.

About a week later, just before Mrs. Ashburner could confront them and tell them of her decision to ask them to leave, Elizabeth and Jennifer paid her a visit and told her that they had planned on asking Ruby to leave just as soon as she had fully recovered. They told Mrs. Ashburner that they were getting someone new to replace her, someone who was highly recommended by Jennifer's mother. Mrs. Ashburner, recalling how sensible these two young women were, decided to give them one more chance and allowed them to stay on.

Ruby, once she had realised how lucky she was to be alive, made a decision to leave for home as soon as she was able to. She told Elizabeth and Jennifer of her decision as soon as they got back from seeing Mrs. Ashburner. With tears in her eyes she told them how sorry she was for being such a jerk and had asked them for their forgiveness. Elizabeth and Jennifer, who earlier were bent on trying get rid of Ruby, felt like jerks themselves but managed to refrain themselves from persuading Ruby to stay on as recollection of Ruby's past promises invaded their minds. They felt that Ruby, who was still showing a mild drug withdrawal symptoms, would be better off amongst her family. A medical student friend of Jennifer told her that treatment of drug addiction was a slow, difficult and painstaking process, requiring much patience and determination, not only the addict but by those who were close to her. At home with her family members around her there was hope that Ruby would be able to kick the habit and to sort her life out. Both Elizabeth and Jennifer have met Ruby's parents when they came to visit Ruby last summer and they seemed like a nice people, who obviously love their daughter. Elizabeth and Jennifer felt confident that Ruby will get all the love and affection that she deserved and the attention she needed. Away from her family there seemed to be little hope that she'll be able to recover fully.

Elizabeth and Jennifer were both relieved and thankful that they were spared the ordeal of having to tell Ruby to leave their flat. They couldn't help thinking how things sometimes have a way of sorting themselves out. The new girl that came to view their flat, two days after Ruby had left for Malaysia, was a Malay girl who wore a *tudung* and was pursuing a course in computer science. She told Elizabeth and Jennifer that she had been sharing a flat in a suburb not far from theirs for the last two years with four other girls, but due to a misunderstanding with one of them she felt that it would be best that she moved.

"What kind of misunderstanding," asked Elizabeth who was more forward than Jennifer.

"She accused me of trying to steal her boyfriend away from her. It was ridiculous really! One day I was coming down the stairs when accidentally tripped and fell down the stairs, spraining my ankle. This girl's boyfriend who was waiting for her in the lounge helped me to my room. As he came out of my bedroom, the girl who had gone to the corner shop for some grocery happened to walked in the door and saw him. She dropped her grocery onto the floor and began screaming at her boyfriend and then at me. She accused me of doing all kinds of things with her boyfriend behind her back. It's ridiculous really because I'm already engaged to very nice Malay boy back home and we hope to get married after we both graduated in about two years' time."

"Did you explain all that to your friend?"

"Of course I did, but she didn't believe me. She continued making all these wild accusations against me. I'm up to here with her, so it's best that leave," said the girl, touching her chin with the back of her hand, her face flushed with anger. It seemed that the girl's mother and Jennifer's were classmates in their senior years in school but had lost touched with each other until recently. It came somewhat of a surprise to Jennifer that her mother had a Malay girlfriend for she couldn't recall having seen a Malay woman in her company before.

"Tell me, what is your mother's name?" Jennifer asked the girl.

"Diana is her name and my father's name is Malcolm Abdullah," she replied.

"Oh, Auntie Diana is your mother! Of course. You look a bit like her. Your father is a Mat...."

"Yes. He's a *Mat Salleh.*"

❧❧❧❧❧❧

CHAPTER TWENTY-FIVE

Elizabeth had loved Alexander the moment she had laid eyes on him. The occasion was a party given by a Malaysian businessman and his beautiful wife at their elegant home in Heidelberg, a posh suburb about thirteen kilometres from Melbourne. She had been with someone else, and so it seemed, was he. She had seen him talking to someone she knew. She excused herself from her partner and walked straight to her friend who immediately made introductions. Alexander was tall, with fair complexion and had dark-brown eyes. Although simply dressed in a sports jacket and a matching pair of pants, he turned a few ladies' heads as he led Elizabeth to the dance floor while his partner was dancing with hers. She knew then and there she did not want to marry anyone else but him, unfortunately his partner was a friend of hers.

Elizabeth cast her eyes around the dance floor and spotted them looking at her and Alexander. As they danced, Elizabeth felt Alexander holding her close to him. She looked up and met his eyes and they were smiling at her. After returning his smile she pressed her head on his chest and closed her eyes. When the dance was over her escort cut in and they dance the next dance and the one after that...until the party finally broke up around midnight when they left. She was disappointed she didn't say goodbye to Alexander. It took Elizabeth Wong six months to get him and a further six before he proposed. And now back in Singapore, she was about to introduce him to her parents.

Although they hadn't set a date for their wedding, they figured that it will have to be after Elizabeth have finished her course at the RMIT at the end of the year. They wanted to make sure that they had the blessings of both their parents first. This trip was for him to meet her parents.

Alexander had left early in order to beat the heavy traffic on the newly completed North-South freeway that stretched from *Bukit Kayu Hitam* at the Thai border, right down to Singapore. He had planned to be in Kuala Lumpur around noon, have a spot of lunch, and then to continue with his journey to Singapore, which he hoped to reach by nightfall.

As soon as he left the Penang Bridge he took the lane that took him to the toll plaza before getting on the North-South Highway heading south. He was excited at the prospect of driving along this highway, which some say, cuts through some of the most beautiful parts of the country.

Alexander thoroughly enjoyed the first leg of his journey which ended in Kuala Lumpur. It reminded him a lot like the autobahn in Germany on which he and his father had driven when they spent a summer vacation together last year. His sister Andrea was supposed to have joined them, but an unexpected visit to Penang by two of her college friends from England had changed her plans.

He smiled when he thought of what she had said over the telephone. "Bring me back a bottle of perfume," she had said to him. "And don't you pick up anything that's contagious while you two are gallivanting all over Europe!" she had added.

"How could I? Father will be with me, remember?" Alexander had laughingly reminded his sister.

"Hah! Knowing you, I'm sure you'll find some excuses to sneak out on your own at night." She had called to wish him a safe journey. That was last summer, almost a year ago.

After Alexander had completed his Master's degree in Business Administration, he had come back to Malaysia to work for a major housing development firm. As their vice-president for Planning and Development, he was kept very busy, so busy in fact, he only managed make this trip to Singapore because all the company's offices were closed for the long holiday weekend. When he had first entered the university he had taken the course in architecture just like his father did but had changed his mind when he found out that he suffered from vertigo. With the trend nowadays for architects to design buildings that literally reached the sky, anyone who couldn't stand heights would be doomed to failure in that profession.

As he cruised at the top speed limit of 110 k/ph., Alexander couldn't help thinking of his sister and the guilty feeling he had felt for not telling her the real reason for his trip to Singapore. He saw the hurt in her eyes when he told her that he was leaving for the trip. She had already suspected the reason for his trip was to ask Elizabeth's parents for Elizabeth's hand in marriage. She felt hurt when she thought that her brother hadn't trusted her enough to tell her that.

Ever since they were little, they had never kept any secrets from each other. Alexander had written to her often while she was still in England and told her all about Elizabeth and their plans to tell her parents about their intention to get married when Elizabeth came back for a short holiday home. And now, after having been back only two days, Andrea found her brother was actually making the trip he had often talked to her about, without mentioning anything to her. She was not only surprised but felt terribly hurt when he hadn't volunteered the information to her. Alexander reproach himself for not telling Andrea the real reason for his trip to Singapore and he hated himself for it. It was the first time he had not confided in her on something as important as this. He made a mental note to telephone her as soon as he and Elizabeth had fixed their wedding date.

Since he had arrived in Kuala Lumpur earlier than he had expected, he decided to tour the city a bit before settling for a place for lunch. He couldn't decide what to have. KL, as it is fondly known, had become quite a cosmopolitan city, just like Melbourne or Sydney. Restaurants of all kinds seemed to have sprung up everywhere all over the city. In the end Alexander settled for his favourite kind of food - Italian. It was at a place not far from where he had planned on visiting after lunch. *Cucina Italiana* was a quaint little place run by a Malay and his Italian wife. It was decorated in a typical Italian fashion with bunches of garlic hanging from fake columns and plastic vines complete with delicious-looking grapes snaking through latticed dividers. Illumination was provided by fluorescent lights hidden behind white Perspex sheets giving it a daylight effect regardless of the weather outside. The walls were covered with framed posters depicting scenes from the various regions of Italy. The shelves that surrounded the four walls of the dining room were laden with wines bottles of all shapes and sizes.

While waiting for his orders Alexander read names like *Chianti, Barolo, Bardolino, Asti Spumante*, off the bottles. There were so many others whose labels he couldn't read from where he was sitting so he decided to ask for the wine list. He thought it odd that the waitress had not ask him whether he had wanted to have some wine with his meal nor did she offer him the wine list. Alexander couldn't help wondering why wouldn't an establishment, that obviously have an ample supply of wine, seem not too keen to promote the stuff. Just as he was about to ask a passing waiter the reason, a small notice printed at the bottom of the back cover of the menu held by a man at a nearby table caught his attention. It simply said - "Digestive aid: Please consult our waiters if you need wine to help with your digestion.". Before Alexander could think more about it a waitress brought him his food which he immediately tucked into with relish.

For his *primo pieta* Alexander chose the *minestrone* - a vegetable soup and *pollo arrosto* - a roast chicken, as his main meal and finally for his desert he chose a home-made Italian ice cream.

After lunch he drove to Taman Tun Dr. Ismail, a suburb not far from the city centre. He wanted to see the house where his father and his two step-brothers used to live. He had no idea why he had wanted to go there but he knew that he'll never forgive himself if he didn't at least take a look at the house since he was in town.

As it turned out, getting there was no easy task. The area had become a very large suburb with a thriving township thrown in, and he lost his way many times. After stopping just as many times for directions, he finally found himself in the right vicinity, by a street vendor's reckoning, but despite the man's assurance, he didn't find the house even though he thought he was in the right street. An elderly man taking a walk with a young boy, most probably his grandson, tried to assist Alexander but unfortunately the man's *Bahasa Malaysia* was thick with a *Kelantanese* accent. Alexander tried his best to follow the man's direction until he found himself lost again. He must have taken a wrong turn for he found himself totally in an unfamiliar surroundings. He was about to give up when he caught sight of Petronas petrol station in the distance. He pulled into it and asked an attendant, this time he found the house without much difficulty.

Months later he told his father about his visit to their old house in Kuala Lumpur. James was taken aback by the revelation.

"Tell me, why did you want to go there?" James asked.

"I don't really know. I thought about it as I was driving towards KL. I was curious, I guess," replied his son.

James looked at his son and wondered about what was on his mind.

"Were all of you happy in that house, father?"

"I think during the early years we were happy but later on things began to deteriorate."

"Why? What happened?" Alexander asked.

"Oh, I don't know, a combination of many things I guess. The money, or rather the lack of it was the main cause. In the middle of the recession people tend to tighten their belts and tried make do with lots of things they may have discarded or replace at any other time, like clothes, for example. I was then in a recreation business, so it was hard to imagine a family spending good money in sports and other leisure pursuits when times were lean?" James asked his son. "My business was badly hit, and even though we managed to struggle for as long as we could, we finally had to cease operating."

"She left you because you had no more money?"

"Well, she tried to convince herself and me that wasn't the only reason: it was perhaps because she no longer loved me, she had said. But she and I knew it wasn't the reason; her love for me during our entire marriage was luke-warm at best. It didn't take me long to realize this but since I was in love with her, or at least I thought so, I accepted our situation as *fait accompli*. The question she should've asked herself was whether she would've left me if I still had the money?"

"Did you love her, father?"

"I did but not anymore. I love your mother...."

"Why is money so important to them, father?"

"Who do you mean?"

"To the Chinese! Why do they worship money so?"

"Money is important to everybody, son, not just to the Chinese. It's just that it shouldn't take precedence over everything else."

James looked across the breakfast table to his very Chinese-looking son whom he adored and who had suddenly gone very quiet. "What are you thinking now?"

"I was thinking of Elizabeth. I still love her, father. I can't help it"?

"I know you do, but think of her as your sister and love her as one and don't ever forget her."

"No, I won't." Unable to hold the dam much longer, Alexander burst into tears. Embarrassed, Alexander covered his face with both hands.

"It's all right to cry, Alex. It's okay." James rushed to his son and put his arms around him. Alex told his father that he didn't exactly know why he went to see their old house in the first place, but he was glad he did. It was as if he had an incomplete picture in his head and finding that house had helped him fill some of the blank spaces. He remembered stopping his car across the road from the house and began to envision in his mind what life must have been like for the four of them there based on stories his stepbrothers have told him.

Alexander had never met his step-brothers' mother, and from what he gathered from them she was a good mother. Both were proud of their family and both of them used to adore their mother until one day, out of the blue, she told their father to leave her brother's house in which they were staying after their father's business went bust. Hurt and confused, their father moved into a rented room not far away from her. At that time his step-brothers were studying in England.

Hoping that they might get back together again, their father hung around Singapore for a while. He even took a lease to operate a Malay food stall at one of the hotels there, but it seemed that his wife was determined to end their marriage of twenty-two years. When all his attempts at reconciliation's proved futile, he finally left for Penang, a place he thought was as far away from Singapore as it could get. He set up a similar food stall, this time it was in the Yaohan Food Arcade. Yaohan was a leading departmental store there in *Kompleks Tun Abdul Razak* or *KOMTAR* as it was normally known. After an initial near disastrous four months in which he nearly lost everything, his saw business begin to pick up. It continued to grow until it came to a level whereby he could just leave it to his capable staff. He would come by once a day for an hour or so with the rest of the day he'd spend writing his novel. Writing was something he had wanted to do for years but had put it on hold due to family and business commitments.

It seemed to Alexander that his two stepbrothers never forgave their mother for what they perceived as her treachery towards their father. They once told Alexander their mother's motto used to be, 'No Money No Talk'. Although they didn't know it at that time if their mother was serious about that motto of hers. Less than a year after their father's business had collapsed, their parents' marriage met the same fate.

When Alexander had asked his stepbrothers how they knew about their mother's motto, they had said they overheard their mother mentioning it to a group of her friends during an afternoon tea at their house.

Although they didn't know it at the time their mother uttered those words in a jocular manner. Unfortunately with eavesdropping one often hears things out of context as they did, but nevertheless her decision to leave their father at a time when he needed her the most, somehow triggered their memory and plunged them back to that particular moment in time when their mother made those remarks. It also marked the beginning of a simmering hatred between them and their mother that hadn't stopped ever since, despite their mother's many attempts at reconciliation. Alexander had deduced from their conversation that it'd be unlikely that they ever will.

It seemed to Alexander his father's life may have come a full circle. He was no happier now than when he was married to his first wife. Alexander suddenly became angry at the thought of what Mandy was doing to James. He shifted down to a lower gear as he overtook the Proton Saga car in front of him, but instead of keeping to the speed limit he put his foot down on the accelerator and watched the speedometer until it reached 200 k/ph., overtaking every vehicle in front of him.

For several minutes Alexander kept at that speed until he noticed a few vehicles travelling in the opposite direction flicking their high-beam lights. He thought nothing of it until he saw in the distance what looked like a police road block. He knew then he had it, the police was going to give him a summons for speeding. At the speed he was going he knew he was in trouble.

As he drew near the road block, a policeman signalled to him to pull to the side of the road and stop. In front of him were two other cars, each had a policeman talking to the driver. Moments later the policeman who had directed him to pull over came by his side and asked for his driver's license. Alexander took it out of his wallet and handed it over to the policeman who took it without a word. Taking the cue from the policeman, Alexander too kept his mouth shut. Pleading innocent when it was obvious he had broken the law was just a waste of time, he reckoned. The moment the officer had taken down all Alexander's particulars, he told him that he had exceeded the speed limit of 110 km/h back there. He asked Alexander to sign on the summons before handing him a copy together with his driving license. As he continued with journey, Alex cursed himself for being stupid. He had no doubt that the few minutes of immature display of temper and reckless driving would set him back by hundreds of ringgit.

The rest of the journey to Singapore, although picturesque, was uneventful. Alexander had kept to the indicated speed limit all the way until he reached Singapore. He called Elizabeth from a phone booth at Woodlands telling her that he was already on Singapore soil. Alex could hear her bubbly voice giving him the direction to her place. A few minutes after 8.00 p.m. he pulled up in front of their place in *Watten Park*.

Feeling slightly apprehensive, Alex got out of this BMW and was about to press the doorbell when he saw Elizabeth emerge from the front door and running towards him. Noticing how happy Elizabeth looked at seeing him made Alex lose some of his anxiousness. Elizabeth gave him a bear hug for a moment before leading him in the house, eager for her parents to meet with Alexander.

Both Sally and her husband didn't know what to expect when their daughter told them that she had invited Alexander to come and stay with them for a few days. From her balcony Sally Wong watched anxiously as her daughter runs towards the BMW car to embrace a tall, good-looking young man coming out of it. She sighed with relief when she saw a Chinese-looking young man, looking very smart in his casual clothes, and not some scruffy Australian *Gwailo*. Sally had mistakenly thought that when Elizabeth had told her she was bringing home a friend from Australia, she had assumed that her daughter was bringing home a *Mat Salleh*. For several days she was nearly sick with worry at that prospect. She had pumped her daughter for some details on this Alexander, all she got out of her daughter was that he was a very nice man who was about six years older than her and she loved him very much. When Sally pointedly asked Elizabeth about his race, her daughter flashed her an annoyed look, ignoring her question completely. Sally decided that it would be best to wait.

Her husband, Steven Wong, was on the telephone talking to a jockey who would be riding one of his horses at the next Saturday's race, a race he was looking forward to for such a long time. Like all the men who had been in this business as long as he had been, Wong could feel it in his veins that one of his horses could end up winning the prestigious *Singapore Cup* the coming weekend.

Winning that cup would be an important step for him towards his rehabilitation back into a society which had rejected and ostracised him for his past misdeeds, and to be sure, there had been many. He knew that his past had been as murky as the Kallang River used to be, but he had vowed never to go back to that life again. To his credit he has done a lot towards cleaning up his image. Like the phoenix, he had arisen from the ashes, and would resurrect himself to be the pillar of society once again.

Towards that objective, Wong had worked very hard to raise funds, and together with own contribution, to help the under-privileged children continue with their education even up to college level. This philanthropic effort on his part had earned Wong a lot of media attention. Then, there was that political party fund-raising committees that he belonged to. This, more than anything else, had gained him a lot of attention by the ruling party. During the last couple of years, he had managed to raise a lot of money for the party, and that had brought him to the attention of the party leaders. At that time he was just an ordinary party member. His ultimate aim, of course, was a post much higher but Wong was willing to wait. He knew that it'll be just a matter of time before he'll be offered something more than being just an ordinary member in the party. After all, almost single-handedly he had raised a lot of money for the party. From there on, who knows? He was forced to cut short his day-dreaming and hung up as soon as his daughter walked into their large living room with Alexander in tow.

"Dad," said Elizabeth, "this is Alexander."

Alexander shook hands with the man whom he thought looked vaguely familiar.

"How do you do, sir. I've been looking forward to meeting you."

Before Wong could respond, they heard the slapping of slippers on their highly-polished marble floor as Sally walked in. Elizabeth introduced Alexander to her mother. Without further ado, Sally Wong released her pent-up, inquisitive energy, by directing it at Alexander with a barrage of questions in her usual tactless manner. Fortunately for Alexander, her husband stepped in and suggested that Alexander must be tired after such a long journey.

"We'll see you at dinner," he said, "we can talk then."

Alexander nodded his head and let himself be guided upstairs by Elizabeth followed by a Filipino maid who had insisted on carrying his overnight bag for him. Since it wasn't heavy, he had let her. His bedroom was modest in size, it had a bathroom attached to it which Alexander was secretly thankful for. He had an aversion to sharing bathrooms. He was always in constant fear of offending other people by being in there longer than necessary, but worst of all, he hated it when finding other people's under-things in there. Maybe with the exception of Manhattan island in New York, a place he had been once, in land-scarce Singapore one would find more tall buildings than anywhere else in the world, as most of the population live in tiny flats scattered all over the island. The government built most of the housing in the island state and ownership were encouraged in order to instil some feelings of belonging and loyalty to the state - a state in which the highly transient Chinese represent the majority of its citizenry.

The Wongs live in a three-storey semi-detached house in an area so clean you could eat off its pavement. Steven Wong had chosen a house in that area because of its close proximity to the Singapore Turf Club in which he was a member. It had been a long arduous climb to get to where he was. Ever since he got out of jail after serving five out of the six-year term, and finding that his brother had left his business in ruins, Wong had worked like a man possessed.

While he was in jail, and in order for Sally and their children to live on, he had told her to take a mortgage on their house from the bank to tide them over until his release from jail. The house had been Wong's family house for generations. His great-grandfather had built it with his own hands when he first came to Singapore before the war. It was in a remote part of the island then and not many people had wanted to live there due to its distance to Colliers Quay, where most of the business activities were done in those days.

At first the house he had built was nothing more than a shack, big enough to accommodate his wife and a son he had not seen whom he had planned on bringing over from China. When he had died, his son - Wong's father, had it rebuilt and made it larger. Like most Chinese in those days who were in business, Wong's father tend to operate his business from his home. In this way every member of the family could lend a helping hand whenever they could to keep the business going.

Eventually their business prospered and with the extra money they added an extension here and a room there. It was the same house in which Wong was born in, and had inherited it on the death of his father. Although it was built before the second-world-war, it was on a huge parcel of land, and in land-scarce Singapore it meant a lot of money. While still in jail Wong had made meticulous plans of what he had wanted to do once he got out. While in prison Wong had dedicated himself to be a model prisoner and had worked very hard in trying to get his sentence reduced, which he eventually got.

As soon as he got out of jail he had his house sold, paid off the mortgage, and put a down payment on the house they presently lived in. With the balance of the money he successfully rebuilt his father's import-export business. As the profit from the business began to accumulate, Wong began once again to acquire race horses. At that moment, as he looked out at his garden through the glass-sliding doors of the living room, Wong felt at peace with the world.

Sally Wong, mindful of their guest's Islamic dietary requirement, had prepared, with the help of her two Filipino maids, a sumptuous meal for that night's dinner. Although apprehensive at first, she was relieved when her daughter, Elizabeth, had said that Alexander's mother was Chinese despite the fact that his father was a Malay. To Sally, Alexander looked very Chinese and she was satisfied.

Sally Wong had wished that her son Tom, and her other daughter Lucy, could also be with them that night. She had missed them terribly especially Tom - her eldest. He had joined the Singapore Air Force and was posted somewhere in Brunei. Her eldest daughter, Lucy couldn't make it because she and her husband John had to go to his mother's birthday party.

"Oh, what's the use!" she mumbled to herself. "Lucy wouldn't come even if they didn't have John's mother's birthday party to go to."

Sally felt she was going to cry and was trying hard not to, knowing how much she would despise that. She sometimes wondered whether her eldest daughter will ever forgive for that bit of indiscretion on her part, which happened at the time while her husband was serving his jail sentence. An indiscretion with Tony, her husband's best friend, which Lucy had inadvertently witnessed when she walked into her mother's room one day when she thought that her mother and her brother were at her grandmother's house.

On that day, due to a power failure at the library where Lucy had been going to almost daily in preparation for her forthcoming examinations, she had come home rather early. She had gone straight to the kitchen for a coke before going upstairs to her bedroom to study. As she walked past her mother's bedroom she thought she heard someone giggling, she stopped and listened. Silence. She shrugged her shoulders and began to walk towards her bedroom. It was just her imagination, she told herself, her mother was at grandma's. Lucy continued walking towards her bedroom when she stopped in her tracks; this time there was no denying that she distinctly heard a man's voice coming from her mother's bedroom. She turned around and headed for her mother's bedroom. And as she came closer she heard her mother's muffled cry. Gingerly she opened her mother's bedroom door.

Lucy was just in time to see Tony ramming himself into her mother. She could see his white arse heaving up and down between her mother's equally white splayed legs. Lucy stood transfixed with a mixture of horror and curiosity at the scene before her when suddenly she heard her mother cry out in the throes of her passion, "Tony, I love you." Disgusted, Lucy slammed the bedroom door shut and ran to her room and locked herself in. Since that day her relationship with her mother had never been the same again. Where once they used to be as close as one can get between mother and daughter, now Lucy hardly spoke to her, avoiding her mother like a plague.

As the three of them sat down at the round dinner table enjoying their dinner, the 'interrogation' of Alexander by Wong and Sally continued. Alexander, as far as Sally could see, seemed to be genuinely fond of her Elizabeth, judging by the attention he was giving her and by the way he looked at her. She was pleased about that.

Sally noticed that her husband too seemed to like Alexander by the way he kept putting food on Alexander's plate, something Wong rarely did. His manner of speaking when directed at Alexander seemed softer too, unlike his usual condescending tone when talking to people outside his circle of friends or people he perceived as not being on the same social level as he was. It was obvious to Sally that the latter not being the case, judging from the car Alexander was driving in, and from his poise and mannerism. Alexander, in Sally's opinion, was like a person who was always in control, and she was pleased about that too, knowing how high-strung her daughter Elizabeth was. She needed someone strong for a husband, if it comes to that, she was thinking. As Sally watched the two men talking, she was struck by the fact that not only they both look so much alike, but so too were their mannerism.

"Alexander, what is your mother's name?" Sally asked suddenly.

"Most people call her Mandy," Alexander replied. "But her real name is May Ling."

Sally felt her heart began to race. She quickly turned to look at her husband to see whether the name had meant anything to him. Apparently it didn't for he kept on eating. Sally, in an attempt to pick up her glass of water, knocked it over and almost soaked the entire dining table with it.

"I'm so sorry," she muttered. "Clumsy of me." She immediately got up and made for the kitchen. Just before she disappeared into the kitchen she shot a look at her husband. Wong, who hadn't recognised Mandy's name, saw the look his wife was giving him. He excused himself and headed for the kitchen. He was halfway through the door when Sally pulled him in and practically dragged him into the breakfast nook.

"I wasn't sure at first," she said excitedly, "but when I saw you two talking I noticed that the young man bore a striking resemblance to you. And on the top of that, there were also certain mannerism you both share. I... I... think he is your son. And that name - Mandy... Wasn't that what you called the young girl you raped?"

Sally abruptly sat down in one of the pine chairs and covered her face with her hands and began to sob. When realization hit Wong, he felt as if he was going to be sick. He lowered himself onto one of the other chairs. Wong couldn't believe it! After all these years, and after what he had gone through, he found that his past could still come back and haunt him. He thought he had all that buried and done with when he had served his jail sentence as demanded by society. He had never wanted that part of his life brought up again - ever! He had worked very hard ever since his release and had painstakingly rebuilt everything from scratch, including his pride and joy - his stable of race-horses.

He felt he had lost everything during the period he had spent in jail. And now, just as he felt that he had succeeded in putting everything back together again, that nice young man outside sitting with his daughter, with whom, he had no doubt, she was in love with, unknowingly had brought back Wong's sordid past with him, and had thrown it back in his face. The realization shocked and numbed him. Not knowing what to do Wong did nothing. Sally, aware that her husband hadn't said a word, stopped crying and began to pull herself together. She suggested that he too did the same. She was afraid that their daughter might walk in on them. She knew that they have to find a way to tell Elizabeth the truth, but for now they have to get back to the dining room and continue with their dinner. Elizabeth, oblivious to the turmoil her parents were going through in the kitchen, was happy to note that both her parents seemed to like

Alexander. She failed to notice anything out of the ordinary when Wong and Sally re-joined them at the dinner table. Elizabeth was hoping that by the time Alexander left for home in a few days' time, both she and Alexander could tell her parents that they planned to get married sooner that what they had originally planned.

ℵℶℵℶℵℶ

CHAPTER TWENTY-SIX

All night long Wong and Sally tried to figure out a way to tell their daughter the truth, but by dawn neither of them was having any luck. It was still fairly dark in their bedroom with the curtains drawn, but Sally could tell from the droning sound of the traffic on *Bukit Timah Road* about a mile away it was time she got up. She gave a bleary-eyed look at the clock on her side table, it was ten minutes past seven. Half-an-hour later she was surprised to find Elizabeth and Alexander already in the kitchen having their breakfast.

"Good morning, mother, would you like some breakfast?" Elizabeth asked her mother.

"Good morning Mrs. Wong," Alexander chipped in cheerfully. Sally noticed that Alexander, who had been sitting down, had stood up the moment he saw her walk in, inwardly she felt pleased. The boy seemed to have such good manners, she couldn't help thinking. Automatically Sally thought of Mandy. She must have been a good mother to have brought up a well-mannered son like Alexander. She found herself wondering what Mandy really looked like. Judging from how handsome Alexander was, and knowing her husband's penchant for pretty women, she concluded that Mandy must have been a beautiful woman. A pang of jealousy went through Sally and a hard, cold look appeared involuntarily on her face. Bereft of any make-up, it made her appear as if she was snarling.

"Good morning, Mrs. Wong." Alexander said again, thinking that she may not have heard him the first time since she hadn't replied nor look in his direction. He was alarmed too, not only at the way she looked, but also at the way she seemed to avoid looking at him. He couldn't help wondering what he might have done to make her react that way towards him this morning.

"Good morning," Sally finally said, still unable to look at Alexander. She went straight to the coffee maker and poured herself a cup. Noticing that Alexander was still standing in front of his chair, she made a tremendous effort to look cheerful and joined him at the table.

"Thank you," she said, when Alexander pulled back a chair for her, she couldn't remember when anyone had done that for her. Not even her husband had done that for her!

"Alexander," she began, as soon as Elizabeth joined them at the table, "Any mother would be delighted to have you as a son-in-law. You seemed like a nice person, you're good-looking and also well-mannered. And from what you've told us, you seemed to know what you want to do in life. I have no doubt that you'll be tremendously successful in whatever you do." Sally paused for a moment, ignoring the looks of alarm that was beginning to appear on Alexander's and her daughter's faces. "However, there is something that I have to tell you that will prevent you from marrying my daughter." Having come this far, Sally was aware that she had to go through with it and say it all, otherwise she might chickened-out altogether. "You cannot marry my daughter because you two are brother and sister."

"What?" Elizabeth was immediately on her feet, looking visibly upset. With arms akimbo, she towered over her mother and glared angrily at her mother. In contrast, Alexander knew almost immediately what Sally was talking about and the impact of that realization immobilised him temporarily. Elizabeth, who was obviously not aware of certain episode of her family history, demanded from her mother an explanation on what she had just said.

Alexander had known the truth because Mandy had told him about her rape by Wong as soon as she felt he was old enough to accept the truth. She had insisted on telling him about the sordid episode of her life despite objections from James. She told James that it was her duty as a mother to tell her children the truth no matter how painful it was. On Alexander's twelfth birthday, she told him what Wong had done to her and had repeated it to Andrea when she too turned twelve.

In reality Mandy's motive was far from noble. She did it in order to propagate the hatred in Alexander what she had felt for Wong. The reaction she got from Alexander, however, wasn't exactly what she had expected. Instead of being angry and filled with hatred for Wong, he became withdrawn and non-communicative. He was filled with regret, shame and sorrow, all at the same time. The lad was utterly confused and for the first in their married life, James reproached Mandy for what she had done. He could tell from her look of defiance, she wasn't sorry at all.

It took Alexander many years before he could reconcile himself to the fact that he was not James's son, and that he was a result of a rape of his mother by someone who had promised her a job. Someone whom he had never met, but had hated nonetheless. From that day onwards, as far as Alexander was concerned, Wong was someone he wanted to hurt so badly if he ever caught up with him.

As the realization began to get hold of him, Alexander felt the anger in him began to flare up. He got up from his chair and strode out of the kitchen. He practically ran up the stairs and headed for Wong's bedroom.

Wong, unaware of what his wife had done, was just coming out of his bedroom when Alexander threw a punch at him. He saw Alexander lunge at him but he was unable to do anything about it, not even to duck.

Wong took it hard on the jaw. He could have sworn he heard a cracking sound just as he fell to the floor. The next instant he felt Alexander grabbing him by the collar of his shirt, he braced himself for the second punch he knew was coming. He passed out when that punch landed. Fortunately for him, he was spared from more beatings when Elizabeth threw herself between her father and Alexander, imploring the latter to stop.

An hour later just as the doctor and his team at the hospital were about to wire Wong's jaws back in place, Alexander was being taken into custody by the police. He was charged with assault. He was bundled into the back of a police vehicle and as it was the procedure, he was hand-cuffed like a common criminal. Elizabeth, her eyes brimming with tears, stood helplessly by and watched at the police vehicle pulled away from the kerb and disappeared out of sight. Sally walked to her and practically dragged her to the ambulance which was waiting to take Wong to the hospital.

At the remand centre, Alexander telephoned James in Pulau Langkawi where he had been living on and off ever since he and Mandy broke off nearly two years ago. And the first thing James did after speaking with Alexander was to call the hotel in *Kuala Trengganu* where his daughter Andrea and her friends were on their way there that morning for a short stay. When told by the hotel that they had not checked in yet, James left a message for Andrea to call him back. About half-an-hour later Andrea telephoned him and he told her what had happened and asked her to catch the next flight to Singapore. He also called his lawyer there and told her what had happened. He asked her to make arrangements to get Alexander out of jail immediately. James then tried to get in touch with Mandy at Mong Kok's residence in Singapore but was told that she had gone to Penang to see her mother who was ill. When James telephoned there, it was answered by her mother. Moments later Mandy was on the line and he told her all that he knew - which wasn't much. Mandy immediately told him that she was taking the next flight to Singapore to be with Alexander.

"You can't be with him," said James. "He's in jail."

"He's my son," she yelled at him. "I have to be with him."

"He's my son too," replied James calmly. "And I'm doing everything I can to get him out of jail. So please be patient. Call me at this hotel as soon as you've arrived in Singapore. My travel agent is trying to get me booked in there as well as a seat on the next flight to Singapore. I'll call you again when everything has been confirmed." James hung up the phone and began packing his clothes. A few moments later his travel agent called and told him that he was booked on the next flight to Singapore. He reminded James to leave for the airport immediately in order to catch it. Half an hour later he called Mandy again from the airport and told her that he was leaving in ten minute's time for Singapore. He also gave her his hotel's telephone number.

James somehow sensed that Alexander had not told him everything over the telephone. Alexander had asked him not let his mother come to see not until after they've talked. James hadn't asked him why, for he knew that Alexander had always a sensible head on his shoulder. He must have a good reason for not wanting to see his mother.

As the plane banked in for the landing at Changi Airport, James couldn't help wondering what was it that Alexander didn't want his mother to know. At Singapore airport, James was surprised to see his daughter, Andrea, waiting for him.

"How did you know that I'd be on this flight?" he asked. "I called a friend at KL airport and asked him to check for me which flight you were on," Andrea replied.

James noticed the worried look on his daughter's face. "Don't worry, darling, everything is going to be all right," he said.

James called his lawyer's office again to find out if they had been in touch with his son. His lawyer told him that their Singapore representative had already seen Alexander. She brief him on what they had learnt from Alexander. It seemed that they too hadn't learnt much from Alexander.

When James had spoken to Alexander earlier all he got out of him was that he was in jail on an assault charge for causing bodily harm to Wong - Elizabeth's father. When James had asked him why, Alexander hadn't said anything. When James had asked him who had thrown the first punch, Alexander had readily admitted that it was he who had thrown the first punch. James was surprised when he thought he detected a slight euphoria in his Alexander's voice. But before James could ask him why he would want to cause his prospective father-in-law any harm, the phone went dead in his hand.

As he was and Andrea was were walking towards the taxi rank, James was paged through the public address system to collect a message. He went to the information counter and was given the same message his lawyer in Kuala Lumpur had given him earlier. Earlier his lawyer had informed him that someone from their Singapore office had already met with Alexander. The name of their Singapore lawyer was Mr. Goh, and he was waiting at the remand centre where Alexander was being kept when James and Andrea walked in. Goh briefed James on what Alexander had told him, but had suggested that James should see his son first before they could talk further, giving James the impression that there seemed to be more to Alexander's story than what he was made out to believe. Andrea had wanted to go with her father to see Alexander but Goh had quietly suggested that perhaps her father should go in alone first. With great reluctance Andrea agreed to wait.

"Hi, father," Alexander said, as soon as James sat down in front of him.

"Alex, how are they treating you here?" James asked. James couldn't help looking at his son with concern. Alexander looked tired. James couldn't believe what was happening, Alex, whom James had always considered to be the most sensible among his four children, whose sense of fair play was well-known not only in the family but also among his friends, a person who wouldn't hurt a fly, was being locked up in a cell like a common criminal. He looked around him and saw how out of place his son was among the rest of the inmates. It seemed like a bad dream to James, and he wished that it would end soon.

"They are treating me just fine here, father." Said Alexander as he concentrated on a spot on the table in front of him, avoiding his father's worried look.

"Tell me, Alex. What really happened. You told Goh you got angry with Wong and his wife Sally, when they told you that you cannot marry their daughter Elizabeth. You then had an argument with Wong and you hit him, breaking his jaw. Is that about it?"

There was a moment's hesitation before he said, "yes."

"Come on, Alex! You wouldn't hurt that bee despite the fact that it bit you in the bottom when you were twelve, remember?" James reminded him. "Oh, by the way, this man Wong, he's just a pint-size squirt, is he?"

This time Alex shot his father an incredulously look. "No, he's bigger than you!"

"Oh, I see. He's bigger than me and you beat the hell out of him because you were angry at him for not letting you marry his daughter - is that correct?"

For several minutes they just looked at each other in silence. James was hoping that his son's trust in him was still strong enough, and that he would open up to him, but it seemed that something was preventing him from doing that now and James didn't know what to do except to be patient.

James had recognised the look on his son's face before, he had seen it many times in the past. Alexander would mull over whatever it was that was troubling him, and when he could see it clearly in his mind he would open up eventually. James hoped that it'll be soon because he couldn't bear to see his son behind the ugly iron bars - not even for a minute longer.

After several more agonising minutes, Alexander looked at James and said, "Wong is my father - my real father. He's the one who...who...hurt mother a long time ago. When his wife told me that Elizabeth and I can't get married because we were brother and sister. I didn't understand it at first, but when it finally hit me, I got so angry I went after Wong and hit him a couple of times before Elizabeth stopped me. To tell you the truth, I wanted to kill him for what he did to mother."

"Alexander, listen to me," James said softly, in an attempt to console him, when he saw how agitated he had become. "What had happened, happened a long time ago, Wong has already paid for his crime, and as far as the law is concerned the case is closed and I want you to do the same thing. I know you can't forget, neither will your mother, and neither will I, but we must move on. I know how you must feel at the moment, but it will pass, believe me. Right now the most important thing is to get you out of here. I'll leave you for now, but I'll be back with Andrea. She's waiting outside with Goh and she wants to see you."

"No, dad! Don't let her see me now. Bring her tomorrow. Tell her anything...tell her visiting time is over...anything..."

James didn't have to lie to Andrea. Visiting time was really over when he reluctantly stood up when told by the policeman on duty that his time was up. He waved his hand in response to his son's wave and left.

All attempts by Goh to get Alexander released that day proved fruitless. He did manage, however, to get him out by noon the next day.

James and Andrea found a worried-looking Mandy waiting for them in the lobby of their hotel. James took them into the coffee house and briefed Mandy as best as he could, knowing full well how delicate the situation was, especially with Andrea being there.

Mother and daughter hadn't been on speaking term ever since Mandy decided to move in with Mong Kok. One look at the both of them told James that their relationship was still frosty. Andrea had avoided looking at her mother and all attempts by Mandy to get Andrea to speak to her were rebuffed. James too had tried his best to coax his daughter to reconcile with Mandy but was rewarded with a hard stare from her.

The next day Alexander couldn't hide his happiness the moment he saw both his parents and his sister Andrea. He felt uncontrollable tears start to flow down his cheeks as they hugged and kissed him. For once in his adult life he didn't care if anybody saw him crying. He noticed that they were crying too and he felt something that he had never really felt before - loved. He couldn't help noticing how easily women cry when he saw how teary his mother and sister were, while his father, even though his eyes were wet with tears, somehow managed to look composed.

Alex was wrong on that score, at least as far as his mother was concerned. Mandy, who hardly ever cry, found herself blubbering helplessly. She looked up at her estranged husband and noticed that he too had tears in his eyes despite his attempt to put on a brave face.

"Come on, let's get out of here," James told his family. They walked to the car park where James bundled them into his rented Mercedes-Benz and drove to an house belonging to a friend. It seemed that Alexander's car was still at the Wongs and he made a mental note to contact Goh and get one of his men to fetch it for him. He had no intention of having any contacts with Wong or any member of his family.

The house that James mentioned so casually to his family was actually a mansion. It had, among other things, a swimming pool, an indoor Jacuzzi and a tennis court. The owner, an old friend of James's and a fellow Malaysian, was a millionaire many times over, and he happened to be abroad at that time. He told James over the telephone that they were welcome to stay as long as they like. As Alexander was not allowed to leave the country until his court appearance, and since his court appearance wouldn't be due for another week, James was grateful to his friend for letting them use their house. Under the circumstances, he thought that a house was better than staying in a hotel, especially when a live-in amah and a gardener-cum-chauffeur came with it. Mandy and Andrea readily supported the idea, while Alexander, on the other hand, just shrugged his shoulders and offered no comments.

Endang, the fifty-year-old housekeeper, who greeted them at the door, showed them to their rooms. James and Mandy were allocated a room while Alexander and Andrea was given a room each. When James saw the look on Mandy's face, he quickly asked Endang whether she could spare him another room where he could work, and perhaps rest too in between his work.

The housekeeper proudly told James that the house had fourteen bedrooms and that he was more than welcome to take as many rooms as he liked. She proceeded to show him the rest of the rooms she mentioned. James chose a room across the bedroom that was allocated to Mandy and him. And as soon as Endang had left, he told Mandy where he would be sleeping. He could have sworn that he saw a look of disappointment on her face and he was puzzled.

𐊡𐊥𐊡𐊥𐊡𐊥

CHAPTER TWENTY-SEVEN

The housekeeper prepared a sumptuous lunch for them, and as she kept hovering in and out of the dining at lunch, James asked her how long had she worked for the Lees. She told them that she and her husband had been looking after Lee, his wife Doreen for more than twenty years. And she had looked after their two children, Patrick and Theresa from the day they were born.

They were originally from Indonesia, she had said. Her husband, Jomo, had worked in a rubber plantations there owned by Lee, while she herself worked as their housekeeper. When the Lee family migrated to Singapore, they were asked whether they would like to come along and work for them. They had jumped at the opportunity. The happiest moment of their lives they said, was when they became Singapore citizens. That was about seven years ago. They thought that they will continue to serve the family until the day they die. She told them that they were treated as members of the family and they were very grateful to Allah. The Lee family, according to Jomo, who prefers to be called Pak Daud, spent a lot of time abroad therefore they had not much to do except to keep the house neat and tidy. His duty, as their chauffeur and gardener, was to maintain the grounds and to drive them around when they were home. Over lunch James told his family that he and Lee had known each other ever since they were in same college in Australia. Back then they were considered by others as inseparable, but once they got back home they went on their separate ways with an occasional letter to each other now and then. Several years down the road, their infrequent correspondence got relegated to just New Year's cards, until one day they finally lost touch with each other.

James have never been a great believer in fate but in coincidences - yes. And he was sure that it must have been a coincident that had brought Lee and him in touch with each other again after such a long time. It was while Goh and James were discussing Alexander's case, when Goh suddenly asked him. "Have we met before? You look very familiar to me and as a matter of fact, so is your name." James gave Goh a long look and then shook his head.

"No ... I don't think so. I'm usually quite good in remembering faces. Name is another matter, but faces I never forget." That was yesterday morning when they met for the first time at the remand centre. And when they met again later that day, Goh asked James whether he knew a Mr. David

Lee. Since many Chinese have names that are similar to one another, James asked Goh a little bit about this David Lee person. When Goh told him that David's family used to be in the rubber business in Indonesia before they migrated to Singapore, but now they were in many things including banking, shipping and manufacturing.

James told Goh that he once knew a David Lee whose father was in the rubber business in Indonesia, Thailand, as well as in Malaysia. They were friends while they were in college in Australia, he had added. As James began to narrate to Goh about his friendship with this David Lee, a smile began to appear on Goh's face.

"Mr. Goh, were you studying in Melbourne too at that time?" James asked, dreading the unlikely possibility that they may have met and that he had forgotten him. James was relieved when Goh shook his head and said, "No, I was studying in Sydney at the time when David, who by the way is my cousin, was studying with you in Melbourne. When I told you yesterday that I thought I had seen you before, I gave it some thoughts. And this morning I remembered where I had seen you. It was in one of my photo albums. A long time ago David gave me a bunch of photographs of him and some of our friends and I had it kept in an album. It was your name that triggered something in my head and I dug out the old albums. I remembered David talking about his best friend James all the time in those days. When I went through the albums I came across your photographs with David. Then everything fell into places - You and David were great friends, weren't you?"

"We were like two peas in a pod," James said to him, smiling at the thought of his long-lost friend. "Although, in temperament, we couldn't be more opposite."

The conversation had taken place in Goh's sumptuous-looking office on the thirtieth floor of a modern office block over-looking the Kallang River not far from the High Court building. It's proximity was obviously the main reason why the building housed so many of the great law firms in the Republic.

"I talked to David last night and he asked me to call him the moment you step into my office," said Goh, reaching for the phone. "He's dying to speak with you." Moments later James was talking to his oldest and dearest friend. The line was loud and clear despite the fact that they were thousands of miles apart, thanks to modern technology. James couldn't help noticing that David sounded just the same to him as he did while they both were in college. He also spoke briefly to Doreen, David's pretty wife. David and Doreen were in London where they were spending their holiday with their two children. They talked for several minutes and when it was over, James told Goh that David had offered him and his family their house for them to stay while they were in Singapore. James couldn't help feeling elated, not only because his son was out of jail and he had just talked to a friend he had not seen for many years and he had Mandy back with him, although he couldn't be sure for how long. He was hoping that the enforced get-together brought about by this twist of fate, might also help to bring about a reconciliation with her. He wanted that desperately especially after seeing her again and the strong yearning he still had for her. He knew that he still loved her.

"I guess I'll never stop loving her until the day I die," James thought to himself. Despite the trouble he was in, Alexander, was pleased that the family was back together again.

"You know, I hope I won't have to go to jail, but if I have to, it'll be worth it." He said to Andrea. They were in the middle of their game of table-tennis when he made the comment. His sister missed her shot when she momentarily looked up at him with a questioning look on her beautiful face.

"I mean, look at us, we're a family again. Isn't that great?," said Alexander. He purposely missed the next shot when Andrea returned his volley. He noticed a fleeting smile suddenly appeared on Andrea's face and he felt reassured that his sister hadn't lost her strong competitive spirit that he had always admired her for. For the next several minutes the white ball went back and forth without any letting up as the two opponents concentrated on their game. So far Alexander had been leading with two games to one and Andrea knew she had needed to win this game badly in order to maintain her position as his potential partner in the forthcoming tournament they were entering for some charity during the Adelaide-Penang week - provided, of course, Alexander was still free to enter the tournament. Otherwise, Sandy, who has been mooning over Alexander ever since they've met several months ago, would take her place. Sandy who had managed to sleep with nearly every boy Andrea had gone out with, was her natural enemy. But at that moment Andrea wasn't thinking of herself, she was afraid that with Alex's present state of mind, he might fall into Sandy's trap all over again. Alex had managed to get away from Sandy once, when he found out about her numerous love affairs, but Andrea was afraid that her brother may not want to get away this time. The event in question was something that was planned some time ago but Alex felt unsure about competing in the tournament under the circumstances he was in. Everyone in the family, including his mother, thought that it'll be good for him; not to mention the spastic children's home which will be the major beneficiary of the prize money if he and Andrea were to win in the events they have entered for. The company that Andrea was working for had not only given her some days off for her to practice, but was also a major sponsor for the tournament.

The organizers anticipated quite a good turnout during the three-day table tennis event. It was to be one of the major events during this year's Penang-Adelaide week.

This annual affair held alternately between Adelaide and Penang, had been the brainchild of a former Premier of South Australia and a former Chief Minister of Penang. It's popularity as well as it's prominence had grown tremendously ever since its modest beginning many years ago. This year it was Penang's turn to host this special extravaganza. And as far as the table tennis main event was concerned, Penang, the current champion, would try its best to retain the title, which it had won the year before, after losing it to Adelaide two years in a row prior to that. Andrea lost in the first set, but in the second set she had already won two games to nil and seeing that her brother was in a sentimental mood Andrea figured that her chance of winning this game too was good. She desperately wanted to beat him three games in a row, something she had never done before, and felt that this could be the first time. She psyche herself into winning this game. All she had to do, she told herself, was to concentrate on the ball and the game would be hers. But it was easier said than done, for in the end they both ended up in a draw.

At the end of their game Andrea was convinced more than ever that any winnings she had scored against her brother had only been entirely due to his generosity with little, if any, due to her skill. She knew she was being unfair to herself, and instead of being angry with her brother, she gave him a fond look and felt blessed to have him as a brother.

Andrea gave a loud whoop when Alexander finally told her that he'll be honoured to have her as a partner for the forth- coming tournament. She ran after him to give him a hug, but when he saw it coming he ducked into the shower to escape her. Mandy, who had been lying on the deck chair by the pool, had witnessed the closeness between her two children despite the fact that they both had different father. Instinctively she looked up at the bedroom above the recreation room where James was working on his latest novel. She could see him keying in on his Compaq notebook in front of him - a far cry from the archaic 286 XT desktop personal computer he had when they had first met. She was aware that she was affecting his concentration, every now and then she'd notice him look her way. And during the last couple of days she was aware of how much he still loved her - James could never hide his feelings as far as she was concerned. She could read the tell-tale signs - by the way he `accidentally' brushed against her, and the way he looked at her when he thought she wasn't looking - a difficult thing to do in a house full of mirrors. There seems to be more antique mirrors of all shapes and sizes than anywhere Mandy had ever been before. No matter where you go in the house, there'd be one starring you in the face. Mandy began to conclude that David's wife, Doreen, must be a very vain woman. Admittedly she did find the mirrors convenient for checking on her hair, her make-up and her attire. Oddly enough, Mandy felt a sudden desire to be in James's arms and to be told, like he used to do, how much he loved her. It can't be, she thought to herself, I can't be in love! And yet, she couldn't deny the fact that her heart seemed to flutter whenever James came near her.

In all the years they were married, she had never once said any endearing words to James, not even in response to his declaration of being in love with her. She couldn't lie because she really didn't love him then. On the other hand, James's love for her had grown stronger each day, of that she was sure of. She wished hers had, at least in his eyes, pretended to love him but she hadn't. Often she had seen the hurt in his eyes, and just as often, she had wanted to lie to him and to tell him what he had wanted to hear, but couldn't. It was too late now, she told herself dejectedly; if only I could turn back the clock, she lamented.

※※※※※※

CHAPTER
TWENTY-EIGHT

Mandy was waiting in the coffee house of the Hilton Hotel on Orchard Road. Unconsciously, she tapped the side of her water glass with her fingernail. The thought of what she was about to do made her extremely nervous. For the last five minutes she had been looking up at every person that had walked into the coffee house. It had caused a lot of speculations among the men and some interesting bitchy remarks from their lady partners as they walked past her table. Mandy looked at her watch again. Five minutes to ten. He had said he'll be there at ten. She was early, something she had rarely done, but what she was about to do was far too important and felt that she should be extra early. Unfortunately, all those who knew her, including the man she was waiting for, never expected her to be punctual, and they in turn never turn up early for any appointment with her. It was the case of tardiness beget tardiness. Mandy was nervous because one thing you can never do to Mong Kok was to go back on a deal, the consequence can be deadly and she was about to do just that. She was resigned to the fact that if she were to die for going back on an agreement, then so be it. At the very least, she told herself, she would die trying to right a wrong, it would be worth dying for. Mandy had come to a conclusion early that morning soon after she had woken up in James's bed. Still feeling the remnant of the after-glow of their night of passion, Mandy had felt good with the decision she had already made.

Seeing that James was still asleep, Mandy quietly slipped out of bed and headed for the bathroom. She locked the door behind her, picked up the telephone extension and began punching some numbers. She spoke quickly and quietly for several moments and then hung up. The call she made was to Mong Kok, a notorious racketeer, involved in smuggling, gambling and prostitution in the Asean region. The authorities in the six countries seemed unable or unwilling to connect him with all these illegal activities. In some of these countries they were afraid of his enormous influence with the top echelon of the ruling class there. On the surface Mong Kok was a well-known businessman who owned and operated a number restaurants in Singapore, Malaysia and Thailand. His other legitimate front was as a property developer as well as an importer and exporter. Through clever manipulations of these legitimate operations, Mong Kok easily funnelled all the funds that came from his other, more lucrative, but illegal operations and in the end all his dirty money became squeaky clean. Despite numerous allegations that he was not what he seemed, the authorities in the six countries were wary about trying to take him on for fear of any backlash. Over the years Mong Kok, through his press agents and social secretaries and connections in high places, had carefully nurtured his image as a man with a social conscience. They helped him to cultivate his relationship with the government and the media, and they in turn helped highlighted his numerous, well-orchestrated philanthropic activities. The media, through careful manipulation by his press agents, adored him because he was news to them. And Mong Kok was never known to turn down an interview with them and they love him for that. As far as the money spent on the charities was concerned. To him it was simply good business sense. He figured that for every dollar he spent on his charities he stood to gain several thousand more from his not so legal activities, not to mention the dollar value he got out of it in public relation and besides, they were all tax deductible. So what if some of these charity organization had, from time to time, suspected that the money that came from him may have been tainted? They seemed perfectly happy to accept the money and ignore any rumours they may have heard. Mong Kok first met Mandy several years ago when he was introduced to her by his onetime jockey at a discotheque in Singapore. At that time she was still with Wong. And Mong Kok, following a time-honoured tradition about not poaching among members of the racing fraternity, as both he and Wong were, he forced himself to forget about her despite the fact that he had fancied her. Tried as he may, Mong Kok, who had found Mandy's beauty so alluring, couldn't forget her. If fact he was so smitten with her from the moment he had laid eyes on her, he had photographs of her taken without her knowledge. These photographs adorned the walls of a special room in his palatial estate, tucked away in a secluded exclusive corner of tiny Singapore. He had often spent endless hours in this room looking the photographs of Mandy. His desire to own her was all consuming and Mong Kok was a patient man. When he heard that Mandy had brought on a rape charge against Wong he thought he saw an opportunity to get close to her then. His lawyers, however, didn't think it was a good idea. They told him that any woman who was willing to shout rape once could do it again and should be avoid at all costs. He was glad he took their advice because during the trial, which took several weeks, a lot of Wong's dirty linen were publicly aired. In the end Wong was given a six-year sentence.

Several years later, during one of his frequent visits to Penang, Mong Kok came across Mandy once again. It was while he was in a pharmacy looking for a tooth paste, and Mandy was seen entering a supermarket across the concourse area not far from where he was standing. He saw Mandy with a very pretty young woman whom he had assumed was her daughter. The younger woman had a certain resemblance to Mandy. Immediately his longing for Mandy rekindled and almost at once it became intensified despite the fact that he hadn't seen her in over twenty years. He couldn't believe that it had been that long, Mandy, as far as he could see, had aged very little during all that time, if at all. As a matter of fact he thought she had looked more beautiful than ever. Mong Kok quickly strode across the concourse area and slipped into the supermarket where he got hold of a trolley and went after them. When Mandy and Andrea stopped in front of a shelf, Mong Kok stopped near them and pretended to look for something on the same shelf. He kept looking at Mandy hoping to attract her attention, but she kept talking to Andrea, ignoring him completely. Unaccustomed to being ignored, especially by women, Mong Kok decided to go for the direct approached.

"Excuse me," he said, looking at Mandy. "Aren't you Mandy?"

Mandy with Andrea by her side turned her head and faced the speaker. When Mong Kok saw that she had not recognised him, he quickly took out his business card and handed it to her. "We met a long time ago, my name is Mong Kok..."

Mandy took the card and after pretending to study it, handed it back to him and said, "I'm sorry, you must be mistaken. I am sure we haven't met."

She then turned to her daughter and said, "Come on darling, we've got a lot more shopping to do." Mong Kok watched them walk away from him leaving him feeling terribly embarrassed. As he strode out of the supermarket, his embarrassment soon gave way to a smouldering anger. Once in her car with Andrea by her side, Mandy gave out a sigh of relief. Meeting Mong Kok again after all these years was something she had never expected. She had heard talks about his interest in her, despite the fact that they had only met once at a discotheque, and it had got her worried. Despite his worldly appearance and urbane manner, she was afraid of Mong Kok. She felt as if underneath all that glitter, something sinister, something evil was lurking. She had met Mong Kok while she was babysitting one of Wong's jockeys who had, later, introduced him to her. It was he who had approached their table. The jockey who she was with that night was nice compared to some of the others who thought that she was nothing but a piece of flesh to them. It seemed that he had once ridden for Mong Kok. Mandy, while working for Wong, had to endure some of the most degrading treatments from some of them. There was one in particular who had demanded continuous sex from her despite the general belief among the fraternity that sex before a race would be detrimental to their performance at the tracks. She couldn't help observing the next day that one or two of her charges seemed to have recovered sufficiently and had performed quite well during the race, while others could hardly raise themselves on the stirrups. More than once Mandy had wanted to kill herself and end her suffering. Wong had made it clear to her that should she renege on their agreement, he would make sure that her entire family would suffer for it. Having no other alternative, Mandy continued to debase herself until she had paid off the money she owed Wong for her grandmother's funeral. Not long after she met Mong Kok at the disco, she heard from several people that he had been making enquiries about her, and somehow it had frightened her. She didn't want to have anything to do with him, and meeting him again at the supermarket rekindled that fear.

"Mother, what's the matter?" Andrea asked Mandy when she saw her mother had looked rather shaken.

"Nothing." Mandy replied as she slid her arm around her daughter's slim waist and they both strode towards her parked car.

The traffic at that time of the morning was light and they managed to reach home in no time at all. As they walked up to their fourth floor flat, Mandy once again reminded herself that she should look for another place to live - one that was equipped with a lift. These thoughts had become a ritual with her, especially if she was tired or loaded with a lot shopping. But each time, once inside, her resolve was soon forgotten - until the next time she had to climb those stairs.

Mandy remembered with a mixture of nostalgia and sadness, how she and James, each had paint roller in one hand, had worked side by side to make the flat nice for her and their two children to move to when she decided to leave him.

It must have been very difficult for him. She admired James for letting her go without making a scene. All she did was to remind him of his promise he had made to her when he asked her to marry him. The promise was that he would have to let her go if she wanted to. She told him that she wanted to be on her own for a while. She told him that she did not want a divorce.

James had tried his best to try to make her stay, but in the end he had concede to her demand when she reminded him of his promise.

Both Alexander and Andrea had been devastated when she told them of her decision to live separately from their father. They had wanted to know why. Mandy couldn't tell them that she didn't love their father and that she never had. All she had managed to tell them was that she wanted some time to be by herself, that was all!

Since both her children were young adults, she told them that they could go and stay with their father whenever they like. She couldn't help thinking how awful it must have been for James to do what he did - to let her and the children go.

Finally when the day came when they were actually leaving James's flat, both Alexander and Andrea had cried, but not her, she remembered she felt relieved. She couldn't lie to herself, she just didn't love James even though she liked him a lot. She knew she had to go, otherwise they might end up hating each other, and she didn't want that.

Although built not too long ago, none of the blocks of flats there had lifts installed in them, and everyone, with the exception of those living on the ground floor, had to use the stairs to go up and down to their flat. How the developer had managed to contravene the by-laws by not installing lifts for any dwelling three floors and above, was anybody's guess.

As Andrea was helping Mandy put the groceries away, she noticed that her mother was rather quiet.

"By the way, mother, who was that man talking to you in the supermarket?" she inquired.

"I don't know." Mandy lied. "I've never seen him before. He must have mistaken me for someone else."

She realised immediately that her voice sounded a trifle strange, even to her ears. She had never lied to daughter before and she dreaded the thought that Andrea might have detected her lie.

Andrea did detect that her mother was lying, and she had wondered why. She paused momentarily from her task of putting some of the groceries into the refrigerator and gazed at her mother.

Mandy caught Andrea looking at her and she quickly turned her head away, but not before she saw the look in her daughter's eyes. Mandy had wanted to rush to her daughter and to embraced her and to tell her the truth. But what good would that do? How could she tell her daughter the truth without hurting her. How could she reveal to her sweet and innocent daughter, who thought the world of her, all her sordid past. And what if she did, will she still have her daughter's respect afterwards? While all these thoughts were going through Mandy's mind, she didn't realize that Andrea had already left the kitchen and had gone to her room and had locked the door behind her. Mandy knew then it was too late. She had missed the opportunity, that split-second opportunity that was available to her was now lost forever. She knew then that her relationship with her daughter will never be the same again.

ཀྵཀྵཀྵ

CHAPTER
TWENTY-NINE

A week later Andrea left for London to continue with her course at the prestigious London School of Economics in which she was in her final year. During the ensuing months she had written to her mother, but unlike all her previous letters, Mandy noticed the lack of enthusiasm in all of them. In contrast, all her letters to her brother Alexander were more in-depth and more chatty. Andrea for some unexplainable reason had switched her attention from her mother to her brother, as if she were sending some kind of message to her mother. She knew that her brother would tell their mother everything she had written, unless she had specifically asked him not to.

Alexander was of course delighted to receive such letters from Andrea, he told her often enough in his replies. Andrea also wrote and told him how envious she was of him that he had now completed his studies and was free to do whatever he had wanted to do while she still had got another year to go. Alexander had recently obtained his Master of Business Administration degree in Australia and had decided to stay back in Australia and work for a while before taking up a job offer by a well-known company in Kuala Lumpur, a place he'd rather be than anywhere else in the world.

He had also written Andrea telling her about a girl he had just met who was currently the love of his life. Coincidentally both Andrea and Elizabeth, which was Alexander's girlfriend, were of the same age. In her reply Andrea had written telling him that she was happy for him.

* * *

Mong Kok was surprised to see Mandy already waiting for him. He thought he was early. He couldn't help wondering what the emergency was when Mandy telephoned him early that morning. It probably had something to do with her son's impending court case. He had already agreed to let her be with her family until it was over. He felt an irritation coming on as he wondered what more could she want now? A sudden arrival of a pretty young waitress put that thought on hold as he openly admired her as she pulled back his chair for him.

Mandy caught the look in Monk Kok's eyes and thought to herself - What a lecher this guy was! She stubbed her cigarette into the ashtray and waited for the waitress to depart.

"I want out of our deal," she said. "I'll pay you back what my mother owed you, but please let me go!"

Mong Kok tilted his head back and laughed, causing one or two heads to turn in their direction.

Mandy, whose nervousness was quickly replaced by anger, picked up the table knife and lunged forward and jabbed Mong Kok in the stomach with it. It caused him to lose his balance, he tipped over backward.

Mong Kok made a grab for the table but grabbed the tablecloth instead. As he fell to the floor, he pulled the tablecloth and everything on it down onto the floor. Mandy, towering over the undignified figure of Mong Kok among the pile of what was on the table before, threw the knife down on the floor near him and said, "I mean it, Mong Kok, I want out or I'll kill you." She then picked up her handbag and stormed out of the hushed coffee house and caught a taxi back to the house.

Not wanting to encounter either Andrea or James, Mandy entered the house through the side entrance. She then walked through the kitchen and then sneaked up to her room. Andrea, who happened to come out of the bathroom opposite, saw her mother slip into her own room. She noticed that her mother looked rather upset and her eyes were swollen as if she had been crying and it puzzled her. She had never seen her mother cry before. Andrea had always considered her mother to be a tough cookie.

Andrea quickly knocked on her mother's door and waited, when no reply came she knocked again. After some moments the door opened and was shocked to see her mother crying, something she had never seen her do before.

"Mother, what's wrong?" Andrea asked, concern was written all over her young and beautiful face. She quickly put her arms around her mother as she implored her mother to tell her what the matter was. For several minutes Andrea, who had led her mother to lie on her bed, couldn't get anything out of her, she continued to sob. Not able to do anything about whatever it was that was causing her mother such intense unhappiness, Andrea sat by her and began stroking her mother's hair.

Andrea recalled her childhood days, and of moments like this when she was unhappy, her mother would stroke her hair and would sing to her. She couldn't remember the words but the tune came easily enough and she began to hum it. Mandy stopped crying and looked up at her daughter and then a smile appeared on her face. She recognised the tune immediately, and remembered how she used to sing that song to her while she caressed her soft hair, just as Andrea was doing to her then. Mandy would sing to her whenever she had cried or had woken up from a bad dream. Mandy had wanted so much to unburden to her young daughter everything that had been troubling her, including her past, thinking that only by doing so she could begin afresh and work on her future. Mandy weighed the pros and cons in her mind for several moments and when she finally convinced herself that it was the only way to go and was about to tell Andrea all about her sordid past, the look of innocence on Andrea's face made her change her mind.

It began to dawn on Mandy that there was no way in the world she could ever tell anyone in her family her story and still expected to be treated with the same respect afterwards. Even James didn't know everything about her past. She knew from her past experience that men could never handle the truth about their spouses' past. Most men, she reckoned, would prefer not to know. It came back in a flash to Mandy on how Andrea had treated her nearly two years ago, when they ran into Mong Kok at the supermarket. Andrea had sensed that she had lied about knowing him, and for months afterwards had treated her as a *persona non grata*. Mandy couldn't put a finger on what was it exactly that was troubling Andrea over the affair - jealousy perhaps. Andrea loved her father very much and it was natural for her to feel protective of James. She couldn't bear the thought of her mother knowing other men besides her father. Andrea must have thought that she was hiding something when Mong Kok had approached them and had called her mother by name.

In hindsight, Mandy realised how stupid it was of her to deny to Andrea about knowing Mong Kok when it was so obvious that he knew her. If only she hadn't snubbed Mong Kok the way she did at the supermarket, none of these things would have happened. Mandy could imagine what her daughter would think of her if she knew that her mother had been Mong Kok's mistress not long after their encounter at the supermarket.

Andrea was still stroking her hair with a touch so soft, and the feeling so soothing, Mandy closed her eyes and her mind began an instant flashback of the difficult days and months that she had with Andrea following that encounter with Mong Kok.

Mandy could recall with clarity how a week later Mong Kok had telephoned her and had asked her to have dinner with him. She was indignant that he had the gall to call her and she had told him so. She had also warned him that should he bother her again she would call the police. A week later, Mandy, who was wearing a light-blue long-sleeved blouse and a navy-blue pair of slacks, was relaxing after spending the whole morning doing her housework. After she had showered, she made herself a cup of tea, and was flipping through the row of the compact disc for something soothing that might help her figure out what she could do to repair her relationship with her daughter. She had, earlier that day, received a letter from Andrea. It contained two paragraphs in which she repeated, more or less, what she had said over the telephone on arrival in London, about five days earlier. In it she had written that she had enjoyed the MAS flight, arriving in London the following morning soon after breakfast. Andrea repeated what she had said about the weather - that it was cold. Finally in the last paragraph she then hinted that she had a lot of cleaning up to do and therefore she had better end the letter then. Oh, yes, she had promised to write again soon - that was it. Mandy folded the letter and placed it back in its envelope before putting it in her handbag. The ringing of the telephone on the coffee table in front of her gave her a slight jolt. She glared at it before picking it up. It was Mong Kok and he sounded belligerent.

"I thought I told you not to bother me? "Mandy barked into the mouthpiece.

"Don't hang up!" said Monk Kok. "There's someone here who would like to speak to you." Before Mandy could hang up the phone, she heard a voice that sounded a lot like her mother's.

"Hello! Hello! Who is this?" Mandy had demanded.

"Hello, May. It's me, your mother," said the voice.

"Ma! What's going on? Where are you?...."

"Mandy, this is Mong Kok here. Look out of your window and you'll see a metallic-gold Mercedes-Benz car. It's waiting to take you to me. Go to it now. When you get here, your mother will explain everything to you. Please don't do anything foolish like calling the police, or your husband. Otherwise you might make things worse for your mother. You do understand, don't you...." The line suddenly went dead.

Without bothering to change, Mandy hurried towards the waiting limousine. It drove off as soon as she had slammed the door shut. Twenty minutes later, the car slowed down as it approached an intricately-designed gate which began to slowly swing open. The Mercedes-Benz began to pick up speed as it drove through it, past well-manicured garden filled with a combination of fruit trees and flowers. A Malay-looking gardener momentarily looked up from his task of watering some plants and gave Mandy a curious look. The limousine finally came to a stop when it reached an imposing-looking mansion, built two stories high, on a hill that overlooked the sea. From the outside, the house was practically hidden from view by tall trees that surrounded it. Mong Kok was already at the doorsteps in front of the imposing facade of house built before the second world war, in the style favoured by the rich at that time. He reached for Mandy's hand to assist her out as soon as the chauffeur opened the car door for her.

"It's so nice to see you again," said Mong Kok as he caressed her hand. Mandy, who quickly pulled her hand back, was enraged by his temerity.

Mong Kok, whose face had an amused look on it, led the way towards the centre of his living room. It was tastefully furnished with several sofas and comfortable chairs on one side of the room, while in the dining area an intricately-carved, oval-shaped dining table stood. It was surrounded by eight chairs all of which were made of rosewood. Mandy's eyes panned the room quickly until they finally settled on the pathetic figure of her mother. She was shocked to see her look rather distraught and fidgety. She tried to avoid, without success, her daughter's probing gaze. When she finally looked up at Mandy, her eyes pleaded for compassion.

Mandy noticed that standing behind her mother's chair were two men who would look more comfortable in boxing shorts than in the tight suits they were wearing. In contrast, Mong Kok, who wore a pair of Bermuda shorts and a short-sleeved Hawaiian shirt, would look more at home on the beach than in the exquisitely furnished living room. Mandy rushed towards her mother.

"Ma, are you all right?," she asked. The old lady nodded her head as she stared at the carpet. She looked as if she wished she were somewhere else.

"Ma, what are doing here?"

But before the old lady could reply, Mong Kok said to Mandy, "I've brought her here so that she can tell you herself what a terrible mother she had been to you". Mong Kok gave Mandy a lecherous look. "You see, she had sold you to me for two hundred and fifty thousand ringgit."

"What the hell are you talking about? Sold me!"

"You see, your mother had been gambling heavily at my club and had lost just as heavily. She had received credit from me because she told me that you'd pay me. And each time I demanded payment from her, she always said that you'd make good all her debts, otherwise, she had said, you are mine. So, have you got two hundred and fifty thousand dollars for me?"

"You go to hell!" Mandy shouted at him. "If my mother owes you money, then let her pay you, not me." Mandy turned her back towards Mong Kok and made for the door.

As she was about to reach the door, she heard Mong Kok say to her, "If I don't get paid, your mother is a dead woman." Mandy stopped in her tracks. Mong Kok, whose lip had worked themselves into a sneer, threw his head back and laughed.

Mandy shot him an angry look, but he kept on mocking her with his laughter. Her mother, whose eyes were filled with fear, kept wringing her hands as she sat at the corner of the sofa. With great reluctance, Mandy walked back into the living room and sat on the sofa opposite her mother. As she sat there pondering her fate, she began to wonder whether this was God's punishment for her for being cruel to James.

Mandy had often thought James was a man without sin and therefore God was on his side. He had treated her with nothing but kindness and in return she had abandoned him like an old dress. Surely, what was happening to her was God's way of telling her that He was displeased with her.

"Don't look so worried," said Mong Kok. "All you have to do is stay with me for two years and we would have squared things up. After all, you're all alone now, aren't you? Your children have grown up and that they are studying overseas now. I can assure you that living here as my mistress is far better that living in that cramp flat of yours all by yourself."

Mong Kok seemed to have done his homework well, he seemed to know everything about her. Mandy shot another look at her mother. No doubt her mother had a lot to do with him being so knowledgeable, she thought angrily. Her mother, wisely, avoided her eyes, studying a spot on the carpet instead.

* * *

"Oh what a tangled web we weave, when first we practice to deceive" was what Sir Walter Scott wrote a long time ago. How right he was, Mandy sighed dejectedly at the thought.

"Ah, Chopin," she said, as she pulled out a compact disc from among the rows of other classical discs. "Perhaps you can help me ease some of my pains."

She took out the disc from its case and placed it carefully in the Sony player before settling down on the sofa. She closed her eyes when *Chopin's*

Fantasy Impromptu began to play and soon began to drift in and out of slumber. Her mind seemed to be floating in step with the movements of the music. Mandy had been an avid listener to classical music ever since she heard Tchaikovsky's Romeo and Juliet Overture at James's place some twenty years ago. And when they parted she took with her hundreds of tapes and CDs, most of them were classical music. In the beginning it was James who, not only had helped her with her selections, but had also cultivated her interest in classical music. She had taken it from there and had developed her interest further by exchanging tapes and CDs among her friends who had similar interest. Her group of classical music lovers would meet regularly in each other's homes. Apart from listening to the music each had brought for the purpose, they would also discuss the background of various composers. Occasionally their sessions could become so lively, it would be hard to imagine that music was their subject of discussion and not politics. Even though James had, in the early days of their marriage, patiently explained to Mandy the technical terms used in describing the various movements and tempos, as well as the composers and their life history, the very idea of dissecting each piece of music like one would a frog, was a bit much for him, but he did nothing to discourage Mandy in the pursuit of her interest in it. Unashamedly, James would shed some tears whenever he heard Tchaikovsky's music being played. Knowing how much Mandy had loved that particular piece by the Russian composer.

Mandy's decision to leave came out of the blue. It rendered James speechless for several moments before he finally asked her why. She quickly reminded him of the promise he had made to her when he had asked her to marry him - that he shouldn't ask why. He had noticed for nearly a week that she was withdrawn and morose. James initially had put it down as nothing more than the usual monthly thing women seem to suffer and had dismissed it from his mind. At that time he had a lot on his mind due to a pending plagiarism case against a publisher who had received, by mistake, of a copy of a manuscript he had sent out to another publisher. They had the book published, claiming that James had given them permission to do so. Despite his lawyer's claim that everything was under control, he was nevertheless still worried. It was unfortunate that the case had detracted him from detecting whatever it was that was troubling Mandy. The simple truth was that Mandy did not love him and she was bored with being married. James on the other hand thought that he should have paid more attention to Mandy's mood change than to his court case. He thought that he should have known better! After all, during the past twenty years, he had witnessed numerous changes in Mandy and somehow they'd always managed to work things out. This time he blamed himself for not paying more attention to her.

James will be the first to admit that despite all their years together, theirs hadn't been a perfect marriage, far from it. Because of his work he had to spend most of his time at home, while Mandy loved to go out. And because of his allergy to a number of outside food, his preference was for home-cooked meal. Mandy, on the other hand, had hated cooking and preferred to eat out. According to general reckoning, the marriage was perhaps better than most. It was due mainly to James's maturity, and also due to the fact that he had a disastrous marriage before and therefore had tried his best to avoid making the same mistake. That, and the fact that he had loved Mandy very much - faults and all - must have helped them ride out the ripple, the midi, as well as the wipe-out waves of the turbulent waters of their life together as man and wife. Yet, despite all the efforts he felt he had put into the marriage, it looked as if he had failed again, and that had added to his depression.

Mandy moved into an flat, almost similar in design as the one she had just left. Alexander and Andrea reluctantly went with her. Seeing how deplorable the condition of the flat was, James offered to help Mandy decorate it. With hardly a moment's hesitant, Mandy had accepted his offer. For three days they were together again. Sometimes, standing side by side, they patched, they painted, and they scrubbed the grime out of the badly neglected flat. The phenomenon of neglecting the upkeep one's rented house or flat was typically an Asian one. To be fair the flat that Mandy had rented had its interior painted before she moved in, but it was so badly done she felt compelled to do it all over again.

Unlike Mandy, most tenants don't give a hoot about their rented flats. They may demand that the premises were up to certain standard before they move in, but even if they stayed there for some years they wouldn't spend a dine on its maintenance. If during the course of time that wear and tear began to show on the walls or the woodwork, they seldom would lift a finger to stem it. To improve on it would be unthinkable, thinking that since it wasn't theirs why should they let the owners benefit. It never occurred to them that the environment they improve may be their own! Anyway, after three days solid work, the flat looked more liveable. Since both Alexander and Andrea were in school all day while their parents were doing they were naturally disappointment that they couldn't join in the fun.

"You call slogging all day and half the night for three days in a row, fun?," asked Mandy.

"Yeah!" Both of them answered in unison. The next day Mandy telephoned James and told him that her landlady couldn't believe what they've done to her place. Needless to say, she was pleased as Punch.

James took the separation hard in the beginning, but with Alexander and Andrea spending most weekends with him, he was able to bear it quite well, and as time went by, he began to adjust to living on his own again. He buried himself in his work and bit by bit his life became normal again.

Mandy was out like a light sometime during the third track, and by the time the disc played itself out she was having such a frightful nightmare she woke up in cold sweats. It took her a while to realize that the phone was ringing, it stopped as she was about to pick it up. Mandy was getting off the sofa where she had been lying and strode towards the wall unit to turn off her music system when the phone began to ring again. This time she picked it up immediately and almost dropped it on the floor when she recognised the voice on the other line, it was Steven Wong.

"Hello, Mandy," he said, "how are you. It has been a long time and you'll never guess who this is." Mandy felt her heart was beginning to race when she recognised Wong's voice. Keeping her voice sounding as normal as possible she said, "I'm sorry I'm not in the mood for games. If you wouldn't tell me who are, I'm going to hang up."

The response came instantly. "This is Steven Wong."

"Wong! how did you get my number," Mandy asked, fighting hard the fear that was threatening to choke her. "What do you want?"

"To offer you my sympathy," he said. "I've heard that you and that Malai Kwai husband of yours have split up and I just want to say I'm sorry."

"Thanks," said Mandy.

"As soon as I've heard, I made some enquiries about you. I think I know now quite a bit more about you than I did then." Wong sounded his usual cocky self. His mocking tone was beginning to terrify Mandy.

"I hate to sound like an old record," said Mandy, trying hard to match his tone, "You still haven't told me what is it that you want?"

"You!" he said. "I want you."

"Obviously you haven't heard," Mandy said, mockingly. "I'm with Mong Kok now."

"Oh, I didn't know that!." Wong answered. "In that case, I'll leave you alone, for now, but I'll get in touch with you again soon."

Knowing a few unsavoury characters in her life, Mandy could still remember the one thing they have in common: they always sounded so cocky when they think they have something over you. And Wong last remark sounded quite sinister to her. Having lived the way she had lived before she married James, she was sure that Wong must have something up his sleeve. She couldn't believe her bad luck - everything seemed to be going against her. Nothing seemed to work, no matter what she tried to do. It was as though she had been cursed. Despite the situation she was in, Mandy couldn't help thinking about James and the way she had hurt him. Even if she lived to be a hundred, she told herself, she'll never find anyone as kind and loving like him again. She had left him because she thought by doing so she could save his career. Leaving him was the hardest she had to do, but she had to do it to prevent him from being destroyed. She had no idea that Mong Kok would take the opportunity to take James's place by using her mother. Now it seemed that even Steve Wong, the man who had raped her, was also keen to possess her. She felt as if she was nothing but a chattel to be owned and used. While she was with James, she had found out that certain quarters had been digging into her past and were about to use those facts that they had managed to unearth to smear his name. James name was being touted as the likely candidate to take over the post as the next President of the country's most prestigious educational council - a kind of think-tank for the government on education. Mandy couldn't let anything prevent him from getting that post. She thought that the best thing for her to do was to leave him and let whoever who planned to destroy him know that she was no longer with James and therefore whatever dirt they had on her would be of no use against James.

Mandy managed to get an interview with a gossip columnist whose speciality was mud raking. With her usual ingenuity the columnist managed to get more dirt on Mandy than what she had bargain for, and had it published in her column with the usual style of nastiness she was known for.

James was nominated, seconded and finally elected with the full backing of the board. It was doubtful whether Mandy's brave attempt at self-mutilation, in which the article in the newspaper was intended, had anything to do with James getting the appointment.

Naively Mandy had thought that after all the wonderful years James had given her, sacrificing herself was the least she could do for him. What she didn't know was how hurt James was when he saw the article in the newspapers, and how little she accomplished. Ironically the people she hurt the most were her two children, the very two people she loved more than anything else in the world.

CHAPTER TWENTY-NINE

Mandy's announcement in the press caused Wong to be riveted in his seat. The calm that permeated his household ever since that explosive scene his family had when his wife had tOld Mandy's son that Wong was his father was about to be shattered. For some inexplicable reason Wong had wanted to get in touch with Mandy despite the consequence and predicable reaction he knew he would get from his own family if they ever knew. His desire to see Mandy was so overwhelming it was beyond logic. All he knew that he must see her at least once before it was too late. Now that he had met Alexander, he needed to tell her how sorry he was. Come what may, he told himself, he must see her!

Mandy was in the kitchen preparing lunch for Andrea and herself when she heard the telephone in the living room ring. She wiped her hands on her napkin and proceeded towards the telephone.

"Hello".

"Hello, is this Mandy?" Wong could hardly contain his excitement on hearing Mandy's voice. He was tempted to reveal himself to Mandy but had quickly changed his mind.

"Yes, this is she," Mandy replied.

"Well, hello Mandy, this is …," said the voice and he hung up.

Mandy hung up the phone and went back to finish her work in the kitchen. Several minutes later the phone rang again, and like before she got up and went to pick it up. Like before, she heard someone clearing his throat several times but made no attempts to speak. This time Mandy quickly slammed the phone down and returned to the kitchen. When the telephone began for the third time, she strode into the living room, picked up the telephone and shouted into the mouthpiece,

"If you don't stop bothering me, I'm going to call the police!" She hung up and was about to return to the kitchen when she suddenly lifted the receiver off its cradle. Instead of returning to the kitchen, Mandy picked up the newspaper, which she had earlier put on the coffee table, and began to browse through it. Her heart almost stop beating when she suddenly saw a photograph of her wearing a most provocative dress which left little to the imagination. The article accompanying it contained very little of what she had given the columnist, but had looked more like an *exposé* of a good-time girl. By the time she had read the whole article, she found herself crying with frustration. She tore the article from the newspaper and hid it in a drawer.

Andrea, who was reading a novel in her room, ran out and headed for her mother's room when she heard her cry. It was alien to her to hear her mother cry. She had never heard her mother cry like that before, and it frightened her.

"Mother, what's the matter?" she asked. "Why are you crying?"

Mandy looked at her daughter's young but anxious face and it made her cry more. The look of innocence written all over her lovely daughter's face inexplicably made Mandy think of her sordid past. She couldn't help thinking that at Andrea's age she had been beaten, starved, locked out of her house and raped. She mentally vowed that her daughter will never face the hardship she had faced.

"Andrea, I want you to know that until I met your father, my life had been nothing but a series of disasters. Your father was the kindest man I've even known and I don't think I'll ever find a kinder person even if I lived to be a hundred."

"But why have you been treating him so badly?" Andrea asked. "Has he done something wrong?" Looking anxiously at her mother.

"I had to, darling, so that he'll forget me," she said. "Believe me, I thought I was doing this in order to protect him from some bad people who were out to destroy his credibility and his reputation."

Mandy wiped her face and went to the desk by the window and retrieved from one of its drawers the article she had hidden and showed it to Andrea.

Mandy watched with dread the change of expression on her daughter's young face and immediately regretting she had shown it to her. But it was too late now. She knew sooner or later she had to tell her children the truth about her past in order for them to have any kind of future.

Mandy braced herself for the worst as she scrutinised her daughter's face for any tell-tale sign of what her reaction would be. All she could see was Andrea's grim look.

After what seemed like an eternity to Mandy, Andrea turned towards her mother and said, "Mother, I'm so sorry. I had no idea what you had gone through. I want you to know that regardless of what you think of yourself, you are the most wonderful mother in the whole world as far as I am concern, and I'm sure I speak for Alexander too. You've always been there for us."

Andrea hugged her mother for the longest time. When she finally released her grip, she continued. "I think I understand why you made that press statement, but what I don't understand is why do you have to leave daddy? You know he loves you very much, don't you?" Mandy nodded her head.

"I was a fool to have said some things to the columnist. She seemed so sympathetic and I must have got carried away. I never thought that she would twist everything I have said! I was so stupid. I thought I was doing it for your father's sake. You do understand, don't you? Your father has done so much for me, I thought that it was the least I could do." Mandy, who hardly ever cried, found herself crying all over again. Andrea cradled her mother's head in her arms and the two ladies gently rocked to and fro.

Andrea didn't understands it at all. How could her mother say that she is doing all this for her father when in reality she's destroying his very existence. Worst of all, why did she have to reveal all the sordid details of her past, to her that seemed unnecessary and most humiliating. All of a sudden it dawned on Andrea that her mother was really a very selfish woman; all she could think of was herself. A scandal of this nature would, without a doubt, cast a shadow on her father's reputation initially, but she was convinced that he'll come out of it unscathed. However, she doubted whether her mother would ever be as pure a driven snow as she had sought out to achieve. Andrea looked down at her mother, whose head was on her lap and was relieved to see that her mother had fallen asleep. She wanted to get away from her to seek some quiet moments to sort out her own thoughts regarding what had been happening. Andrea reached for a cushion and very gently lifted her mother's head from her lap and rested it on the cushion on the settee they had been sitting on.

Before she walked out of the living room, Andrea turned to look at her mother once more.

She couldn't help feeling sorry for her. On one hand she was saddened at the thought of what her mother had gone through and on the other, she was angry at her stupidity. By the time she reached her room, she was determined that she should try to do everything possible to save her parents' marriage. She was hoping that her father's love for her mother could stand this sudden upheaval that had befallen their lives.

Andrea couldn't help it, the more she thought of the newspaper article, the more angry she became with her mother. How could she be so stupid?

The first thing she should have done, Andrea told herself, was to tell her father everything her mother had told her after she had shown her the newspaper article, and to try persuade him not to accept her mother's proclamation on its face value. She had to convince him that her mother was only doing what she thought was right in order to protect him.

As it turned out, James, who was unaware of what Mandy had done, was about to deliver a lecture on the virtues of the institution of marriage versus the modern practice of couples living together and even to the extent of having children out of wedlock. He was unaware that many among his audience had already read the article in the newspaper. James looked rather perplexed when some among his audience had sniggered during the lecture. He was saved from further embarrassment when someone from the rear came forward and showed him a newspaper cutting. He quickly read it and put it aside after thanking the young woman who had given it to him. He then removed his reading glasses and continued with his lecture with the same enthusiasm he was known for in the lecture circuit. At the end of the lecture he found himself close to tears when they gave him such a standing ovation. As it turned out the young woman who had given him the newspaper cutting, was also a reporter sent by her newspaper to snoop on James. In the end she was so impressed with the way he conducted himself during and after his lecture, she wrote such a flattering article on him in her paper the next day. Dozens of people who had known James telephone her office and congratulated her for an article well done. Some had even suggested to her to read up on Mandy's rape trial which she had already done.

Mong Kok had just finished reading the article on Mandy and was about to take a sip of his brandy in the lounge of his sumptuous villa when one of his servants brought him the telephone. He put his drink down and spoke into the mouthpiece of the telephone. When he finished, he had a satisfied look on his swarthy face. He had just been informed that Mandy's mother had lost rather heavily again at one of his gambling dens. He shook his head in amazement at the thought at why anyone like Mandy's mother, who played Mahjong so badly, would be stupid enough to play against some of the best players in the country. He took out a notebook from his desk and noted that the old woman had already owed him more than ten thousand dollars. He felt that it was time for him to tighten the screws further. He knew in his heart that it will be just a matter of time when Mandy will come crawling to him. The thought gave him some satisfaction and involuntary smile appeared on his face.

Mong Kok poured himself another drink and began savouring both the expensive brandy as well as the thoughts of having Mandy naked in his arms. Both gave him complete satisfaction. After a while he got up from the sofa and rang for his chauffeur. In his car Mong Kok formulated his final plans for the complete capitulation of Mandy.

"It won't be long now, my dear," he muttered to himself. He leaned back in his seat and smiled.

ﻙﻙﻙﻙﻙﻙ

CHAPTER THIRTY

For the second time since that morning Mong Kok was summoned to the entrance of his new supermarket only to be told that it wasn't the *Menteri Besar's* car that was approaching, but another Mercedes-Benz that belonged to a rival supermarket owner.

Unaccustomed to wearing a suit, Mong Kok was perspiring profusely. He tugged at his collar nervously, trying to accommodate his thick neck in a shirt that was one size too small. He cursed himself for not thinking of buying a new shirt for this special occasion. He cursed too, the establishment, for making people like him feel alienated. It had taken a considerable effort on his part in order to get the *Menteri Besar* to officiate the opening of his supermarket.

When he had been told that the *Menteri Besar* do not, as a rule, officiate any opening of supermarkets, he had telephoned everybody he could think of who had owed him favours and began pressuring them. Unfortunately all these efforts brought him to nought. In the end only the good old fashion bribery of one hundred thousand ringgit to the *Menteri Besar's* party finally brought the desired result. The opening ceremony of

Mong Kok's new supermarket took less than half-an-hour.

The *Menteri Besar*, unaware of Mong Kok's seedy reputation, made the usual appropriate noises about how much the people had benefited from the government's ongoing efforts to improve the living standards of the people. He couldn't help but touch on the favourite subject of most of the politicians: How well the economy of the country was doing, and the need to expand it further. As he emphasized his points home with usual manner of using both hands, he noticed that his audience were mostly of familiar faces that seemed to appear in most of the public functions he had officiated. And to his astonishment, he saw one of them actually mouthing his often-used phrases. Angrily he cut short his speech and practically stormed off the dais and headed for his car. His startled entourage almost tripped among themselves in trying to catch with him as he strode towards his car.

Mong Kok quickly rushed to the *Menteri Besar's* side and shook the latter's hand just as he was about to get into his rather large imported car. Moments later, with outriders resplendent in their black and white uniforms astride their Japanese motor-cycles and with their sirens blaring, they cleared the way for the *Menteri Besar* official car and those of his usual hangers-on, to make a quick departure away from the gaily-coloured bunting that festooned Mong Kok's supermarket entrance.

* * *

Mong Kok's slightly stooped figure in the shadows brought a sudden fear to Mandy as she lay on the bed waiting to be taken by him as part of the deal she had made.

Mong Kok had telephoned a few days ago and had threatened to put her mother in one of his brothels unless she agreed to become his mistress for one year. She had offered that she'll agree to be his mistress for three months. He disagreed; he demanded six months. In the end they compromised to four months, whereby Mandy will have to stay with him at his house to do what he will with her, and at Mandy's insistence, there would be no appearance with him in public.

As it turned out, that after four months with him, it seemed like four years of hell on earth to Mandy. Mong Kok's taste in sex was so perverted, just the thought of it now rendered Mandy to vomit uncontrollably. Mandy had wanted so badly to erase it from her mind, the horrors of four month's imprisonment in Mong Kok's gilded cage - his mansion on the hill.

The memories, however, kept coming back to her like a bad dream, leaving her only to reappear whenever she tried to close her eyes to sleep. She kept telling herself that it was over and she need not have to see him again. Mong Kok had tried his best to be nice to her towards the end of her stay, expressing in his crude manner, his desire that she should stay on. He tried to sweeten the offer by suggesting to Mandy that should she stay, there was to be fifty thousand ringgit fixed deposit for her in the bank. Not wanting to antagonise him in any way, at least not until she was safely out of his house, Mandy told him that she'll think about it, but for the time being, she had said, she would like to take a break and stay with her mother.

Back in her mother's house, Mandy found it hard to sleep. Her mother who had been the cause of her sufferings under Mong Kok's hands seemed reticent in her presence. Due to lack of sleep, Mandy knew that she was losing a lot of weight. She also couldn't eat properly because vivid scenes of Mong Kok's sex in her mouth would appear as soon as she put any food in her mouth. Night after night Mong Kok would make her take his tool in her mouth, and when he came, he'd force her to swallow his sperm until she felt that she would choke. Night after night she would throw up after each of these sessions.

Mandy knew she needed help, but she wasn't sure whom to turn to. She had thought often of James and her daughter Andrea, whom she had persuaded to live with her father. Her son, Alexander, who was in Australia had not been in touch with her since he left soon after his court case was over.

Although James and Andrea were but a short taxi ride away from her, Mandy had not made any attempt to approach them for help. She felt that she had lost the right. She knew then that part of her life was over, she had to start anew somewhere - a new town perhaps, and a new name to go with it. She needed a new beginning, and she needed to do it now.

Meanwhile in a hotel coffee shop about a mile away from their flat, James and Andrea had just finished their lunch. It was their last Sunday's lunch together before Andrea left for London. Sunday lunch was a ritual they had been following for the last several months. And it looked like it had to be postponed until Andrea came back from her studies abroad. James had hated the idea of her leaving but he knew that there was no choice, Andrea had to finish the rest of her course in London. It was part of the twinning arrangement the Malaysian university had made with another university in London.

"Would you like some coffee, Miss?" the waiter asked Andrea.

"Yes, please." The waiter refilled her cup. He looked at James, who nodded his head to indicate that he too would like a refill.

"Daddy," said Andrea, as soon as the waiter was out of sight. "Are you sure you want me to go to London? I could stay and look after you?"

"I'd like that very much, but you must think of your future." James looked at his daughter's concerned face and smiled. "Go to London and complete your course, and while you are there learn much as you can about the business of high finance. London is still the business centre of Europe, contrary to what others may claim. Besides, your two brothers are there. And subtlety, of course, try to impart some of your religious knowledge to them. As a father, I failed them that."

"It would be nice to see them again," said Andrea. "However, I'm not sure about the religious knowledge part though. They probably know more than I do."

"I doubt that very much," said James. "Nobody reads and understand the Koran better than you do. I guess what I am trying to do is to pass my responsibility to you. It's not fair I agree, but I can't think of any other way of doing just that." James took a sip of his coffee before continuing. "I have this feeling that once you three have met, you'll all get along famously."

"I hope so, Daddy", Andrea said softly.

* * *

The announcement over the aircraft's public address system had just been made informing all the passengers to return to their seats and to fasten their seatbelts. The aircraft, it seemed, was about to land at Heathrow airport. Andrea couldn't help feeling slightly apprehensive about landing at a new place while at the same time looking forward to see all the sights of London she had only read about.

All week long she felt giddy with excitement just thinking about the prospect of working for a big London bank while finishing her course. It was part of her practical course. Andrea was excited when she was told that the bank she would be attached to was right in the City itself. Just think of it, two years in one of the most exciting cities in the world. As Andrea proceeded slowly towards immigration, her thoughts were of her father and Alexander who was down-under, way down-under, in Melbourne.

She hadn't thought of her mother ever since they that row over her decision to move in with Mong Kok, whom she considered most contemptible. Once Andrea had the misfortune of meeting her mother with Mong Kok at the same restaurant she and a couple of her friends had gone to. Mandy had seen her and had indicated her intention of coming over to their table. When she got up from her chair Andrea had turned her back towards her and had carried on with her conversation with her friends, pretending that she hadn't seen her.

Mandy had stopped in her tracks, feeling terribly hurt and humiliated, and had just managed to avoid making a fool of herself by allowing Mong Kok to pull her back on to her seat.

At Heathrow Airport, Andrea was both surprised and pleased to see her two step-brothers waiting for her as she emerged from Customs. It was something she hadn't expected and she was glad. She figured that their father must have telephoned them and told them her flight number and ETA.

They saw her first and waved. The warm smiles they gave her looked as if they too were pleased to see her. That, if nothing else, helped ease her apprehension a little. She smiled back at them as she struggled to keep her trolley moving in the direction she wanted it to go instead of being led by it. It had a defective wheel or something, all it wanted to do was to keep going to the left.

There seemed to be a lot of people waiting outside the barrier where friends and relatives eagerly awaited the new arrivals. Andrea's two step-brothers rushed to her and shook her hand. Their hand-shakes, to Andrea, seemed stiff and formal and all of a sudden her apprehension returned.

The two of them relieved Andrea of her baggage, and in between small talks regarding her flight to London, they made for their car which they had parked in the multi-storey car park nearby. Andrea had a hard time trying to keep pace with them for their style of walking was more of a march. Determined not to be outdone, Andrea began marching herself.

In the car, after a brief conversation in which they enlightened Andrea with quirks of the British weather, and some of the familiar sights along the way, the rest of their journey to their flat was done in silence.

Their flat, as far as Andrea could see was typical of what a bachelor's flat would be. The furnishing was Spartan to say the least. It looked to Andrea as if the furniture that her two brothers had chosen were chosen for its practicality, with scant regards to design or colour coordination. No attempts were made to match any of the pieces in the lounge. Further excursion in the flat confirmed what she had rightly concluded after she had opened the refrigerator, her two step-brothers were not only terrible at decoration, but at shopping as well. They seemed to buy all their groceries by the cartons.

She found an unopened carton of oxtail soups and another containing instant noodles. Elsewhere in the pantry were open cartons of foodstuffs and toiletries. In a tiny kitchen adjoining the living room Anthony, the younger of her two step-brothers, made some coffee, while Ronald who was three years older, took out some cakes they had bought, most probably at the airport canteen, and began putting them onto a plate which had flower decoration around its rim.

Inwardly Andrea found the scene quite amusing. The picture of domesticity in which her two strapping step-brothers, both nearly six feet tall, didn't seem to fit. A smile appeared involuntarily on her face. Anthony, conscious of the look she was giving him, looked up and said, "What's so funny?"

"Nothing," she said. "I'm so happy to have met you two at long last."

"Me too," replied Ronald.

"And Me," said Anthony who walked into the living room with the tray in his hands.

Andrea walked towards Ronald, stood hesitantly in front of him for a moment and then gave him a hug. She then went to Anthony and gave him a hug as well.

To her dismay, Andrea found her tears beginning to well up in her eyes, and without further ado, they burst their banks. though she couldn't see it, her two step-brothers were trying hard to hold back their own tears. In the end, all three ended up crying on each other's shoulders. Andrea couldn't help wishing that Alexander was there too.

That afternoon they took Andrea for a drive around the city, telling her this was only an overview of London. Tomorrow, they said, they were going to spent the whole day visiting some of the various sights London was well-known for. Earlier in the car, while Ronald, who was driving, pointed out some of the familiar sights to Andrea, Anthony, who was into music, was telling her all about the music scene in the country. When Andrea showed some interest in a particular band, Anthony quickly offered to take her to one of their concerts.

Andrea observed that Anthony had the gift of the gab and would prattle on about anything and everything while Ronald was more reserved, choosing his words more slowly and precisely. In looks, she and Anthony seemed to have some traits in common which they shared with their father, while Ronald looked very much like his mother. There was a picture their mother on the mantelpiece and Andrea had studied while both of her brothers were in the kitchen.

The hotel in which her office had booked her in was at the Holiday Inn in Swiss Cottage, a suburb not far from the West End of London. After her two brothers had dropped her off, Andrea rang personnel at the bank and told them who she was and that she had just arrived in London. The personnel manager, who introduced himself as Mister Stewart, bid an unenthusiastic welcome to Andrea and told her to come to see him first thing Monday morning, which gave her the weekend to spend with her two brothers. Andrea assured Stewart that she'd be there, but before she could say anything else, she heard the line being disconnected. So much for English hospitality, she thought to herself.

"Never mind," she said cheerfully to the empty room. "I've just met my two brothers and they were positively happy to see me!"

Mr Stewart was exactly as what Andrea had figured on how he would look like. Dressed in a dark-grey pin-striped three-piece suit, white shirt and a polka-dot maroon-coloured tie, Stewart tried to look exactly what he was not - a dashing figure. Instead, he looked more like a typical union man - which was what he was - until the management kicked him upstairs to make him more malleable. In the beginning he had a hard time trying to come to grips with the various new terminology his branch of management had spawned, let alone understand. He had no idea that modern management could be so complex and he feared that he may not be up to it. He seemed to have persevered, nevertheless.

Stewart recognised his shortcomings and got himself enrolled in an evening course in personnel management. Now he understood why the bank had offered him the job, they had wanted him to make a fool of himself so that they could kick him out in disgrace. In the end it was he who had laughed when he finally earned himself a degree.

With a new-found confidence the degree had brought him, Stewart began to put to the top management proposals on how to streamline the various departments, which included cutting down the number of staff. Among his proposals were the early retirement of some of the senior staff, people who had made his life miserable at some stage during his working career with the company.

Needless to say, it made him highly unpopular with his former union. They promptly kicked him out the moment he accepted the management post and had replaced him with another unionist who was fanatically married to the cause.

Andrea's meeting with Stewart, as it turned out, was short and sweet. She had come early that Monday morning, and while in the lift she had the good fortune of meeting her Malaysian boss, who apparently was on a visit to the London office. And when they had got off on the same floor he offered to introduce her to Stewart.

Stewart was startled at first when he saw McNeil, a person whom he had long respected and admired, had walked into his office with Andrea. McNeil introduced Andrea to Stewart and when he spoke of Andrea as if she was his prodigy, Stewart was smart enough to take notice.

Every new recruit who had joined the bank and who had gone to see Stewart without exception tend to experience mild nervous disorder afterwards. Most will eventually recover from it, some felt that they couldn't get away fast enough from the imposing-looking building and never to return. Andrea on the other hand felt that Stewart was rather perfunctorily with her during the meeting with him. She didn't think very much about it except that she was glad that it was over, and was looking forward to what challenges her new job would bring.

⚜ ⚜ ⚜ ⚜ ⚜

CHAPTER
THIRTY-ONE

Andrea did find her new job most challenging indeed, and she was grateful for that. She found that her 9.00 AM to 10:30 PM day did not allow her much time to think about anything else, least of all about her mother. Andrea couldn't help feeling terribly disappointed and sad whenever she thought of her mother. To her she was a person whom she had always adored and respected. She couldn't understand how her mother could just throw away her values, her self-respect and her morality by going to live with Mong Kok.

As of late, Andrea had often thought that perhaps her mother never had any moral values in her in the first place. After all, her own mother (Andrea's grandmother) had never bothered to marry the man she was living with. Mandy was just emulating her mother. Will she herself be like her mother some day? Will she throw everything that was good and decent out and live like her? Andrea shuddered at the thought.

Looking back, Andrea could see clearly that everything about her mother seemed to be fluid. She never believed in permanency in anything, and certainly not in any relationship. Outside the family Andrea couldn't recall her mother having any other friends. And of late too, Andrea had often thought of her father. What a decent man he was. She smiled at the thought of how he had struggled to try to impart some of his religious knowledge to her when she was small. His anxieties seemed to derive from his limited knowledge on the subject initially, but later on as he began to research more and more on it, the more overwhelmed and worried he became.

He was unsure how to impart, what he had learned from the books, to his pragmatic daughter. James was apprehensive because in the Muslim religion, according to the Koran, was based on a dogma, a body of narratives and moral and juridical injunctions – all of which must be accepted without questions.

Central to the dogma is the belief that there is no god but God (Allah) and Muhammad was His Apostle and the last of the prophets. It became particularly difficult for him to try to explain to Andrea that in the Koran, Muslims were also enjoined to believe in the previous prophets and their scriptures.

As it turned out Andrea, an avid reader just like her father, and who had read all the books he had brought home including the Koran, seemed to have accepted the dogma without difficulty. Determined to decipher everything what the

Muslim holy book had to say, Andrea had taken a course in Arabic. By the time she had completed the course, Andrea was able to read the Koran loudly and fluently, as most Muslims were disposed to do, whether in their homes or at functions such as a wedding or thanks-giving. But unlike many Muslims who were only able to read the Koran fluently without understanding a word of it, Andrea understood its meaning quite well. It was without a doubt an enviable achievement and James was proud of her.

At the graduation ceremony, which included a reading of a short verse from the Koran, James had beamed at his daughter when she had walked away with the first prize. He knew then his fears had been unfounded.

Andrea didn't like living in Swiss Cottage at first. She felt that it had nothing to offer: no famous monuments to speak of and it didn't even have a decent restaurant, apart from the ubiquitous MacDonald's and some Chinese and Indian Takeaways.

Worst of all, it did not even have a proper High Street like most towns in England do. The only thing she liked about it was its close proximity to Central London. Although the Holiday Inn was convenient, just a short walking distance to the station, but after two weeks staying in one of its cramp rooms, she was delighted to be able to find a decent flat in nearby St John's Wood.

The ground floor flat was among several blocks of flats that was located in a decent area not far from Regent's Park, and it had a balcony that overlooked a quaint back garden. But the best thing of all was that it had a decent size bedroom, which she was going to use herself, and another bedroom, a smaller one, which she visualised would be nice as a study-cum-guestroom. She was thinking of Alexander or even her father, who might want to come and visit.

With the help of her two step-brothers, Andrea managed to make her two-bedroom flat bright and cosy. Once her learning curve at the bank seemed to have tapered off – meaning she was beginning to know her job better, her working time became regulated from 9.00 to 5.00, but a week later her lectures began at her college. This time she had to make the rush from work right across town to her college.

Andrea found that she had only the weekends to do up her place. At first she tried to do it on her own, but after having to clean up spilt paint from her entire staircase one weekend, and after bruising her knee when she had fallen off the stepladder during another, Andrea decided to solicit the help of her two step-brothers. Not wanting to impose on them at first, Andrea gave them only light jobs to do. Seeing what she was trying to do, Ronald asked her point blank what exactly she was trying to accomplish in her flat. When she told him what she had in mind, he quickly drew up a work schedule and after discussing with them the scope of the jobs to be done, he made three lists and each of them took one each. Andrea gave him a smile and nodded her head. She felt so relieved at being able to relinquish her job as work leader to her elder brother.

For nearly six weeks, working on weekends only, the three of them finally completed the transformation of Andrea's flat from a damp and dingy one into something that was bright and cosy.

To celebrate their accomplishment, Andrea told her two brothers that she was going to invite them to a dinner party the following weekend. She also invited some of her colleagues at work to come.

To her credit, it turned out to be a great success even though some of the food came from a Chinese and an Indian Takeaway nearby.

As the months wore on, Andrea got to know her two brothers more and more and their friendship became stronger and stronger. She couldn't be sure whether she had managed to impart any of her religious knowledge to them or not, as her father had suggested, but when she asked them to breakfast at her place during Ramadan a few months later, she was pleased to learn that the both had been fasting without missing a day ever since the fasting month began. And when they pulled out their prayer mats out of a bag Anthony had brought with him, they could have knocked her down with a feather.

Despite her efforts to try to keep images of her mother out of her thoughts, they always come crashing in uninvited. And the most disgusting thing of all was that the images of her in the arms of that despicable man, Mong Kok.

Andrea could still remember the time when she and her mother had met Mong Kok in the supermarket a long time ago. She remembered too how her mother had lied to her when she had said that she had never laid eyes on him before.

What a liar she was! It turned that her mother had known him long before she married her father. Andrea was sure that they had been lovers. She found the prospect utterly repulsive. She couldn't understand how her mother could even bear to be in the same room with the likes of Mong Kok. To think that she would be in the same bed with the man was beyond her. To Andrea, Mong Kok, despite his enormous wealth, could never fit in their world.

She recalled what her father had told her once about money. *"Money is like a tool, use it as you would any tool, nothing more nothing less".*

People like Mong Kok use money to corrupt and to debase the morals of men and women who were weak. What Andrea couldn't understand was why would her mother do what she did. Perhaps she did it because of fear. What was she afraid of? What sort of hold did Mong Kok have on her?

Suddenly that macabre idea gave her some comfort. It surely was a possibility, she told herself - her mother was coerced into doing what she did! Andrea felt elated suddenly and decided to call her mother, but when she looked at her watch and saw that it was almost ten o'clock, she changed her mind. It would be six o'clock in the morning, far too early for her mother.

Andrea waited for a couple of hours before she made the attempt to call her mother. She had hoped that Mong Kok wouldn't be the one who'd answer the telephone. A lady answered the telephone and when Andrea asked her if she could speak with Mandy she was told that Mandy no longer lived there and hung up.

Andrea was filled with gladness at the news that her mother was no longer living with Mong Kok. She picked up the phone again and this time she tried her mother's flat. She heard the ringing tone and waited. She waited for several moments and was about to hang up when she heard her mother's voice.

"Hello," Mandy sounded as if she had just woken up.

"Hello, mother. Are you all right?"

"Yes, darling, I am now." Her voice began to break up and Andrea could hear her crying. "It's so nice to hear your voice. First of all, I'd like to apologize for everything...for not seeing you off at the airport...for not writing to you...or phoning you..." Mandy covered the mouthpiece and blew her nose in a tissue before continuing. "I couldn't face you after what I've done and I didn't know what to say to you in writing or over the telephone. Will you ever forgive me?"

"There's nothing to forgive, mother. I understand."

"No, you don't understand!" said Mandy. "You couldn't possibly understand. How could you? When you get back I'd like us to get together so that I can explain everything to you - Okay?"

"Yes, mother. I'd like that very much." They talked a while longer, and when they hung up Andrea felt so relieved that she and her mother were on speaking terms once again. Tears began to roll down her cheeks uncontrollably.

Mandy too felt so grateful to the All-Mighty that Andrea had telephoned. To be able to say to her daughter the things that she had been wanting to say to her all this time was such a relief to her. When all her crying was done, Mandy did one thing she never thought that she could never have the courage to do - she called James. She had often thought what a fool she had been for leaving him. He was the best thing that had happened to her and she was too blind to see it.

"Hello, it's me," she said softly, as soon as she heard his voice.

"Hello Mandy," he replied. "It's nice to hear your voice again."

Mandy couldn't help thinking how much alike father and daughter sounded, and sometimes both would use the very same phrase with her. Mandy tried desperately to suppress an unwanted tear that she knew would soon be followed by others. She didn't want to have to cry again. When James asked how she was, she managed to answer clearly how she was. But when he said to her that he had missed her and had often thought of her, she abandoned herself to her emotions and cried like a baby.

"I've missed you terribly," she finally managed to say.

James, aware how vulnerable he could be when dealing with his emotions with regards to Mandy, threw caution to the winds and asked her whether they could have dinner together the next night. James tried in vain to suppress his tears that soon flow when Mandy had said yes.

James knew that he could be in for another dosage of pain if he ever saw Mandy again. But his heart overruled his head, and so he gave in to his heart. Mandy went shopping for a *Malay baju kurung* with accessories to match. James will be shocked to see her in a Malay dresses instead of the Western attire she had most preferred.

She had said a silent prayer for a second chance with James. She knew that her chances were very slim indeed knowing James and his set of principles. She had walked out of him and their children and to James that would be pretty hard to forgive. Still, she was clinging to the hope that perhaps that he might forgive her this time; after all, didn't he invite her to dinner?

James picked Mandy up at her flat in a Mercedes-Benz instead of his *Proton Perdana* Mandy knew he had owned. Mandy had once jokingly remarked that it was not a car but just a vehicle. The truth of the matter was, James had only recently sold his Proton Perdana and had bought the Mercedes-Benz, not because of the glamour and the prestige it might bring him, but it was a damn sight more reliable car than all the other cars put together. He had bought the Perdana when it first came into the market out of pride that it was the first Malaysian made car that looked like it had some substance and he hadn't been disappointed.

Mandy couldn't help noticing that James had bought the Mercedes in the colour she had once remarked to him that she had liked. They had often joked about how one day when they could afford it, they'd go and buy themselves a brand new Mercedes-Benz.

"You did it!" she said. "You bought a Mercedes-Benz in the colour that I like."

"Yes, I did," James said, smiling as he opened the door for her.

Mandy couldn't help thinking what a crass slob Mong Kok was compared to James. Not once would he open the car door for her nor would he pull back a chair for her in a restaurant or wherever.

Once they were out of the car, he'd be the one walking miles ahead of her, and invariably he would seat himself long before Mandy had even reached the table.

And whenever he ate he had table manners of a pig. He would spit out bits and pieces of food onto the table making a molehill-size pile by the time they had finished their meal. What Mandy found so disgusting was that he'd do this as if it was the most natural thing to do. And he would be totally oblivious to the stares of nearby diners.

To make things worse, at the end of the meal he would invariably ask for some tooth-picks. He would pick his teeth with the same intensity and temerity as he had done with his food - all to utter disgust of the diners around them.

Sitting across the table from James, Mandy could feel her heart was about to beat wildly. It was a rather pleasant sensation, one she had rarely experienced before. She was wondering whether this was what being in love was like. She recalled having read of similar experience her heroines from Mills & Boon novels had felt, and they all seemed to put it down as being in love.

"My goodness!" James exclaimed. "You are looking more beautiful now than you were when we first met."

"Thank you," replied Mandy, thrilled at the compliment. "You are looking not so bad yourself."

"For a man of my age, you mean?" James gave her a smile.

"James, you're ageless, you know that, don't you?"

A couple had walked by and gave them a look which both of them had seen before. It was a familiar look which used to cause Mandy considerable discomfort before.

Today it was different, she felt proud to be in James's company. And that was something new too. Two new experiences in one day, experiences she had never felt before.

As they ate, Mandy kept glancing across the table at James. She noticed that he had lost a bit of weight, and the lines at the corners of his eyes seemed more prominent than before. They were hardly noticeable when they were living together. She noticed something else too; James was gripping his fork and spoon as if they were something heavy. It was then when she noticed the tell-tale swellings that she had seen before when someone was suffering from arthritis. Mandy turned her attention from the swelling on James's hands and focussed it on his face. There was no doubting the pain he was suffering as he struggled to cut the steak on his plate. It was written all over his face.

Mandy quickly put down her knife and fork and asked James quietly if she could cut his steak for him. He gave her an embarrassed smile before nodding his head in a dejected manner.

Mandy reached across and began cutting the meat into small chewable pieces for him. He nodded his thanks before slowly picking up his fork and stabbed the nearest chunk of meat on his plate and brought it to his mouth. Mandy returned to her own plate and pierced a slice of carrot and put it in her mouth. They ate their meal in silence, each deep in thoughts.

Mandy wished at that moment that she had ordered a glass of wine. She felt that she could do with a slightly stronger drink than the glass of orange juice that she was having. She was about to order one when she realised that it was James she was having a meal with and not Mong Kok.

With Mong Kok she would prefer to be slightly drunk in anticipation of what was coming. And what was coming was something she knew she couldn't avoid.

Mong Kok had never refrained from having sex with her even when she was having her period. She felt nauseated the first time he had plunged into her despite the fact that she was particularly bloody with a heavy period.

Mandy had learned the hard way never to deny Mong Kok sex. It was the time when she had just moved in with him and at that time she was having her period. She told him that he could not have sex with her because she was having the curse.

"That's all right," he said. "You have more than one hole." The oral and anal sex that he had forced her to endure that night was so horrible, she knew she'll never forget it for the rest of her life.

Mandy soon learnt that by having a few drinks before going to bed with Mong Kok was the only way she could endure his sick love-making. Sometimes, while still in the act, and if the drink had worn its effect and she had become sober, she would pretend that it was gentle James who was making love to her and not the horrible Mong Kok and the act became tolerable. And on very rare occasions it even helped her reach her climax. It happened very rarely though; most of the time she would just lay there and pray for it to be over soon.

Looking across the table at James, Mandy knew then that she was looking at the only man she had ever loved and most probably the only one she ever will.

All of a sudden Mandy felt a great sense of remorse for having let all the years go wasted by, and to her dismay she felt her tears were beginning to well up in her eyes, and before she could reach for her handkerchief they began to roll down her cheeks uncontrollably. In a flash James was by her side, looking very concern.

"Mandy, are you all right?"

"Yes, I'm all right," she said.

James's gentle hand on her shoulder had a soothing effect on her. She wanted so badly to have him hold her in his arms. As if he had read her thoughts, James pulled her up gently from her chair and put his arms around her and kissed her right in the middle of the crowded restaurant. There was silence at first.

Some of the patrons were embarrassed at sight of seeing an older man embracing a woman who seemed to be young enough to be his daughter. However, soon, some of the younger ones were thrilled at the sight and they wolf-whistled at them, while others began clapping their hands.

James, oblivious at first at the attention given to them, became embarrassed when he saw people looking at them. It dawned on him that the claps were meant for them. He slowly pulled away from Mandy. Mandy, who'd finally become aware of what was happening around them, clung on to James and kissed him again. That action brought a spontaneous, thunderous response from the crowd.

"I love you," she said to James. "I guess that I've always loved you and didn't know it. Please forgive me for all the hurt that I've caused you. I know that I have no right to ask, but if you'd give me another chance I'd like us to try again."

James, without saying anything, took her hand in his and looked at her. Mandy, not knowing what was in his mind, was close to panic when his answer did not come immediately. She felt her cheeks were beginning to feel hot as embarrassment encroached.

"Yes. I think we both should give ourselves another chance," replied James finally, much to Mandy's relief. "Let's go home." Amidst loud applause from the crowd, they embraced for the longest time before leaving the restaurant holding hands.

❈❈❈

CHAPTER THIRTY-TWO

Alexander's court appearance was short and sweet. Steven Wong, at the advice of his own lawyer, agreed to drop all charges against Alexander. Goh, Alexander's lawyer, had contacted Wong's lawyer and had reminded him that should they go to trial, he would not hesitate to rake up Wong's rape case since it was the mitigating circumstances in which his client had acted the way he did.

* * *

James was still about two blocks away from his flat when he heard the sound of sirens which sounded odd to his ears. It didn't sound like the ordinary police sirens nor the siren of the ambulances, it was more like a cacophony of sirens. As he drew nearer to his home, it grew louder and ominous and for some reason he felt uneasy.

Without realising it he began to accelerate, and felt at the same time his heart too began to race. As soon as he entered the front gate to the flats he found a crowd of people blocking the entrance to the inner court car park. He sounded his horn but was told by someone amongst the crowd that the car park was closed. James reversed his car slowly to avoid hitting people that seemed to be coming in from everywhere. James drove his car to the rear car parking area and parked. A neighbour he whom he recognised by face and not by name, tapped on his window.

"There had been an accident at your flat," he blurted out to James.

Before he could continue, James was already running towards the lift. On reaching there, James found a notice stuck on the lift's door which informed everyone not to use the lifts but to use the stairs instead.

James ran up the stairs to the fifth floor where his flat was located. What he saw on reaching there almost made his heart stop. Debris were strewn along the entire corridor, and the walls on both sides close to his flat were all blacken up and pock-marked. Up ahead, right in front of his flat stood two policemen. They seemed to be conferring in earnest with each other, and judging from their uniforms James knew that they were senior police officers.

They looked up questioningly at James as he approached them. One of them, the junior of the two, raised his hand indicating to James that he was not to come any closer.

"What has happened?" James asked. "My name is James and I am a tenant in there," pointing to the flat behind them.

The same policeman quickly walked towards James and tried to stop him from going any further. James ignored him and kept on walking until he reached his flat. The other policeman who was standing right in front of James's flat saw what was happening became alert immediately and was about to draw his gun but for some reason changed his mind.

He stepped forward and gently prevented James from entering his flat.

"I'm sorry, you're not to go in there. The bomb squad people have not finished with their investigation yet."

"Look, this is my flat. I have the right to know what happened," James shouted at them.

Despite hearing the words coming from his mouth, it was obvious to James that something terrible had happened. His charred front door was off its hinges and the front room had all its windows blown off. Shards of glass were strewn all over the front passageway.

"I'm so sorry," said the policeman, "there had been an explosion. A body of a woman had been found..."

"My wife...? Was there anybody else?"

"We found only one body," replied the policeman. He was about to ask James if there were anyone else, but stopped short when he saw James starring at the covered body on the stretcher. He gently put his hand on James's shoulders and said,

"It is necessary for me to ask you to identify the body. Tell me if you're not up to it...."

James apparently did not hear him for he kept starring at the inert covered figure on the stretcher. The officer kneeled down and lifted the covering which caused James to flick back in horror. The sound coming from James sounded more like a wounded animal than from a human being. Despite what the bomb did to her face and parts of her body, James recognised the rings on her fingers and the watch which she had a habit of wearing on her right wrist instead of her left. The watch was present he gave a week ago, a day after they got together again.

Later at the morgue James was about to touch Mandy's badly disfigured face when he heard commotion coming from behind him. He turned his head to look behind him and saw Alexander and Andrea being restrained by an attendant at the door.

"It's all right, they are my children," said James as he quickly zip up the body-bag that contained Mandy's remains. He wiped away his tears with the back of his hand. He stood up and went to his children trying his best to steer them away from the remains of their mother.

"There had been an accident," he began, but before he could finish his sentence, Andrea had pulled away from his clutches and had run towards the body-bag and began to pull at the zip. James ran after her but by the time he reached her, Andrea had already unzipped the body bag. Moments later a loud wail pierced the air.

James quickly held her in his arms and with a considerable effort, gently led her away from the scene with Alexander, looking rather shocked, in tow. As he drove his car towards the city amidst a lot of crying from Andrea, who was sitting in the back seat, and his son sitting next to him in front, James was trying to think of why anyone would want to kill Mandy, or was that bomb meant for him? He shook his head as if to stop it from going into a tailspin. The killing seemed so senseless and his mind kept going back to the scene where he found the two policemen standing in front of his flat. He kept hearing the words "We found no other bodies among the debris. We found no evidence of other than the woman being in there," said the senior of the two policemen. He remembered the mixed feeling of anguish and relief on hearing those words.

Unaware to James the senior of the two policeman was watching him with a curious expression on his face. He remembered how angry he was when one of them asked James, "Where were you during the last couple of hours?" For a split-second James had wanted to throw a punch at him.

Fortunately for both of them the situation diffused itself when James realised what the policeman was trying to do. He shook his head in disgust at their technique and wondered whether it ever produced any tangible results.

"At the university," James replied curtly.

"If you wouldn't mind, we'd like you to come to the station with us and give us a statement," the officer said.

All of a sudden James sensed that the police officer's mannerism had changed. He had dropped all pretence of politeness and he seemed to be all business. It began to dawn on James that he had now become a suspect and he became angry.

"Am I a suspect?" he asked angrily.

"At this stage, everyone is a suspect,' he replied without showing any emotion. "Please come with us."

They led James towards the staircase where he found himself walking down the stairs with one policeman in front of him and another behind him.

At the station James had to give details of his movements from the time he left Mandy and his two children, Alexander and Andrea, soon after they had breakfast together, until he came running towards the two policemen right in front of his flat approximately two hours after an explosion ripped through his flat killing Mandy. His two children apparently had left the flat soon after he did and had spent the whole day out with their friends. They didn't know about their mother's death until they came home not long after James was conducted to the police station in the company of the two policemen. A policeman that stood guard in front of their flat told them what had happened and was asked to go to the same police station where they took their father to.

Alexander took it quite calmly at first, but a few minutes later, tears were seen flowing down his cheeks as he sobbed silently. Andrea on the other hand had wailed uncontrollably on James's shoulders. Seeing how distraught James and his two children were, the officer who had been hostile towards James began to relent somewhat. He asked whether any of them would want anything to drink. None of them wanted any, and after several more minutes of questioning they told James that he and his two children were free to go.

Both Alexander and Andrea had wanted to go back to their flat but James told them that it wouldn't be a good idea. Besides, he told them, he doubted that the police would let them in. Instead, he took them to a hotel where they took two rooms. He shared one room with Alexander while Andrea took the adjoining room.

James headed for the bathroom as soon as they got in their respective rooms. He hadn't shown any emotion in front of his children so far but felt that he couldn't contain it any longer as he locked the door behind him. He didn't want Alexander or Andrea to see him break down. It was something he couldn't afford to do because he felt, at this moment, his children needed him to show courage. As soon as the bathroom door closed behind him, all the emotion that he had managed to contain so well from his children released itself like an escape valve of a steam engine, and he found himself babbling like a child.

Unknown to him, Andrea had entered their room and both she and Alexander couldn't help but hear their father crying in the bathroom. They looked at each other with sad eyes and soon both of them broke down and cried too. On hearing some noise outside the bathroom door, James quickly pulled himself together and came out only to find his two children crying on each other's shoulders. He went over to them and gave each of them a hug.

Unlike Andrea, Alexander was spared from having seen the mangled body of their mother at the morgue, where one of the two policemen had taken James to soon after they had taken a statement from him at the station.

James was angry at being treated like a suspect at first, but later on he felt glad that they were taking their investigation seriously. He for one had wanted to know who could have done such a terrible thing to Mandy. Despite what the bomb did to her face which was blown beyond recognition, James recognised the wedding band and the engagement ring on her finger and the watch she had a habit of wearing on her right wrist instead of her left. The watch was a present he had given her a day after they got together again.

For almost a week James had felt he had lived again. And last night when they had a wonderful dinner together at a French restaurant, Mandy had told him how much she had loved him and had vowed never to leave him again, James felt that life had never felt so good to him and he didn't want it to end.

This morning when they had breakfast together they had talked about the possibility of going on a holiday to the Philippines and Hong Kong with the kids. They were going to surprise Alexander and Andrea this evening over dinner. It was during the preparation of that dinner when Mandy was called to the door to receive a parcel which had a type-written note that said `not to be opened until dinner - signed H'. She smiled when she had read the note, assuming that it was from James. She took the parcel into the kitchen with her and placed it on the kitchen table close to where she was working. Half-an-hour later the explosion demolished the entire kitchen and part of the living room, shattering all the flat's windows along the corridor.

Fortunately no one was passing by at that time. The corridor was the favourite place for children to ride their tricycles in. If the bomb had exploded an hour later it would have been a different story. As it were, at the time of the explosion, most, if not all the residents in the adjoining flats were in their respective flats cooking their dinner or taking their afternoon nap and not outside hanging about along the corridors while waiting for their husbands or their children to return home from work and from school.

"Daddy, when can we bring Mommy's body home?" asked Andrea. James looked at his daughter for the longest time before turning to his son.

"I want you two to be very brave," he began. "Mommy was killed by a bomb, which according to the police must have been remote-controlled. And it must have exploded not too far from her because the force was so severe. It did a lot of damage to her body...her face was beyond recognition...." James tried unsuccessfully to continue. He ended up covering his face with both hands and cried.

Andrea rushed to her father and tried to console him as best as she could. Alexander too came forward and stood by his father's side. He placed a hand on his shoulder and said, "Don't cry father, please don't cry."

Alexander was trying desperately not to break down again but failed. Tried as he may, he couldn't stop his tears from flowing from his already red eyes.

All night long James found himself asking the same questions. Why was Mandy killed? Who could have wanted her killed? Was the bomb meant for her only? Or was it meant for him? How about Alexander and Andrea, are they free from any danger? All these questions were swirling in his head and by morning he knew then that he could not take any chances with regards to their safety.

He had to find a safe place for them to stay while the investigation into Mandy's murder was being carried out. Despite protests from Alexander and Andrea, James sent them off packing to his friend's place in Singapore. David had asked James to come too, but James had declined telling his friend that he should stay just in case the police may need his help with their inquiries. In reality he had stayed back in order to assist his friend catch Mandy's killer.

"By the way, do you know of a man called Mong Kok?" James asked his friend as they sifted through the debris for some clues the police may have missed.

"Mong Kok? Sure I know of him. He's the man the police had been after for all kinds of criminal activities. Only they couldn't pin anything on him," replied Rahim Rahman, a retire police superintendent. When James did not say anything further, Rahim stood up from his crouching position and turned to James and said, "Why do you ask? Do you think he has anything to do with Mandy's death?"

James gazed at his friend for a moment or two before replying. "I'm not sure, but Mandy telephoned him about a week ago. I found his name and telephone number in her hand bag, and when I called that number it turned out to be a company but Mong Kok wasn't in at that time. I asked the lady over the telephone what the company's general activities were. She was not very cooperative except to say that they were importers of goods mainly from Thailand. With a help from a friend in the Customs and another from the IRD, I found out that the company was the biggest importer of Thai durians in the country but when I checked from the records my friends in the IRD gave me concerning the income declared, it did not commensurate with what my friends in the Customs said they were importing."

"So, Mong Kok did all that work for nothing, is that what you mean?" Asked Rahim.

"Something doesn't smell right and I don't mean the durians", James added. "Can you find out a bit more about him?"

ℵℤℵℤℵℤ

CHAPTER THIRTY-THREE

Mong Kok was watching the evening news on television when a knock on at the front door brought two of his maids running into the living to see who could be visiting at this hour. Although it was only a quarter to eleven, Dow and her younger sister Sunee, who had just turned sixteen, had always considered the hours after eight in the evening the unearthly hours. In the village close to the Burmese border where they, their parents, and their ten other siblings had lived, they tend to go to bed rather early. Admittedly they haven't been in Singapore all that long, but they still can't get used with idea that people here sometimes do not sleep at all.

Mong Kok couldn't help looking at Sunee, whose features were so delicate and she looked so ravishing in her short silk cheongsam, which he specially picked out for her. She looked especially sexy in her tight-fitting, semi-transparent clothes Mong Kok had insisted they should wear while they were home alone. He had bought the two of them from their parents when he heard about them from his contacts in Thailand and had brought them to Singapore, officially as maids. He did that because of his need to console himself in their arms when Mandy had walked out on him.

"Stop!" he shouted at them and they froze in their tracks. "Go back to your room," he said to them. "I'll get the door." At first they gave him a questioning look, then they giggled when they realised that they were about to open the front door when they practically had nothing on. Still giggling, they tore down the corridor and disappeared into their room.

"Boss, everything had been taken care of," said the first man who walked into the room. He was about thirty-five years of age, five feet ten in height and heavy set. He looked like a former boxer. The man behind him couldn't be more opposite to him for he was short and scrawny, a man who could not get through the day without his usual regular dosage of opium.

Mong Kok led them straight to the den through the side door, without going through the living room. Without offering them a seat, he went to his desk and took out an envelope and handed it to the burly man who took a peek in it before handing it over to the thin man. They nodded their thanks. A few moments later they left the villa through the back door escorted by two of Mong Kok's ever-present guards.

Mong Kok went back to the living room and poured himself another generous lashing of Martel before settling on the couch to resume watching the news. But instead of listening to what the newscasters had to say, his mind was on Mandy, who in his opinion, had one of the most perfect body of her species. Making love to her was like enjoying a good meal. Each morsel had to be tasted with relish, leaving the best for last.

In his life he had many women but none can match Mandy in bed despite the fact that she didn't even like him. Suddenly the thought of her making love and being made love to by the *Malai Kwai*, James, made Mong Kok very angry. He sent his partially empty glass flying across the room to the wall opposite the sofa with a crash. His jealousy of James or the *Malay Devil* as he preferred to call him, whom Mandy was so obviously madly in love with, caused him to tremble with rage.

The sound of the glass crashing against the wall brought not only the two sisters running back to the living room, but practically his entire staff had followed suit. After telling them that there was no cause for alarm, that he had only accidentally dropped a glass, he quickly sent them off. With his arms around the waists of the two sisters, the three of them walked towards his bedroom.

* * *

Although the repair to his flat was completed, James found it hard to concentrate as he sat at his desk trying to do some work. He kept on thinking about Mandy and the way she had died. The thing he couldn't understand was why she had to die. Had she done something so terrible that she had to die that horrible death? That question kept nagging at him.

He went into the kitchen to make himself a cup of tea and when he came back another name began to appear in his head. Wong - the man who had tricked Mandy into becoming his mistress with a false promise of a job - the man who had his jaw broken by Alexander. Wong – Alexander's biological father - was also the man he would like his friend, Rahim, to dig deep into.

James picked up the telephone and called his friend again. Rahim picked up the telephone immediately.

"Rahim, I have another name which I think could be involved in Mandy's murder. His name is Wong." James told his friend what little he knew about Wong.

"All right. I'll check him out and let you know of the outcome as soon as I can. In the meantime take extra care yourself, we really don't know if Mandy was the only target, do we? As far as Alexander and Andrea are concerned, I have my friends across the causeway keep an eye on them. It's you I'm worried about."

James thanked Rahim and promised him he'd be extra careful. He took a sip from his cold tea before making another call, this time he called David in Singapore and had a few words with him before talking to his children. They seemed glad to hear from him and that gladdened his heart for he really loves them.

Two days later, a knock on the door brought James to it, but before he opened it he took a peeked through the peephole. Rahim had a smile on his face when he walked in.

"Well, it seemed that your Mr. Wong checked out clean. He had nothing to do with Mandy's death. As it turned out he was near death himself at the time when Mandy was killed. He's suffering from cancer and the prognosis is that he will die before the year is out, which means he's got about three months more to live. He had been in and out of surgery for the last several months." Rahim said. "So, I think you can rule him out as a possible suspect in Mandy's death. It seemed that he had been sick for such a long time. The thing was, he didn't know that there was anything wrong with him until Alexander broke his jaw and the blood test done at the hospital prior to the surgery to wire his jaw back in place, reveal that he had cancer. I doubt that he had the time or the energy to plan anything like this."

"What about Mong Kok?" James asked.

"Well, now, Mong Kok is another kettle of fish," Rahim accepted the proffered cup of coffee from James before sitting opposite James.

"I have a theory that this character...this philanthropist, this saviour of the downtrodden, the man who had been importing durians from Thailand may also be bringing in something else besides durians into the country..."

"Drugs, you mean?" James interrupted.

"A very strong possibility," replied Rahim. "Remember, these fruits have such pungent smell, even the dogs tend to keep away from them."

"All right! I think we should work on him," said James.

"No, no, I should work on him. You continue to do whatever you're doing - be a university professor. Teach those young minds creative writing or whatever, like you are paid to do and leave all these police work to me."

"But you're retired!"

"Retired, yes, but not dead. Besides I have a score to settle with that bastard Mong Kok, so I'm doing this for me as much as for you. *Mengerti?*"

As soon as Rahim left, James wondered whether he should tell Alexander know about Wong's condition. After all, Wong is his real father. After a long while he realised that Alexander had a right to know about his father's illness. And it was up to him to decide what to do with that information. He had no right to tell him what to do.

He picked the telephone and punched David's number in Singapore. While waiting for David's servant to fetch Alexander, James pondered on what his son's reactions would be as well as his own if he were in Alexander's shoes. He hadn't come to any conclusion when Alexander's voice came on the line. James told him what his friend Rahim had told him about Wong's state of health.

"I thought you should know," James added quietly.

"Dad, do you think I should go and see him?"

"It's not for me to say whether you should see him or not. You have to decide that for yourself."

"All right, I'll think about it and let you know of my decision."

"Fair enough. Now let me talk to your sister." Andrea must have been listening in to their conversation from the extension. She came on the line almost immediately.

Without any preamble, she came in loud and clear. "Dad, I don't think Alex should go to see Wong. I, for one, am glad he's dying. I think this is God's punishment to what he did to mother. Good riddance to a bad rubbish, I'd say."

James was taken aback by the venom in his daughter's voice. He had never for once thought about what she felt about what Wong did to her mother. After all, it was something that had happened long before she was born. To hear such hatred coming from her mouth rendered him speechless momentarily.

"Dad? Did you hear what I've said? Forbid Alex from going to see this Wong!"

Andrea knew that she was being rude to her father, something she had never done before, but for once she didn't care. She, somehow, blamed James for bringing up the subject of Wong. She felt that her father should not have told Alexander about Wong's illness in the first place; Wong had nothing to do with the family.

"Andrea! What is the matter with you?" asked James. "All I did was to tell Alex about his father's illness, that's all. Aren't you jumping the gun a bit? Alex has not indicated that he was going to see Wong, has he? And even if he is going to see him, it's his right," James suppressed his anger at his daughter's impudence.

"Right! What right?" Andrea retorted, fully aware that she was now treading on thin ice. Throwing caution to the winds, she continued, "What right has he to consort with the enemy? To me that's tantamount to betrayal to mother's memory."

Before James could reply, he heard loud voices over the telephone, convinced that his daughter and son were having a verbal battle and there was nothing he could do about it except to yell impotently into the mouthpiece for Andrea to calm down.

After what seemed an age, Alexander's voice came over the line, "Dad, I had no intention of seeing Wong before, but now I think I will. This is to teach someone in this family not to second-guess me in future." The line went dead in his hand.

James wanted to call them back but after a moment's consideration, he decided not to, knowing then that it was not the time to lecture his children. He'd talk to them again when they have cooled down.

James couldn't help thinking at the way Andrea had reacted when Wong's name was mentioned. Her hatred for him seemed boundless and he was worried what it might do to her close relationship with Alex if he really decided on going to see Wong.

As it turned out, Alex did pay Wong a visit at the private hospital where Wong had been rushed to a day earlier. The nurse on duty told his that Wong's condition had turned for the worse. Fortunately for Alex, none of Wong's family member was there at the time of his visit. The nurse had looked at Alex and had automatically assumed that he was a member of Wong's family. The resemblance was unmistaken, she thought to herself as she ushered Alex into Wong's room.

As Alex stood in the semi-darkness, he was aware that his heart was beginning to race; he turned around and headed for the door.

"I never expected to see you again, but I am glad that you came," said the voice behind him.

Alex spun around and looked in the direction of the bed, still unable to see clearly the figure on it. He stood still by the door waiting for his eyes to get adjusted to the dimly-lit room. He couldn't believe his eyes at what he saw, Wong had looked so emaciated Alex could hardly recognize him. The head and the face that appeared above the hospital blanket looked more like a skeleton he had seen in horror movies. Mustering all his courage, Alex walked unsteadily toward the foot of the bed and stopped. "I came to see how you are..."

"Not good, Alex, as you can see," Wong said in a voice that seemed surprisingly strong for a frame that seemed so frail and brittle. "The doctors gave me months to live before, but it looks like they are wrong. I think I have only days to live."

Wong began to cough, slow at first, but it reached a crescendo whereby he began to splutter. Alexander rushed to his bedside table and handed him the glass of water Wong was desperately trying to reach.

After a few sips of water, Wong's cough began to subside. A few minutes later Wong became, more or less, normal again.

"Shall I call a nurse for you?" Asked Alex.

Wong shook his head and said, "No, it's all right. I get these coughing fits now and again, nothing to worry about."

Alex had wondered why he came in the first place. He was once again in the presence of the man he had hated for so long, a man who was racked in pain, a man about to die. Alex suddenly found that the hate which had been burning inside him for so long had almost disappeared. Pity seemed to have taken over as he watched the skeletal head move in a jerky manner, its sunken eyes cast a look at him.

"How is your mother?" Wong asked weakly.

"She died a week ago."

"Died? But she's so young. What did she die of?"

Wong began to cough again, and as usual it went like it did before, until the sips of water that he took began to produce its desired effect and he was calm again.

"Someone placed a bomb in our flat and had it detonated by remote control while my mother was preparing dinner in the kitchen." Alex gave him a grim stare and demanded, "You had nothing to with it, did you?"

"Me? Of course not! You can take my word that I have nothing to do with it."

Wong suddenly went into his coughing bout again. But this time, even another full glass of water that Alex had given him, which he had poured from a flask on the bedside table, couldn't stop the coughs.

Alex pressed the button and almost immediately the same nurse who had shown him came rushing into the room. She went into action like a pro that she was and few moments later Wong was back as his old self again.

When Alex saw this he quickly slipped out of the room and headed for the basement car park to retrieve his car.

ⵣⵣⵣⵣⵣⵣ

CHAPTER
THIRTY-THREE

Mong Kok was most resourceful when it comes to bribery. He would, for example, seek people in various government departments who might be eligible to be his informants. People who are high in rank but low in self-esteem, with little or no principle, were those he sought. But the most important ingredient of all was that they must be greedy enough to do anything for money.

Fortunately for Mong Kok, there are many people who fit the bill in almost every government department and in every state in the country. Some of them epitomised the ideal citizenry: people who were upright and obviously the pillar of society. Most, if not all, could be called very religious too, which never fail to amuse him. What humbugs they all were, he kept telling himself. To some, the more pious they seemed to be the more corrupt they really were. It was as if they were trying to balance things up within themselves.

Mong Kok's strength was derived through the weakness of others, whether it was with the civil servant who wanted to be rich without really trying, or the little pushers who wanted to make it to the big time by peddling their poison as hard and as furious as they could. They all play an important role in Mong Kok's plan to control the drug distribution trade in Asia. The Colombians may have their cartel, but here in his neck of the woods he was the Kingpin and had no desire to share this exclusivity with anyone else.

He wished he had control of its production too, but alas, that was not possible for now. An ageing warlord named Koonta was very much in control of the opium production in the golden triangle area. Mong Kok was getting wary of the Old Man of late due to the latter's habit of going back on his words regarding delivery. Sometimes terms and condition regarding shipment which had been meticulously worked out before, could, at the last minutes be changed, and there wasn't a damn thing Mong Kok could do about it except to grin and bear it.

He had tried to get his Thai partner, Som Phong, to try to get someone to bump off the Old Man but he was told to get such foolish notion out of his head for there was no way any outsiders could even get near him to do any damage. Only his most trusted men could get within one hundred yards of him.

However, there was one thing they could do, Som Phong, said to him. They could send a strong message to Koonta that if he did not mend his ways, some members of his large family could get hurt. Mong Kok agreed that they should send that message to him straight away.

Koonta, as a warlord had many mistresses and all of them, without exception had many children. What if Koonta were to receive the head of one of his children as a warning that should he fail to deliver the drugs on a timely basis, more heads will surely follow.

The news of the death of the youngest child of his favourite concubine, hit Koonta hard, and to prevent more deaths to any his children, he instructed his men to ensure that Som Phong, whom he had suspected was responsible for the killing, got his supplies without any delays.

It seemed that the youngster who had his throat cut was about sixteen years old and was one of Koonta's favourite sons. He was one of several he had groomed to join his inner circle when the time came.

Koonta went into mourning, refusing to see anyone for several days, but when he came out of his self-imposed isolation, he sent a message to Mong Kok. In it he mentioned that due to perhaps errors of his ways, or perhaps due to the sins he may have committed in the past, one of his sons had recently been taken away from him. And after much prayers and consultation with the monks he had been told to appease the gods by doing some good deeds. And so with that in mind, he said, he would like to start by giving Mong and his

Thai partner not only a substantial discount for their next orders, but their shipment will be expedited to ensure early delivery. He hoped that this humble act will help to dispel some of the black clouds that seemed to be hanging over his head.

Mong Kok and Som Phong immediately replied by offering their condolences for Koonta's loss and thanked him profusely for his generous offer which they, following age-old custom where one must show great humility when accepting gifts of any nature, reluctantly accepted with great show of respect for Koonta for his generosity.

Unlike Som Phong, Mong Kok thought nothing more of the incident and went on with business as usual. Som Phong, on the other hand, was not easily taken in by Koonta's conciliatory utterances. He was sure that Koonta had suspected that he and Mong Kok must have been responsible for his son's death. He was afraid of what Koonta might do once he had ascertained their guilt.

The thought of what his men had done to Koonta's son brought fearful images of his own son, his only son, lying in a pool of blood with his throat cut - just like Koonta's son. He gazed at his face and saw the look of surprise on it and blood was oozing from the gaping wound that stretched from one ear to the other.

Som Phong broke down in cold sweat, and when he finally recovered he quickly rushed to his son's bedroom only to find him sound asleep.

He returned to the study where he had been working and poured himself a stiff drink. His wife, who had been awaken when she heard the door opened and shut from her son's bedroom, came into the study and found her husband slumped in his chair behind his desk. One look at his face told her that all was not well with her husband.

"What is wrong, my husband?" she asked as she stood by his side.

"Nothing," he said, without looking at her. "I am just feeling tired, that's all. I won't be long. Why don't you go back to bed."

Without looking at her he knew that she knew that something was wrong. Despite his many mistresses, he considered Kanya more than just a wife. She was someone he had trusted more than any of his mistresses put together; she was his confidant. Kanya started to open her mouth to speak, but after having married and living with her husband for the last eighteen years, she knew when not to pursue the subject any further. She'd know it soon enough, one has to be patient, that was all. Kanya turned to look at her husband once more before retreating to their bedroom. On the way she stopped to look into their son whose bedroom was at the end of the corridor with a view to the back garden of the house.

Despite the distance she had to walk, Kanya was always looking forward to seeing their son when he was asleep, besides, she had been doing this for as long as she can remember.

Sunan was their son, their only son, whose emergence into this world had brought joy and happiness to both parents. For a long time both of them hadn't thought of having another child because they felt that Sunan was all they had wanted. They were contented with him and he in turn brought them happiness. It wasn't until Sunan reached his twelve birthday when they decided that perhaps another child would not come amiss, but to their great disappointment, they found out that they had left it too late and she would not be able to conceive.

Kanya had cried until her eyes became red and swollen. Wild thoughts began to enter her mind, blaming herself for not being able to give her husband another child. What a disappointment she must be to her husband, she kept telling herself. When she finally ended her self-incrimination, Kanya disappeared from their home for the whole day, came home just before her husband returned. Right through dinner Kanya narrated to her husband what she did the whole day beginning with the mundane things like what the greengrocer's wife had told her about her daughter-in-law's parent's eating habits.

Her husband looked up at Kanya but said nothing even though he had heard that tale the day before when Kanya had told it to him over breakfast. He was quite used to her forgetfulness by now. The next thing she told him was also not news to him, he heard that one several days before that.

But when Kanya started to tell him about a visit she had made to her cousin May Choo's house in the next town, he almost choked on his chicken porridge. May Choo was the last person on earth his wife would want to visit especially after she had found Som Phong and May Choo in bed not too long ago.

May Choo had just turned sixteen at the time and was still a virgin when she and Som Phong made love. It was the first row Kanya and Som Phong ever had. Caught in the act, Som Phong knew he had no excuse whatsoever to offer Kanya. Kanya had made a big production of showing Som Phong the stained bed sheet before telling him that he could no longer share the bed with her. Som Phong moved to a guest bedroom at the opposite end of the corridor to their son's bedroom. He was to stay in that bedroom for exactly one year before Kanya asked her maids move Som Phong things back to their bedroom. As far as Som Phong knew Kanya had not spoken to her cousin since that day, so to hear from her mouth that she had made a special trip to see her made him stop and stare.

"Why?" He had asked after a long while when Kanya hadn't offered an explanation.

"I went to ask her whether she'd be willing to have your child."

"What?"

"I want you to make love to her so that she'll be pregnant with your child. After she or he is born I'd like us to adopt him or her," Kanya said to her husband.

"Why?" Som Phong was beginning to sound like a one word man.

"Since I can't have a baby myself, there's no reason why May Choo can't have it for us," said Kanya simply. "It's not as if you two are strangers or anything like that. Except that this time you two will make love with me around, as a matter of fact she will share our bed. I've already ordered a bigger bed for us. It's custom-made to accommodate the three of us and it will arrive here tomorrow and so will May Choo."

Som Phong gave his wife an incredulous look and felt that he should protest, or at least say something appropriate. Little did his wife know, Som Phong had already heard about her little plan from the younger of their two maids, who came storming to him one morning when his wife had gone to the market with the other maid. It seemed that she had heard the conversation between her mistress and the other maid who was in her mid-forties and who happened to have a niece who had just turned sixteen, whom she thought, would be perfect for the master.

Little did his wife know the younger maid had been serving her husband more than coffee and croissant whenever she and the elder maid were out to the market. Because the younger of their two maids had just turned thirteen, no one in the household had suspected her for any wrongdoing except for her clumsiness when it comes to washing the dishes. She had almost gone through a perfectly nice set of dinner wares during the nine months she had been with the family.

In reality it was she who had initiated the illicit love affair with Som Phong when he found her in his bed one day when everyone else was out of the house. From that day onwards they had made love at every opportunity they get. For a twelve-year old, Som Phong found her to be very experienced indeed. When he asked her how she knew so much about making love, she told him that at the age of nine her uncle had come to her bed and told her that he had come to teach her how to make love and how to please men in bed.

He had told her in all seriousness that it was his duty to see to it that she was well versed in this aspect of her upbringing. He had warned her that it was something very sacred, and that she was not to tell anyone in the family about this. As a matter of fact, he told her that it was something that every young girl had to go through, and usually it is an uncle's duty to teach and since he was her only uncle, it fell upon himself to take up this responsibility.

He kept repeating to her during the course of their liaison, which only had stopped when she came to work for Som Phong, that talking about it would demean his status as an uncle and would ruined his reputation as an honoured teacher.

She has sworn to her uncle that she'll never divulge it to a soul. She had kept the secret until Som Phong had asked her, but then he wasn't a member of her family or anything like, she had reasoned. She had made him swear not to repeat it to anyone. She told him that after having been in his home for nearly a month she felt that she should continue with her lesson but since her uncle wasn't around she had wondered whether Som Phong would mind continuing to teach her. Since he had readily accepted her in bed the first time, she knew then that she had found herself a teacher and she was very glad.

Som Phong had a hard time trying to suppress a chuckle she had told him all this, but he somehow managed it. In all solemnity he had told her that he'd be honoured to be her substitute teacher, but had cheekily added that he feared that he might not be as good as her uncle.

She told him that he needn't worry about that because she felt that she had been a good student of her uncle and had learned her lessons quite well.

She felt certain that she must continue practising in order to keep in shape so to speak.

He assured her that he'd be there whenever she needed him for practice, and had added that he'll try his best not to disappoint her. When that was said and done, they had made love once more: Like they say, practice makes perfect, who was he to question such wise dictum.

"May Choo's body is made for bearing children as you can see," said Kanya as she and Som Phong examined her while she laid on their pink-coloured satin sheet.

Kanya was exalting all May Choo's virtues like a seller would when trying to sell a merchandise. She would run her fingers along the contour of May Choo's hips, over her flat stomach and she even caressed the tips of May Choo's breasts to emphasize their shape and size as being not too big for the baby to suck. Then with both hands Kanya had encircled one by one May Choo's breasts to point out to Som Phong that since they are firm, they should produce ample milk.

When it came to her sex, Kanya had spread May Choo's legs apart for him to see how clean and pink her slit was and had declared that it was not too big for him either as she inserted two fingers in it and moved it around.

After having made that pronouncement, instead of removing her finger out of May Choo's sex, she continued to rub and massage the inside and its outer rim. After a few minutes Som Phong could see how wet her fingers had become. And when she finally pulled her fingers out they looked saturated with May Choo's juice and gleamed in the glow of their bedside lamp. By this time Som Phong was on the verge of coming in his pants, but somehow he had managed to play along with Kanya by giving her appropriate comments here and there.

When Kanya finally had removed her fingers from May Choo's sopping wet sex and her monologue stopped, she asked Som Phong whether he was up to it to make love to May Choo there and then - just to test her suitability, she had said.

Som Phong had wanted to tear his pants off but felt that such uncouth display of eagerness would not go down well with Kanya at that moment. He waited as long as he could before telling his wife that if she insisted he might as well go ahead and test May Choo for her.

Fifteen minutes later both Som Phong and Kanya seemed pleased with May Choo. And by the look at her flushed face and her quick breathing, May Choo seem pleased too.

Nine months three days later May Choo gave birth to a bouncing baby boy who weighed eight pounds. Both Som Phong and his wife were at her bedside at the private hospital when she awoke. Beaming with obvious joy, both of them told her all the good news about the baby. A few minutes later

May Choo was shown her baby, who, with his eyes closed, was already fed and wrapped like a cocoon with only his head showing. On his left leg a tag was firmly in placed with his particulars on it. In his birth certificate it had put Kanya as its mother and of course Som Phong as the father. He had made sure that everything was done legally and the money had pressed into appropriate hands had ensured that.

During the months and days preceding the birth, both Som Phong and May Choo had to follow strictly to the chart that Kanya had prepared for them, which in turn had been prepared for her by her doctor who had mistakenly thought that it was for her own use.

The dates therein were dates when Som Phong had to make love to May Choo and Kanya was there to make sure they made love on the prepared schedule dates. The moment the act was over, Kanya in a white nurse uniform, which she had made, would wipe her husband's member thoroughly with a wet cloth, which smelled of Dettol. And when he was done, she'd repeat the same ritual with May Choo. With that over, May Choo would then retire to her bedroom next to theirs? Kanya would then get into bed with her husband, who, more often than not, would be sound asleep by then. A few minutes later she herself would be fast asleep, contented like a mother would, after looking after a well-behaved child. Right through pregnancy, Kanya would be there to look after May Choo.

Som Phong, who had neglected his little maid while doing his service duty to May Choo, quickly resumed his duty as a teacher to her, especially when making love to May Choo was out of the question due to her advance stage of pregnancy.

Som Phong at the same time could not neglect his wife whose appetite was normal for a woman of her age, which was just approaching forty-five. Each day Som Phong couldn't thank his lucky star enough for his good fortune.

Sunan, following the family tradition, was away attending a boarding school in England while all this was going on. He was naturally thrilled when told by his parents that he now had a baby brother and the photograph accompanying their letter was now among all the other photographs he had on the mantelpiece above the mock Adam fireplace.

Sunan, like his father when his age, was not too clear as to what his father did for a living, except that he must be doing all right. Back home they lived in a house that was palatial in comparison to other houses in their area or in their province for that matter. Then there was that house in Bangkok and the beach house in Pataya.

All the three houses had a full-time staff looking after them, including armed guards, and drivers who seemed to be at their beck and call twenty-four-hours a day. His father had a habit of appearing unannounced at any one of these houses. And apart from the cars, Sunan couldn't be sure how many there were; his father also owned a helicopter, which he used frequently.

Like his father before him, Sunan will eventually be inducted into the family business on his return from England. Perhaps like his father he might be unwilling, at first, to accept the fact that his family business was in all kinds of illicit trade including drugs, prostitution, smuggling of not only contraband goods but dealing in human traffic as well. And like his father, after sometime at the helm of the company, he'd begin to see the perks that came with the job. He too would find the enormous power that went with the job was akin to an aphrodisiac. And like his father, Sunan would find that he had connections in high places that included government ministers, civil servants, military leaders, customs and immigration officials.

He will eventually learn that these people do earn their keep by ensuring that none of his father's operations were hindered in any way - they would make sure of that.

Although Sunan didn't know it, his father, at the time of taking over from his grandfather, was fantasizing with the same lofty ideas about how he was going to use the money to uplift the livelihood of the poor people in his province - a sort of Robin Hood-type activities which he envisaged on doing once he had full control of the company. However, when the time came it didn't take him long to get sucked into the system, whereby life of wealth and luxury had made him put his original goal of being a Robin Hood on hold indefinitely.

And on his father's death, Som Phong had forgotten about his earlier plans to help the poor in his province. Instead, like his father before him, he had exploited them by selling them things they did not need just to get them in hock to him.

Som Phong, like his father, continued to spent the millions of dollars greasing the right palms. He made sure that the people he had been bribing do not forget him or his favours. In return he had made hundreds of million out of his illegal activities. He could see that with his knowledge, he could easily quadrupled what they had been making. The rest, as they say, is history.

And in about two years' time, history will repeat itself with the return of his son, Sunan. He had nurtured the hope that with his degree in Business Administration and Sunan's added knowledge in computers, their business could match what he had done or even surpassed it when his time came.

On his return to Thailand, Sunan, not unlike his father, had accepted his father's offer to take up his post as his father's under-study with the same intention his father had of legitimising it one day. It looked like history was about to repeat itself in the family. It must be something to do with having the same blood. What else do they say - blood runs thicker than water, or was it like they say like father like son. Now, how appropriate the saying was. In the end both father and son acted no differently with one another, and their lofty ideas in trying to help the poor people of their province will have to take a back seat.

In the final analysis, and with the help of Mong Kok who was their best distributor in Malaysia, Singapore and Indonesia, their business grew from strength to strength.

CHAPTER THIRTY-FOUR

The powerful engine under the bonnet of his German sedan purred like a well-tuned engine should, and Sunan, who had just left his girl-friend's place, leaned back against the luxurious leather seat and was listening his latest CD which he had recently brought home from London.

Ten minutes later he eased back on the accelerator, turned on his indicator to show that he wanted to turn right, and finally stopped in front of the noodle house whose green neon sign flicked on and off with equal regularity.

As he manoeuvred his car into an empty spot in the crowded parking lot, a single shot was heard reverberating in the still of the night. It took approximately thirty seconds before he slumped forward onto the steering wheel as if he was just going to rest his head.

Blood that oozed from the side of his head streaked down his grey shirt and on to the carpet of the car forming a pool. At first nobody paid any attention to the loud sound of the car horn, thinking that it might be just another badly installed car alarm that had accidentally gone off. But when the sound had persisted for several minutes, a patron in the noodle house got up from his seat and peered through the plate glass towards where the sound was coming from. At first he did not see anything out of the ordinary until his eyes began to focus on the still figure whose head was on the steering wheel of his big BMW car. He shook his head and returned to his seat - some drunk who must have passed out, he thought to himself. Another patron who was sitting across the crowded noodle house also found the continuous noise from the car horn irritating. He too stood up and peered out of the window. Like his predecessor he saw the BMW with a man whose head was resting on the steering wheel the car. But unlike the other guy, this man could see blood oozing out of the fellow's head and told everyone within hearing range what he saw.

Within minutes several people rushed out of the noodle house and rushed towards the BMW. One of them tried to open the car door but found it locked. In fact all the car doors were locked, it had a central locking system. The police was called in, and when they arrived several minutes later with an ambulance preceding it, they too tried and failed to open the car door. It took another forty minutes before a fire department people arrived. They came with their special tool which was designed to wrench open locked car doors in an emergency. By this time the crowd had swelled into several dozens, most was consumed with curiosity. And when the car door was finally opened, some gasped back in horror when they saw the blood-soaked body of Sunan Som Phong.

Needless to say he was already dead. Koonta was still in bed when the youngest of his four common-law wives woke him up and told him that Leepong, his most trusted underling, was waiting downstairs.

Despite his age of seventy-one years, Koonta, that morning was bright and sprightly as he got out of his bed and walked briskly towards the bathroom. Fifteen minutes later, as he sipped his strong coffee, he listened to what his two trusted underlings had to say, which was short and to the point, and it sounded very sweet indeed to his ears. When he heard the telephone ringing in his study, he walked briskly to answer it.

He recognised immediately the voice of the senior member of the police force who had been his paid informer. He told Som Phong of his son's death. Som Phong and Kanya had rushed to the hospital in a convoy consisting of three cars. His men, armed to the teeth, drove in two cars: one in front of Som Phong's car and the other followed close behind.

Accompanying Som Phong in his car were two more armed men making it an even dozen. These were men who were trained to kill on orders. The leading car set the pace by driving at break-neck speed breaking every rule in the book, as they sped towards the hospital.

On arrival, Som Phong's men practically took over the entire hospital, preventing people from entering or leaving they brushed aside protests from the hospital authorities. Pandemonium broke out when his men roughed up and prevented people who had wanted to visit their sick relatives.

The precinct's police chief found himself in a bind because of his loyalty to Som Phong on the one hand and to his superiors on the other. He was finally saved from further torments when Som Phong, on finding his son and heir was already dead, decided to leave the hospital taking the remains of his dead son with him.

Mong Kok had just wakened up from a night of lovemaking with his two young concubines and was in the bathroom when he heard the telephone ring. Some nights before, the news about the death of one of Koonta's sons, was a big turn-on for him and had satisfied himself with the sisters. He was satisfied of what Som Phong had done and everything was going according to plan.

Mong Kok was rinsing his mouth when he heard one of the two sisters answered the door. As he waited for her to poke her head in the bathroom to tell him that he was wanted on the telephone, he continued to lather his face. When the bathroom door opened behind him a few minutes later, expecting one of the two sisters, he was shocked to find a man pointing a gun at him.

He slammed the door shut just as the man was about to squeeze the trigger. The shot that followed missed him by inches. Fortunately for Mong Kok, his bodyguard who had been rendered unconscious by a bump on the head began to regain consciousness and he appeared just as the gunman was trying to blast the bathroom door open. The bodyguard opened fire and hit the gunman in the back of the head. Needless to say the gunman was dead before his body hit the floor. His accomplice, who had been waiting in a car parked just outside the high wall, heard the shots, decided to investigate by climbing onto his car roof and then over the wall.

A surveillance camera had moments earlier zoomed in on him as he was about to climb onto his car and two guards were dispatched to apprehend him.

The moment he had jumped down on to the well-trimmed turf, he was immediately picked up the two guards. The third man, whose presence was unknown to neither the first nor the second gunman, slipped past the guard that was watching the back entrance of the house when he was momentarily distracted by all the commotions. Once inside the house the third man lost no time in locating the bedroom he was looking for. He stood outside the door with his ear pressed against it. He tried the door but found it locked. He tapped softly on it with the tips of his four fingers. The door opened a crack and a pair of eyes peeked at him.

Moments later the door opened wide and he was let in. As soon he was in the room the twins embraced him all at once. He looked at his watch. He had four hours to kill before he had to make his move. That should give him plenty of time, he was thinking as he began to undress. The twins giggled softly as they too began to undress.

Mong Kok was an ugly mood. He never had his security breached before and the experienced of nearly being killed had unnerved him and he didn't like that. After he had dressed down his chief bodyguard, he personally went down to the cellar to interrogate his intruder.

Despite the beating he received from Mong Kok's men, the intruder refused to talk. He was repeatedly beaten until he passed out. Mong Kok had returned to his room fuming with anger. He poured himself a stiff brandy and downs it in one gulp. He poured another and downed that in two gulps. He rang for the twins before stripping naked and lay on the bed. When the two sisters came, he ordered one of them to take him in her mouth, while he fondled and kissed the breasts of the other. An hour later he was sound asleep. He had taken one of the twins the normal way and the other he sodomized.

The third assassin had no trouble entering Mong Kok's room through the electronically controlled door, using the combination the twins had given him. Mong Kok, who was security conscious, had spent a fortune installing combination locks in his house. Only those he trusted had access to them.

The twins, besides his chief bodyguard, of course, had access to most parts of the house, As the assassin stood over the sleeping figure of Mong Kok with a gun in his hand; the assassin was startled to find the twins sisters in the bedroom with him.

"How did you get in?" He mouthed the words.

"Through there," one of them said. Indicating a door behind the bookshelf. He quickly put a finger on his mouth to indicate to the other to be silent.

"Don't worry," said the other twin. "He won't be awake for some time yet, we spiked his drinks." Her sister giggled before digging into a pocket of her dressing gown.

Moments later he saw her pulled out a kitchen knife as she walked towards the bottom of the bed. The other flashed a smile at her sister and walked the head of the bed. She too had a similar knife in her hand. She turned her head towards the man and said,

"When I give you the signal, shoot him through the heart."

The assassin watched as the one at the bottom of the bed lifted up the bed cover and put the blade against Mong Kok's member while holding up its tip with her left hand.

The other sister had her knife on Mong Kok's throat with her other hand gripping a handful of his hair.

"Now aim the gun at his heart...and when I give the signal, you shoot...understand?"

The assassin saw what they were trying to do and was about to protest when he heard the same twin who had spoken to him yell, "Now!" He heard his gun go off with a thud through the silencer.

When he saw what they had simultaneously done to Mong Kok, he turned around and fled the room. He threw up just outside Monk Kok's door.

The next moment the bullet from Mong Kok's chief bodyguard caused him to keel over and fall motionless, face down, onto the carpet.

As soon as the twins heard the sound of gunfire outside the door, they quickly returned to their room through the secret passageway and pretended to be asleep. The chief bodyguard found them huddled together when he had the door opened. They rubbed their eyes sleepily and asked him what was the matter. When told that Mong Kok had been killed, they had wailed and pulled their hair in grief and had cried on until their eyes had puffed up. They were inconsolable the whole day. They continued to cry until their voices were coarse and had refused to eat anything.

A few days later, a member of Mong Kok's family, seeing how distraught the two sisters were, gave them some money and told them to go home. They thanked the middle-aged lady profusely. They left for the airport where they took a direct flight to Bangkok and from there they got on to another plane to Chiang Mai. The twins wisely took a bus instead of a taxi to their village. It wouldn't do to show off their wealth, they thought.

Placed at their feet was a nondescript-looking holdall made of PVC. In it contained their meagre possessions which the customs at Dong Muang Airport only paid a cursory look before passing them through. What customs didn't know was nearly ten thousand Singapore dollars the twins had painfully stitched in the linings of their clothes. Money they had quietly taken, over a period of time, from Mong Kok's wallet while he was asleep, money they knew he would not have missed. They had no qualms about stealing the money from Mong Kok; they felt that they had earned it.

Koonta was waiting for them as they disembarked from the rickety old bus. They smiled at him as soon as they saw him.

"You did well my children," he said. "You two have avenged your step-brother's death and I'm proud of you."

Koonta cleared his throat several time before speaking again. "What do you want to do now? Do you want to come back and stay with me?" The twins looked at each other before one of them answered. "No, father. We'd rather stay with our mother. Someone has to look after her."

"All right then, here's some money. Look after your mother well and take care. Call me whenever you need anything".

"Goodbye father," said one of the twins.

"Goodbye father," said the other. "Remember, you owe us now!"

With that they turned and walked towards an imposing looking house surrounded by wrought iron gate, beyond which grew tall trees that practically surrounded the house. The architecture of the house was typically Thai and the mistress of the house, the mother of the twins, stood gracefully at the top of the staircase. As soon as the twins walked through the front gate, two maids rushed to take the holdall from them.

The twins smiled as they approached their mother. They hugged each other.

"You've done well, my children," she said. "Your father was here, and he seemed pleased. Did you see him?"

"Yes, mother," said one of the twins. "He was pleased and he told us to take good care of you."

"He did? That was nice of him." She looked pleased.

"And, mother," said her sister. "You'll be pleased with us too. Here is the list of the dealers Mong Kok had been supplying to. Do you think you'll know what to do with this?"

Their mother took the list from her and looked at it for several moments.

"You know, with this list someone could become very rich. I think I know someone who would be very interested in this list." She looked at her two daughters and smiled.

CHAPTER THIRTY-FIVE

The news of Mong Kok's death went through the underworld's grapevine faster than the Internet. His enemies were glad that he was gone, while others, like his drug dealers, were frantic because their supply had, all of a sudden, dried up. Alternative source had to be found pretty quickly, otherwise there'd be trouble in the streets. Some dealers could find themselves in mortal danger from junkies desperate for a fix.

* * *

Suparman was a small-time dealer supplying drugs to schoolboys in the streets of Jakarta until one day he had the good fortune of meeting with Mong Kok. At that time Mong Kok was looking for someone in that teeming city of eleven million people who could lay the groundwork for his impending foray into Indonesia. It didn't take long for Mong Kok to rate Suparman as a dealer who could make it big if only he had the resources. He seemed to have contacts all over the place, but the thing that impressed Mong Kok most was the man's ability to get along with the authorities, whether it was the police or the customs and even the immigrations. In other words, he had the ability to stay out of trouble.

Mong Kok had wasted no time in recruiting Suparman as his man in Indonesia, and within a year Suparman saw the business grew beyond his expectation. The news of Mong Kok's death hit Suparman hard at first. He knew his supply will be delayed but for how long? Within two weeks his supply was cut by half and he was getting desperate. His down liners were screaming at him and he knew he had to do something fast.

Unable to take much more of the hassling from his dealers, Suparman decided to go direct to the source in Thailand, by-passing Mong Kok's office in Singapore altogether.

Koonta received Suparman well when he paid him a visit. But when Suparman asked him whether he could supply his needs, Koonta balked at the idea, saying that he had a long business relationship with Mong Kok. Even though he was dead, according to Koonta, he must honour the deal they had made when he was still alive. Suparman, according to Koonta, must still buy his stock from Mong Kok's office in Singapore. Unfortunately, he said, the price would have to be much higher now. With that, Koonta begged to be excused, citing pressing business as the reason.

Suparman felt the slight, but had kept his cool. The Javanese in him had taught him to accept insult with restrain in other people's home, unless a declaration of war had been made. Suparman left Koonta's house with revenge in his mind, but he managed to calm himself by reminding himself that he had not fulfilled what he had come for. News about Suparman's disastrous visit with Koonta reached Koonta's twin daughters' ears within the hour and they told their mother about it. The twins decided that one of them should make contact with Suparman but not at his hotel. They were sure their father, Koonta, would have the place under surveillance. They managed to send Suparman a note, through a cousin who worked at the hotel, telling him to go to a fruit stall they named at the night market not too far from his hotel.

As soon as Suparman reached the fruit stall, he was whisked through the back door where a taxi was waiting for him. After a short ride, the taxi dropped him off near a klong where a boat was waiting for him. Inside the twins were already waiting for him. Suparman had seen boats like this plying the Chao Phraya but never sat in one before. The moment he stepped in he noticed that the interior were divided into two sections. The front section where he was had been tastefully done up meant for recreation. There were comfortable seats placed strategically against the walls and there were two rectangular tables placed in the middle. However from where he was standing all he could see of the other half of the boat was part of a table protruding.

The twins invited him to sit on one of sofas opposite them. On the table in front of him were cans of Pepsi-Cola and young coconuts which had straws protruding from the openings. One of the twins gestured to Suparman to have a drink. Suparman chose the unopened can of Pepsi-Cola. One of the twins casually asked Suparman if his meeting with Koonta had been satisfactory? Suparman shook his head but said nothing. He pulled the tab from his can of drink, raised it with cupped hands and nodded at them before he took a sip from it.

The twin waited until Suparman looked at them again before telling him that if he so wish to do so, from now on they will be happy to supply him with all his needs. For the moment there were no increase in price and the terms will be the same as what Mong Kok was giving him. Suparman asked them if they can deliver immediately? The one sitting opposite him nodded her head. Suparman shook their hands and waited for their signal to leave the boat.

"But where will we get the drug from?" asked her sister as soon as Suparman had left.

"From the same source your father got it from," said their mother who had been listening in on their conversation from her small cabin next door.

"But how?" Asked her other daughter.

"It's all very simple," replied their mother. "The headman from the Shan community is interested to have you two as his wives. All I have to do is to send word that you two have agreed to become his wives. The rest should be easy...." Without completing her sentence she left the room. Knowing her daughters, she knew that they will discuss it among themselves, and once they had come to a conclusion they'll come to her.

That evening Suparman couldn't have been more delighted when a courier came to see him with a sample of the purest heroin he had ever tasted. He smiled at her ingenuity when he saw her pull out the packet out of her briefs. He had expected to pay at least fifty percent more for heroin this pure but since they had agreed not to increase their price to him, there was no reason why he could not charge more back home in Jakarta. Suparman told the courier that he was ready to pay a deposit of one hundred thousand Singapore dollars and the balance to be paid on delivery of the drug in Jakarta.

That afternoon the two sisters departed for the headman's village in the remote mountain village near the border of Burma and Laos. That night a big feast was being prepared to celebrate their wedding in which most of the villagers, as well as his four other wives, attended. Late that night the headman, after much drinking and eating, staggered into the two sisters' bedroom and officially consummated his fifth and sixth wife respectively.

He was delighted when he saw how lovely and petite they were. He had earlier guffawed loudly when they had asked him if he could grant them one request. He eyed them suspiciously before asking them what that request was. They said they would like all three of them to make love together. The Old Man had always wanted to experience that but none of his other wives had ever wanted to make a threesome with him.

Koonta, not knowing what his two daughters were up to was at first delighted at the prospect of having his biggest drug supplier as his son-in-law. He saw visions of having unlimited source of drugs whenever he wanted. No more haggling about price with the Old Man, he told himself and no more begging for the extra kilo or two of the stuff, and most important of all, with the headman as his son-in-law, he could fix the price himself. The Old Man's had always driven a hard bargain with him and he found that exasperating. He had always referred to the headman as the *Old Man* even though they were of the same age.

A week later, Boonchai, his right-hand man, rushed into Koonta's office and told him about a big drug shipment that was going to Indonesia.

"Where was the stuff from?" he asked.

"Where else? From the Old Man, of course!" replied his lieutenant.

"Do you know who the buyer is?"

"No, sir, I don't, but I'll know soon enough," he said, waving his cellular phone in the air. "I've sent Chapchai to find out for me."

For nearly twenty minutes he watched his boss paced the room, his face solemn. Boonchai had been drinking a lot of beer with his cronies and had forgotten to relieve himself before he came into the room and now, with the air-conditioning going at full blast in the room, he was desperate to go. But seeing how black a mood his boss was in, he daren't make a move. To his relief the telephone in his hand gave out a loud shrilling sound. He pressed a button and spoke into it.

He turned towards Koonta and said, "It's Chapchai."

It was apparent to Koonta that the news he was receiving wasn't good. With his face contorted with rage, Boonchai barked further instructions in a rapid-fire manner into the receiver and then broke off the connection.

"The name of the buyer is Suparman," said Boonchai softly.

"Suparman?" Koonta's voice caused a minor sonic boom in the room. "I thought you told me that he had agreed to deal with us now that Mong Kok is dead?"

"Yes, sir," said Boonchai in a whisper. "But now he's buying the drugs from your two daughters..." Boonchai had neglected to tell Koonta that he had met Suparman again at his hotel and had demanded a price that was doubled what he had paid Mong Kok before. That extra was what he had wanted for himself. All of a sudden, despite the air-conditioning was running at full blast, Boonchai found himself beginning to sweat. He knew he was dead man if this fact is known to Koonta.

"My daughters!" Another sonic boom reverberated throughout the house.

"Yes, sir..." Boonchai could see that he was in for a verbal lashing.

"Come on. Out with it, what else are you holding back on me?" Koonta asked calmly.

Koonta had suddenly remembered what his doctor had told him about getting a grip on his famous temper. Not too long ago he had suffered a heart attack that nearly killed him. That was the time when he and Mong Kok were feuding over territorial control over the region. It was also the time when Koonta had wanted to expand his drug operation into neighbouring Malaysia, which had long been Mong Kok's territory. The short warfare that erupted following his incursion and the simmering feud that followed may also have been the contributing factor to one of his son's death. Panrit was Koonta's heir apparent. Despite having many more sons, Koonta still grieved for Panrit even though it has been over four years. It was only money Koonta kept telling himself whenever he felt he was about to lose his temper. And what good is money if you're dead. So far he had managed to stay alive by clinging on to that philosophy. But the news that his own daughters had thrown their lot with the *Old Man* was too much for him. To his credit, Koonta had managed to put a lid on his famous temper. Koonta was an insensitive man, unable or perhaps, unwilling to change from the old ways in which the perception that a son was always better than a daughter was. In his case - his two daughters.

Although Koonta didn't know it, his twin daughters were far more intelligent and more resourceful than his son Panrit was. He didn't know it because he never had time for them, never beyond a pat on the head once in a while. Like all his generations and those before him, he considered having daughters nothing than a nuisance. His twin daughters were close to their brother, Panrit. They never felt jealous of him despite the fact that their father had often ignored them especially in Panrit's presence. They had accepted the fact that this was the way things ought to be. They had never question their father's decision on anything, even when it concerned them. Even when they were treated like chattels and were sent to live with Mong Kok as appeasement to him, they accepted it without question. Koonta had told his two daughters that he would consider it a great favour if they would agree to be Mong Kok's mistresses so that they could let him know everything about his activities.

Having been taught at an early age that women's main role in life was to make men happy, the twins accepted their father's decision without question.

However, while they were staying with Mong Kok in Singapore and with help of television, magazines and newspapers that Mong Kok had in his house, they began to improve their English both written and spoken. It didn't take the twins long to realise that what their father had done to them was wrong and they were furious. Their anger became so intense after they began to realise that their father had never once ask them about their welfare or had anything nice to say to them.

From that day onwards they plotted revenge on their father as well as on Mong Kok. During Mong Kok frequent absence from home, they put their plans into action. By observing and asking seemingly insignificant questions, they had a good picture of how Mong Kok's operation had run. They made sure they took down the names of all the buyers Mong Kok had written in a special book hidden in a false panel behind the electrical fuse box. They will one day soon return to their beloved Thailand and to take their rightful place in Koonta's organization. They had loved their brother Panrit and they would have no trouble accepting him as the head of the family had he been alive, but he had since long gone. They had grieved for him and now they felt that it was time that they stop mourning.

* * *

Boonchai, who stood with his head bowed, could tell by the silence and the way Koonta was pacing the room that his fate was in a balance. It could fall either way. On the good side, his boss may remember that he had once suffered a heart attack and may try to curb his temper and might let him off the hook. On the other side, his boss may chew him up for not anticipating what his two daughters had in mind when they were eager to become the *Old Man's* fifth and sixth wives.

Koonta stopped pacing the floor and stood in front of Boonchai and asked him once again. "Is there anything else you want to tell me?"

Boonchai took a deep breath and said, "Lee from Singapore and Kassim from Malaysia have cancelled their order with us and are now buying from your daughters too." Boonchai instinctively took a step backward and braced himself for the tirade that could soon follow. In the past he had often been on the receiving end of these tirades, and they would normally be filled with expletives about what a useless human being Boonchai was and so on. He remembered that it could go on for as short as fifteen minutes or it could go on for half-an-hour to forty-five-minutes.

To Boonchai's surprise, Koonta only gave him a thoughtful look before leaving the room. As he quickly followed close behind, Boonchai couldn't help noticing how stooped his boss had become. And that was not all, he was also walking with a noticeable gait in his stride, something he hadn't seen before.

The house in which Koonta had built was in an up-market residential area of Bangkok. It was built along Thai traditional style with its distinctive pagoda roof and decorative woodwork on its doors and windows. A high iron fence completely surrounded it; their sharp spikes on top are to discourage any would-be intruders from climbing over.

Nopharat however wasn't just an ordinary intruder. Born in Korat amidst poverty and hunger during the Vietnam war, he had run away from home after he got fed up with continual thrashings he got from his father, who was always moaning about the meagre sum he brought home after a hard day's work as the resident beggar on a street in Patpong.

Nopharat had managed to pull himself out of the gutter he had been occupying when he ran from home and began working in restaurants washing dishes at night while he continued begging during the day. As a sixteen-year old, with only a few Bahts in his pocket and no friends, Nopharat had no idea how he was going to survive in a big city like Bangkok. Nevertheless he was determined to make it, he told himself. The alternative would be to stay at home and to be continually abused by his father. It didn't take him long to learn that in a big city like Bangkok not to trust anyone, not even adults who looked as if they wouldn't hurt a fly.

On his first night, after having walked aimlessly all day, he decided to take a rest at a bus stop. The street in which the bus stop was in was deserted except for an elderly couple waiting for a bus. They asked him whether he was waiting for the bus to the city centre. Not knowing where in the world city centre was, Nopharat nodded his head in reply.

After a few minutes of waiting, the heat and the tiredness got to him and he promptly fell asleep on the hard wooden bench close to where the couple were sitting. He remembered them smiling and nodding their heads benevolently at him and he remembered feeling that it was all right to close his eyes for a while since they there sitting close to him.

When Nopharat woke up several hours later, he discovered not only his money was gone, but so were all his belongings - a plastic bag containing his spare shirt and another pair of trousers. The toothbrush and a cake of soap that he had stolen earlier that day from a supermarket, were also gone. He couldn't think of anyone else except the elderly couple who could have taken his things. Unlike the small village where he had been born and raised, where people would go out of their way to help one another, here in the big city, as he had quickly learned, not only that no one will lift a finger to help you, but they'll steal anything that's not bolted down.

Nopharat soon realised that Bangkok's hostile environment was no place for a boy who was alone and trusting. The shopkeeper across the street, who saw everything from his cashier's desk, took pity on Nopharat by giving him some food to eat and a place to stay for the night.

The next day he introduced Nopharat to his brother who owned a restaurant in Korat. The proprietor of the restaurant, after having heard the boy's plight from his brother, was quick to capitalize on the situation. He quickly offered Nopharat a job at a pay no one in the city would touch with a ten-foot pole. Nevertheless Nopharat was grateful for the job, especially it came with a place to stay.

Determined to make a better life for himself he worked hard with hardly any days off. That pleased his boss very much because he thought he had a dumb, hard-working peasant in his employ that was willing to work long hours for nothing. Little did his boss know that Nopharat was not spending all that extra hours for nothing. He was learning all he could learn about the trade because one day he was hoping of opening a similar restaurant.

CHAPTER THIRTY-SIX

The opportunity, however, came sooner than he had expected. While he was tidying up his boss's office one day, in came a lovely young woman, whom he reckoned was about a couple of years younger than him, and introduced herself as owner's daughter.

"And who the hell are you?" she demanded, her hands akimbo. Nopharat immediately detected from her manners that she was spoilt and arrogant. It immediately provoked a retaliatory reaction from him. Although it was the first time he had met her, he had often heard his co-workers talking about how beautiful their boss's daughter was and that she was constantly chasing after the local film stars. Nopharat's sharp mind sprang into action and he immediately grasps the situation with both hands.

"I'm Nopharat," he said. "You may have heard of me. I've just come from Bangkok to do a scene for a movie here in Korat."

"Are you an actor?" she asked. This time her tone was more cautious and it was tinged with curiosity and her mouth was slightly parted.

"Yes I am," replied Nopharat. "I am waiting for Mr. Wongprasong to discuss the possibility of filming part of our scene here in his restaurant."

Nopharat observed the noticeable change in the young lady. Her mouth had not only opened a mite wider but her nostrils began to flare sensuously and her eyes had that glitter he had seen in many young girls who had come into the restaurant in the arms of some of the American airmen from their air force base nearby.

The young girl walked up to Nopharat with her hand extended. "I am Lisa, Mr. Wongprasong's daughter," she said. "I can tell you right now that my father will not have any objection to your shooting your film in our restaurant."

"Really? That's good," he said. "I can't tell you how grateful I am to you for allowing us to film in your restaurant. If you have a free moment perhaps we can go somewhere where I can tell you about the scene we'll be doing in your restaurant."

"I have some free moment now," she replied. "Perhaps we can do it now?" by this time her face was already flushed and she could feel the palpitations of her heart.

"Excellent," Nopharat replied. "Let me phone for a taxi to take us somewhere where we may talk in private."

"There's no need for a taxi," she said. "My car is parked just outside and I know just the place where we can talk."

Nopharat couldn't believe his good fortune at this turn of event. As he led Lisa towards the door, his mind was racing at full throttle trying to hone the strategy that was beginning to germinate in his mind. "Where are we going?" he asked he slid onto the front seat of the young girl's blood red Honda Civic.

It had often been said that a person tends to change his, or in this case, her personality, once she got behind the wheel of her car. Nopharat was about to witness the statement being put into action as he braced himself for the action to roll before his very eyes.

Lisa pulled out of the kerb in such a manic fashion; she only missed the bumper of the parked car in front of her by inches. Despite the notorious traffic snarl Bangkok was known for, the street that morning was quiet and practically free of cars. Lisa didn't fail to take advantage of the lull in the traffic by going at least fifty mph, hardly slowing down when she took the right turn two blocks down the road.

Unfortunately for her not all roads in Bangkok that morning was as quiet as the ones they had left behind. Ten minutes later they found themselves bogged down in the middle of the worst traffic jams Nopharat had seen since he left his idyllic village nearly two years ago.

Nopharat had often thought of his younger brother, whom he adored, and his two elder sisters, one of whom he could not get along with. She was constantly on his case, forcing him to do all her chores - pinching his stomach until it turned blue whenever he refused. His other sister was all right, as far as he was concerned. She would help him with his chores whenever she saw how tired he was, or help him ease his pain by applying some ointment, she had concocted herself, on the numerous cigarette burns his drunken father had often inflicted on his body.

He remembered once how his father had become so enraged with him when he accidentally spilled his father's glass of Mekong whiskey. That day his father burned parts of his hands and legs as well as his neck and face with his lighted cigarette. His sister counted a total of eleven burn marks on his body, not to mention the two kicks he had received in the stomach. As the matter of fact he was grateful to the blows he received in the stomach. It knocked the wind out of him; he hardly felt any pain when his father applied the red-hot tip of his cigarette on him.

Lisa's sudden acceleration, when she pulled out of their lane and got onto the path of the incoming traffic, caused Nopharat to snap out of his painful thoughts. He gripped the dashboard with both hands and said a silent prayer when he saw the container lorry loomed hugely in their path. He shot a glance in Lisa's direction and wondered if she had suddenly become suicidal. To his relief, he saw her pulled into an empty space in front of a car that had broken down seconds before the lorry roared past them with horns blaring.

Nopharat was convinced that the lorry had no intention of slowing down if Lisa hadn't pulled away from its path. The house that Lisa had brought him to was in the outskirt of the city by the river. Inside it was well furnished and it had a lived-in look about it.

"It's our family's country retreat," said Lisa, reading his thoughts. "No one will disturb us here."

Nopharat playing the role of a film actor, proceeded to inspect the place. When Lisa was showing him the bedroom she normally occupies, according to her, he sat on the bed and said, "very nice." As Lisa was standing close to him, he extended his hand to her.

Lisa took his hand in hers and Nopharat slowly pulled her towards him. He kissed her and she returned his kiss with passion. A few minutes later they made love.

"What role will you be playing in the film?" asked Lisa as she nuzzle up against him, enjoying the sensation as their two naked bodies rubbed against each other.

"As a bartender," he replied. He suppressed a smile when he said that. In real life he was the bartender in her father's restaurant - had been for the last one year.

It was as a bartender he had known many women. They would normally come into the bar with an escort; either an American serviceman or the local who had a bit of money for the restaurant was an up-market one whose prices were exorbitantly high. Some would find Nopharat's primitive ruggedness very attractive. Many would end up in his arms in their beds if not his.

With all the other women he had made love to Nopharat had the necessary precaution, but with Lisa that night he had not. He wanted her to love him and he wanted her to be pregnant, the sooner the better.

The next night Lisa came to her father's restaurant and found Nopharat working behind the bar. As he hadn't expected her he almost died when he saw her sitting at bar in front of him.

He was about to confess to her that he was nothing but a bartender in her father's restaurant when she suddenly covered her mouth to one side in a conspiratorial manner and asked,

"Where is the camera?"

Nopharat blinked his eyes and looked at her quizzically.

"Are they rolling the film now? She asked.

"No, not yet," he replied. He almost kicked himself for forgetting what he had told her.

"You shouldn't be here. These are actors, besides you don't want your father to see us together, do you?" He looked at her, pleading with his eyes for her to go away.

"Why don't we meet tonight at your place - say around midnight!"

"All right," Lisa replied. "I'll see you tonight." That night Lisa asked him to move in with her. A few weeks later she told him that she was pregnant.

Nopharat smiled at her and said, "In that case I think we should get married."

"Married? We can't get married! My father will kill me. Remember what I told you about what he feels about actors? He doesn't think much about them."

He remembered. How could he forget, she kept repeating it over and over again. How about a bartender? What will he think if his own daughter were to marry a bartender - his own bartender? Nopharat smiled at the thought. "Do you want to marry me or don't you?" He asked her seriously.

Lisa gave him a long look before nodding her head. "Yes, I want to marry you, but how?"

"Simple!" He said. "First we'll get married in secret, since I'm not acting in any movies now, I'll find a job, an ordinary job which your father will not object to."

He paused and began pacing the room, his face looked as if he was in deep thoughts. A moment or two later he stopped pacing the floor and rushed to her side, his hands holding hers.

"How about if I work as a bartender in his restaurant? I think Tan, the manager, will give me the job. He had jokingly said that I could have the job anytime I want. I'll ask him tonight."

"What are you going to tell my father?" Asked Lisa, giving him a rather sceptic look.

"I'll think of something," said Nopharat. "You know what I'm trying to do, don't you? I want your father to know that you had respected his wishes by you not marrying an actor, and I, who was an actor, am willing to sacrifice my career to marry you - a girl whom I love very much. Besides, we don't want to deprive him from seeing his own grandson."

"Grandson? How do you know it's going to be a boy?"

"Granddaughter or whatever. I'm sure he'll be thrilled just the same." With only a few friends present, Lisa Wongprasong and Nopharat got married.

Despite her excitement being married to a film star, as Nopharat described himself to be, Lisa couldn't help feeling a little forlorn for deceiving her father. She had loved her father very much. He had always been there for her ever since her mother died several years ago. I'll make up to him as soon as the baby was born, she told herself.

While Nopharat continued working at a bartender at the restaurant, Lisa worked very hard trying to be a good housewife. She had no idea that the job that Nopharat was holding on to was the only job he had got. She had believed the story that he had told Lisa that the only way her father will have any respect for him was for him to continue to work under his nose as a bartender.

He said that they should wait until their baby was born before telling her father everything. On the day their baby boy was born Nopharat went to see Wongprasong and told him about their marriage and about their baby boy - his grandson.

At first Wongprasong did not believe him, telling him that he can dream. People like him, according to Wongprasong, do not marry into families like his. Besides, his daughter Lisa wouldn't dream of marrying him even if he were the last male on earth, he added.

Nopharat became angry, but Wongprasong's reaction was just as he had expected and he was ready for it. He dug into his shirt pocket and showed Wongprasong a couple of photographs of he and Lisa with their baby.

With his face slowly turning red like a lobster, Wongprasong snatched the photographs from Nopharat's hand and tore them into bits before throwing them in Nopharat's face.

Nopharat took a step forward and grabbed Wongprasong by the collar of his shirt and began twisting it until Wongprasong began fighting for air. Nopharat continued twisting the collar knowing full well that if he kept that up another couple of minutes, Wongprasong will passed out.

Wongprasong made some futile attempts to fight off Nopharat but to no avail. He was no match against his adversary, who was much bigger and younger too. Just as Wongprasong was sagging to his knees, Nopharat released him abruptly. Wongprasong lay at Nopharat's feet gasping for air, the noise he was making was loud enough to cause Nopharat some concern about being heard. He moved back a step to give himself some room and gave Wongprasong a hard kick in the stomach. Unknown to Nopharat, Wongprasong's heart was not strong. Wongprasong clutched at his chest, moments later he closed his eyes and was still.

Nopharat checked Wongprasong's pulse and found none. He was sure that the kicks in the stomach he had given the Old Man wasn't hard enough to have killed him, and neither would that twisting of his collar. He reckoned that Wongprasong must have died of a heart attack. He bent forward and began to lift the body onto the chair behind the desk. As soon as he had arranged Wongprasong's body with his face down, he made a telephone call to the company's doctor to whom most of the employees had gone to see at one time or another.

The doctor, a middle-age man, whose white hair was cut military style and whose middle pouch showed noticeably through his not-so-white coat, lost no time in examining inert body of Wongprasong.

"What happened to him, Doc?" Asked Nopharat, going into his act. "He was dead when I came into the office. I found him slumped on his desk just as you see him now when I came into the office. I had an appointment with him, but when I knocked on the door and received no reply, I walked in and saw him lying there. I telephoned you immediately." You told your wife that you are an actor, now act, Nopharat thought to himself.

"Heart attack," said the good doctor. "He died of a heart attack. I had warned him before about eating and drinking too much, I guess he just couldn't help himself. Being the owner of a restaurant known for its good food must be hard on him. He loved his food, and you should know about his drinking being a bartender."

"Yes, he loved his brandy," replied Nopharat sombrely. The doctor put his hand on Nopharat's shoulder and said, "I'm sorry about your boss. I'll inform the authorities straight away. Will you notify his family? or shall I."

Nopharat nodded his bowed head. "I'll let his family know." After the doctor had made his telephone call, Nopharat called Lisa at the house and told her about her father.

Her wails caused him to push the telephone away from him. As soon as she was calm enough he told her to leave the baby with their servant and to come to the restaurant immediately. He told her that the doctor had arranged for her father's body to be moved to the hospital. Nopharat assured her that he wouldn't allow them to remove the body until she arrived.

While waiting, Nopharat searched Wongprasong's pocket for the keys to the office safe. He opened it and found a bunch of other keys among which was another set of the safe key. He took the bunch from the safe and pocketed it. He also took a large sum of money but made sure there were still enough money left behind. He returned the key he had taken to Wongprasong's pocket. He also went through Wongprasong's wallet where he lifted some money and pocketed it. Lisa came few minutes before the hospital van arrived.

Nopharat comforted her and told her to be strong. He told the same story he had told the doctor - that he had found Wongprasong slumped on his desk when he open the office door after knocking on it several times. As requested by the people from the coroner's office, Lisa removed all her father's personal effects from his body such as rings, watch, the gold chain with an amulet which her father had always worn, and the wallet and some loose change from his pockets.

To her dismay, they also removed his shoes and gave them to her, saying that they looked expensive and it wouldn't do to leave them on his person while at the hospital. Lisa nodded her head at the logic of what they were saying. They also wanted to remove the Dunhill belt and socks from her father's body but Lisa had insisted that they should be left alone. The hospital staff told Lisa that they were only doing this because they could not guarantee their safe return afterwards. Angrily Lisa told them that she'd hold them personally responsible.

CHAPTER
THIRTY-SEVEN

The coroner's report confirmed what the company's doctor had concluded earlier. The funeral was a grand affair attended by many people from the business sector as well and from the government.

Wongprasong, it seemed, was a well-known figure in both circles. Nopharat played his role well during the entire period so much so that even the chief priest had assumed that he was now the person he should be dealing with. When all the rites had been said, the chief priest handed over the cremated remains of Wongprasong to Nopharat. He slowly brought the beautiful urn and handed it to Lisa who held it against her bosom. As a mark of respect, the restaurant, as well as numerous other enterprises, in which the late Wongprasong owned, was closed for a week.

Nopharat lost no time in getting Lisa to agree to take over the entire operation with him as her trustee. Lisa, who hadn't done a day's work in her life, was glad to hand over all the responsibility of running her father's entire operation to her husband. To prevent any unsavoury speculation from being aired, a press release was made to explain Nopharat presence including a coloured photograph of the couple with their baby.

The presence of a baby in any situation of this nature was like oil over trouble waters. Any dissent among some of the minor shareholders in Wongprasong's huge business holdings was soon won over by various means, including insiders' tips on a couple of flotations the company had made. While others were given large bonuses or expensive gifts, and even holidays to a neighbouring country.

The company continued to prosper under Nopharat's leadership. Despite his lack of formal education, Nopharat was a fast learner and a natural when it came to making money. He seemed to be able to smell a good deal out in a sea of bad ones. At the end of five years he was able to triple the company's profit and everybody within the company loved him. At home front too it seemed that he could do no wrong, as a devoted husband, and a loving father of three wonderful children, he was a consummate actor worthy of an Oscar.

However, unknown to everyone else including Nopharat, there was a speck in the ointment. Koonta, the late Wongprasong's sworn enemy, became more and more irritated when the authorities, a number of whose members were on his payroll, had failed to honour their undertaking not to disturb his drug-related activities.

It seemed that they were under pressure to try to stem these activities on United States instigation to do so or risk losing some of the privileges the country was enjoying. Koonta tried every which way to get the heat off his drug business but to no avail. The country, it seemed, was in love with the new breed of entrepreneurs like Nopharat, and Koonta despised the likes of him. He reached the limit of his indignation one night when the police raided all his massage parlours and prostitute joints. It was too much for Koonta when even the sanctity of the good old fashion flesh trade was being violated.

"What will the country come to if decent young men and people like you and I can't find young women to sooth away their woes?" he fumed at his assistant. "It's people like Nopharat that was giving prostitution a bad name!"

"You are right, boss," said his assistant looking up from his newspaper. "It says right here that he's planning to develop an industrial park similar to the Silicon Valley in California right here in our village."

He continued to read with lips moving as he had done before. He turned the page and resumed reading to himself when all of a sudden he gave out a whoop and looked up excitedly at Koonta.

"He also said that he'll compensate the landowners handsomely for the land that his company may acquire. You know what Boss? My mother has some land in that area...I'm going to be rich," he said.

Koonta snatched the newspaper from his assistant and began pouring over the article himself. "Damn the bastard! The area where he's going to turn into an industrial park is also where I get most of my opium from." He folded the newspaper and tosses it back to his assistant; his face was red with anger.

Koonta's assistant tried to catch the newspaper but failed. It landed on his massive chest before falling down onto the floor where he picked it up and took it to the dining table at the far end of the room. He pulled up a chair and resumed reading the article when he was so rudely interrupted.

Koonta in the meantime paced the room until a maidservant entered the room and announced to him that he had a visitor. He asked her to show him in. A few moments later a medium-built man with a noticeable pouch walked into the room. He had a briefcase in one hand and a copy of the same newspaper Koonta had just read in the other.

"I'm sorry to drop in on you like this," the man said. It's just that something of importance has cropped up which I think you should know."

"Mr.Thanom, please don't apologise. You're welcome in my house anytime," Koonta told his visitor. "Please sit down. May I offer you some tea? Or if you prefer, something stronger perhaps?"

"No, no. Tea will be fine thank you," said the other, taking the proffered seat after he had carefully placed his brief case onto the marble-topped coffee table in front of him.

His manners as well as his dressing were impeccable, something he had learned while studying agriculture in the United States. In a country whose mean temperature was around thirty-two degrees Celsius, Thanom was wearing an immaculately tailored suit, white shirt and stripped tie. His expensive pair of shoes looked as if they had been polished military style - another legacy he had acquired when he joined the army as soon as he returned home from the US. With his degree plus six months of basic training, Thanom emerged as a second lieutenant in the army. In a country where the military had a lot of say in running it, being a military officer was the most logical thing as far as he was concerned. He stayed with the army until his term expired. By that time he was already a captain with a substantial acreage of land. Land which he began acquiring almost as soon as he had finished basic training.

With his knowledge of agriculture, Thanom grew opium of the finest quality in the country, surpassing even those that came from the two neighbouring countries that made up the so-called Golden Triangle. As an officer in the army he was able to operate without much trouble from the authorities. His biggest buyer was Koonta, in whose living room he was.

"Have you heard of a man called Nopharat?" He asked his host.

Koonta nodded his head. "I have heard of him but I have not met him." He faced his guest and waited. His face revealed none of the anger and turmoil that was inside of him a few minutes ago.

"Nopharat had somehow managed to convinced the civilian government who is now running our country that time has come for us to increase our industrial output by opening up more industrial parks especially in the country side and conveniently he had earmarked my farm and those of my friends for one of the his projects. And you know what'll happen when they do that, don't you?"

"Yes, Damn him!" To hell with niceties, Koonta was thinking. You'll be compensated handsomely for your land and so will the others, but what will I get except a lot of heat from my buyers. First my daughters stealing my customers away from me, and now this!

"How long have you got? Will they wait until after the next harvest?" Asked Koonta.

"I don't think so," replied Thanom. "They've already got their bulldozers on site."

Koonta turned angrily at Thanom and said, "You dirty bastard, you've sold me out!"

"No, no, that's not true. Look! I've got some money for you." Thanom leaned forward and flipped his briefcase open to reveal the money. "Fifty thousand dollars in United States' currency... all yours."

"Fifty thousand! Are you kidding? That's peanuts compared to what I've been making!" shouted Koonta.

"I'm sorry, that's all I can give you," Thanom replied, flinching visibly at Koonta's sudden outburst. Without bothering to close the briefcase, he walked out of the living room and left.

"Nopharat, I'm going to get you for this!" Koonta slammed his fist on his desk.

Nopharat was still in his office when he received Lisa's frantic phone call telling him that their son had been kidnapped from his kindergarten.

Lisa had arrived at her usual time to pick up her son when she saw a man, and a woman who had looked vaguely familiar to her, walked out of the school with her son in tow. She tooted her horn and sped up to them, but as soon as they saw her car coming, they drove off quickly and were soon out of sight.

She tried as best as she could to follow them but she soon lost sight of them at an intersection. As she couldn't be sure which way they went Lisa took the left turn only to find it ending up in a dead end. She made a U-turn and proceeded to look for the car the other way.

After about half-an-hour of fruitless search, Lisa decided to abandon it and called her husband at his office. He informed her that he was on his way home and asked her to do the same. If their son was kidnapped, he told her, he'd expect whoever it was who kidnapped him to call them at home.

An hour later they received a telephone call from a woman telling them that they had their son and that he was safe. However, she warned, his safety depended on Nopharat carrying out her instructions to the letter. He waited for the instruction, but when he heard nothing, he shouted into the phone, "What are your instructions?" But the line was already dead.

Just as he was hanging up the telephone, a servant came in with a letter in her hand saying that someone on a motorcycle had hand-delivered it a few moments ago.

Nopharat grabbed the letter from her hand and ran out to their front gate. All he could see in the distance was a lot of smoke and a glimpse of the rider all in black in the distance.

Nopharat ripped open the letter and with hands slightly shaking, read its content. It had a single sheet of A4 paper with a typewritten message on it that says: `ABANDON YOUR PLAN TO BUILD THE INDUSTIRAL PARK IMMEDIATELY AND YOU MAY SAVE YOUR SON. OTHERWISE YOU WILL ONLY SEE HIM

AGAIN IN BITS AND PIECES THROUGH THE POST. YOU'VE GOT TWENTY-FOUR HOURS'.

Within the hour Nopharat had all the bulldozers out of the area. Working like a man possessed, using methods that could only be described as ruthless, an hour later he and his men had managed to pinpoint who the kidnappers were. Finally after he had used up a lot of his resources and manpower, he ultimately narrowed it down to one man - Koonta.

Nopharat had got to where he was not only because he was clever and resourceful, but he had also learned long ago that if you want something done right, you've got to do it yourself. In this case he knew that he had no choice but to go and rescue his son himself, otherwise he may not see his son alive again. He had no doubt that Koonta had no intention of ever releasing his son even he had stopped with his plans to develop the industrial park. He figured that Koonta would want his son kept alive to ensure that he would not reneged on his promise. It would mean that he'll never see his son again and he couldn't let that happen.

After assembling enough men and firepower, Nopharat had Koonta's villa encircled. He even commandeered all the houses surrounding it. He achieved all this in less than four hours after he had received the ransom note. After telling his men to wait for his signal, Nopharat looked up at the wall and told himself that he should be able to climb over that easily enough. Sure enough, he went over without much difficulty. But once he was on the other side, he found himself facing another fence.

This time however, instead of having smooth steel vertical bars to hold on to, he found razor-sharp barbed wires ready and waiting to shred his hands and clothes to a bloody mess.

Unknown to Nopharat, the six feet wide corridor with its well-turfed carpet grass was also guarded by a pair of ferocious bull-terriers that could tear a man's flesh off its bones with no more than a jerk of its head.

It was precisely in the middle of this no-man's land, at the back of the house, Nopharat found himself facing one of the bull terriers. It had sneaked up on him, as he was about to cut the barbed wires with a pair of wire cutters. He had no inkling of it being there until he saw a shimmering reflection at the corner of his eyes. He turned to look at what it was but saw nothing, so he continued with what he was doing.

A few moments later he saw the shiny reflection again, this time there was no mistaking the bull terrier's shiny, well-brushed coat of hair.

The shock of finding the animal standing just a few feet away from him caused Nopharat to pull back his hand clumsily. The sharp edges from the barbed wire cut deeply into his gloved hand. At the smell of the blood, the dog lunged at Nopharat, Barking loudly to attract its companion.

Nopharat managed to grab hold of its collar with one hand and with his right hand he plunged the wire cutter repeatedly into the dog's eyes. Blinded, the animal backed off from him and into the barbed wires hurting itself badly before running to where it came from.

Nopharat was about to make another attempt at the wires with his bloodied wire-cutter when he was set upon by another bull terrier. It was identical in look and in size with the other one, except this one looked madder and more ferocious than the one before - if its growls were anything to go by.

Instinctively Nopharat raised his hands to protect his face from the animal's teeth. The wire cutter was knocked out of his right hand and out of his reach when the sixty-pound dog landed hard on him. The impact from the dog knocked the wind out of Nopharat and it took him several moments before he managed to struggle up his feet. Fortunately for him, he had managed to push the dog away from him when they fell. It must have hit its head hard on the steel fence; it became disorientated for several seconds before it tried to make another attempt to attack Nopharat. By this time Nopharat was ready for it, for when it lunged at him, he grabbed it by its neck and swung it towards the barbed wires.

The dog landed in between the rolls of the razor-sharp wires. Nopharat turned his head away when saw what the wires had done to the poor animal. Its cries brought an immediate response to whoever was in charge of the security at Koonta's house.

Floodlights around the house and its compound came on all at once and Nopharat found himself bathed in it and nowhere to hide. He did the only thing he could think of, and that was, to beat a hasty retreat. Unfortunately for him, the dog, although badly mauled by the barb wire, was faster than he was and he found himself on the ground with the dog's teeth firmly gripping his calf.

He led out an involuntary yell that promptly alerted his second-in-command who saw his boss struggling with the dog. Praying that he would not hit his boss, he took careful aim and pulled the trigger. He knew he had hit the dog in the head where he had aimed for. Moments later he saw his boss limping towards where he had begun to cut the barbed wire before. After waiting for what seemed an eternity, he finally saw Nopharat cut through the barbed wires and moments later he disappeared out of view.

Nopharat managed to slip out of sight when two men suddenly appeared at the scene. He dipped his hand into his bag-pack and took out his gun with the silencer on. He shot dead one of the guards and hit the other in the shoulder with his second shot, forcing him to drop his weapon.

"Where are they keeping the boy?" Nopharat demanded from the guard, pressing his gun against the man's temple.

"Upstairs," the man said, jerking his head in the direction.

"How many men guarding him?"

"Two. One outside the door and the other is with the boy inside the room."

Nopharat pulled the trigger and the man slumped on to the floor. Nopharat silently ran up the stairs and crept up to the guard that was standing in front of the door. He pressed the nozzle of his gun against the back of the man's head and whispered to him to tell his friend inside to take over a while so that he could take a leak. Nopharat told the man to drop his weapon as soon as he opened the door. Relieved to see that his son was all right, Nopharat quickly took out a couple of handcuffs from his backpack and cuffed the two men to the window grille.

He then took out the flare gun he had in his backpack and fired in the air to signal his men to make their move. Several earths moving equipment suddenly appeared and drove straight for the walls. Behind them, and on foot, were several of Nopharat's men, many were armed with AK-47 riffles. The moment the walls were down they went into co-ordinated action killing a number of Koonta's men who seemed to be badly outnumbered and outgunned. Nopharat's second-in-command

and his men reached their boss and his son and within minutes they were quickly taken out of the villa where a car was waiting to take them to the safety of their own home. Before leaving the scene, Nopharat whispered his final instruction to his lieutenant who nodded his head before giving his boss a wide grin.

CHAPTER THIRTY-EIGHT

There was nothing in the press the next day about the rescue by Nopharat of his son, nor was there any news at all about the incident. It was as if the whole thing didn't happen - the kidnapping, the ransom note and its incredible demand and finally the heroic rescue - all these didn't seem to have taken place.

Nopharat's instruction to his second-in-command the night before was to destroy Koonta and to raze his place to the ground. While he and his son were on their way home, his men sought and found Koonta hiding under the floorboard in basement of his huge villa. Systematically they ransacked every room for anything they thought that might be worth something before razing it to the ground with their bulldozers.

When they found Koonta in the basement he was clutching a briefcase full of money and was shaking like a leaf. He offered them the money for his life.

Unfortunately for Koonta, Nopharat's men, unlike his, were either not interested in money, or that they feared Nopharat more. Once again he was unfortunate, he was shot in the head before he could find out. The money, nevertheless, was retrieved from his hand and handed over to Nopharat.

By morning, what was once a beautiful villa amidst an equally beautiful landscaped garden, an empty flat piece of land was in its place. Everything had been levelled to the ground, with all its rubble pushed into a depression nearby as landfill.

* * *

The *Old Man*, a creature of habit, was up as usual at six o'clock that morning. Five minutes later one of his men had telephoned him to give him the news of Koonta's death.

Even though he and Koonta had never been close, he felt some sadness when told of his death and the circumstances surrounding it. It was with a heavy heart that he had to tell the twins of their father's death. And despite the quarrel they have had with their father, he was surprised to see how anguished they were at the news.

The *Old Man* had already suspected that Nopharat might have had Koonta killed but he had kept that piece of information to himself knowing how impulsive the twins were. The last thing he wanted was for them to go gunning for Nopharat.

Although they had never met, the *Old Man*'s estimation of Nopharat had, during the last twenty-four hours, went up a few notches as a man who shouldn't be taken lightly. He hadn't known about the kidnapping of Nopharat's son by Koonta, of course, although he had suspected it. He blamed himself for not confronting his late son-in-law the moment he heard about it. He should have, if he did, perhaps he could have prevented the disaster from happening.

When told by his men how Nopharat had had Koonta's place razed to the ground, the *Old Man* hadn't expected it to be literally razed to the ground. As he gazed through the spotlessly clean windscreen of his Mercedes-Benz car, he could visualize the anger Nopharat must have felt and awesome power he must have wielded in order to destroy what was literally a landmark in the town.

Koonta's villa, not un-similar to those that belonged to the Hollywood Stars in the United States, was one of those sights that got mentioned as the tourists passed through the town on the way to or from the airport. A local architect, at the cost of several million US dollars, beautifully built it. It dwarfed the Governor's Mansion nearby, making it look more like a guard's post in comparison. And now the ground looked so level it was as if a football field was to be built on it. All that was needed was the turfing to be done and in a few months' time soccer games could be played there.

"I've seen enough," said the *Old Man* to his chauffeur. "Let's go home."

He picked up that morning's newspaper from the top of his briefcase beside him and leaned back against the soft leather seat. He flicked quickly through the newspaper for the article he was sure would be in it. To his dismay he found that Koonta's death and that of his men, and the total destruction of his exquisite villa was not even mentioned in it.

One hour later his car drove in through his own front gate with his guards passing them through in a rather lackadaisical manner. The *Old Man* lambasted them for their sloppiness and threatened to send them back to work in the poppy fields for the rest of their lives should they let anyone in without checking with him first.

He made a mental note to come up with some sort of signals they could use as part of the security measure and to discuss with his son in Singapore about beefing up security at their place in the light of what had been happening at Koonta's place.

* * *

From his first floor study David heard Endang mentioning his father's name and he automatically placed his hand on the telephone extension on his desk.

He picked it up the moment it rang. "Yes?" He spoke into the mouthpiece.

"Your father, sir, on line one," said his housekeeper in her thick Indonesian accent.

"Hello, father," said David. "Is everything all right?" For nearly ten minutes, the *Old Man* told his eldest son all that had been happening in his neck of the woods and the need for them to beef up security at their place including their farms. When they finally ended their conversation David confirmed with his father that he would be home for the reunion's dinner the following week.

Next the *Old Man* called a Kuala Lumpur number and was soon answered by another son - his number two son. Like his older stepbrother he was also a lawyer, and he was attached to the Attorney General's department there. The son too agreed to be home for the family reunion's dinner.

The third call he made was to another son, a lawyer working in his own law firm in Hong Kong. Finally he called his youngest son, another lawyer, working in a major law firm in Vancouver, Canada.

Even though the *Old Man* never spoke for more than ten minutes to each of his sons, the combined calls took him more than two hour to make. The reason was each call was made from a different phone booth covering a distance of over twenty miles.

The reunion dinner, which normally would be held at his villa, took place in a restaurant that the *Old Man* owned. It was located high above on a mountain top not far from Chiang Mai.

It was chosen because he was sure it would be safe, for no one can go in or out of the place without going through a tight security check since it was a favourite haunt of the rich and famous. Apart from the restaurant, it also has a number of chalets as well as a golf course, and the temperature up there was comfortably cool.

In the plush decor of the restaurant the *Old Man* sat impassively at the head of the table. Opposite him at the other end of the table sat David, his eldest son from Singapore. With the exception of the seat on his right, which was meant for his guest, he told his sons, all the other three seat were occupied by his other three sons.

The *Old Man* could see that all his sons were curious about who his guest might be. Earlier when he was about to enter the dining room, he heard them speculating about who the mystery guest could be. They wondered why their father had invited an outsider to what was purely a family gathering - an annual event they had been attending for as long as they could remember.

"Surely this must be the first time an outsider was invited to our gathering," said George, the youngest of the clan.

At exactly eight o'clock, while the waitresses were filling their glasses with water, a stunning-looking woman wearing a traditional Thai dress was shown into the room by the restaurant manager himself. She wore her hair short but not too short, but in a style that suited her beautiful face well. She wore little jewellery - a pair of earrings, two strings of pearls around her neck and a diamond ring and a wedding band on her left-hand's third finger. The manner in which she greeted their father suggested to the sons that they were no strangers to each other.

Seeing other women with their father, other than their mother, was nothing new to the boys, but watching a faint but a noticeable sign of deference from him towards the woman was something they had not observed before, and they were burning with curiosity about her.

"Boys," said the *Old Man*, "this is May." Collectively they said their "How do you do" to her.

She nodded at them before taking her seat. Following the Asian tradition of not mixing business with pleasure, at least not at the outset, they ate in silence. Whatever little comments made were made with regards to the food.

When dinner was over, David was first to speak by addressing his question to their guest. "I take it that you're not from here, Miss May?"

"Please call me Mandy," she replied, flashing him a smile. "Yes, you're right, I'm not from here. I'm from Penang originally."

"Oh! I go to Penang often," said David. "Which part of Penang are you from?"

"Batu Ferringhi."

"Is your family still living there?" David was beginning to sound like a lawyer that he was.

Before Mandy could reply, the *Old Man* interrupted by saying,

"Mandy is a dear, dear friend who has come to give us a hand to eliminate a serious problem we are now facing."

"Oh! What problem is that, father?" Asked his son from Vancouver, pointedly ignoring Mandy.

It was glaringly clear to her that she did not charm the *Old Man's* son named Samuel like the rest, nor did she impress him. She wasn't even sure whether he liked her by the way looked right through her throughout dinner. Besides, his *'you're are beneath me'* look was a giveaway; even a blind man wouldn't fail to notice. She smiled inwardly at his surmising. Samuel saw the smile and was furious.

"It's not what, but who," replied his father. "And his name is Nopharat."

"I don't like what he did to Koonta. He must be stopped before he thinks he can do what he likes." It was David from Singapore who made the acid comment. He looked at everyone at the table for support. They in turn nodded their heads in agreement.

"Father, you've brought forward the family dinner for a reason," said his son from Hong Kong. "Could you tell us what's all this about?"

Before the *Old Man* could explain, his son from Kuala Lumpur suddenly stood up and faced Mandy.

"I know who you are," he said, pointing a finger at Mandy. "You're the woman who is supposed to had died in a explosion at a flat in Penang not too long ago, aren't you?"

He waited for a reply from Mandy, when none came, he continued. "You're married to a Malay - a lecturer at the university there - right? He's also a writer, I believe, and you have two children. Is that correct?"

"Allan, please sit down," said the *Old Man* to his son from Kuala Lumpur. "You are right, Miss May is the one you must have read about in the press recently. We staged that accident so that she could come here and help us. However, I would like to ask all of you not to harass her with any more questions regarding the affair."

"Help us to do what, father?" Asked David. "I can ask that, can't I?"

David suddenly remembered Mandy was also the name of his friend, James's wife. Could she be the same one? They had stayed at his house in Singapore while he and his family were in London.

He remembered that it was during the time when their son was in custody there for assaulting a man called Wong. David remembered all these details because his cousin Goh was the son's lawyer, and he had mentioned all these things to him when he had returned to Singapore. By that time his guests were already back in Penang. It seemed that Wong suddenly dropped the charge against their son.

When David glanced across the table, he saw Mandy looking at him; it was as if she was trying to remember where she could have seen him. He wished he had read in more detail on the so-called accident. He had no idea that the young woman that was supposed to have died in the explosion in a block of flats in Penang was James's wife.

David was afraid that she might remember him from the various pictures of him at his house. Beside the pictures, there was also large painting of him and his wife in the living room. He shot a glance at her again. He was pleased to see that she had ignored him and was concentrating on what the *Old Man* was saying about the meteoric rise of Nopharat in the community. The last thing he wanted was for her to recognize him. David tried to return his concentration to what his father was saying about how Nopharat had managed to convince the government to covert large tracts of farmland into industrial parks. It seemed less of a coincidence that a number of these farmlands were growing poppy plants among their usual crop of tobacco and other vegetables. And that the main chunk of the farmers income were derived the opium from the poppy plants and not from the rest.

The *Old Man* was explaining to his sons and Mandy that even though Nopharat's background was a bit of a mystery, there was definitely no mystery as to what he was aiming for - a high political office. The noise he had been making about drug trafficking near schools had hit the right chords among the parents, and many had begun campaigns of their own to lobby the government authorities to stamp out these potential killers from the schools and their environs.

"Nopharat even had hot-lines for spotters of drug pushers to call. Rewards were sometimes offered," said the *Old Man*. "Ever since he had Koonta wiped out, he had become some sort of celebrity. Some people had been aping him by taking the law in their own hands. A few petty criminals had been hacked to death after they had been caught in the act, and pushers were beaten. We can't allow this to continue," said the *Old Man*. "Can you imagine what would happen to good old fashion crime if everybody got into the act, huh!" He shook his head as if to clear the unpleasant thoughts. "It would be a disaster."

"What can we do to stop him," asked George, looking very concerned. "We can't," replied his father. "None of us can. If we lay a finger on him, the backlash could be devastating. People would boycott all our businesses, and our fields would be burned to the ground. It would be People's power all over again, just like in the Philippines under Marcos."

"But I can," Mandy Interjected. "Nopharat's wife, Lisa, and I are friends. We've known each long before she and Nopharat were married. The funny thing is, she never mention Nopharat to me before. Out of the blue she telephoned me and said that she was married to this Nopharat - a former actor, according to her. I asked some people I had met while I was working for a horse owner in Singapore before, people who worked in film studios in Hong Kong whether they'd heard of Nopharat, none of them have. These people were gamblers who used to come to Singapore for the races." Mandy picked up her glass of water and took a sip from it before continuing. "Soon after your father had arranged for that *'accident'* in Penang and had me smuggled into Thailand, I began to get curious again about Nopharat. It was soon after I saw my friend, Lisa, sitting in a car next to her husband. The moment I saw him, I'd recognised him immediately as one of the stable boys that had worked for a Thai horse owner I once met. Horses are either flown in or transported by road to wherever races are being held most weekends in this region. I suspect drugs are sometimes brought in from Thailand this way..."

"I've put Mandy as a branch manager of our travel agency here," interrupted the *Old Man*. "Her office, by the way, is next door to Nopharat's. Her idea is to get Lisa to see her husband for what he is and have him thrown out."

"How are you going to do that?" David said, directing his question to Mandy.

"I don't know," replied Mandy. "But I'll think of something."

David looked sceptically at her. As he scanned the faces around the dining table, he was dismayed to see that, with the exception of their father, all of his brothers had the love-struck look on their faces as they looked at Mandy. When he looked at his father, he saw not a look of love or lust, but a look of unmitigated pride and he was puzzled.

The dinner ended with everybody feeling quite contented - all except David. He was so busy speculating about Mandy and his father's relationship with her, he hardly ate anything, and drank very little. As he got into his room at the villa, he told himself that he ought to dig deeper into Mandy's background. There was something very suspicious about her, and the look of pride his *Old Man* was giving her was most perplexing.

David was pleased that their next day's meeting was without the presence of Mandy. It seemed that she had left for town early that morning. Without her David was more relaxed and was his old chatty self. He wanted to bring up the subject of Mandy but suddenly remembered how everyone was mooning for her the night before, he decided to skip it for the time being. He was sure he'd have plenty to say after he had her investigated.

The *Old Man* too seemed pleased with himself this morning. Even his manner was different. He treated every one of his sons with deference instead of his usual gruffness. Although they found his behaviour baffling, they nonetheless welcomed it and hoped that it would remain as a new permanent feature in their father's psychological make-up.

The meeting ended just before lunch with everyone feeling quite happy with the performance of his business to date. By nightfall all of the *Old Man*'s sons had departed for their respective homes.

David, who had been booked on a SIA flight to Singapore that evening, sneaked out of the airport terminal building as soon as his father's chauffeur had dropped him off. He took a taxi back to the city and booked himself in a second-rate hotel - a walking distance away from Mandy's office. He went into the foyer's coffee shop that overlooked the lifts as well as the staircase to the upper floors of the well-appointed office building and waited.

Twenty minutes later Mandy came out of one of the lifts and strode out of the building. David hastily went after her. As he came out of the door he saw her get into a taxi. He had to wait for nearly five minutes before another one came. He figured by that time Mandy could be anywhere.

He couldn't believe his luck when several minutes later his taxi was caught in one of the famous traffic jams of Bangkok. And about three rows in front of them, and two lanes to their right, stood Mandy's taxi. He smiled when he saw her peered out of her window. He told his taxi driver to keep to their lane and to follow Mandy's taxi, which he pointed out.

The driver jerked his head in the direction where David was pointing. When he saw what a beautiful woman Mandy was, he looked at David through his rear-vision mirror and gave him a knowing smile. When he saw what an excruciating slow ride it was turning out to be, David began to relax and took out his hand-phone and gave his friend James a call.

"Hello? Is this James?" he asked the moment he heard a man's voice answered.

"Yes, it is," came the reply. "Who is this?"

"How are you, James. This is David."

"David, how are you?"

"I'm fine, thank you. Are you really all right? I've just heard about your wife...Mandy, wasn't it? Right. I am so sorry to hear that she had died. What did happen?"

James gave David the account about Mandy's death. How one day he had come home and found it in shambles when a bomb had exploded and Mandy, who was alone at the time, was killed. The firemen found her charred remains soon after they had put out the fire. Her body was so badly burnt; it was difficult to identify except by jewellery she was wearing and by bits and pieces of her clothes that the fire had not completely destroyed.

David detected how difficult it was for James to recall the gruesome detail of Mandy's death; he quickly cut short his telephone conversation. He promised to come and see him soon.

Twenty minutes later Mandy's taxi finally discharged her at a house in an up-market area of Bangkok. From the inside of his taxi parked across the street, David could see a young woman about Mandy's age opened the door to Mandy. Moments later the door was closed shut leaving him wondering as to whom the house belonged to.

As if reading his mind, the taxi driver said the house belonged to Nopharat - the industrialist. Like Mandy said, she and Nopharat's wife were good friends. And the way they seemed to greet each other was a testimony to that. Satisfied that so far Mandy seemed to be telling the truth, David instructed the taxi driver to take him back to his hotel.

On the way there they were stuck once again in a traffic jam, only this time it was worse. He took the opportunity to think things out with regards to Mandy. First of all, he told himself, he reckoned that she had the capability of breaking up Nopharat's marriage with his wife, Lisa. Secondly he must assumed that she had recognised him. The question was what would she do about it? Will she turn him in as a menace to society, or will she turn a blind eye since she owed his *Old Man* a favour. And another thing, why did she want everyone, including her two children and her husband, to think that she was dead?

It was obvious to David that his friend James, was very much in love with her? And talking about love, is his father in love with her? Vivid picture of how his father had looked at her last night came to his mind.

The trip back to his hotel took David almost twice as long due to the traffic jam which was getting worse. As he stepped out of the air-conditioned comfort of the taxi, he felt hot and clammy. He picked up his keys from the lethargic-looking desk clerk and headed for the lifts. He was looking forward to a long cold shower despite the fact that he already had one early that morning. Having just come back from London where he had a home, and being an Anglophile that he was, having more than one shower a day wasn't a done thing. Bangkok in the middle of July, however, could get unbearably hot and humid, with hardly any breeze for respite, having more showers was the way to go.

CHAPTER THIRTY-NINE

Sitting in a car across the street from the hotel were two men. The American, sitting in the passenger's seat, unused to the heat, despite having the car's air-conditioning running, was fading in and out of sleep, while his Thai partner, sitting in the driver's seat, was the first to spot David as he stepped out of his taxi. The Thai gently woke his companion by tugging at his shirtsleeve. As a reflex action the American went automatically for his gun which he had tucked in his hip pocket. He smiled sheepishly at his companion when he realised what he had just done and where he was. He quickly returned his gun to his hip pocket and his eyes in the direction where his partner was pointing. They got out of the car and began to follow David along the crowded pavement.

David couldn't be sure but he thought he was being followed. In order to draw out whoever was following him, he increased his pace and turned the corner away from the direction of his hotel. The American and the Thai immediately broke into a run. David spotted them instantly. He ducked into a Chinese restaurant and went through their kitchen to the back lane that led him directly to the service entrance of his Hotel.

The duo followed him in the restaurant and after spending a lot of precious time looking for David among the crowded diners, they finally went through the kitchen only to be told that a man had through there moments ago. They realised they took a wrong turn when they ended up in a street that sold anything from designers' Jeans to Dunhill briefcase; from Gucci's shoes to Guerlain perfume - all products of a thriving backyard industry that produced cheap imitation goods ranging from Rolex watches to Levis Jeans.

"Damn it! We've lost him," said the American, his face covered with sweat and his shirt clung to his body like a tight-fitting glove.

"Don't worry. We've got men watching out for him at all the airports," replied Akit, his Thai counterpart.

Lawson, an American narcotic agent, looked at his partner with scepticism but said nothing. He had been warned by his boss in Washington not to antagonize their Thai counterparts.

"We need their cooperation more than they need ours," he had said to Lawson. "If the Thais decided to close their eyes to all the drugs that flowed through their country, we'll be inundated with that stuff. And if Mexico were to do the same thing, can you imagine what will happen to this country?" He shook his head violently for several minutes as if he was unable to discard the unpleasant thoughts from his mind.

Dejectedly they returned to their car and headed for their downtown office. Lawson picked up his jacket from the back seat and dipped his hand in its pocket. He reread the extradition papers that authorized him to take David back to the United States to stand trial for drug trafficking and other related offences. If convicted David would spend at least thirty years behind bars. Somehow the thoughts reassured Lawson that what he was doing was what Uncle Sam wanted and he eased up a bit. He felt that ought to compensate for all the personal inconveniences he had suffered ever since he arrived in Bangkok. Lawson was one of the few Americans who didn't think much of Bangkok. He couldn't understand how anyone could put up with such hideous traffic jams which could snarl-up everything for hours on end. And as a contributory factor, he had read, the traffic jams also had caused people to die from respiratory and other diseases. Tons of pollutants were emitted from these vehicles.

Involuntarily he dipped into his hip pocket for his handkerchief and pressed it against his nose. He wondered how badly affected his lungs had been and began brooding about all the way to their hotel. On the top of that, during his first week out, Lawson had suffered from what was generally known as the *'The Travellers Bugs'*, which confined him to his bed for two days, and that was despite the precaution he had taken by not drinking the local water. Unfortunately he hadn't counted on the local ice he had in his Coca-Cola to be contaminated.

David, who managed to give the two narcotic agents the slip, was unaware that narcotic agents in the UK had stumbled on to his drug smuggling activities there too by accident, when on his last trip there the fuselage of his executive jet was dented by a baggage handler who had carelessly reversed his cart into the side of David's jet. In an attempt to repair the damage on the sly the authorities at the airport stumbled on a secret compartment filled with drugs.

The British authorities checked the plane's flight plan. They found out that it was bound for the Kennedy Airport the following night. They alerted their American counterpart and a trap was laid for David as they followed David wherever he went.

Fortunately for David a security guard that had been on his payroll tipped him off regarding the accident on his plane and was told that an army of men had worked frantically to get it repaired. David became suspicious and decided to dump the whole shipment of drugs into the sea the minute he was over international waters.

As he had expected, David found his plane surrounded by narcotic agents the moment he landed at Kennedy International Airport. After examining his entire plane from top to bottom, and having found nothing that resembled drugs, except for the few tablets of aspirin he always carried in his shaving kit, they had to let him go.

From that day onwards he had never handled any shipment of drugs himself. He had left it to others to do the work. His task was merely to plan how to get the goods from point A to point B without being caught. He came up with some winners with one or two lemons in between. The end result was that he was shipping more of the stuff than ever before.

As he sat sipping his coffee in a dingy coffee shop in the heart of Bangkok's China town, he was contemplating on how to get the mother of all shipments of the purest heroin into the United States without being caught. With the Thai and American narcotic agents on his tail, he worried that after months of preparation he may not be able to do it this time.

It would be a great blow to David for he had planned it to be his last deal before retiring in Australia where a number of his compatriots were enjoying their retirement. This planned shipment, if only he could get it through, would be worth millions of dollars. He thought he'd set up a law firm there dealing mainly in corporate law, nothing messy, or aggravating like criminal law. He snapped out of his reverie when he suddenly heard a crashing sound behind him. David jumped to his feet thinking that his two pursuers may have caught up with him. When he turned around all he saw was a young Caucasian had fallen onto the floor near him.

The coffee shop proprietor, an old man of undeterminably age, suddenly appeared through the kitchen door and went to the young man's aid.

David, being the only other customer there, approached the inert figure lying on the floor. He watched as the Old Man felt for other's pulse. After a few moments, he turned towards David and shook his head and said, "This young man is dead. I'd better call the police."

His last remark was made with such distaste; it was obvious to David that he had no love for the police force. And during that split second David saw a way he could solve his problems.

"I think I know this young man," he said to the old man, pausing to see if he had detected the lie he had dished out. When he saw none, he continued, "Why don't you leave everything to me. There's no need to involve you with the police, is there? I'll call for assistance to get him out of here and I'll get in touch with his family. In the meantime, why don't you close up for the rest of the day."

The old man looked so relieved, he practically ran to the front door and shut it quickly. "If you want to use the telephone, here it is." He pointed to the phone on the counter next to his ancient cash register.

David made a phone call and within half-an-hour a van with four men arrived at the back entrance and took the body away with them. Before he left with them, David handed the old some money saying it was to make up for his loss of business. The old man couldn't believe his luck when he saw the amount of money David had shoved in his hand. It was more than doubled his whole day's takings. He thanked David profusely, giving him the traditional Thai sign of homage.

* * *

In a funeral parlour across town David was examining the contents of the wallet that was in the hip pocket of the deceased. Apart from a single piece of hundred-dollar travellers' cheque, the only other money the dead man had was some loose change in his pocket. They also found a packet of heroin hidden in the heel of his shoes. David was looking for some identification as to the nationality of the dead man. He finally found a driver's licence tucked in the zip pocket of his PVC hip pouch. He put it in his pocket and left.

Working from a safe house not far from Don Muang airport, David began working out the details for his last project. It was over two hours later before he was finally satisfied with the plan. On paper it looked like it could work, but a lot had to be done at the United States end. He was debating whether to let his brother from Vancouver in on his plan. Finally after much soul searching, he decided to let him in on a condition that their father wouldn't be told about this shipment. David told his brother that their father is suspect at the moment because of his relationship with this Mandy woman, as he put it.

* * *

K.K.Lee, whom everyone in the community had always referred to as *The Old Man*, was a small time pusher in Penang when he had to run for his life when the authorities there were about to nab him. Under the strict Malaysian laws, if convicted as a drug trafficker, Lee could be sent to the gallows. He knew then that they'd be on the lookout for him at all the exit points. He knew he had little choice but to leave the country which meant leaving his wife and three children.

The only way out for him was to cross into Thailand and to try to make contact with his supplier. He was caught at the checkpoint at the Malaysian side of the border. He had hidden in a special compartment in an empty palm oil tanker. He suspected that someone had tipped off the police. He managed to escape from a drug rehabilitation centre where he was put as a drug addict and not as a pusher. That had cost him several thousand ringgit, but it was worth every cent. If he had been charged as a drug trafficker, it would have been a different story. Sometime later he overpowered a guard and he escaped into Thailand.

Being bright and quick, in no time Lee worked himself to being a supplier himself. With the connections he had in Singapore and Malaysia, he began to streamline his network of pushers. Soon it became too big for him to handle from Thailand and it became apparent to him that he needed a distributor in the area to cover Malaysia and Singapore.

Mong Kok at that time was a small time pusher just like he was while in Malaysia and at the same time dabbling in loan-sharking and prostitution. During a meeting in Bangkok, Mong Kok revealed to Lee his ambition to venture into the retail business like operating supermarkets and restaurants. This way, according to him, it will stop people from speculating where he got his money. Lee saw the logic in Mong Kok's ideas and gave Mong Kok his moral support. He saw in Mong Kok what he saw in himself – a person whose ambition may not be limited to just being a down liner to him solely. He saw in Mong Kok as a person who will stop at nothing until he had achieved all, in other words: a dangerous man. He made the decision not to deal with Mong Kok directly but only through his number one dealer in Bangkok – Som Phong.

* * *

Mandy had woken up early and had breakfasted and was waiting in the study waiting for the *Old Man*. A maid had brought her a cup of Chinese tea in a cup with a blue motif around its rim and an exquisite lid with the continuation of the same motif on it. When closed together it showed an outline of a well-define lips on its rim where one take the sips from. The sofa she was sitting on was made of leather whose woodwork was carved but the design escaped her. She leaned back to savour the tea and found it to her liking.

The *Old Man* appeared wearing a bush jacket and matching pair of pants similar to the ones favoured by officials of His Majesty's government. She wondered why he was wearing it since he wasn't in the government.

"Good morning, May," the *Old Man* said cheerfully.

"Good morning father," replied Mandy.

"We have a lot to talk about, haven't we? I'm sure you must have a lot of questions you want to ask me."

He paused to accept a cup of coffee from the maid who appeared as he was about to sit in the armchair opposite Mandy. She also brought two plates containing some glutinous rice and mangoes and placed them on the table in front of them.

"I don't know what your mother have been telling you," the *Old Man* began. "I did not abandon you all, but I was told to leave by your mother because she found out that I was dealing in drugs.

She told me that she didn't want ever to see me again."

"And you were such an obedient person, you did what you were told to do, right?" Mandy replied sarcastically.

"No, I had no intention of obeying her as you put it," he said calmly. "I left because I thought it would be best if I could make some money first and then come back for you all later. Unfortunately the police caught me the following night. Fortunately for me, at that time, the mandatory death sentence hadn't been passed yet and I was spared the gallows. They took me to a drug rehabilitation centre where I spent some time before I took off and headed for the Thailand border."

"You decided to take off, just like that!" Mandy noticed he didn't take her sarcasm well that time. She saw an angry flash on his face. It disappeared almost immediately.

"No, not just like that." Snapping his finger. "Little did the authorities know that some of the guards were getting rich by growing marijuana in jungle not far from the centre. They were using the inmates to work the farm on a rotation basis. Some of the harvested crop was sold to those inmates at the centre who needed them while the rest were sold to dealers outside the centre. Pretty neat, huh! Anyway, one day while working at the farm, I overpowered one of the guards who was dozing off the effect of smoking too much ganja, and I made for the hills."

The *Old Man* paused and took a sip of his cold coffee. "I want to emphasize this to you so that you'll understand what I was up against. Because of what we know, no inmate had ever escape from this detention centre before had managed to stay free or alive for very long. Five inmates that I knew of who had managed to escape were all hunted down and killed within a matter of weeks. You see they'd managed to do that not all by themselves, but with a lot of help from informers and dealers on the outside. None of the inmates who had escaped ever come back alive. You see, we knew too much. Beside the Mafia in Sicily and those in the USA, I can't think of any other group who were more efficient or ruthless than the guards at these detention centres."

He took another sip of his coffee before continuing. "I know you are angry and not in a mood to hear any explanation from me. But please hear he out, all right?

I knew that in order for me to survive I had to make sure I was as far away from the rehab centre as possible. The uniform we were provided with was bright orange, so first thing I had to do was to find a house where I could steal some clothes. On that score I was lucky, the first kampong house I encountered happened to have a pair of Jeans and two T-shirts hanging on their line outside which fitted me perfectly. It seemed that luck was still on my side because about half a kilometre away I stumbled upon a van which was being loaded with coconuts by two men. I managed to sneak into it as it was pulling away. By this time I was very hungry but there was nothing in the van except coconuts, so I took two coconuts and smashed them against each other until it cracked open. After drinking the water and eating some of the meat, what with the sway of the van from side to side as it took the corners plus its droning sound, tiredness must have overcome me and I fell asleep. The first thing that hit me when I awoke was that the van had stopped. I had no idea where I was because the van's door was still shut. And so with extreme caution I opened it slightly only to find the shaft of bright light had hurt my eyes. I quickly shielded them from the sun and panned the view in front of me. What I saw gave me hope - all round me was trucks and lorries with mainly Thai number plates, which could only mean that we must be close to the Thailand border. Without any hesitation I left the sanctuary of the van and began looking for the coffee shop or food stalls that must be around somewhere - otherwise these trucks and lorries wouldn't be there. I saw it among the cluster of trees - a rectangular building made of timber and zinc roof with food stalls lining one wall, and tables and chairs placed in rows in front of them. By this time I was very hungry but I had no money. I went to the back of the building thinking that maybe I could work for a meal. As I entered the kitchen, a woman who was frying some noodles, turned her head momentarily and ask me when I've come to deliver the coconuts. I told that I was and asked her how many would she want. She told me all she had was in the wheelbarrow back there, jerking her head in the direction of a green coloured wheelbarrow in the corner. She asked me to bring a wheelbarrow full of coconuts. Without any hesitation, I emptied the wheelbarrow of the few coconuts and began wheeling it toward the van I came in. After ascertaining that no one was around, I began filling the wheelbarrow with coconuts. With it full I brought it back to the restaurant where I should it to the lady who began to count it. She then dug into the pocket of her blouse and gave me some money. Without counting how much she had given me I put it in my pocket and got the hell out of there. I didn't even bother to get myself some food for I didn't want to take a chance of encountering the van owner who may be the one she was expecting. Once again luck was on my side. Just as I got out of the kitchen door, a truck with a Thai number plate was about to leave. I ran after it and jumped into the back and prayed that it was going back to Thailand instead of coming from there. The truck was filled almost three-quarter-full with cartons and I wanted to check what was inside when it suddenly stopped. At that moment I knew that it was heading towards Thailand because it was stopping at the Malaysian - Thailand checkpoint in Padang Besar. When I heard a voice asking what was in the truck, I quickly got into one of the cartons which was half full and burrowed myself underneath what looked like cut flowers and tried to close it as best as I could. Moments later the truck door was opened and I heard someone climbed onto it and stood next to my carton. I held my breath when I heard the lid of my carton being opened. Whoever it was that was peering into it said something about the flowers being nice. After what seemed like an eternity the lid was finally closed back and I heard footsteps moving away from me. A few moments later the truck door was slammed shut and the truck pulled away not long after that. After I got out of the carton I began to panic because my legs seemed to have gone to sleep. It took me long while, rubbing my legs vigorously, before I could get the circulation going again. I had hoped that the truck would stop as soon as it crossed the border so that I could get something to eat. By this time I was so hungry I was ready to eat the flowers. The last meal I had was so long ago I had forgotten when it was. Unfortunately for me truck went on and on for several hours. I thought of jumping off the truck but in the state I was in I'd probably would break my legs or worse.

In order to keep my mind off food I played a number of games I had learnt in my youth. It worked half the time, the other half I just laid on the cartons in order to make myself comfortable and fell in and out of sleep. In my sleep I'd dream of food, lots and lots of food, and while I was awake I'd think of more food, and the more I thought of food the more hungry I became. At one stage I tried to nibble on the leaves of the flowers, then I remembered about what my father had said about multi-coloured leaves - most of them tend to be poisonous. Same with wild fruits. Weak with hunger, I must have fallen asleep again. I did not wake up until several hours later. It seemed that the truck had stopped and was in a warehouse and with great caution I got down from the truck and tried to find out where I was. The moment my feet touched the cement floor, two men who came from nowhere and pointed their guns at me. They led me to a room where a group of men were playing cards. They forced me to sit on the floor while one of them fetched for their leader. The men who were playing cards continued with their game as if nothing had happened. They only stop playing long enough to give me a cursory glance.

Their look of indifference was puzzling to me. And another curious thing about them was their seemingly lack of enthusiasm in their game. A moment later I saw the reason for their lacklustre performance in their game of cards. Beyond them, in the shadows, sitting on a chair, was another man who had what looked like an Ak47 in his hands. I recognised the riffle because the guards in the rehab centre used them. He met my gaze with a look that was devoid of any emotion in his eyes. He was hugging that gun as if he was in love with it and I felt cold sweat running down my spine. When he saw that I was looking at him, he pulled his chair into the light and sat down again. Despite the fact that he was sitting down I could see that he wasn't very tall. About average height, I would say, but he was well built. He had an Afro hairstyle - well trimmed like his beard and moustache. He wore a checked shirt and a pair of Jeans and boots. All in all, he wasn't the sort of man you'd want to encounter in the dark.

I was terrified of him but I was also thirsty and hungry, and I was about to ask him for some water when I heard footsteps behind me. A man wearing a dark bush jacket and matching trousers appeared with the guard. The bush-jacketed man asked me a lot of questions. I answered by telling him more or less the truth that I had run away from a drug rehab centre in Malaysia. I emphasised the point that I was a pusher and not a user. He looked at me and then at the group at the table as if for verification. I couldn't tell whether he believed my story or not. Nevertheless, he told the guard who was with him to bring me some food. When it came, he sat at the far end of the table and watched me eat. By the look on his face, after watching me eat, I think he was convinced that I was telling him the truth about not having eaten for several days.

Even the guys at the table stopped playing cards to watch me eat. It didn't take me long to wipe everything clean from my plate. Someone at the table offered me a cigarette, which I gratefully accepted. It was somewhat stronger than my usual brand of cigarette, but I enjoyed it all the same.

The next day the boss, this time wearing not a bush jacket, but a short-sleeved shirt and a pair of grey slacks came to me and took me aside. He told that he had decided not to turn me in but to offer me a job doing more or less the same thing I was doing before I got caught. This time he assured me that I wouldn't be caught provided I follow his guideline on how to do things. As I listen to him talk I realised that I was talking to someone who was smart and probably learned too. Sure enough, as I got to know him, I learned that he was educated in the USA with a degree in Business Administration and that he was a son a dirt farmer whose land was so small, he barely eke out a living to support his wife and son, let alone trying to send the son, his only son, to the United States of America to study as he had hoped. Somehow he managed it, and the son, knowing how hard his father and mother had to work to keep him there, worked just as hard. He graduated at the top of his class four years later. On his return he found their house in such a state of disrepair and his old man dying from tuberculosis. Despite her denials to the contrary his mother too was suffering from kidney failure. He took them to the hospital and the doctors there told him that both his parents needed medical care that would require a lot of money.

The cash crops that his father had been growing on their small plot of land could not generate enough cash for their livelihood, let alone the enormous sums required by the hospital. Knowing that there was no one he could turn to for the money he required, he decided to grow poppies for its opium instead. With only the hoe as their tools, the son with the help of one worker worked the land from early morning till dusk. With his first harvest of opium he found out that not only he was able to pay his parents medical bills, he still had some money left to pay his worker and for food. Needless to say, the son had never turned back.

With his educational background he applied modern techniques in agriculture to his small farm. He was pleased with the result of his next harvest and in no time at all he was able to increase his yield two-fold. With the extra cash he invested on modern equipment. Both his parents recovered fully from their illness, and to make sure that they at least had a better chance of beating their illness from reoccurring, he modernised their house by installing better sanitation facilities, had electricity connected, and had running water.

The solitary worker that he had in the beginning was none other than your old dad. He was kind enough to give me a job with no questions asked. You see I could not go back to Malaysia, I was a hunted man. I just couldn't face the thought of being caught and returned to that rehab centre. I'd rather die...you do understand, don't you?"

Mandy looked at her father with tears in her eyes. Finally she nodded her head. "Yes, I think I understand."

"Thank you," he said. "I've often thought of you and your two brothers. How are they? Have you got a photograph of them with you?"

Mandy dug into her handbag and took out her wallet. From it she removed a colour photo of her and her two brothers and handed it to her long lost father. A father she never thought she'd ever see again. A father who knew that she was in danger even before she did, and had arranged for her to be rescued from a man he had known very well - Mong Kok.

Mandy's father took the photograph from her with both hands. She noticed that they were trembling slightly, not because he was old, but because he was eager to see what his sons look like. She saw in the way he was looking at the photograph that he was thrilled. Lee then took out his wallet and lifted a photo and showed it to Mandy. It was a photo of her taken at a race course, most probably at one of the courses in Thailand where she used to go to when she was with Wong.

Mandy couldn't be sure how old her father was, but she heard some of his workers affectionately referred to him as the *Old Man*. He was strongly built but of an average height. However, his hair had gone grey and it was cut short - military style which gave him an elderly look. Jealousy could the other reason why some people refer to him as the *Old Man*.

For a man who was supposedly old, he had had something like sixteen wives in Thailand alone, most of whom were fairly young, and between them he has fathered sixty-five children. Excluding herself and her two brothers, and the four she had already met. At that moment she couldn't decide whether to hate him or to have him recommended for a medal for being such a productive man. She smiled inwardly at the thought. At that moment she realized that she had lost her hate for him and she was glad.

There was no doubt in Mandy's mind that her father must love all his children, but only in his peculiar ways. His love for them did not go beyond physical contacts. Nevertheless she was grateful he had saved her from Mong Kok.

Mandy had learned how her father had sent someone over to Penang to rescue her as soon as he heard that a contract had been put on her by Mong Kok. It so happen that the hired assassin was someone he had known and whose family he had helped once. When the assassin was given the photograph of his target, he had immediately recognised her as his friend's daughter. He was the one who had photographed Mandy at the race course in Bangkok at the behest of Lee.

He had contacted Lee and between them they came up with a rescue plan that not only saved Mandy from a certain death but also at the same time satisfied Mong Kok that she was dead.

With a recently buried corpse, which they had dug up from a graveyard, wearing Mandy's clothes and jewellery, they then placed it in candy's flat. After making sure that no one else could be hurt, the assassin then had her place blown up using a remote control.

Mandy in the meantime was safe and sound in Thailand where she had been smuggled to earlier. Unknown to Mandy, her father had arranged it for her to stay at one of her stepsisters' house and her family. Mandy of course didn't know that the young woman whose husband was a military man was none other than one of her stepsister. She had liked her and her two daughters, but her husband, for some reason, seemed a bit cool towards her.

"Tell me again, father, how many brothers and sister have I got in total?" Mandy asked.

"Presently, Seventy-two," he replied.

"Do you take care of all of them, or do you just leave it to their mothers to fend for themselves, like mine did?"

"I was young and very foolish then, but I did try my best to take care of you, your mum and your two brothers. I'm sorry if you thought that I had abandoned you all. I'll try to make up to you and your two brothers."

"But not to my mother?"

"No!" He replied vehemently.

"Why?"

"I'm sorry, but you have to ask your mother that."

"Did my mother do something wrong? Was she unfaithful to you? Is that it?"

Instead of replying, he got up from his chair and went to the cupboard and took out a fresh pack of cigarettes. He unwrapped the top of the cellophane wrapper carefully by pulling the red strip around it. With the tip of his fingernail, he lifted a corner off the foil paper to expose the cigarettes. He then tapped a cigarette out and fitted it in a holder before lighting it with a disposable lighter. He was standing by the window and he had his back towards Mandy.

Feeling affronted and angry, Mandy got up from her chair and strode purposely out of the room. She remained in her room until her two stepmothers, who were presently living with Lee at the villa, came to ask her to have lunch with them.

Mandy told them that she wasn't hungry, but somehow they managed to coax her to come and have lunch with them. During a sumptuous lunch prepared by her two stepmothers, Mandy asked what prompted them live with Mong Kok.

"Because our father asked us to," one of them replied. She gave Mandy a stony look.

"Why did you?" she asked her other stepmother. Her stare matched the other.

Despite their obvious anger at being asked such impertinent question, Mandy plodded on and asked them, "Did your father asked you two to marry my father? Marry is probably the wrong word to use, but you know what I mean don't you?"

This time both looked coldly at her. "No, he did not asked us to come and live with your father. It was your father who had asked our father for our hands in marriage and we accepted."

"Why?"

"Why what?"

"Why did you want to marry my father? He's got so many wives already. Were you two so desperate that you cannot find someone else younger to marry you?"

Mandy suddenly realised that this time she had gone too far. They looked as if they were about to strike at her. Their faces looked red with anger. One of them began to clutch and unclench her hand in an effort to control her temper, while the other sat rigidly in her seat with her hands clutched in a fist, her knuckles white. What Mandy didn't know was that most of these mistresses were daughters of his trusted lieutenants who had given their consents willingly when he had asked for their hands. This was his strategy to avoid infighting within his inner circle.

For several minutes the three of them sat there rooted to their seats like a Sphinx with Mandy on the receiving end of her stepmothers' venomous stare. The dark mood in the room was fortunately broken when Mandy's father came into the room with a beautiful young lady in tow. Mandy gave the young woman a cursory glance but to her father she gave an unmistaken look of contempt. The young woman gave Mandy the traditional Wai which Mandy returned emulating the other before she realised what she was doing.

The *Old Man* immediately sensed the electrified atmosphere in the room, but after having lived with many women in his life, he chose to dismiss it as nothing more than transitional which he was sure would soon come to pass.

"May, this is your sister Ratana," the *Old Man* said as he introduced the young woman to Mandy.

"Ratana, this is your sister from Malaysia. She doesn't speak our language and she's not familiar with our custom. I want you to take good care of her?"

The young woman clasped her hands together in a traditional Thai greeting and bowed towards Mandy. Mandy replied by giving her newfound sister a similar Thai greeting but did not bow to her.

The *Old Man* gestured to his two wives, and the three of them quietly left the room leaving

Mandy and her sister alone. He was sure, that despite their obvious inability to communicate with each other, they'd get along fine. He had long ago recognised Ratana's special gift, and had used her to get his message across to the hill tribes he had under his employ, whom he had learned, could be as stubborn as a mule when it came to doing something they did not like, or against their beliefs. Somehow she had always managed to persuade them to go along with her ideas.

As they sat facing each other across the coffee table, Mandy could see how relaxed her sister was as she began to point out to Mandy the Thai names for various things such as coffee pots, saucers and so on. And to her surprise Mandy found herself repeating after her in Thai. Her sister in turn asked her for their equivalent in English, this way Mandy felt less like a student and a little more like an equal. It was novel idea and she admired her sister for it. She suddenly felt that not only she was learning a new language from her sister but also in turn she was teaching her English. It seemed like a fair trade to her and she felt suddenly at ease. Despite the fact that they had different mothers, Mandy could find that they had many similarities in features as well as in mannerism.

Despite her earlier reservations, Mandy found herself liking her sister Ratana very much. The weeks passed by, followed by the months. Enveloped by comfortable circumstances without any cares, Mandy hardly noticed their passing. She had long reconciled with her two stepmothers and had made peace with her father. Other relatives too liked her; they first came to see because they were curious, but soon they came to see her because they liked her. However, with the exception of Ratana, she had no close friends.

Recently her thoughts were of James, of her son Alexander and of Andrea - her high-strung daughter.

"We're two of a kind, you and I, Andrea my darling," she softly said to the ceiling as she lay on her bed. Realising she had just talked to herself, Mandy at once became embarrassed.

Although her bedroom door was closed and she was alone in the house, all the walls in the house were made of wood and were thin. Sound travelled easily throughout the whole house. It would be a source of gossip if any one of her sister's two servants were to hear that she had talked to herself. After all, she was a *Farang* or a foreigner, and everybody knows that all foreigners were a crazy lot.

Mandy had moved out of her father's house and into her sister Ratana's house soon after they had met. Sensing that all was not well between Mandy and their two stepmothers, Ratana had asked her father's permission for Mandy to move in with her. The *Old Man* had given his consent when he heard from his two wives that Mandy had been difficult and quarrelsome with them.

Thinking about James and her two children had brought sudden tears to Mandy's eyes. Funny how prone to crying she was nowadays, she thought to herself. Mandy was wondering how they were getting along without her. Do they miss her as much as she had missed them? Or, have they forgotten her as if she had never existed; after all she wasn't much of a mother to them, nor a wife to James, she lamented silently.

When Ratana had told the *Old Man* how morose and moody Mandy had been lately, he called on Mandy at her office. It didn't take him long to find out that despite her unhappiness, Mandy was good in her work. She had learned how to transact business affairs, to exercise power over people, to learn to use people effectively. He noticed that people seemed to like her; they came to her if they needed advice, be it business or personal. However, with the exception of Ratana, she had no close friends.

It didn't take Mandy long to realise that her father's travel agency seemed to have a lot of repeat customers with a number of them being issued outward bound tickets almost as soon as they got back from one trip. As first she didn't think anything about it until she picked up a few names and ran them through her computer. The printout showed that these same people make trips to all parts of the world and all without exception had made at least one trip each to the United States.

Mandy also found it incredibly fortuitous for the company to have so many customers who lived in Malaysia and Singapore to be issued tickets from her office in Bangkok. These air tickets were specially couriered to contacts in Kuala Lumpur and Singapore for distribution to the travellers in these two countries.

Suspecting that something was amiss, Mandy made special efforts to be at Don Muang Airport to see some of these customers off. After chatting with a number of them at their respective check-in counters, Mandy found out that very few of them could give her a good reason as to the purpose of their trip and what did they know of the country they were going to. She noticed too that most of them seemed to be checking in almost identical suitcases and carrying almost identical hold-all.

Suspecting that these people were donkeys for her father's drugs, Mandy decided to exchange a suitcase and a hand-luggage from one of her customers without the traveller knowing about it. In her room at her sister, Ratana's house, she emptied the contents of the suitcase. She found nothing unusual about the contents - clothes any traveller would pack for an overseas trip. However when she gave the suitcase a thorough check, she discovered false compartments at the bottom as well as the sides where she found packets of white powder which she suspected being heroin packed in manner that would fool even the dogs used by most drug squads.

Using her hand phone Mandy called her friend, Lisa, Nopharat's wife, and asked her if they could meet. Lisa invited Mandy to her house, telling her that her husband was away on business and wouldn't be back till late that night.

Suspecting that her driver would report to her father all her movements, Mandy walked through the back door of her office and hailed a taxi about a block away to take her to Lisa's.

The hug that Lisa gave her revealed to Mandy that she was welcomed, and despite her apparent wealth, all was not well with her. Mandy came straight to the point and asked her friend if she could remember the name of the policeman who was keen on her, Mandy, during the time when she was still with Wong attending the horse racings in Thailand.

"Of course, Inspector Teerapat", she replied. "Nopharat and I met him recently at a dinner. Oh, Mandy! Are you keen on him now?"

"Maybe". Do you know how to get in touch with him?"

"Most certainly. Why don't I make arrangement for dinner, just the four of us. You haven't met my husband, have you?

Mandy shook her head. "No, I don't believe I have". She dug into her purse and took out her business card and gave it to Lisa. "Why don't you ask him to give me a call first. For all we know, he may have forgotten about me or he may not want to meet me now?"

As soon as Mandy left her house, Lisa made that call to Teerapat who seemed thrilled that Mandy had remembered him. He called while Mandy was still in a taxi stuck as usual in a traffic jam. Teerapat invited Mandy to have dinner with him that evening and when Mandy accepted his invitation, he practically gave a whoop and Mandy laughed.

Teerapat, who Mandy had remembered as rather skinny, had put on some weight. He had picked her up in his Toyota Camry and had asked Mandy what she would like to eat. Mandy suggested a seafood place she had been once, where one make a selection of what one would like to eat just like one would in a supermarket by pushing a trolley along the vast array of all kinds of seafood and vegetables. Mandy made the selections for the both of them. She selected some fish, about a dozen crabs, a kilo of clams and a large lobster she wanted cooked as lobster thermidor – her favourite, and some vegetables.

The white wine Teerapat ordered went well with their meals and finally when they had finished their dessert, Mandy told him about her discovery.

ꛯ꛰ꛯ꛰ꛯ꛰

CHAPTER FORTY

The flight with the body of the young American was about to touch down at the Los Angeles International Airport. The hearse was ready and waiting for the signal to be given for it to approach the aeroplane. The driver, an Oriental, sitting in the driver's seat smoking a cigarette oblivious to the NO SMOKING sign no more than a few feet away on the wall in front of him. He was nervous and he needed the cigarette to calm his nerves. His companion, a Caucasian, sitting next to him gave him an angry stare and pointed to the sign, but he ignored him and continued puffing at his cigarette. The other was about to make an issue of it when an uniformed guard banged on the roof of the hearse and told them to proceed to the aeroplane which by now had parked on the apron. The driver absent-mindedly threw his cigarette but onto the ground and raced his vehicle towards the aeroplane. The Caucasian, although still angry at the driver, pulled himself together and presented himself to one of the ground crews who looked at his papers and led him to the ramp at the rear of the plane.

"This man here has come for the stiff," the ground crew yelled to his colleague up on the plane. The other nodded his head; a few minutes later the coffin was rolled down and was quickly transferred into the hearse.

The driver muttered a silent prayer when the guard at the gate waved them through. Their spat forgotten, the duo smiled at each other as they drove to their rendezvous; the success of their mission seemed to have brought the two together again and they were friends once more.

Unknown to them David had another team were watching them all the way to the warehouse where the drugs were to be removed from the corpse after which it would be taken to the funeral home where it would have a proper service with his family in attendance. David, as a friend of the deceased, will be there to give comfort to the bereaved family. Although he had never known the deceased, he gave a convincing lie to the grieving family, telling them that he and the deceased had been like brothers. The family, who had never known other Orientals before, felt very touched, shook David's hand a long time. A handsome aunt of the deceased gave David a warm hug and a kiss on each cheek and was told to come and visit soon. David gave her his vague promise; he watched them walked slowly back to their cars before heading for the airport.

David felt an ultimate high as he boarded an airline later that day back to Bangkok. Even though he had made plans to settle down in Australia and retire completely from the drug business, he knew he wouldn't be able to rest easy until he had taken care of one more unpleasant business in Thailand.

Not wanting it known to his family that he had come back to Bangkok, David hired himself a car from the Hertz counter at the airport. It didn't take him long to realize that driving in Bangkok in fact was worse than they made it out to be. Knowing how important it was for him to tie the loose ends here, he endured the two-hour journey to his sister Ratana's house where he heard was where Mandy was staying.

Before arriving there, David had made one stop at a one-bedroom flat he had kept in which even his wife nor his father knew nothing of its existence. He picked up a bottle of *Singha* beer from the refrigerator and headed for the bedroom. The mustiness assailed his nostrils the moment he opened the bedroom door. He turned on the air-conditioner and left the room closing the door behind him. In the living room David pushed the sofa away from its position and lifted a floorboard from underneath the rug and removed the gun he had stashed there. He checked to make sure it was loaded, satisfied that it was, he went back to the bedroom and drank the beer he had left there as he lay on the bed. By this time the mustiness in the room had almost disappeared, and found the room's coolness most soothing to his body; soon he fell asleep.

It was dusk when David finally woke up. Disoriented he found himself wondering where he was; the ceiling looked so unfamiliar to him. As he gazed around the room he became more awake and the more awake he became the more alert he became. By the time he took in the room completely he was fully aware where he was. His watch indicated that he had slept for nearly two hours. He got off the bed and headed for the bathroom. Half an hour later, with the gun in the pocket of his trousers, he got into his rented car and drove towards his sister Ratana's house.

The old caretaker, whose quarters were beside the garage, took a peek at the gate when he thought he heard a car coming. When he saw nothing he return to finish his dinner consisting of rice and some tom yam soup in which he had put in bits of chicken, a piece of fish and some small prawns to make it tastier.

As far as Ratana his mistress, was concerned, he was there to take care of the large ground as well as being the general handyman around the house, but his real job was to be her body guard. It was the *Old Man* who had given him the job after Ratana's husband was killed during a heroin smuggling operation into Malaysia.

The *Old Man* was certain that someone in his organisation must have tipped off the Thai authorities that in turn tipped off their Malaysian counterpart. They seemed to know exactly where and when to hit; not only had he lost the entire shipment worth several million dollars, he lost several good men including his son-in-law as well. He had never given up hope in trying to track down the culprit who had betrayed them. He had suspected that it would be someone close to them.

Through a back window David saw Mandy wearing a midnight-blue silk robe come out of her bathroom. She had a towel on her head and with both hands she was drying her hair with it. He took out the gun from his pocket and aimed it at Mandy who by then was sitting on a stool by the dressing table. He could see her reflection in the mirror and felt his palm began to sweat. He had never realised how beautiful she looked before, and to his dismay he felt a hard-on coming on. This can't be happening to me, he was thinking. Perplexed, David sat on the cement floor with his back against the wall just underneath the window. He dug into his hip pocket and took out his handkerchief and wiped his hands dry before picking up his gun again. By the time he peered through the window again, he noticed that Mandy was no longer in the room.

With extreme caution he went round the house and peered into every window he was able to look into when suddenly he heard someone moving about in the dimly lit kitchen. David peered into the window to see if it was Mandy in there and not someone else. Although he could not see the person's face clearly he had recognised her midnight-blue dressing gown. Without any hesitation he took aim and fired.

At the sound of the gunfire, the guard was suddenly alert. He reached for his riffle, slipped quietly out of his room, and headed for the back of the house where he was sure where the gun-fire was coming from. As soon as he turned the corner, he immediately saw the shards of glass below the kitchen window. He peered in and saw his mistress lying prone on the floor. His immediate reaction was to go to her, to smash down the back door to get in if necessary. His animal instinct - his years as a guerrilla fighter fighting for the Vietcong had horned his instinct like that of an animal - gave out a signal that indicated that an enemy was close by. The next instant he saw a reflection among the bamboo trees close to the fence on to his right. He rolled his body on the ground and landed in the drain that encircled the house just as a bullet zipped by him. Having been shot at many times in the past he could tell that the bullet was too close for comfort, and providence may not hand him a second chance. He raised his riffle and aimed it at general direction of the bamboo plants and the moment he saw the movement he was waiting for he pulled the trigger. The sickening thud that followed told him that his bullet had hit its mark.

Mandy who had heard the first gunfire ran to her stepsister's room to find out what was happening. When she couldn't find her there she went through the rest of the house with Ratana's two maidservants. They too had heard the gunfire; scared out of their wits they ran to look for their mistress. They later met with Mandy on the ground floor near the front door and when she told them that Ratana wasn't in her room, they went to the kitchen. It was there where they discovered Ratana's body in a pool of blood in front of the refrigerator. An empty glass, miraculously unbroken, was still clutched in her hand. It looked as if she was about to get a glass of water from the refrigerator when she was shot from behind.

The riffle-shot coming from outside the house brought the three of them scurrying for cover. For several moments the three women laid flat on the kitchen floor as if by doing so they would escape from harm. Mandy was the first to get off the floor when she heard some furtive rustlings outside the house. She peered through the broken glass of the kitchen window. What she saw made her run for the telephone and tried to call Teerapat at the police station. Unfortunately for her she couldn't make herself understood. After several attempts at trying to make herself understood, she finally said, "*Karuna ya waang hou*".

She then ran back into the kitchen and practically dragged one of the two maids with her. She told her to tell the policeman on the line to come here quickly.

"Tell them there had been a murder and the gunman is still outside the house, and don't forget to give them our address."

The maidservant repeated to the policeman exactly what Mandy had told her. Mandy had mistakenly thought that the caretaker had killed her sister Ratana and her brother David whom she saw lying on the ground at the back of the house. She saw through the kitchen window Ratana's caretaker standing over David's body and he had a riffle in his hand.

The police came with an ambulance and after a while the ambulance left taking Ratana and David's bodies with them. The police stayed behind and continued with their investigation. Based on what Mandy had told them the police had the caretaker brought into the house and questioned. He answered their questions simply and to the point. While he was being questioned the forensic boys from the police department went to work by scouring the grounds and came up with the empty shells from the two weapons used in the two killings.

A few minutes later the police officer in charge received a call from the medical examiner who told him that the woman was killed by the bullet that came from a hand gun while the man was killed by the bullet that came from the riffle. It verified what the caretaker had said thus exonerating him.

As soon as Mandy heard this she apologised to the elderly caretaker who accepted her apology with a bow, touching his palms together. He asked softly if anyone minded if he left and get on with his work. Mandy looked at the police officer who shook his head. She apologised once more to the caretaker as she walked with him to the front door.

At the door he turned to Mandy and said, "It's alright, my lady, everything is going to be all right."

The police officer that spoke passable English asked Mandy about the similarity about hers and her sister's dressing gown.

"My sister gave me this dressing gown," replied Mandy. "Why do you ask?"

"Was your brother David and your sister on a friendly term?"

"Yes, I think so."

"What about you? Did you and him get along well?" Mandy could see what he was getting at.

"We got along all right."

"But not too well, I gather."

"No, not well." Mandy was about to add that she and David hadn't known each other for very long when her father walked in. Apparently he heard the tail end of their conversation and was afraid that Mandy might tell the police more than she should.

"Officer, I overheard what you've just asked my daughter," said the *Old Man*. "Would you mind telling what you're getting at?"

"It's just a theory of mine, sir. I thought that it might be possible that your son had shot at your daughter Ratana when he mistook her for Miss Mandy. After all they both wore identical dressing gowns."

The *Old Man* must have accepted the theory for he became visibly shaken, his authoritative posture gone, and slumped into a chair. Despite the dent in his facade, the *Old Man* turned the reality into his and Mandy's disadvantage.

"It's all my fault," he said. "I should have nipped it in the bud when I saw the rivalry between the two of them when they were young." The *Old Man*, anxious to get rid of the police, decided to agree with the young officer.

The officer seemed pleased that he was able to solve this crime so easily, and he was doubly pleased that such a distinguished gentleman like the *Old Man*, whom he had often heard of, but hadn't had the pleasure of meeting, seemed to agree with his theory. He strutted about like a peacock, telling his men to pack up.

"Right then, sir, we'll be on our way," the officer said to the *Old Man*. He then turned towards Mandy, touched the brim of his cap and left through the front door escorted by the *Old Man* who put his palms together in response to the officer's farewell gesture.

"Papa, why do you think David was trying to kill me?" Mandy asked the *Old Man* when he returned to the living room.

"That's the first time you've ever call me that," the *Old Man* said, beaming at her. "I don't know why David tried to kill you. I didn't even know he was in the country."

The smiled that had appeared briefly on his scraggy, well-tanned face disappeared completely, and its place was one that showed a great concern.

"I think that it is time that I went back to Malaysia," said Mandy. "I've missed my husband and I've missed my children. I've realised something since I've been here, there's no wealth greater that the wealth that comes from the love of one's family. I know mine had loved me but I let greed rule my life. Money is no use unless you have someone to share the joy it may bring you, and you should know very well that it doesn't always guarantee to bring you joy."

"Your family thinks you are already dead," said her father. "Why not make a new life here. I saw the look on that young officer's face just now, why not give him a call tomorrow to thank him for his prompt response to your SOS."

"No, father, I've made up my mind. I'd like to leave as soon as you could arrange for me to get across the border. As you know I have no passport." She spoke quietly but firmly, letting her father know that she was serious.

"I have a better idea," said her father. "I'll have a Thai passport made for you. You can leave Thailand on that. If you decide to stay with your family, destroy it. Use it only if you decide to return to Thailand."

"No, father, that's not a good idea. If I decide to stay then I'll be considered as an over-stayer and I don't want that. I'd rather be smuggled across like the way I came. Please make the arrangement for me, father, that's all I'll ever ask of you."

The *Old Man*, seeing that Mandy was serious, nodded his head. "All right, I'll make the arrangement. After all, you can always come back and see me as a Malaysian and not as a Thai. Promise that one day you'll bring your family to come and see me?"

Mandy went to her father and gave him a hug. In his arms she failed to hold back her tears and she cried like a baby. Her first real cry as far as she could remember.

"I loved Ratana, Papa. She was so good to me...so patient. Why did she have to die? She didn't deserve it, I do... I'm the rotten one... I'm the one that deserved to die...not my sister..."

What Mandy had uttered in her misery hit the *Old Man* like a ton of bricks? For the first time in his life he realised that many people had died while many more must have suffered because of him, and yet he still walked the earth, seemingly untouched by all that misery and suffering. And yet, his daughter Ratana who wouldn't hurt a fly, was sweet and gentle and good natured, was no more. Where was the justice in all this! Could it be true what they say that only the good die young while people like him who had thrived on the misery of others would go on living.

His eyes misty, he looked at Mandy whom he had abandoned when very young, and he thought of her two younger brothers whom he vaguely can remember, and he wondered how they and their mother had managed to cope all these years. It was obvious to him that they had somehow managed. And now he was married to the two sisters, daughters of his former rival and archenemy. This marriage too was far from having been made in heaven, but came from his desire to revenge himself on their father. It was true that he liked them, but what he liked most was the novelty of being married to two sisters at the same time, not just any sisters but an identical twin. He must admit that he hadn't counted it to be that tiring. Perhaps if he were ten years younger.... Nevertheless, once a week for each of them was all he could muster these days. To make things worse he wasn't all that keen to have sex nowadays. Realising that Mandy was looking at him in a curious manner, her father quickly snapped out of his reverie.

"How will you explain your death and resurrection to your family?" he asked.

"I don't know, I'll think of something," she replied. "The easiest way would be for me to tell them the truth."

"If you are sure this is what you want I'll arrange for you to get across to Malaysia tonight."

* * *

As the water tanker was slowly making its journey along the twisting road towards Malaysia, Mandy, lying in foetal position in a specially made compartment inside a water tank, couldn't help wondering how many had had to endure this claustrophobic journey before her. Despite the uncomfortable position, and the annoying vibration she felt from the truck's engine and the bumpy road, Mandy's mind began to wander. Like a homing pigeon it always seemed to zero in on James and her two children. She tried to picture how they would react when they saw her again. The picture she got, however, was fuzzy. She couldn't see their faces, and for the first time since she got into the smugglers' boat and thereafter in this long uncomfortable ride in the water tanker, she began to panic and it took a considerable effort on her part to try to get herself together again. Mandy tried to concentrate on her family again and just when she finally became calm again, she began wondering what she would do if she detected hostility from either James or from her two children when they met.

Despite the tears that the thought had brought her, she told herself she was determined to go on living somehow and to try to do everything in her power to regain their love. She didn't care how long it would take - she'd try anything to get them to forgive her. To be forgiven and to regain their respect was all that mattered to her.

Mandy was picked up by a man and a woman as soon as she felt the water tanker had stopped several hours later. When she was finally dropped off at Kota Bahru Airport where all the bookings had been made for her by her father, she was tempted to call James but soon changed her mind. As soon as she had boarded the plane and had settled in her seat, she became impatient for the aircraft to take off. All of a sudden everything seemed to be going in slow-motion for her - the passengers seemed to take forever board the plane, while some seemed to take their own sweet time to deposit their belongings into their overhead compartments, and just as the air hostesses were about to close the doors, an announcement came over the PA system telling them that they'd delayed for a few more minutes due to the late arrival of a VIP who apparently had been held up in a traffic jam caused by an accident on the road to the airport.

When the VIP finally arrived and the aircraft's doors were finally shut, Mandy gave a sigh of relief. She peered out of her window and watched the plane began to taxi towards the runway for the take-off. Mandy, for the first time since she boarded the aeroplane, was able to relax as she slowly leaned back on her seat. She closed her eyes as the plane began its run for the take-off; at that moment, when the world around her began to melt away, she felt alone like a star in the heavens, overwhelmed by a feeling of icy despair, but at the same time became firmly resolved with herself than ever before. She felt the worst was behind her now.

"There's nothing I can do about the past," she whispered to herself. "But if I were given another chance...."

❧❧❧❧❧❧

CHAPTER FORTY-ONE

Andrea heard the doorbell the first time but she dismissed it thinking that it must have been the television. But when she heard it the second time, she lumbered towards the front door as if she had a ten-kilo dumbbell in her hand instead of the Time magazine she had been reading while watching the television. In reality she had been reading it while the television was on.

Andrea couldn't believe what she saw through the peephole. She dropped the magazine onto the floor and backed away from the door while screaming for her father. James Rashid, who was working in his study, rushed to the living room and found his daughter, white-faced as if she had seen a ghost, pointing an unsteady finger at the front door.

James took a peek at the peephole, but when he saw nothing out of the ordinary he opened the door only to find a woman walking away towards the lifts. Although her back was towards him, James was sure it was his beloved Mandy who was walking away from them.

"Mandy, if it is you, please come back," he said. But the figure kept walking slowly towards the lifts. "We need you," James repeated softly.

Andrea, who was standing gingerly behind her father, and who by this time had fully recovered from her initial shock of seeing her mother through the peephole, said in a loud clear voice,

"Mum, we all need you, please don't leave us again."

Mandy tears flooding her eyes, stopped and turned around to face them. The moment she saw James and Andrea she half-ran towards them until she was in their arms.

Once inside their flat Mandy lost no time in telling them everything - leaving nothing out, certain that it was the right thing to do. Many times during the telling of her tale she had doubts about the wisdom of being truthful.

She remembered a song, an old song, about a man who implored his love, not to confess. It was never revealed in that song whether she had confessed or not. Confession may be good for the soul, they say, but Mandy could tell that the hurt she was inflicting on her husband and her two children was more than she could bear. She wanted to stop many times or cook up a better story, but she felt that the only way she could live with herself again was for her to tell them the truth and nothing but the truth.

Alexander, who had been playing tennis at one of the tennis courts, had finally joined them. He had on his face a look so cold; it sent shivers up and down Mandy's spine. James had a look in his face in which she couldn't read. The only person who seemed to have a trace of sympathy on her beautiful face was her daughter. She sat on the sofa next to James; her hands folded in her lap, nodding encouragingly to Mandy from time to time, as she listened to her mother's incredible story.

* * *

That night, over dinner, she told them how her father had helped her escape from Mong Kok's death squad and how she was smuggled into Thailand and then out again. When she came to telling them about Ratana and how she had died, Mandy was once again in tears. Finally she told James and her two children how much she had missed them and had given them her solemn word that she would never leave them again.

Andrea, who had been keeping quiet all this time, went to her mother and took both her mother's hands in hers and said, "Mom, we're a family, remember? We should never keep anything from each other. Whatever problem each is facing could always be solved when the four of us put our heads together, I'm sure of that."

"Yeah, mom. Like our namesake Harun al-Rashid, he was a warrior, wasn't he?" added Alex.

"No, you dope! He was a caliph." Andrea ruffled her brother's hair, which she knew he hated.

"Oh, yeah! Just how do you get to become the main man unless you were good in combat, huh?" He pushed his fingers through his hair in a futile attempt to groom it back in place.

Mandy turned and looked at her son. His dark curls, thick as wires would need a brush to tame, noticed the eyes full of humour and his sensual, sensitive mouth - she was so glad that the painful episode her Alexander had endured was now truly buried, he seemed his usual self again. She was grateful to James for looking after him like his own son. Ashamed at herself at what she had done, at her selfishness, and at the way she had taken for granted his love for her. Her daughter never looked so beautiful to Mandy, something that never ceased to amaze her. She automatically looked at James and remembered thinking a long time ago that if they ever had a daughter together, both of them had wondered: would she look like Chinese or Malay? As it turned out Andrea looked simply beautiful.

Mandy walked to her two children and gave each one of them a big hug. She told them how terribly sorry she was for all the hurt she had caused them and asked for their forgiveness.

James, who had never ceased loving her, took Mandy in his arms and kissed her briefly on the lips, acutely aware that their son and daughter were watching them.

James would always remember till the rest of his days how un-attracted he was to her when he first saw her. Over a year later, the image of her sitting there all alone in the pizza parlour, staring at her glass of orange juice and toying with her spaghetti Bolognese was becoming vivid in his mind. That was the first time he felt the attraction which was so strong then, it was as if he had lost all control over all his senses, and he was being pulled towards her like a metal pin would to a magnet. Perhaps it was more like seeing a kitten and having a compelling desire to pet it. A rather inappropriate analogy perhaps, he thought, but an accurate one. Over two decades later he still felt the same way about her.

Time had been kind to Mandy; not a line could be seen on her face. The scar on her chin was still prominent, perhaps more so on that day because she wore no makeup, and despite looking slightly thinner, which did not suit her, Mandy still looked beautiful, and as far as James was concerned she was the most desirable woman he had ever known. The way Mandy had responded to his kiss, he knew that she had come home for good. He longed to hold her in his arms again and kiss her but stopped short when he suddenly realised that his son and daughter were still in the room with them.

Alexander, as if reading his father's thoughts, gave Andrea a knowing grin, the next moment both of them quietly slipped out of the living room.

As soon as they had left, Mandy quickly led James to their bedroom, where they made long passionate love, followed by having a shower together. Not long afterwards, they heard a knock on the door of their bedroom. When Mandy went to open it she found a trolley laden with food with a note saying,

"Welcome home, mom", signed, Andrea and Alexander.

* * *

It happened all too fast: one moment they were driving leisurely towards their favourite seafood restaurant, the next moment James saw the white Proton Saga on their lane speeding towards them. James swerved to the left to avoid it but unfortunately the other car was hurling towards them at such a great speed, it hit the side of James's car. The impact sent their car out of control and they landed in the ditch by the side of the road. Mandy escaped unhurt but James was pinned underneath the steering wheel. The other driver did not fare too well, he had died on the spot.

Other drivers who saw the accident stopped and tried their best to extricate James from the position he was in while they waited for the ambulance, but all their attempts were in vain. It took the fire department's personnel, who came almost at the same time as the ambulance, another thirty minutes before they could remove James from the wreckage. Due the Malaysian drivers' bad habit of using the emergency lane on which the ambulance could not use they've managed to arrive more than forty minutes after the accident.

By that time James had lost a lot of blood and was barely conscious. In the ambulance Mandy kept telling James, who had passed out, over and over again to hang on in there and not to die on her.

The paramedic tried all they could to keep James alive; they even radioed the hospital to let them know that James would need a lot of blood and letting them know of his blood type.

On the way to the hospital, Mandy held back her tears and prayed. She remembered the times James, who could have easily slammed the door in her face each time she came to him for help, but as sure as night follows day, he had never failed to extend his hands in friendship to her.

A friend she once confided in told her that she must have done all the nasty things to James in order to get back at her father for abandoning her when she was only six years old. James was about the same age as her father, so to her, in her sporadic confused state of mind, James was the father figure and therefore must pay for what he did to her.

The sudden opening of the ward door jolted Mandy back to the present as she moved aside in order to allow the nurse to do her job.

Mandy moved to the bottom of the bed, out of the nurse's way and watched her replace the near-empty fluid bottle from its rack above James's head. When the nurse approached her at the bottom of the bed in order to write something on the chart, Mandy moved to the head of the bed and pressed her hand on James's shoulder. A moment later James opened his eyes and smiled at her.

"How long have you been here?" he asked, his voice strained.

"Oh, not long - about two days," Mandy replied, bending down to give him a kiss on the lips.

"You shouldn't have stayed here all this time, you should have gone home. There was nothing here for you to do, except maybe, and watch me sleep. What fun was that for you?"

"More than you know. You've done so much for me. Even if I live to be a hundred, I could never repay you for what you've done for me, so please don't tell me that I'm wasting my time here, or that there's no fun for me. For as long as I can remember, all I ever did was to have fun - fun at other people's expense, fun at any cost. It's not fair! I should be lying there instead of you. I should be the one who should be suffering, not you."

"Ahem", said Rahim who had entered the room without either of them hearing his knock. "The man in the Proton Saga was a hired killer look[ng for you, Mandy. In a bizarre twist of fate, he literally bumped into both of you when one of his tyres burst and he lost control of his car and smashed into your car, James".

"How do you know all this?" James asked.

"He had died on the spot and he had all the incriminating evidence on him including this". Rahim held up a photo of Mandy for them to see.

Mandy took the photo and looked at it and saw the photo of her with the police captain, Teerapat. That was the night she had dinner with Captain Teerapat at that fish restaurant; the night she gave him the printouts going back several years of all the couriers her father had used to smuggle his drugs practically all over the world.

"Captain Teerapat and I are friends", said Rahim. "We attended a course together at the police academy in Kuala Lumpur some time ago. He mentioned to me the list you had given, Mandy, and he acted on it. He made several arrests including K.K.Lee also known as *the Old Man* who was later shot by the police. It looked like the courier service provided by Lee is now closed for good. Lee was shot to death when the police raided the place. It looked as if he had gone there to destroy what was in the office safe. When he took pot shots at the police in an attempt to scare them away long enough for him to destroy all the incriminating evidence, the police returned fire and hit him in the chest and head. He died on the spot."

Mandy let out an involuntary gasp. James looked at her and saw the stricken look on her face. "Are you all right, Mandy?"

"Lee was my father", she said. Involuntary tears welling up in her eyes.

Unable to control it, Mandy started to cry. "All I ever did was to hurt people… you in particular", looking at James. "Not once you showed your hurt but I know now how much I must have hurt you. Can you ever forgive me?"

"Ahem", Rahim cleared his throat for the second time. "I'd better be off. Got a lot to do today". He walked to James and pat him on his good shoulder. He turned towards Mandy and said. "Goodbye, Mandy".

As soon as Rahim closed the door behind him, James reach out his hand to Mandy who grasped it with both hands.

"There's nothing to forgive!" James said to her.

"Why did you put up with me all these years?" Asked Mandy.

"The answer to that is simple", he replied. "I was in love with you from the moment I saw you, although I knew it wasn't right according to the eyes of the law at the time. You were too young."

"I was seventeen then. How old was I when we got married?"

"You turned twenty-one about a week before we go married," replied James.

"I'm truly sorry you didn't get much out of this marriage, did you," she said. Mandy gave James a studied look.

"Who said so? I've got plenty out of our marriage," James retorted sharply. "First of all, I was in love for the first time in my life. Many had claimed that they had been in love, but very few were really in love. Secondly, look at our two children. They've turned out to be the most loving, level-headed, well-adjusted young adults I've ever known, and I'm very proud of them, aren't you?"

"Yes, I am, very." Mandy replied, her voice was filled with emotion.

"And I think I know what you meant about being in love because right now I feel I'm madly and deeply in love with you. I've never felt this way before ..."

ABOUT THE AUTHOR

 The Author lives in Perth, W.A., and Melbourne and in Bandar Baru Bangi, in Selangor, Malaysia. Whenever he is in Malaysia he lives with his two children and wife.

He's an engineer by profession, had been a Marketing Director of two companies, and a COO of a subsidiary of a Bottler of Pepsi-Cola in Malaysia. In retirement, he became a Sales Advisor in a Mazda Dealership in Malaysia.

The author had published a book called the Thirdway Factor.

The author hopes to complete a follow-up with two more books to The Thirdway Factor while in Australia, after the launch of this present book.

You can reach him at www.hamidyusof.com

www.ingramcontent.com/pod-product-compliance
Lightning Source LLC
Chambersburg PA
CBHW022231020726
47496CB00004B/852